Discover *All Seeing Eye,*
a heart-pounding new thriller by

ROB THURMAN

. . . the sensational writer whose gripping work
New York Times bestselling author Charlaine
Harris described as always having "an engaging
protagonist, fast-paced adventure, a touch of sensu-
ality, and a surprise twist that'll make you blink."

Only *don't* blink—because here, you believe the
unseen at your own risk. . . .

———

More praise for the *New York Times* bestselling
novels of Rob Thurman

"[*Nightlife*] is like the illegitimate love child of
Lenny Bruce and H. P. Lovecraft. . . . Dark fantasy
fans who enjoy their novels with plenty of smart-
ass attitude will find this chaotic and raging debut
refreshingly unreserved and impenitent in its over-
the-top narrative style."

—Paul Goat Allen,
Explorations: The BN SciFi and Fantasy Blog

"As good as an urban fantasy series can be. Buy it.
Read it. I defy you not to love it."

—*Penny Dreadful* on the Cal Leandros series

"Supernatural highs and lows, and a hell of a lean over at the corners. Sharp and sardonic, mischievous and mysterious . . . the truth is Out There, and it's not very pretty."

—*New York Times* bestselling author
Simon Green on *Nightlife*

"The combination of Chandleresque detective dialogue and a lyrically noir style of description is stunningly original. The reader's attention is captured and held from page one."

—*The Green Man Review* on *Nightlife*

"The plotting is tight and fast-paced, and the world building is top-notch."

—*RT Book Reviews* on *Moonshine*

"Thurman continues to deliver strong tales of dark urban fantasy. . . . fans of street-level urban fantasy will enjoy this new novel greatly."

—*SFRevu* on *Madhouse*

"A touching story on the nature of family, trust, and love lies hidden in this action thriller. . . . Thurman weaves personal discovery seamlessly into the fast-paced action, making it easy to cheer for these overgrown, dangerous boys. . . ."

—*Publishers Weekly* on *Chimera*

"*Chimera*—a contemporary thriller with science fiction underpinnings that blends elements of medical speculation à la Cook and Crichton with the breakneck pacing and psychological suspense of novels by Koontz and Kellerman . . . powered by Thurman's signature acerbic wit."

—Paul Goat Allen,
Explorations: The BN SciFi and Fantasy Blog

"If I had only three words to describe this book? They'd be: Best. Twist. Ever. . . . Go. Buy this book. It will floor you."

—*New York Times* bestselling author
Lynn Viehl on *Trick of the Light*

"Just enough action, angst, sarcasm, mystery, mayhem, and murder to keep you turning the pages to the very end."

—*Bookspot Central* on *Madhouse*

"A beautiful, wild ride, a story with tremendous heart. A must-read."

—*New York Times* bestselling author
Marjorie M. Liu on *Trick of the Light*

Also by Rob Thurman

———

The Cal Leandros Novels

Nightlife
Moonshine
Madhouse
Deathwish
Roadkill
Blackout
Doubletake

The Trickster Novels

Trick of the Light
The Grimrose Path

The Korsak Brothers Novels

Chimera
Basilisk

ALL
SEEING
EYE

ROB
THURMAN

POCKET BOOKS

New York   London   Toronto   Sydney   New Delhi

Pocket Books
A Division of Simon & Schuster, Inc.
1230 Avenue of the Americas
New York, NY 10020

First Pocket Books paperback edition August 2012

POCKET BOOKS and colophon are registered trademarks of Simon & Schuster, Inc.

For information about special discounts for bulk purchases, please contact Simon & Schuster Special Sales at 1-866-506-1949 or business@simonandschuster.com.

The Simon & Schuster Speakers Bureau can bring authors to your live event. For more information or to book an event contact the Simon & Schuster Speakers Bureau at 1-866-248-3049 or visit our website at www.simonspeakers.com.

Designed by *Kyle Kabel*

Manufactured in the United States of America

10   9   8   7   6   5   4   3   2   1

ISBN 978-1-4767-8623-0

This dedication can only go to
Adam Wilson, Jennifer Heddle, and Lucienne Diver.
You believed I could make the leap.
Watch me *jump*.

"The eye of the master will do more work than both his hands."

—*Benjamin Franklin*

"Truth lies at the bottom of a well."

—*Democritus*

ALL
SEEING
EYE

PROLOGUE

I never saw it coming.

Pretty ironic for a psychic, isn't it? People would say it was what I was paid the big bucks for. It was my job. I should've whipped out my damn crystal ball. I should've known, but I didn't. Sometimes you don't. A sky that turns from blue to green in a heartbeat, while a tornado with your address lands like the hand of God to swat your house to pieces that scatter half a mile away. A simple cough shows up on a chest X-ray as the future shadow of a grave marker. The ocean inexplicably retreats miles from the beach, only to return at a thousand times the fury and blot out the sky itself. And there are days you wake up surrounded by family, and by the time twilight creeps in, you're alone.

For the rest of your life.

No matter how careful you are, sometimes the bad . . . the horrific, they sneak up on you. Sometimes they come boiling out of the shadows, out of the dark corners, and there they are. There they goddamn are.

There were no shadows today, but there was darkness, the kind you bury six feet under—in the dirt and in your mind. It doesn't do any good. That darkness never stays down. It digs its way out, handful by handful. It may take years, but it always comes back. You feel the bloody fingerprints of it on your subconscious as it rips its way free. You hear its choked and gleeful laughter at how you thought you'd left it behind—that you'd dare imagine things could be different.

Because in the end, it would always be the same as before.

It *was* the same as before.

Right now. Right this moment.

That guy who said you can never go home again? What an asshole.

The sky was the same blinding blue. Exactly the same. The air still with the same choking heat. The grass an identical faded green splotched with crisp dead brown. I'd lived every summer of my life until I was fourteen with that sky, that heat, that ground. I'd lived every day of every year since then knowing I'd never see it again.

Wrong.

Unlike the sky and the earth, which belonged although I didn't, not anymore, the knife and the shotgun shouldn't have been there. *Couldn't* have been.

It didn't stop the bright sliver of metal lying on a dusty kitchen counter. It didn't stop a hand from yanking a shotgun out of a closet with a warped wooden door. Everything in its place—just as it had been the first time.

I saw the slash and spill of blood as the knife—her best knife, her meat knife—hit a throat and sliced. I felt the lead pellets rip into my ribs under my arm as I lunged at a man who had lost his mind to carry the mind of a dead boy instead. It hadn't done much good. I was on my feet, and then I was falling. I went from the sight of the worn boards and dirty window glass of a rundown shack to that of a stained ceiling. I wished it had been blue summer sky.

From standing to lying in a house as dead as the people who'd lived in it.

From whole to a little less than.

I touched the pain, a player all its own in this game, and my hand came away red. Who knew agony had a color? It did, though, and it made sense that it would be the same as blood. Crimson as the ever-present Georgia dirt turned to liquid mud, the kind to run like a river after a hard rain. I closed my eyes, but the red remained.

The knife had happened before.

The shotgun had happened before.

I didn't like guns. I didn't have to be on the receiving end of one to realize that oh-so-fascinating bit of news. I'd recognized that since I held one for the first and last time sixteen years ago.

I heard the shotgun being pumped again. An echo of the past. My past.

I'd known this whole nightmare would end in violence, I'd known it would finish in a pattern of blood and brutality, but I didn't imagine that it would end here. My own place of violence—my own personal hell.

Home.

And I never saw it coming.

1

A lost shoe. That's how it began.

It was nothing more or less than that. A shoe, just one small shoe.

At first, I didn't recognize it, although I should have. I'd seen it hundreds of times on the front porch or lying in the yard, its shine dulled by red dust. Tess was a typical five-year-old, careless with her things. Not that she had many things to be careful with. The pink shoes had been her only birthday present. I'd been with Mom when she'd picked them out at the secondhand store in town. She'd paid two dollars for them, but that didn't stop me from thinking she'd gotten ripped off. Pink patent leather with bedraggled ribbon ties and rhinestone starbursts on the sides, they were ugly as hell and louder than Aunt Grace's good church dress.

Tessie loved them, of course. She wore them everywhere and with everything, even when we went blackberry picking. With hands stained berry purple and hair in lopsided pigtails she'd done up herself, she would skip along in denim overalls, shirtless, ignoring the thorn scratches on her arms, and beam at the sight of those damn awful shoes.

That's where I was walking home from, selling the blackberries. I had a stand up at the main road. It wasn't much to look at, a few boards I'd clapped together. A strong wind could take it down and had once or twice in a good old Georgia thunderstorm. I sold paper bags full of plump, gnat-ridden berries for a dollar to people driving by. Sometimes Glory and Tess hung around and helped, but usually not. Five-year-old twin girls don't have much patience for sweltering in the sun in the hopes of making a couple of bucks. Besides, today was a school day. Glory was at kindergarten. Tess, with a bad case of chicken pox and spotty as a Dalmatian, was stuck at home, and I was skipping. I'd get my ass busted for it, no way around that, but it was for a good cause. A skinny teenager, I was two years away from my license and probably four years away from filling out. If I ever wanted to date, money was all I was going to have going for me. Cast-off clothes and home haircuts weren't the way to any cheerleader's heart, not in my school, anyway. Not that cheerleaders were the be-all and end-all of what I wanted out of life. They weren't, but they'd do until graduation.

Mom worked bagging groceries; it was the same place she'd worked since she dropped out of high school pregnant with me. Boyd, my step-dad, worked on holding the couch down. He was on disability, a "bad back." Yeah, right. I remembered when he'd gotten the news. It was beer and pizza with his buddies for a week. You would've thought the fat bastard had won the lottery. That bad back, along with a near-terminal case of laziness, might have kept him from working, but it didn't keep him from other things. I rubbed the swollen lump on my jaw as I walked and then fingered the four dollars in my pocket. I liked the feel of that a lot better.

"Dirt poor" wasn't a new phrase, not in these parts, but it was a true one. That wasn't going to be me, though. I sold blackberries, delivered papers in a place where most houses were at least half a mile apart, and had an after-school job at the same grocery as my mom. It was hard work, and there wasn't much I hated more than hard work. But I did like money. One day I was going to figure out how to get one without doing too much of the other. I had plans for my life, and they didn't involve rusted-out cars or jeans permanently stained red by Georgia mud. I had plans, all right, and plans required money. But it wasn't going to be made by sponging off the government like Boyd. No, not like that sad sack of shit.

He was lazy. I could swallow that. No one knows lazy like a fourteen-year-old kid. But if I could make myself work, so could he. Instead, he squatted on the couch, scratching his balding head and blankly watching whatever channel happened to be coming in that day through our crappy antenna. He yelled a lot at the girls and me, during the commercials. And on occasion, if he was drunk or bored enough, he would lever himself off the worn cushions to back up his bark with some bite. He was careful not to break any bones. Boyd might not be smart, but he wasn't stupid, either. Coyote-sharp cunning lay behind the cold blue eyes. That same cunning held his large fists from doing the type of permanent damage that would draw the eye of the police. He hadn't touched the twins yet, and he wouldn't. I wouldn't let the son of a bitch get the chance. Girls were different. Girls were good . . . well, I amended as I scratched the bite on my calf, *mostly* good.

As for me, black eyes, bruises, some welts. No big deal. Teenage boys were troublemakers, right? We needed keeping in line. I might not have believed Boyd about that, but my mom didn't say a word when he pounded the message home. She'd only smooth my hair, bite her lip, and send me off with ice wrapped in a worn dish towel. She was my mom. If she went along with it, it must be true. Boys needed discipline, and a good smack upside the head was the usual way to go about it. I told a kid at school that once, not thinking anything of it. Why would I? It was the way things were, the way they'd been as long as I could remember. But the look that kid gave me . . . it made me realize, for the first time, that wasn't the way things were, not always. And when he called me trash, I realized something else. We *were* trash, and trash hit each other. It was the way of the world. The law of the trailer park. Being trash, I promptly punched that smug punk in the nose so he'd know what it was like to be me.

I didn't hate Boyd. He wasn't worth hating. I did despise him, though. He was worth that. A mean-spirited, beery-breathed sponge that did nothing but suck up money. He hadn't even wanted to make Tess lunch and take her temperature for a couple of days, but he gave in rather than have Mom miss work and bring home a day less paycheck. He hadn't wanted to be bothered, that was Boyd all over. Just couldn't be bothered about anything. Tess and Glory were hell on wheels, no getting around that, but taking care of your kids is supposed to come with the territory. Sure, Tess chattered nonstop from sunup to sundown about anything and nothing, while Glory was sneaky and wild as a feral cat, but that's who they were. You had to accept it. That's family. I knew I'd done a lot of accepting in my time. The bite that itched on my calf was courtesy of Glory, and the cartoon Band-Aid over it was from her twin. Two halves of a hellacious whole.

I was heading home in the lazy afternoon, still idly scratching the Glory bite, when I first saw the gleam of pink. I'd cut through our neighbor's property, twenty-five acres of scrubby grass, black snakes, and the foundation of a hundred-years-gone icehouse. Rumor was a plantation had been somewhere around there in the day. Now there was only scattered rock and an abandoned well.

The neon flash came from a foot-long scraggle of yellowing weeds. Hideously bright and a shade found nowhere in nature, it caught my eye. Curiously, I moved toward it, stomping my feet to scare off any snakes. As I bent over to study it, the smear of color finally shifted into a recognizable shape. A typically girlie thing, it was cradled in the grass as bright and cheerful as an Easter egg. Tessie's shoe.

She'd lost it. When had that happened? It was far from the house. Yet Tess had lost her shoe way out here. I reached out and picked it up. The plastic of it was shiny and sleek against my skin. The only scuff was on the toe, and I traced a finger over it. It weighed nothing in my palm, less than a feather, it was so small. Tess's favorite shoe, and she'd lost it.

But . . .

That was wrong.

My grip spasmed around the shoe until I heard the crack of a splitting sole. It was all wrong. Tess hadn't lost her shoe. The shoe had lost her. *I* had lost her. Tessie was gone. Smothered in water and darkness, her wide blue eyes forever open, her hands floating upward like white lilies as if she were hoping someone would pull her up. No one had. My sister was gone.

God, she was gone.

How did I know? Easy. It was as simple as the river being wet, as obvious as the sky being blue. Unstoppable as a falling star.

The shoe told me.

2

They painted the walls pink.

They didn't call it that, of course. They called it coral or salmon, more like Salmonella, or some such shit. Call it whatever you want, it was still pink. It was the last straw. Stupid, a simple color driving me over the edge. It wasn't the bad food or the mind-numbing sameness of the rules. It wasn't the bored, empty eyes of the teachers who could barely force themselves through the motions for kids they'd already written off. It wasn't even the vicious fights or the fear of getting gang-raped in the communal bathroom in the middle of the night. Life in a state home wasn't for the weak . . . it wasn't for anyone who hoped to remain whole and undamaged, but I could've toughed it out for two more years until I was eighteen. I'd learned to hold my own. I was still skinny, but I'd picked up a whole bagful of dirty tricks that involved kicking or jabbing with my elbows. I could go toe-to-toe with your average son of a bitch and never have to touch him with my hands. That was another thing I'd learned. Touching people with my bare skin had gradually become a not very good idea. Even the split-second contact of fist against face would tell me things . . . *show* me things that I didn't want to know. So I took my brawling in a different direction. It worked. The nickname Shotgun Jack didn't much hurt, either.

Or the fact that I'd come by it honestly.

Yeah, I could've put up with it. Crappy meals and frequent doses of violence, it wasn't so different from home . . . but home had been two years ago. The pink, though, that I couldn't deal with. Every day I woke up to the reminder that home didn't exist anymore. It stared at me with the blush of a cheek, the glow of a spring dawn . . . the bubblegum shine of a little girl's lost shoe.

"I hate this goddamn color," I growled, rubbing the sleep from my eyes.

"Maybe it's supposed to be calming," Charlie said reasonably from the other bed.

He was always reasonable. Charles Allgood lived up to his name. He was all about the books, polite manners, and staying out of trouble. Unfortunately, the Cane Lake County Home for Boys wasn't the place for the good and wholesome. With those labels tacked to his character, he would've been better suited to a Boy Scout troop than Cane Lake. It wasn't surprising that he'd been through the front door less than an hour when he was knocked flat by a certain Ryder Powell. That was my first sight of

Charlie, lying on his stomach surrounded by text-books and clothes. The guy who'd taken him down, a small-eyed punk with an unlikely soap-opera name, had unzipped Charlie's duffel bag and dumped the contents on the floor to see if there was anything worth stealing. I'd rushed forward, pushed Ryder aside, and helped the new kid up. We picked up his stuff, exchanged hugs, and swore undying friendship.

And if you believe that story, you're going to love the movie version.

Truth was, I just kept walking. I was no one's hero. Besides, this sort of thing happened on a daily basis. Superman himself would run his ass ragged trying to clean the place up, and Superman I was not. Primary colors, not my style. But as I moved on through the commons area, not giving Ryder's fallen victim another thought, I heard a loud thunk from behind me. Turning, I saw Powell waver, then collapse to his knees. The hand he had clasped to the back of his head slowly became stained with small rivulets of blood. Charlie was standing over him with a large book in his hands—biology, I think it was. "I told you to leave me alone," he said calmly, as if it were the most rational request in the world. Maybe it was in the outside world, but here ... Allgood was going to have to keep swinging those books.

He was put in the Quiet Room that night, which didn't bother him in the slightest. Charlie was perfectly happy with his own company. The next day, he was assigned to my room. Shotgun Jack and Book-Thumping Charlie, one helluva dynamic duo. In the beginning, I ignored him. I wasn't there to make friends. I was only marking time until I could get out and find my sister. I couldn't do anything for her now, just as I hadn't been able to do anything for Tess, swallowed by water, but when I was eighteen, they'd have to let me see Glory. I was her brother, her only remaining family. That meant something. It *had* to.

Charlie didn't mind the rejection. He only fixed me with his odd blue eyes, smiled, and reached for the next book. He was seventeen, a year older than me. A little short for his age and wiry, he had a close-cut pelt of intensely black hair that whispered of Asian or Hispanic blood. That might have been belied by the pale color of his eyes if it weren't for the slightly almond shape to them. Despite that exotic feature, he had a face typically referred to in the South as five miles of bad road. And the hair, while short, was always disheveled, as if distracted finger-combing was the most attention he could spare it. Pleasantly homely was what Granny Rosemary would've called him. If she'd still been around.

He kept to himself, studied nonstop, and left me alone. Once in a while when I was erasing holes in my paper with frustrated force, he would offer to help me with my chemistry homework. Usually, I said no, but once . . . hell, it only takes once. Math I got. It was just numbers, like money was numbers.

For that, I had an innate skill, and it was one that I still planned to use to make a life far different from this. People left you, people died, but money was forever—if you knew what you were doing. And when it came to money, unlike everything else, I always knew what I was doing.

After the chemistry, he started to creep in, bit by bit. I put it down to boredom. I mean, it wasn't as if I needed anyone. I didn't. But when you spend the better part of your day with someone in a nine-by-twelve room, you eventually have to talk . . . talk or kill each other. And Charlie wasn't as annoying as some. He was quiet, he didn't steal, and he kept his shit on his side of the room, which kept me from accidentally touching any of it. And two months later, he was still swinging a mean book.

I grinned to myself as I moved my eyes from the hated pink to the neutral tile of the ceiling. Charlie said he wanted to be a doctor, and that's why he carried so many books around. It was true enough; the kid had his nose stuck in one 24/7, but they also came in handy reenacting his first day. Thick and heavy, they were better than a sock full of pennies. Charlie might be a few inches shorter than I was, but he took care of himself fine.

"I saw Ryder in the library yesterday, believe it or not," I said, hands behind my head. Hunger was a junkyard-dog growl, even at the prospect of a breakfast of leathery scrambled eggs and petrified mystery-meat sausage.

"Library." Charlie snorted as he turned over in a rustle of sheets. "Five books in a milk crate isn't a library."

"Whatever, geek boy. I think he was looking for a weapon. Maybe he's going to challenge you to a duel." Dusty yellow light began to creep across the ceiling like the incoming tide. "Lab manuals at fifty paces."

"If it got that idiot to pick up a book, it might actually be worth it." There was the sound of his bare feet slapping against the floor. I expected him to follow his usual routine. Up to squeeze in ten minutes of studying, then off to the showers. But he didn't, not this time. Instead, he said quietly, "My birthday's next week."

"You saying you want five bucks in a card?"

There were eighty-four tiles up there under the shimmering light. Correction, there were eighty-four spaces, and one was empty. Underneath the missing tile was a black hole that blew sour air directly over my bed. In the middle of the night, I could easily imagine it was the tainted breath of death itself. Not for one moment did I think he'd come to take me away. That would be too easy. No, he was only paying a visit to a junior varsity player, clapping my shoulder with an approving bony hand.

"No, I don't want a card." His foot tapped on the floor, the bump of heel then slap of toes. "I just wanted you to know, Jack. That's all."

He would be eighteen. Eighteen and free. Charlie had told me that his parents had both been killed in a car accident several months ago. With no other relatives in the picture, he'd ended up here, but as of next week, he could walk away. As solid and logical as he was, I was sure he already had things worked out. An apartment, school . . . like me, Charlie had his plans. They were different plans with different goals, but we were both looking to get away from our here and now.

"So, now I know." My eyes dropped back to the pink wall. Next week was as perfect a time as any to leave. It would give me time to squirrel away some supplies, maybe steal some money from one of the teachers. Neither Charlie nor I would have to break in a new roommate. It was good . . . right. No more bullshit, no more being at the mercy of people who were damn deficient in the emotion. And no more goddamn pink.

"Sorry, Tess," I murmured under my breath. She'd loved it, but the color reminded me of too much.

"How much longer for you?"

Exhaling, I sat up. The morning was moving along, and if I wanted any breakfast, I'd better get moving with it. "Two years," I answered absently. It wasn't surprising that he didn't know. I wasn't one for telling personal details. As for my story, how I'd gotten here, he probably did know that . . . from the grapevine but not from me. Whether he knew or not, he didn't treat me any different from how he had since the first day. He didn't stare, and he didn't ask prying, greedily vicarious questions. A good roommate, all right. Damn good.

"Two years," he repeated, the corners of his mouth tightening. He'd experienced two months in Cane Lake; he could certainly imagine two years more of it. "That's a long time. Maybe I could write you sometime, see how you're doing."

I slid him a look that wasn't half as scornful as I meant it to be. "You're not a doctor yet, Allgood. You're not getting paid to take care of me or anybody." I didn't have a problem not telling him that I wouldn't be around to receive any letters. He had a conscience, Charlie did. As bad as Cane Lake was, it was possible he might think that being on the streets was worse. A runaway from the state didn't have many opportunities in the way of legal jobs or housing, and Charlie was smart enough to know that.

"They say they might let Hector come live with me," he said, changing the subject, or so I thought. "I just have to prove I can provide a stable household."

I could hear the bitter emphasis on the last two words. Even easygoing Charlie knew that the places the state sent kids were anything but stable. Not enough foster homes. Blah blah blah. Like any excuse could explain away places like this. Skimming my sleep-rumpled T-shirt off, I grunted noncommittally. Hector was Charlie's brother, younger by a year. He was in another facility. Charlie said Hector was more of a jock than he was and capable of watching his ass. Not that he had put it quite like that, Mr. Prim and Proper. Still, I knew the separation bothered Charlie, like being apart from Glory bothered me. They were all either of us had left.

"I wish they'd let you come, too." He said it with such sincerity. He meant it; he really did. The guy would take a killer like me into his home because he thought it was the right thing to do. Because he thought he was my friend.

It wasn't going to happen, of course. There were rules. Strict rules, fair rules, the kind that put children back with their biological parents to be beaten to death all in the name of keeping the God-given *natural* family whole. Rules to keep people like me away from good, wholesome folks until I was old enough to do some real damage. But even if those rules were different, I wouldn't go with Charlie. Couldn't. Depending on someone else only got you in trouble. I'd learned that the hard way at fourteen, and it was still true at sixteen. Trusting your parents, trusting your friends, it just wasn't a route I was going to go. Not again. I liked Charlie, I did. But like wasn't anything more than that. Like wasn't trust. I was going to be there for Glory, one day, but I didn't plan on anyone being there for me. Depend only on yourself, and you won't be let down. That was a rule of my own. An iron-fucking-clad one.

"It's the thought that counts," I said with an honesty that I rarely bothered with anymore. You didn't need the truth when you couldn't be bothered to waste words on anyone. Charlie had made himself the exception to that when I wasn't looking. Sneaky little bastard. It wasn't trust, but it was something. Yeah, something. Slapping the warm feeling back down to the murk where it belonged, I grabbed a towel and a melted bar of soap wrapped in plastic wrap before heading toward the door.

The week passed quickly, for both of us, I think. Charlie spent his time finishing off paperwork, talking to his brother on the phone, and neatly packing his few belongings. Or putting together his bookmobile, as I told him. It was something to see, Allgood in action. With all their corners lined up in anal-retentive cheer, the books were piled around his bed three high and two deep. It was hard to believe they'd all fit into a duffel bag to begin with, even if it was one bigger than Allgood himself. He tried to give a couple to me, but I didn't plan on organic chemistry being a big part of my future.

I was busy, too. I didn't steal any money; I'd wait on the last day for that. They took that shit seriously here. There would be room searches. Hell, strip searches if the former didn't turn anything up. I'd lift what I could on the day I left. By the time the staff noticed anything, I'd be gone. I'd hit Mrs. Candy Tidwell first. Candy, shit. You'd think with a name like that, she'd be sweet as homemade peach pie. Cheerful as a puff-chested robin welcoming the dawn. Far from it. She squatted on the other end of the spectrum and squatted hard. With the jowls of a bulldog and the cold, round amber eyes of a muck-eating catfish, she had probably cried a river when corporal punishment was taken out of schools. Cried and promptly got a job at a place that ignored an occasional slap or shake, and that place would be here. She had a fist as big as a ham and as heavy as a falling rock. Act up in one of her classes, and it was likely to come crashing down on the back of your head. I'd seen guys bust their noses in a spray of red on their desk from one of her blows.

Who the hell named their kid Candy? A girl like that had three choices when she grew up. Stripper, hooker, or sadistic teacher with a dark line of fuzz on her upper lip. Wasn't it my luck that I was saddled with the third option? Squeezed into a gray polyester pantsuit like a summer sausage popping from its skin, she was the thick, choking smell of chalk, lilacs, and blood. She was frozen stares, cracking knuckles, and the voice launched by a thousand cigarettes. In other words, she was not a good time. I would take her money and piss in her empty purse.

After her, I'd drift by the offices, see if any were open and empty. It didn't happen often, but once in a while, someone would take a bathroom break and forget to lock their door. Except for our beloved leader and administrator, Lewis Sugarman. He

never forgot. With an eerie smile that had been frozen on his face for the two years I'd been at Cane
Lake, he always kept a careful distance from the in-
mates. And that's what we were, really. Prisoners,
unwanted scum—at least that's what you'd think
from the look that would blossom in Sugarman's
eyes if he thought he might actually have to interact
with one of us. Pure, unadulterated disgust. He
would pass through the rec room as fast as his fancy
shoes could take him. And if he saw a kid on the
floor getting the living shit kicked out of him—
well, he'd just keep walking. Tall and thin, he had
shiny shoe-leather brown hair that owed a lot to a
dye more expensive than the drugstore kind. They'd
missed the eyebrows and lashes, though; pale gray,
they were all but invisible. He looked like a surprised Chihuahua but with the poisonous scuttle of
a fiddlehead spider.

Did he care about us? Hell, no. He'd walk
through a lake of our blood in those shiny shoes
and not blink. It was about the paycheck for him,
nothing else. Indifference and malice, sometimes it
was one and the same. Charlie had said that, him
and his big words, but he was right. Too bad Sugarman was so paranoid about locking that door; I
would've liked to take a slice of that check with me.

"I *will* call."

Charlie's stubborn voice interrupted my
thoughts. Sticky-fingered thoughts but misde-
meanors at best. Cane Lake was a mix of all kinds.

Some kids were just victims—of parent-killing car wrecks, bad luck, or relatives who liked to touch too much—but some were a little rougher than that. I'd learned a lot here. Not much of it good, even less of it legal. I was getting an education, all right, just not the kind that got you into college.

"Don't waste your money, Allgood." It wasn't the first time he'd said it. He'd been on this kick for the whole week. "Hair gel doesn't come cheap."

His hand automatically smoothed the bird nest on top of his head. "Funny," he said sourly. "But I'm serious, Jack. I want to call. Just take them, all right? Don't be such an obstinate ass."

"I was thinking the same about you." I leaned back against the wall, math book in my lap. The room wasn't big enough for a desk. Wasn't even big enough for two people to fart in at the same time without blowing the walls down. "Only with smaller words."

"You never have a nice thing to say about anyone, not even yourself." Charlie's books were disappearing into the duffel bag, two at a time and cradled with the same care you'd show a baby. "You're smart enough, Jack. Damn smart when you want to be." He gave me a flash of white teeth. "Except in chemistry."

"Yeah, yeah. Rub it in," I growled.

The last book disappeared, and I was disappointed when I felt a pang at the sight. I was tougher than that. I stood apart, a lone wolf. If it took getting down on all fours and howling at the moon to prove it, then that's what I would do. Just watch me. The rasp of the duffel bag's zipper was unnaturally loud, but I did my best to ignore it. Charlie was harder to ignore. "Take the calls, Jack. Please?"

I gave in. Gave in and told him what he wanted to hear. It was a lie, yeah, but so what? I'd done worse. Much, much worse. "Okay. Jesus. I'll take the calls. Damn, now give it a rest, already."

"Good." Charlie eased the bag to the floor. I would've tossed it. "You'll meet my brother some-day. You'll like Hector."

"Hell, Charlie, I don't even like you," I said impa-tiently, moving on to the next problem in the book. Another lie; this time, it was for both of us.

"Uh-huh." The pale eyes were bright. "Want to wait downstairs with me for my cab?"

The math problem was harder than it should've been for some reason. I gave up on it and tossed the book aside to roll over onto my stomach on the bed. "A cab. Aren't you rolling in the dough?"

He didn't pay any attention to the swipe. "You don't want to come?"

I shook my head, eyes on that goddamn pink wall. I didn't particularly want to watch Charlie get into a beat-up yellow Ford and disappear down the street while I peered through the seven-foot-tall chain-link fence. Not my idea of a good time. "See ya, Allgood."

I heard him heft the bag, heard the faint grunt of

exhalation at the weight of it. It had my lips curling slightly. Such a little guy but such big ambitions. I hoped he held on to them. It's always you against the world, and the world cheated like hell. But it might be that Charlie could fight it to a standstill. If anyone could . . .

"I'll call," he repeated, and I felt the faint knock of knuckles against my shoulder. "And if you don't take them, I'll call Mr. Sugarman instead and tell him you love the pink. Adore the pink. You want to volunteer to paint the *outside* of the building pink."

"Go home, asshole." I laughed. It came out a little thick, probably from those lingering paint fumes, but it was a laugh. My first since . . . since a long time.

He laughed, too. "Talk to you soon, Jack." Then the door closed, and he was gone, leaving nothing but an overly clean bed and the feeling that the room had grown into an empty, echoing space. Hard to imagine in a room the size of a broom closet, but that's what it felt like. I could've jumped up, shouted my name, and not been surprised to hear echoes for days. One smart-mouthed kid lost in a space the size of the Grand Canyon. I turned back over, pulled a corner of the blanket over me, and closed my eyes. There was nothing here I wanted to see right now.

I never saw Charlie alive again, but I did meet his brother, Hector. Charlie was wrong. I didn't like him. I didn't like him one damn bit.

3

I ended up in a carnival, a happy place for a happy kid.

Shit.

Although the place was a lot like me, really. There were the bright colors, the cheerful, tinny music pumped out by a mechanical calliope, all glossy surface to please the eye. Okay, none of that was like me. I was still everything I'd been two years ago at fourteen, red-haired country trash in T-shirt and jeans fished from a bin at Goodwill. Beat you like a redheaded stepchild, a good old-fashioned saying that Boyd had delighted in repeating to me over and over, snickering at his own "humor." I had sullen dark eyes full of wary suspicion and chips on both shoulders with spares in my pockets. No, I didn't have the external flash of the carnival, but I had the internal secretiveness and matter-of-fact larceny.

To live, you need money. There were things I wouldn't do for cash, but not many. Practical to the very edge of ignoring my conscience altogether, I did what I had to do. I lifted a few wallets if the risk seemed low. The last thing I wanted was to be picked up and sent back to Cane Lake or someplace even worse. So while I lightened some pockets, my main source of income came from the con. There was no danger there. The rubes weren't expecting anything but a little entertainment when they crossed my palm with silver.

I'd seen that in a movie once. "Cross my palm with silver," a gypsy had said with dramatically arching eyebrows and hot breath fogging her crystal ball. I didn't have a crystal ball. They were expensive, thirty bucks at least. I made do with a bowling ball. Laugh if you want. It worked. I'd found it in a garbage dump. It was chipped and cracked around the finger holes, but I simply turned that part down against the table and concealed it in the nest of threadbare velvet that cradled it. It wasn't transparent, but the marbleized pattern was odd enough to catch the eye. Twilight blue with a glitter of silver swirling through it, it reminded me of the old days. Lying in a field of sweet-smelling clover and watching as a spray of comets crossed the night sky. I could hear the girls in the distance, laughing and squealing as they helped Mom bring in the laundry. Could feel the bread of my peanut butter sandwich give softly under my fingers as I raised it to my mouth for a bite. It was a good moment . . . yeah, good. And if I tried hard enough, I could live in that moment, just that one, for a while as I stared at the ball.

For two years in the carnival, years that passed more quickly than the ones in Cane Lake had, I dealt the cards and waved a hand over the make-shift crystal ball just like that movie gypsy. At first, I didn't have a tent of my own or a trailer. I would pick a spot on the carnival outskirts, lay out my strip of velvet, ball, and cards, and wait for the ladies to come. And it was always ladies. They'd take a look at my hand-lettered sign that said a dollar a reading, my hair so very earnestly slicked back, my robe that had once been a Halloween Dracula cape, and my fake gold hoop earring that fit the lobe I'd pierced myself, and melt into a maternal puddle. At sixteen, I'd looked younger, an Opie who'd lost his way, and the women couldn't wait to throw their money at me. I could've said you'll meet a tall dark alien who will carry you off to his mothership to be his egg-laying hive queen, and they wouldn't have batted an eye. It was all in fun . . . for them. For me, it was survival.

The carnival owner tried to run me off in those days, more times than I could count. He'd stomp after me, four hundred pounds of arm-waving fury. "Shoo, boy! Shoo!" he'd squeak in a voice oddly high and sweet for such a big man. "Shoo," as if I were a stray tomcat spraying the place. It was safe to say that "Shoo" didn't score too high on my list, damn sure not high enough to actually scare me off. A balled-up fist, a hard and heavy boot, that might've had me moving on. "Shoo"? Jesus. That was kiss-my-scrawny-ass territory. When I saw him coming, shaking the ground like a cranky elephant, I usually had plenty of time to gather my stuff and disappear. Half an hour later, I'd pop back up somewhere else, behind a hot-dog stand or next to the freak show. And that's where I met Abigail.

"Why do you wear gloves all the time?"

I paused in the absent shuffling of my cards. They weren't tarot, just a normal deck, slick and yellowed from a thousand fingers. It didn't matter. I could've played at tarot until the end of time and not seen a goddamn thing. Not from a factory-fresh deck of cards, anyway. It had taken a while to learn to shuffle with the gloves on, but it was time well spent. I could've spent the two-fifty on a new deck and handled them with my bare hands, but it wasn't worth it. I could've touched the cards, but I couldn't have handled the money or the occasional brush of a customer's hand. Gloves were just safer all the way around. Now I looked up at the girl who wanted to know why. I'd been lurking and working the carnival for two weeks, and she was the first person to actually talk to me . . . other than those unbelievably fascinating "shoo, shoo" conversations.

She was younger than me by four years at least. Eleven or twelve, probably. Dressed in a white unitard that was spangled from neck to ankle, she had a cascading mass of pale blond hair that reached her narrow hips. She also had a horn. Yeah, a horn. It was planted right on top of her head and protruding from the thick hair. Obviously papier-mâché and not fastened as tightly as it could've been, it wobbled precariously when she tilted her head to look at me. "Do you have warts? Huge disgusting warts all over your hands?"

There in the sweltering heat and stink of roasting mystery meat, sitting cross-legged on the ground, I looked up into round amber eyes and felt my heart stutter with a painful squeeze. It wasn't love. Hell, she was a *kid,* barely past the Barbie stage. No, it wasn't love but a surge of homesickness so strong that the card in my hand bent double before falling to the velvet. I'd seen the look in her eye before. Curiosity, impatience, troublemaking through and through, she would've skipped hand-in-hand with Tess and Glory . . . perfect synch. She was older but had the same spirit, the same "Look at me, world. Just look how amazing I am." It would've been annoying if it hadn't been true.

I let my eyes drop and swallowed against the strangling heat in my throat. God, I missed them. "No." I cleared my throat, and the next words came out a little more smoothly. "It's hair. All over my palm, just like Granny said would happen."

She scowled, pale eyebrows pulling into a confused V. "Huh?"

"Never mind." I picked up the card and tried to straighten it out. "I just like gloves, okay?"

A pink shoe and gloves. One led to the other.

The shoe had been the first time. I'd picked it up

and known . . . just like that. I'd seen Tessie's strawberry blond hair floating in a cloud, her blue eyes wide and empty, her mouth open just wide enough to show a flash of tiny white teeth. Tess was dead. Tossed into the old well as if she were garbage. Everything in her that made Tess Tess was gone. The fits of giggles, the smell of ninety-nine-cent honeysuckle shampoo, the absolute loathing of Brussels sprouts, and the forever love for her shiny pink shoes. All of it, gone forever. There was no more Tess, and it didn't take any big jump of logic to know who was responsible for that. Chicken pox, Boyd playing babysitter, Boyd who would get bored easily, Boyd who drank until it was coming out of his pores, Boyd who'd thought Mom was a little too old when he married her at seventeen . . . so many thoughts in such a short moment of time as her shoe had tumbled from my hand.

So very many.

It had slowly gotten worse since that first time. In the beginning, I could touch something and see only a flash, a current slice of time. Hand me someone's keys, and I could tell you where they were right then, but that was all. That changed. Little by little, I would see more of the past, until eventually I saw it all. I'd never much cared for history in school, and here I was condemned to relive it constantly. Wasn't that a bitch? The past was all I saw, though, and I was glad of it. The future . . . who would want to see that? Unless you could change it, and it was safe to say with the way things worked, that wasn't possible. Forget physics and math and all that geek crap, that wasn't what would stop you. It was the universe, uncaring and oblivious, that was holding the cards on this one. It wasn't about to let you change the shit coming your way.

"I want a pair of gloves," the girl said imperiously. Quite the princess, this one was. She held out her hands in front of her, palms down, and looked them over seriously. "White, I think. With diamonds. *Real* ones," she emphasized. "To match my costume."

I gave a snort. "Sorry, kid. I'm all out of diamonds." Picking up the stray card, I shuffled it back into the pack.

She gave an exaggerated sigh and flopped down opposite me, skinny legs folded beneath her. "That's okay. They'd be too hot, anyway. My name's Abigail." Sticking out her nonexistent chest, she fluffed her long hair and preened. The horn wobbled so strenuously I was surprised she hadn't put an eye out yet. "Abigail the Amazing Unicorn Girl." The capitals were as clear as if they'd been letters of fire.

"Is that so?" I tried hard to stop the quirk of my lips. She was just a bored girl, bugging me for no good reason. She wasn't Glory, and she wasn't Tess. She was just a girl.

"Yep." She touched a curious finger to the midnight-blue curve of my "crystal" ball. "First I was the One and Only. Then I was Unique. Like the

Unique Unicorn Girl. But Daddy decided Amazing was better. 'Cause that's what I am." Actually, she was probably all three, and I was glad she had a daddy who knew it. "What are you?" she went on, eyes bright and curious.

"What am I?" I laid out a row of solitaire. Business tended to be slow this part of the day.

She shifted, pulling her knees up and resting her chin on them. "You know. Are you Stupendous or Super or Marvelous? You're doing the whole psychic thing, you need *something*." Hastily, she cautioned, "But Amazing is mine."

My lips twitched again uncontrollably, and I agreed, "Amazing is yours." Maybe she was right. Maybe I did need an Amazing of my own. Jack the Psychic didn't quite get it for flash and flair.

"So?" she demanded impatiently. "What are you?"

I stared at the cards blankly for a moment, and then it came to me. "All Seeing." Jackson Lee Eye, the All Seeing Eye. That was who I was. Blind as a bat in the past but all seeing now. Talk about your too little, too late . . . no one was better at that than me.

"All Seeing." She didn't seem too impressed, sighing and shaking her head. "Well, okay, but there's no pizzazz." The hands she threw out gave the word its own special effects. "That's what Daddy says you need in an act, pizzazz." She lingered lovingly over the word, emphasizing the *z* in a sizzle sound.

"I'm sure he's right." Giving my own sigh, I put the cards away and began to fold up the velvet. My stomach was growling loudly enough to scare any potential clients away. It was time to invest in a hot dog. "It was nice meeting you, Amazing Abigail. I'm going to grab some lunch. See you later." Actually, I wasn't quite sure that I wanted to see her again, but in the small confines of the carnival, there was probably no avoiding it. Not that she wasn't a nice kid, but she reminded me of things I'd rather not be reminded of. Life was a helluva lot easier to bear when you could forget.

"Lunch?" She bounced up, surrounded by a cloud of hair. "You can have lunch with us. My mom loves company, and Daddy can help you think of a better name."

I was happy with the name I'd come up with, but somehow I ended up being pulled in her wake. Not caring could work against you sometimes. When you didn't care, it was hard to muster up the energy to stand in the face of Hurricane Abby. Not giving a shit: as philosophies went, it had its flaws. Two years later, I was still going to lunches and dinners at Abby's trailer.

I stuck with the name, though.

Then I was eighteen and had a small tent that was my home. I didn't buy a trailer. I was saving my money for bigger and better things. Abby's parents had smoothed over things with Mr. Toadvine, the carnival's owner, and I'd been allowed to eke out a little corner of the place for myself. When I wanted to shower or clean up, I went to Lilly and Johan's place and locked the door. Abby had dumped enough cold water over the shower curtain to do a good imitation of Niagara Falls. Following me like a puppy, she'd adopted me wholeheartedly as her older brother. Every time I had that thought, my chest ached fiercely. Two years with Abby was still four years without Glory and Tess. That truth was inescapable.

But now I would be leaving soon, and that led to another inescapable truth. I'd be losing another sister, no matter how hard I'd tried to make sure she didn't creep her way into my heart. She was fourteen now, the same age I was when it had happened. When it had all happened. I buried the thought and carefully covered the table in imitation silk. The velvet had long since raveled away. Abby . . . I'd been thinking about Abby, fourteen and thought she was all grown up, although she was still stuck in a training bra to her mortification. A sound of the tent flap being raised had my head coming up. Speak of the devil . . . if the devil were a flat-chested teenage girl in sequins. "Hey, Amazing, what brings you around?" I drawled as I polished the tried-and-true bowling ball of the future.

"I'm bored." She flounced into a folding chair, then grimaced and pulled her tail from beneath her. Johan had decided the horn wasn't enough and had added a full fall of white polyester hair in a cascading tail. Abby had swished it with enthusiasm for a day or two before getting tired of it. Twisting the end of one blond strand, she said with a hesitancy that was completely un-Abigail-like, "Somebody said you were leaving."

"That so?" I took a rubber band from the pocket of my black jeans and pulled my hair back. There was barely enough to make the stubbiest of tails, but I was getting there. I'd pierced my other ear to go with it. Small gold hoops and a hokey billowing black shirt completed the look. There weren't many red-haired gypsies out there, in real life or the movies, but I gave it my best shot. "What's Lilly say about you listening to gossip?"

"My mom is the one who told me." The lip was out in full force, pouting and sullen.

Lilly was one to know and tell every little thing going on at the carnival. Gossip with a side of grocery-bought cheesecake. Overly sweet with a rabidly red strawberry topping, you would eat it anyway to please Lilly. Gossip being her only vice, she was a nice woman, and she loved Abby. Took care of Abby, would never let anyone hurt her. Never. Good intentions only went so far in this world. It was the actions behind them that mattered. Yeah, a nice lady. The nicest. She would've been a mother figure to me if I'd let her. I wouldn't.

Couldn't.

I sat down opposite Abby and fell into a now old and established habit. I reached for the cards. The thin silk gloves slid with comforting grace over the surface of the slick cardboard. Shuffling them from hand to hand with a skill more suited to a blackjack dealer than a psychic, I exhaled, then shrugged. "Nothing is forever, Amazing. You're old enough to know that." It was a bitch of a thing to say, whether it was true or not, and I didn't have any excuse for having said it. I dropped the cards back onto the table and with a feeling of acid self-disgust started to apologize, "Ah, hell, I'm s—"

I didn't get any further than that before small bony fingers cut me off with a sharply painful pinch to my forearm. Luckily, I was wearing long sleeves, and she hadn't touched bare flesh, or I'd have had more than a pinch to deal with. Ignoring my yelp and glare, she ordered angrily, "You're being mean. Stop being mean."

I rubbed the abused flesh of my arm through the cloth. "Okay, okay. I *was* saying I was sorry before you tried to rip off a piece of me as a souvenir. Jesus."

She leaned back in the chair with thin arms folded tightly across her nonexistent chest. "You know what you are, Jackson Lee? An asshole," she said triumphantly, so obviously proud of her daring that I had to smother a grin. "A big, flaming a-hole. Just ask anybody."

"Is that so?" I said with careful gravity. "Makes me wonder why you're hanging out here, then, Miss Amazing. By the way . . ." I checked my watch. "It's time for your first show. You better get out of here, or there won't be any cheesecake for you tonight." As far as I could tell, that was the worst punishment Abby had faced in her short life, and that included the time she'd turned the poodle trainer's entire curly pack loose. The vicious little ankle biters had spent hours terrorizing the entire carnival until they'd been cornered after they took the Dog Boy down. Ten tiny sets of furry hips humping against both of his legs, Artie had never quite been the same. For that escapade, Abby had been sent to bed an hour early. With a big piece of cheesecake.

Shaking my head, I repeated, "Go on, Amazing. Be nice to your parents; they're damn nice to you."

She slid out of the chair and rocked back and forth on her heels. "Will you . . ." Chewing her lip, she scowled and tried again. "Will you write me?"

It would've been easier to lie, kinder, too, like I had done to that kid Charlie at Cane Lake, but I didn't. My entire childhood had been a house of cards built of lies. I was tired of it. I wasn't going to build my own house of the same. "I don't know." The flash of utter hurt in her eyes was a harsh kick, to the head, to the stomach, to the balls. It didn't matter. It was still painful as hell. "I'll try," I amended. "I can't make promises, though, Amazing. I'm . . ." I was what? An outsider deep down? Someone better off alone? A psychological study that would have a grad student pissing his pants in joy? A screwed-up son of a bitch who already had sisters, one dead and one lost, and didn't want to take that risk again? I didn't have a clue. But I did know I couldn't make promises I didn't have the inner resources to keep. "I'm not much of a letter writer," I finished with a faint curl of my lips. "But I'll give it my best shot, Amazing. For you." She wasn't Charlie, not old enough to know that sometimes things don't work out. After a few months, she would forget me, anyway, mostly. She'd find a boyfriend or discover some new hobby besides a messed-up psychic. She would pass the way of all sisters, one way or the other. I could write a letter or two until then. It wouldn't kill me.

"You'd better. You'd better write." She moved toward the tent flap and slipped through, trailing hair and unicorn tail behind her. A split second later, she stuck her head back in and said, "Oh, I almost forgot. I hate you." And then she was gone.

I returned to the cards. They didn't talk to me; they never would. I wished the same could be said about other things. "So long, Amazing," I murmured, the comforting flow of a solitaire game dealt out before me. "I'm sorry, but I have plans." I did, too. Plans for a house that didn't smell of booze and cabbage. Plans for money and independence. Plans for a life where I could walk down the street and not automatically be labeled white trash. Plans where I was somebody. A big fish in a small pond, it didn't matter. I would be somebody. I would be Jackson Lee, the All Seeing Eye.

Not the redheaded bastard from down Rooster Pike way. Not the boy with thrift-store clothes and the homegrown haircut. Not the kid with the occasional black eye and the smart mouth. No, I was done being that kid. I was going to change that for good. I had plans, all right.

I never thought that Abby did, too.

4

There's a sucker born every minute.

Someone really on top of their shit had said that once. Some said it was the great con artist of his or any time, P. T. Barnum. Others said it was one of his competitors who coined the phrase. Not that it mattered. What mattered was the message, the inner truth of the words. There's a sucker born every minute. It was staggering in its simplicity, heart-stopping in its beauty. It was also a personal mantra, my nightly prayer. Picture it, if you will. Me, on my knees beside my bed, hands clasped earnestly as I asked for nothing more than people as dumb as a box of hair to chase me down the street and throw money at me. More angelic a picture you couldn't find.

Of course, it was a nice image but not strictly true. I didn't have to beg. Sliding green out of sweaty palms came naturally to me, an instinct so strong I probably popped out of the womb with it. Lifted the doctor's wallet before he had the chance to slap my ass. Outright stealing and unabashed conning were long behind me, though. The tricks I'd picked up in a state-sponsored home for the tragically un-adoptable and the permanently screwed had gotten me through some hard times, but I'd moved on to other things. That long-gone carnival had taught me a better way, a safer way.

I was the real deal now. I genuinely earned the money I made. If people chose to pay me more money than they had, hey, whose fault was that? If they used what I gave them as an uncertain prop to a shaky life, that wasn't my lookout. My product was solid for what it was—I never lied to a client. If they took it to be something else, took *me* to be something more than I was, all I could do was lean back and rake it in. I never claimed to be a saint. What you did with what I gave you wasn't my concern.

What was my concern was an absent secretary. Abigail, who had never given up on me and had written enough letters to fill a steamer trunk, was off visiting her family. It was a different carnival but in the end just the same. It had come to roost for a while in a podunk town about an hour south of At-lanta, and she'd jumped at the chance to see her parents. Sticky cotton-candy fun for her, but for me it was a different story. No secretary meant calls would be missed and walk-ins turned away. That, in turn, meant a steady stream of twenties and fifties flapping their wings elsewhere. It wasn't a mental image to put me in a good mood as I opened the office. Neither were the horns, curling mustache, and pitchfork some Bible-thumping delinquent had drawn in marker on the glass over my poster. Displayed prominently in the picture window, my face stared back at me with uncannily penetrating eyes. A brown so dark they appeared black, they delivered a gaze both brooding and knowing. Impressive, and it should be. It took me a good hour in the mirror to get that look down pat.

The rest had been easier. Dark red hair was pulled back tightly into a two-inch ponytail, and my work wardrobe was exclusively black. I'd decided a goatee might be pushing the envelope and went clean-shaven, but I still looked like every Hollywood image of what I was. On that note, I tilted my head and reconsidered as my hand hovered to rub the marker lines away. Who was I to say that the devil wasn't a good look for me?

It *is* all in the advertising.

Snorting at a conceit that was pretty big even for me, I went ahead and wiped the glass clean with my glove . . . including the "Repent" sign above my head. I had some older clients. It wouldn't do to scare them into heart palpitations on the sidewalk. Unlocking the front door to the office, I walked in with a shadow following at my knee and dumped the mail on Abigail's desk. Small and dainty, it was all whites, golds, and ornate curlicues . . . much like Abby herself. Twelve years, and she hadn't changed all that much, the same Amazing Unicorn Girl. The

rubes hadn't minded her glaringly fake special effects then, and their equivalent still doted on her
today. There hadn't been many kids cuter than
Abby had been, and there weren't any women more
incandescent.

As for my truth, a runaway from the state who
could see what lurked behind the mundane, I'd
been different from Abby. Not as cute, for one. As
for the seeing, it's sad but true that most people
have done things they regret. Add to that people
who have done things, hideous things, that they
don't regret, and it was a lot for a homeless kid to
know, to see. That's why I'd gotten the gloves, wore
long sleeves. It was why I'd only conned them at the
carnival, but I'd known that if I wanted to move up
one day, that would have to change.

When I left the carnival, I sucked it up. I used my
ability; I didn't fake it. I started when the people at
Social Services weren't as cooperative as they
could've been when I was searching for Glory. I
learned to handle the uncomfortable nature of it. I
broke out the goods and went to work. It hadn't
helped me find Glory, but it had helped me start the
business. It wasn't wine and roses, but it was beer
and barbecue. That had been a start. It had only
snowballed from there.

After opening one of the envelopes from the
mail, I fanned out fifteen twenties and grinned
darkly at a whole new classification of lunch money.
I stuffed the money back in and dropped the enve-

lope into Abby's in-box to be sorted later for a reading. I might charge an arm and a leg, but I did deliver. Moving back to my separate office, I propped open the door with a plaster cast of a head and got ready to greet the day. I had several appointments before noon, although I'd kept the next few days light until Abby was due back. I could've taken a short vacation, too, but a raging Atlanta summer left little to do but sizzle on the asphalt. Even sitting on my dock at home would be like enduring a sweat lodge. The breeze off the river was nonexistent, and the mosquitoes were carrying off water-skiers. The Ninth Circle of Hell had nothing on Atlanta in August.

Even with the air conditioner going full blast, it was still overly warm in the office. I pulled at my black fake-silk long-sleeved pullover shirt. No billowing sleeves—that much into the look I was not, and real silk showed Atlanta sweat stains if you merely looked out the window. It was my costume of choice—it shouted psychic or movie-style spy/assassin, but lightweight as it was, I didn't think it was going to survive, air conditioner or no. My palms should've sweated under gloves of real silk, better fit, but they were long used to being covered. They stayed cool. Protected. I'd settled in behind my desk, a much more massive affair than Abby's. A deep, dark cherrywood, it came direct from the factory. That's the way I liked my things, new. Untainted. It kept my life simpler. Slipping off my shoes, I propped my feet up next to a crystal ball on a brass stand and reached for the nudie mag I'd bought at the corner store. A man had his needs. Being in touch with the pulse of the Universal friggin' Soul wasn't going to change that.

The jingle of bells and a strong hello had me shoving the magazine into a drawer and swinging my feet down. Placing my hands flat on the desk, I cleared my throat and said, "Mrs. Eckhardt, prompt as always." I didn't bother to deepen my voice, but I did flash her an appreciative eye. It was faked, but Ginger was an established client. She might already be hooked, but it paid to invest in her continued satisfaction. "And looking gorgeous to boot. Blond is a good color on you."

A wrinkled hand automatically fluffed the buttercup-yellow bouffant hair as Ginger came into my office and sat in the plush crimson chair opposite my desk. "You heartless flirt. Always the same with you." Pink lips peeled back to reveal the bright and shining smile you didn't need to be psychic to know rested in a cup in her bathroom overnight.

It was hard to say whether Ginger kept coming back for the information from beyond or for the flattery. I didn't care which it was. It was her dime, and either one paid the bills. "How could I not flirt with a woman so stunning?" I said with a sly wink. "It would be a crime against God and nature." She threw back her head and gave a bawdy laugh that

revealed that in her day, Mrs. Eckhardt had been
something, indeed. Of course, I didn't have to guess
that by her laugh—I knew her original hair color. A
rich chestnut brown, it came through clear as day. I
had seen her stuff her first bra, kiss her first boy, and
skinny-dip her way into a reputation she didn't
once regret. When she married the love of her life,
I was there. She gave him three healthy children
that I watched grow up. I also saw her husband
die—a stroke while playing golf. I stood at her side
at the funeral as they lowered the coffin to disappear into the ground, never to be seen again. That
part I could've done without. I'd seen enough of
that magic trick in my own past.

Now you see them. Abracadabra. Now you don't.

I tossed a few more compliments her way, which
she caught like a pro, before I peeled off my right
glove and held out my hand. "What is it today, gorgeous?"

This time, it was a lost necklace. It wasn't the first.
Ginger lost things on a near-weekly basis. If it wasn't
my charm drawing her in, then it was a bad case of
Alzheimer's. I cradled her keys in my hand for a second, and the image bloomed clearly. Tucked away
in a lovingly polished cedar chest and very pur-
posely put there when Ginger was craving company
and a big dose of flattery from her favorite psychic.
With a twitch of my lips, I delivered the news, and
soon Ginger was on her way after promising to call
back and make another appointment with Abby.

The next client didn't show up. A first-timer, no big deal. It happened. It did make me appreciate the fact that Abby wasn't there to say I should've known that was going to happen. She never tired of that joke. Twelve years, and it still tripped from her lips as if it were the first time. Now that I thought about it, a few days' vacation might not be enough for my devoted secretary. A little alone time wasn't always a bad thing, even when it came to someone I'd come to think of, no matter how reluctantly, as a sister. Abby's sense of humor might leave something to be desired, but she was all softness, bright eyes, good heart, and bubbling laughs. Not much like my real sister. Glory was every bit the greedy soul I was, but she went about her larceny in a more proactive fashion. Not averse to danger, she balanced on a knife edge of amorality and violence.

Cute little girls with strawberry blond hair go to foster homes, while gangly teenage boys who knew how to use a shotgun are swallowed by state institutions. At the time, I'd thought Glory had the better deal. It wasn't the first time I'd been wrong. Probably wouldn't be the last. In the end, I wasn't sure which of us could lay claim to being more fucked up—by societal standards, anyway. Those standards had always seemed excessively lofty to my way of thinking, but when it came to Glory, maybe society was on to something. The little girl I'd once sworn to save was gone. And what was left in her place was someone who, if you crossed, it was safe to say you'd regret it.

Too late to change now. Wasn't that the story of my life?

I was just thinking about what to do with my free hour thanks to my no-show, but someone tried to rob me instead. This was also not the first time this had happened to me. He was about seventeen, skinny, twitching for a fix, with a shaved head and a black tribal tattoo on the dark skin of the back of his hand. It was the same hand he used to hold the knife, no doubt thinking it was concealed by laying it flat against his leg.

Kids.

By the time with darting eyes he checked out the place for other people, he was way too late in the game. He turned toward me and lifted the switch-blade, opening his mouth to say something he saw in a movie or a TV show—something that was damn sure going to scare the living shit out of me. The entitled, lazy youth of today. They couldn't even come up with their own piss-your-pants threats. It was a shame. But as his mouth opened to deliver whatever plagiarized obscenity-filled de-mand, he noticed the gun I was pointing at him.

I kept the porn drawer closed so as not to offend the ladies, but I had a holster for one big-ass Glock studded in place to the underside of my desk so as not to offend my undertaker with a difficult-to-conceal slit throat. It was easy to pull, easier to point. I aimed at his scrawny chest. I didn't think because he was skinny and underfed that he wasn't dangerous. In some situations, back-to-the-wall ones, it made people like him—a kid like I'd been— more dangerous, if anything.

His eyes widened, the whites of them tinged more toward yellow. Hepatitis. Not long for this vale of tears. I didn't wait to see if the gun made him back off. I went directly to defense line two and used my left hand to activate the alarm system. The button on the closest corner of the desk was red, simple, and small—the results weren't. The wail threatened to puncture eardrums and bring the police in minutes. It was so loud that, forget Georgia, it might bring every cop in the tristate area to arrest me for disturbing the peace.

I had a third option, but that one I hadn't had to use once. The first two always did the trick. The guy was gone so fast, flinging the front door open with such force, that he shattered the glass encasing the chicken wire. When I'd seen my defaced poster, I should've known it was going to be a bad day.

I turned off the alarm. It wasn't connected to a service. Wasted money. The noise alone was enough to send the thieves running. I replaced the Glock in its holster, but not before noticing the concealing black paint was chipping off the orange tip that was a dead giveaway that it was a fake gun and less lethal than a BB gun. But it was the only gun I would have. I didn't like guns, and I didn't like knives, which made it more awkward when I noticed the thief had dropped his in the middle of the floor as he ran for it.

Because, unlike my gun, it was real.

The body holds eight to ten pints of blood. I saw that on some stupid crime-scene investigation show where everyone is attractive and everyone wears sunglasses at night. I'd been channel surfing one night and wasn't fast enough to keep surfing before I heard that unnecessary fact. I didn't know pints or liters or anything like that, but I knew how much blood poured out of your mother when a knife was jammed into one side of her throat and out the other. In three minutes, give or take, it was a lake of blood. A lake you never forgot; a liter was just a word. I'd lay a thousand bucks not one of those actors had seen anything close to what they were blathering about. They were only reading their lines, and not once did it go through their empty heads that what they were saying and pretending was reality to some people.

A head popped in through the doorway as I dug out the Yellow Pages to call the glass guy to come fix the door. It was Luther, fifty and graying, from Pie and Puds three shops down. The pie was the best in Georgia, and Pud was for when you ordered Luther's special brew of coffee with a slice. Thick as mud with enough caffeine to guarantee you didn't sleep for a week. Pie and mud. Pud. I didn't get it, either, but each to his own. Luther had a faithful elderly clientele that came every day. "Damn, boy, you get robbed again? And can't you get an alarm that plays Barry White? I got old people in the place. You done made them soak their Depend diapers and scared 'em so bad the false teeth were flying around the room like some cheesy damn horror movie."

"Sorry, Luther, but Barry wasn't in the selection." I eyed with grim unease the knife on the floor. "The kid dropped it. Would you mind tossing it into the Dumpster on your way out? I've got a customer coming and they're already five minutes late. I have to get my mojo in gear." I passed a hand in front of my face and reappeared with smooth features, mysterious fathomless gaze, and one raised eyebrow. "Huh? You think?"

He shook his head, grabbed the switchblade, and headed back out the door. "You are one strange white boy. That's all I'm saying."

Once he was gone, I finished calling the glass place. They were used to calls in this area. The office was in a well-traveled, artsy-funky part of town. It was up and coming, not as well known or expensive to rent as Little Five Points, which meant it was still rough around the edges, which had just been proven. That didn't stop people from coming, and walk-ins were common. That didn't mean the man who opened the door while I was sweeping up small pieces of glass wasn't what I considered a member of my usual clientele. Not that I didn't get men in, I did. But they were usually an older crowd or dreadlocked twentysomethings who smelled of incense and goat cheese. The man at my door didn't fit. He looked to be in his early thirties and wasn't being dragged along by a giggling girlfriend or sporting flip-flops and a tie-dyed shirt. On the contrary, he was wearing a suit. In this weather, the man was wearing a goddamn suit. Unbelievable.

Okay, there was no tie, and the shirt was open at the collar one whole button, but it was still a suit. I felt the sweat prickle the nape of my neck at the very sight of it. The guy was tall and solid, with short blue-black hair and almond-shaped pale blue eyes. I'd only seen that combination once before. A couple of months of my long-gone past, and here it stood before me. But this wasn't the real deal. Years had passed, and except for the unusual coloring, I probably couldn't have picked out my old acquaintance on the street. But I did remember that he'd had a helluva nose and was short. This guy had a nose of less than anteater proportions and was tall, taller than me. He wasn't a good-looking guy, with a face of harsh angles and planes, but he had a quiet power about him. An air of competence. I wouldn't have wanted to run into him in a dark alley. Abby, on the other hand, would've finagled his phone number in a heartbeat.

Power and competence. It made me think of Cane Lake and cops. I'd had my fill of cops when I was fourteen, including the sympathetic ones. None of it made for good memories.

"Are you the . . ." He closed the door behind him and waited for the tinkling bells to quiet before he finished the question. "Are you the resident psychic?"

I'd long slipped my glove back on. Resting the broom against Abby's desk, I folded my arms to regard him suspiciously. The disquiet I kept to myself. He wasn't the past, but this guy was someone, all right. Someone who wanted something from me, and it was more than where Auntie Liz had hidden the family silver before she died. He wasn't a cop. He didn't quite have the tinfoil bite to him, but he was *something*. And whatever that might be was pinging hard on my radar.

"That depends on your definition of psychic," I drawled. It was my show, but there were times the trappings of it grated. "Walk-ins are twenty-five bucks extra. Rates are posted in plain sight per Chamber of Commerce rules." I jerked my chin in the direction of the black-and-gilt cursive, Abby's doing, on the wall.

He wasn't put out by my rudeness. "I'm not here for a reading," he said politely with a vaguely Northern flavor to his voice. "Not yet, at any rate. I would just like to talk."

"I charge by thirty-minute increments," I droned on as if he hadn't spoken. If he wasn't here for the talent, I wasn't going to waste the usual routine on him. "I have an hour window in my schedule. You want the whole thing or not?" I didn't care either way. On one hand, I wasn't one to turn away money.

On the other, well, I wasn't one to turn away money. I suppose that meant there was only one hand, a moneygrubbing paw blithely unaware of my caution. Or simply resistant to it.

"You'd charge to talk?" He blinked, torn between a tightly drawn amusement and mildly righteous outrage. "I'm not sure my expense account will cover that."

"I'd charge to flip you off in traffic if I could work out the logistics." I straightened. "My time is valuable. You can pay or you can walk. It's your choice."

He reached for his wallet without further argument, only saying, "There goes my dinner money."

Yeah, cry me a river. I accepted the hundred dollars he forked over and repeated, "Twenty-five extra for walk-ins."

He raised an eyebrow but passed more bills over. "Could we sit down?"

"Sure," I said as I counted the money in a fast riffle. "Knock yourself out. You've got thirty minutes on the meter."

Making his way past me into my office, he sat in the client chair and looked around. The doorstop immediately caught his eye. "Do you have an interest in phrenology, then?"

Wasn't he up on the whole ball of wax? "Nope." I sat back in my chair, slouching a bit and linking fingers across my stomach. "Bought it at a yard sale. A buck fifty. Good for propping the door open." And it made me laugh at people's gullibility.

"You don't put stock in reading a person's character by the bumps on their head, I'm guessing?" He was serious, even with the faintly dry flavor to the question. It only made him seem more out of place. In this business, you usually have two categories: slobbering believers or foaming-at-the-mouth skeptics. This guy didn't come across like either one. He didn't have the fire of a zealot or the cynicism of the doubting Thomas. In another lifetime, I might have been curious. In this one, I only wanted to see the door hitting his ass. Curiosity killed more than cats, I'd learned that the hard way. And if that made me the only closed-minded psychic in the Western Hemisphere, I'd learn to live with the title.

"Only if I put them there." I opened the top drawer, pulled out a deck of cards, and started to deal them out. "So talk, already. I'm on a schedule, pal, even if you're not."

His eyes followed the cards as he said firmly, "I did say no reading."

"It's solitaire." I lifted eyebrows at his insistence. "The only thing I'll pick up from this is paper cuts." If I weren't wearing my gloves. The deck was clean and new. I was the only one who'd touched it, but I wasn't taking a chance around this one.

He gave a rueful smile and apologized smoothly. "Sorry. I'm a little sensitive to maintaining the integrity of the experiment."

Great. He was one of *those*. Now it made sense, although he still didn't quite fit the profile. For all that they tried to be unbiased, most researchers, to use the word loosely, were either skeptics or believers. Trying to prove or disprove, one or the other. This guy, however, was so buttoned down that where he fell I simply couldn't tell.

I flipped over three cards and said matter-of-factly, "I'm not one for poking and prodding, Mr. . . . ?"

"Dr. John Chang." He offered his hand and said, "I apologize again for the rudeness." It came out so easily, so naturally, that I was almost tempted to believe it. Almost. This wasn't a man who spent a lot of his life apologizing.

"Yeah, you're all about the rudeness," I said sarcastically. The guy was doing an imitation of upstanding that was so stalwart and upright that it made my teeth hurt. I nodded my head at his hand. "I thought you didn't want to compromise whatever project you've got going on."

"I was guessing you wear those gloves for a reason." And a good guess it was. He pulled his hand back when it was obvious I wasn't going to shake it. Money bought my time; it didn't buy any manners to go along with it. Especially not for someone who was very probably lying to me. "And you are?"

I was positive he already knew who I was long before he stepped foot across my threshold, but I shrugged mentally and went along with it. My name certainly wasn't private information around the neighborhood. "Jackson Lee Eye." Corny, eh? I was an extra from every Southern-fried, squeal-like-a-pig movie ever made. Despite my urban appearance, I still had the good-old-boy drawl . . . only I wasn't particularly good, and I had learned to speak "purty" enough to flirt with the older clients. But they liked the drawl, and I kept it. Smooth as molasses.

He glanced over his shoulder to look at the painted letters on the tiny lobby's picture window. "Ah, the All Seeing Eye." The corner of his mouth quirked up. "Clever."

"It pays to play to your audience," I replied with an edge of mockery. I had no interest in proving myself to a possible academic who had nothing better to do with his time or to someone even more annoying like a flat-out liar, and it was pretty evident in my voice. If he thought I was a fake, my feelings wouldn't exactly be hurt. He'd certainly spend less time sniffing around. "Time's ticking away, Doc. Do you actually have anything to discuss besides my window treatment?"

"Sorry again." Yeah, right. He turned back to face me with a rub of his finger across his upper lip. "I have to admit that I've researched you somewhat, Mr. Eye. Were you aware that you have a completely clean slate with the Better Business Bureau? Not one complaint. That's unheard of in your profession. None of the others could make that claim."

"Others?" I felt like groaning. This guy wasn't messing around. Not content to focus on one fish, he was throwing a wide net out to catch whatever he could. It did, however, reinforce the conclusion that he was an academic, if a slightly shady one. The doctor probably came from a PhD rather than a medical degree. "You've visited a few of my esteemed colleagues?"

His smile transmuted to one more wry, mocking, and slightly predatory. If I had to put a label on it, I'd say it was that of a lion counting antelopes. When was enough enough? When was that belly full? Decisions, decisions. "A few," he affirmed, noncommittally.

I was liking all of this less and less. The nearly inconceivable notion of refunding his money crossed my mind. Just shove it back into his hand and hustle him out the door. "What exactly do you want, Chang?" I asked flatly as I scooped up the cards and shoved them back into the drawer. "You're beginning to make me nervous." I flashed teeth in a predatory grin of my own. "And Houdini doesn't like it when I get nervous."

Houdini was my third option behind the fake gun and the alarm.

Dr. Chang didn't have to ask who Houdini was. The full-throated growl that emanated from under my desk was introduction enough. Eyes dropping toward the floor, he carefully pulled his feet back a few inches and with a raised eyebrow asked, "German shepherd?" It was a good guess. The back panel of the desk kept Houdini hidden from sight.

"He's damn sure not a wiener dog." Actually, Houdini was a mix. He had the distinctive shepherd bark, body, and ears but the smooth black coat of a Rott or a Lab. He came from the pound, same as me, and neither of us had learned to love people yanking our chains. "And both of us would appreciate you getting to the goddamn point."

Leaning back in his chair with slow caution but no discernible fear, he commented, "Wasn't Harry Houdini the ultimate skeptic when it came to psychic phenomena?"

"I like skeptics. They keep me humble." I slapped the top of the desk, and Houdini came out. Black lips skinned back from ivory teeth, he fixed his pale russet eyes on Chang. "And that's not what I call getting to the point." Houdini had been with me for some time. There were times when Abby was alone in the office if I had to run out for a while, but only with the door bolted and Houdini sitting behind it baring his teeth at whoever walked by. He loved that. It was nothing more than a game to him. Abby suggested we get a real gun so she could keep the office open. That was a flat no, hell no, get the fuck out of town no. Guns were as bad as knives. I didn't like what they could do to the meat of a human body, no matter how deserving that body. The cloying smell of blood, the chunks of raw flesh and yellow fat splattering away from the flying metal, it wasn't must-see viewing. Not for me.

Not again.

And who needed an actual gun when my own personal security force was up to the job? From the dog's flattened ears and rippling growl, you'd never know that Abby called him Harry Bear and used him as a footstool or that the regulars brought him treats on a frequent basis. In one of my more cynical moments, I'd taught him a trick that was a huge hit with his fans. When asked "What does my future hold?" he'd drop to the floor and cover his eyes with long legs. I'd thought about having him simply roll over and play dead, but I somehow doubted that would be as popular.

"Sometimes I do have trouble getting to the point." Careful not to move too quickly, he lifted his wallet from inside his suit coat and laid it on the desk. "At least, my students said so often enough in my class evaluations."

I picked up the wallet and gave serious thought to peeling off my glove and getting all the info I wanted and then some, but I had the feeling he'd make a grab for it if I did. And "Harry Bear" would change from pretend attack dog to the real thing. He, Abby, and I were family. We watched one another's backs. Sighing, I decided to escape an assault charge and do things the hard way. I opened the wallet and examined the contents. "So you're a professor?" I asked absently as I pulled a university ID free. Maybe he was and maybe he was something more. I wasn't forgetting that tinfoil bite to him.

"Not anymore. I've moved to the private sector,

but I am still affiliated with the school. I do quite a few research projects with them. It keeps me in touch with the scholastic world. The freedom of thought, pushing the boundaries of accepted theories . . ." His lips curved with dark humor. "The academic backstabbing. How could I give all that up completely?"

"Fascinating," I said blandly. The rest of his wallet was the usual: driver's license, credit card, auto card, all reading John Chang—curious. Curious but getting boring. There was also the picture of a laughing woman. It was an older picture, from the late sixties or early seventies judging by the dated clothing. She had purely Asian features, probably Japanese or Japanese-American judging by the delicacy of her bone structure. "John Chang" assumed I couldn't tell the difference between someone of Chinese and Japanese heritage. Careless.

The woman wasn't beautiful, but she was pretty, with a glow that would have drawn people to her without effort. "Your mama." My drawl became a little thicker despite myself. "She's been gone for a while." I didn't need to be psychic on that one. He would've had an updated picture if one had been available. Not waiting for a comment, I returned the wallet to him. "No video card? Where do you get your pornos?"

"I'll look into getting one," he said in a distinctly humoring tone. "Have I passed inspection? Do you believe I am who I say I am?"

"No one is who they say they are. Even if they don't know it." I laid a hand on a sleek black back and gave Houdini a subtle down signal. "I'm still waiting to hear what you want. Not," I added instantly, "that you're going to get it. Keep that in mind."

Deciding to ignore my automatic rejection, he replaced the wallet and rested his hands on his knees. "I want you, along with many of your fellow psychics, to participate in a study. The usual, really, trying to measure psychic activity. But our controls will be very strict. We'll also be testing psychics with every known variety of talent."

"Are you sure it won't be like the movie? Where you zap us with electricity if we answer wrong?" I scoffed lightly.

He obviously had no idea what I was talking about, pop culture, Dr. Venkman, and great movies apparently not his thing, but was able to tell that I wasn't serious. "The university couldn't afford that kind of utility bill," he said with a gravity that was betrayed by the glitter in his eyes.

Despite myself, I smothered a grin. Maybe he wasn't a complete doubting Thomas, but he did have some common sense about him. That would be nice to know—if I had any plans on knowing him at all. I didn't. "Yeah, lights would dim all over the state with what you'll dredge up." I checked my watch. "Sorry, Doc. Like I said, no poking or prodding for me. I don't like it, and I don't see any profit in it."

"You don't have any interest in furthering the understanding of the paranormal field?"

None whatsoever. I couldn't be less interested if it *did* involve electricity with a proctologist and an IRS audit as a cherry on top. Besides a near-pathological love of my privacy, just the thought of yukking it up with my so-called colleagues gave me a headache. If I wanted to rub elbows with that many nuts, I'd hit the peanut butter factory over in Macon.

And all of that wasn't counting what the contents of his wallet meant, and they meant a great deal.

"We'll make a psychic of you yet." I grunted, tapped the face of my watch, and stood. "Time's up. It was nice shooting the breeze with you. Tuesdays are two-for-one readings. Tell all your friends."

"You won't even think about it?" He seemed disappointed. "I have to say you seemed one of the more promising candidates. I talked to the woman who left just as I arrived. If it hadn't been so ungodly hot standing there on the sidewalk, I think she would've gone on for hours praising your work . . . and other attributes." He quirked another half smile at that, then came to an inner decision. "It shouldn't take more than a day, and we would pay you."

"Pay?" I still wasn't wild about the idea of being put under a microscope. Wasn't wild meaning that my spine twitched uncontrollably at the thought, but my traitor palm itched almost as much. I ignored it.

"You couldn't mention it to the other subjects. They're doing it for the academic good," he pointed out with a slightly critical air.

"Doing it for the publicity, you mean." Naiveté, thy name is Chang, except it wasn't . . . on so many fronts. And whatever was lurking behind those pale eyes had not even a passing acquaintance with gullibility.

"There won't be any publicity. This is a serious study. It will be years before anyone besides other researchers see it." He stood, too, although he was obviously reluctant to leave, while I couldn't wait to see him go. I thought I might treat myself to that beer after all in celebration.

"Do my fellow psychics know that?"

"Ah . . . no," he commented blandly. "Not exactly."

"Yeah, thought so." I indicated the door with one dark gloved finger. "You can ponder the selfless quality of human nature on your way out, Dr. Chang. And if that gets you too down, Luther makes a killer apple pie at the coffee joint three doors over. Best you'll ever have. It'll fix you up, right as rain." I changed my mind about hearing the exact cash offer. It would only tempt me in a stupid, stupid direction.

He could've been a professor with nothing more than knowledge as his goal. Could've been, but he wasn't. It wouldn't have mattered either way. I wasn't a rat in a maze; I wasn't a *subject*. And I wasn't going to be under anyone's thumb again, no matter for how short a period of time. Look at this, show me that. No, thanks.

"You get a percentage there, don't you?" he said without surprise. "For every slice of pie sold, I'd guess."

"You know it." It was free meals, actually, but I didn't mind some shining of my reputation. "Watch the door, Doc." I didn't mention the glass. "The spring's loose. Wouldn't want it to hit you in your academic ass, now, would we?"

He left. He didn't want to. I expected him to argue further, but he didn't. He either read my set expression correctly, or it was the saliva dripping from Houdini's muzzle as it edged out from under the desk and around the corner to flash bared teeth. One of the two did the trick.

The rest of the day was spent doing what I liked best: making money. And I made it with no one looking over my shoulder, no one telling or even suggesting to me what to do. I made it without owing anyone or depending on anyone for anything.

Just the way I liked it.

5

Home.

If you'd asked me when I was fourteen what my perfect home would be, it wouldn't have been this. And I'd thought about it then—a lot. A mansion with a manicured lawn pampered against the heavy-handed Georgia summer. Not that I would do the pampering. I'd leave that to the professionals. After all, didn't they come with the big house? People to take care of the outside, people to clean the inside. Surely they were part and parcel when the bank handed over the keys. The neighborhood would be as fancy as they came, with towering gates, paved roads, and not a single kid selling half-fermented berries from a four-board stand. The dreams of a fourteen-year-old. A place like that would've driven me nuts. Associations, rules, fees for anything and everything . . . hell, they probably even had one against scratching your ass after ten P.M. No, once I grew up, that dream wasn't for me.

My reality now was better than that. Worlds better. My house was average-sized but paid for and was outside of town, north. It sat directly on the Chattahoochee River. The road was paved, barely, but my neighbors were out of sight around a bend in the shoreline. I saw them only rarely. Most likely they rented their cabin out to tourists the majority of the year. Many river folk did. It was all right. I valued my solitude. After delving into the private lives of people all day, every day, the quiet, the *stillness,* was welcome. Sitting on my deck with a frosty beer and watching the undemanding river flow by, it was the closest thing to heaven I was ever likely to experience.

The house itself was nothing to look at, not from the outside. Weathered cedar siding worn to a nondescript silver blended into the surrounding yellow poplar and sweet gum trees. You could be a hundred feet away and almost not see it, if not for the betraying sun-spangled glitter of a window. The inside, however, was more eye-catching. The ceiling was high and paneled in poplar, reddish brown wood with mellow streaks of gold. There was a lofted area edged with a banister over which were thrown two blankets of red, black, and gold. The walls were painted the same gold, the color of the late-afternoon air.

There were two leather couches—one for me and one for Houdini. I was willing to share, but he wasn't as agreeable. Evil dog.

The kitchen was just that, a kitchen. When I cooked, I tended to try to burn the place down.

Spending money on shiny new appliances would be a waste. The oven had been singed but good on only its second day, and it had only been downhill for it from there. The refrigerator was defrosted on a nearly daily basis. Houdini would sneak in the middle of the night to open it and root his big nose in the cold cuts–drawer. In the morning, I'd find a puddle on the tile floor and the stink of spoiled milk. I'd tried blocking the door with a chair. That lasted about two seconds. Then I'd tried securing it with a chain and padlock. That morning, I woke up to another puddle, and this one wasn't water or melted ice cream. It was yellow and pungent, and it soaked through my socks before I saw it.

Houdini won that battle. As a rule, he won them all. A brain the size of a fist, and he outmaneuvered me every time.

The bedroom was in the loft, which made night-time bathroom breaks a bitch of stumbling stairs and stubbed toes. But it was worth it when I woke up every morning to the green, yellow, and blue explosion that lay outside six-foot windows. Earth, sun, and sky—it was all that was eternal. In comparison with the rest of us, at any rate. In my business, you saw everything that was fleeting, you were shown that most things pass. It was nice to be reminded of the few exceptions. Abby had helped me with decorating the entire place. I might cultivate my personal look, but when it came to decking out the house, I was like most guys. I bought what was functional and closest to the checkout counter, so to speak. If I could sit on it or sleep in it, that's pretty much all that mattered. Or at least so I thought. Abby straightened me out quick on that front.

I'd liked what she did with the rest of the house. It was bold and masculine and comfortable. The bedroom had been a different story. She and Gemma, her British girlfriend at the time, had wanted to do the room in white. For peace and moral purity, they'd said, Gemma in all her feng shui seriousness and Abby with a naughty wink. I think Abby was under the impression that I got more action than I actually did. I'm not saying I hadn't gone through my share some years ago. After a while, that kind of tomcatting had gotten old, but not for the more noble and mature reasons most might eventually reach. I simply had gotten tired of the trying to tune out women's life stories—stories they'd be horrified to find out I knew. Some guys, dumb-asses usually, bitch that their dates won't shut up. Try multiplying that by a thousand, a million. I'd learned over the years to hold things off to a certain extent in my day-to-day life, keep it at arm's length where it was a persistent whisper instead of a loud, constant drone. I'd gotten good at it. But during sex, all bets were off. All that skin-to-skin contact combined with the usual brain shutdown, arm's length was hardly an option. Try doing your business with a person shouting her life story in each ear. I'm not saying it isn't doable, but it's a challenge, no doubt about it.

Abby, on the other hand, worked both sides of the fence. Men or women, they were both fair game. She was monogamous and honest to a fault with whomever she ran with, but there was no denying she had a healthy dating and sex life. And she wasn't averse to sharing the details. Half the time, I didn't need that nudie mag in my desk. Abby was all the entertainment that money needn't buy. Once-long hair was now cropped to short platinum curls. That and the tiny diamond stud in her nose had changed her style considerably, but she was still Abby through and through. She had just grown up, and grown up damn fine.

Was I jealous? Hell, yes, I was jealous. Being a human ask-the-eight-ball wasn't exactly compensation, no two ways about it. The moment when scarlet stars burst behind your eyes and the base of your spine melts into warm pudding, to feel that and nothing else—how could I not envy that? To hold someone tightly in a tangle of warm limbs and heated breath without seeing the cheap green tile of an abortion clinic and hearing the sobs of a scared and sad sixteen-year-old girl, I couldn't even begin to imagine it. That was the thing. To her, that memory might be ten years old, melancholy but faded to a rain-washed watercolor. To me, it was fresh as the day . . . the very minute it had happened. The sound of the vacuum. The nurse's hand warm and tight on hers. The fact that her boyfriend hadn't shown up even though he had promised. The ache, strange and different, like none she'd felt before. That was just one memory, one among numbers uncounted. Good, bad, indifferent. Everyone had them. If that weren't bad enough, and it was, the women who knew what I did for a living always had this *look*, this wary, corner-of-their-eye expectation, when we were in bed. Whether they actually bought the whole psychic package or not, they still had the look. Does he know I wore the underwear with the ripped elastic because it was laundry day? Yeah, I did. Does he know who I'll marry? When I'll die? No. Thank God or the lack thereof . . . no.

So, moral purity was less of a problem than I wished it were.

For the bedroom, I'd vetoed white. Anything but white, I'd said. I should've been more specific. They went for the country look. Not surprising, considering where I lived. Imitation oil lamp, braided rug, and quilt, it was uncomfortably familiar. Of course, the quilt was hunter green, wine, and cobalt blue on a cream background. Nothing like the one I'd slept under for nearly eleven years. That one hadn't come from an upscale department store. It had been sturdy and ugly as hell. Drab brown, rust orange, and whatever scraps happened to be on sale at the fabric store the day Granny Rosemary got her monthly check from the government. I should've cherished it, no matter how hideous it was, because it was made with love. For all that my stepfather was—who he was—his mother was a gentle woman. Loving and quick to give hugs and home-made cookies. I should've loved it because it came from her, but . . . I didn't. I had been a stupid kid, resentful and ashamed of the way I lived. I wanted a bedspread with superheroes or cowboys or, as I grew older, a plain comforter in navy blue or stripes. I never got either. Instead, I'd later learned to do with a thick, itchy institutional blanket of faded gray that had seen hundreds of homeless kids before me. The soft worn cotton of a shabby, homely quilt was missed more than I could've dreamed.

I'd complimented Abby on her choice, nodded as she bragged how she'd gotten it for only two hundred and fifty dollars, then folded it up and put it away in the cedar chest at the foot of the bed the moment she drove away. A simple solid-colored comforter replaced it. It handled the dog hair better, anyway, and it was machine washable. That was helpful for getting out Houdini's drool stains on a weekly basis. I was damn talented when it came to making money, but that dry-cleaning bill would've broken me.

It was a comfortable house and a helluva lot better than my childish fantasy. I planned on staying there until they zipped me up in a body bag. I only hoped I was watching the river and drinking a cold one when it happened.

This night wasn't one for that, though, not unless

I wanted to sit in a pool of my own sweat and inhale bugs instead of air. It was a good decision. The moment I stepped inside, it began to rain, turning the muggy air into an almost impenetrable soup. Listening to the hiss and gurgle of water in the gutters, I decided on reheated pizza and a movie. I'd just popped the veggie special into the microwave when there was a knock on my door. Houdini was so flabbergasted by this unprecedented occurrence that while his head swiveled in the direction of the sound, he remained frozen in his favorite dozing position, on his back on his couch with all four feet in the air. I was nearly as thrown. Except for Abby and Glory, people didn't show up at my place uninvited. It wasn't welcome, and, quite frankly, it wasn't a smart thing to do. Between Houdini and the occasional visit from my sister, my house wasn't a place for the unwary. And that wasn't factoring in my annoyance at having my space invaded.

I threw a jaundiced eye at the unmoving Houdini and went to the door. I wasn't too surprised to see that it was good old Dr. Chang from that morning. I'd been fairly sure I'd see his lying ass again; I'd just been hoping it wouldn't be so soon. Or here.

"Oh, look," I said, snorting, hand resting on the knob, "someone more persistent than a Jehovah's Witness. What fun."

He was less put together than he had been that morning. Rain had flattened his hair, and the suit jacket was a shapeless sodden mess. He was trying to protect a white box with a curved arm with only limited success.

"Could you take this, please," he said with exasperation.

I hesitated. My gloves were off, lying on the kitchen counter. Everything in my house was new . . . safe. No one had been in contact with anything long enough to leave an imprint. Still, it was only a cardboard box, brand-new—chances were it hadn't had time for anything to imprint on it, even from Chang. I took it from him, noticing that he was careful to keep his hands from touching mine. The study, still with the study. Yeah, and who was really running that study? Cradling the box that was mercifully mute in my hands, I continued to block the door and watch the water drip from the eaves onto his head and down his neck. "So, do you want a tip or what?" I asked innocently.

"What I want is to talk to you. And if I could do that without half drowning, I would consider it a bonus." The blue eyes were narrowed grimly as drops of water drizzled down his face.

"Then maybe you should've called first. Oh, wait, I didn't give you my unlisted number." I bounced the box on my hand and took a sniff. It smelled familiar. "Or my equally unlisted address. Huh, you'd almost think you weren't wanted. Go figure." I opened the lid. Apple pie . . . from the same neighborhood diner I'd mentioned to him. I recognized the thick cinnamon-crumble topping and the wide chunk of cheese nestled in a cardboard corner. "I don't suppose you brought coffee."

He continued to fix me with an unwavering and demanding silent gaze.

Unmoved, I shrugged. "That's all right. The caffeine makes Hou a bitch to live with, anyway." I opened the box and set it on the floor. Houdini instantly catapulted to his feet and raced over to bury his snout in the pastry. At the last second, I saved the cheese from his gaping maw. Canine constipation is never a pretty sight.

Chang sighed and wiped a palmful of rain from his face. "So much for my goodwill gesture. You're not going to let me in, are you?"

"Keep this up, Doc, and you'll put me out of a job," I drawled, and started to slam the door in his face. Chances were good that it would take off the end of his nose. Let us count the ways in which I did not care.

His foot stopped the door with a skill I found it hard to believe that college professors, even only professed part-time ones, possessed. "I wanted to do this the easy way, the civilized way," he offered with grim regret. "I hope you try to keep that in mind."

For a moment, I had no idea what he was talking about. The easy way? He might be quick with the old salesman foot, but did he honestly think he was up to pissing me off? I'd learned more when I was a teenager than the superiority of quilts over scratchy blankets or how to spot a mark with one eye and the cops with the other. I could take care of myself. More to the point, I could take care of some dickhead who mistakenly thought I was caught between his foot and an apple pie. I might not want to run into him in an alley, but I would take care of business if I did. "You know, *Dr*. Chang, you've been so careful to avoid contaminating your precious study." I balled my hand into a fist and bared my teeth in a humorless grin. "What a shame, because I'm about to get one helluva reading off your face."

"Maybe you should try reading this instead." Not precisely impressed with the threat, he held up a picture. It was rain-splattered in the dim light that spilled from the doorway, but I made it out. A face nearly as familiar to me as my own.

Glory.

My sister. The numbers she held up beneath a blindingly bright smile were almost a fashion statement for her, she wore them so often. With her perfect cheekbones, hair the color of a handful of new pennies, and eyes the unfathomable green of well water, she looked more like a beauty contestant than a criminal. Hometown girl done good in the big Peach Queen festival, or ex–high school cheerleader who was as fresh and sweet as the day she graduated.

But Glory hadn't finished high school, leaving when she was fifteen some six years ago. The school board frowns on throwing your rival down on the bathroom floor, tying her up with her own bra, then cutting off all her hair with a switchblade. It wasn't the first time my sister had terrorized her classmates, I would guess, not that I was around to know for sure. However, this time, she was caught in the act by a teacher, a female one. Otherwise, she would've wriggled her way out of it with an innocent fluttering of lashes and a not-so-innocent twitch of her ass. Glory had never been quite . . . right. Even at two and three, she made her own rules and flatly refused any others. Self-centered was part of it. Glory just didn't connect with people around her much. Only one person could ever reach her: her sister. And Tess had been gone nearly as long as Glory had been alive.

I know she never listened a damn to me. Before or after. And by the time I was old enough to give what would probably be a futile try for custody, she was gone. Her foster family, and I use the word "family" in the Charles Manson sense, had disappeared with her and several other children. The state does such a great job at those background checks, don't they? Despite years of searching and private detectives, she was the one who found me. That had been about three years ago. She'd asked for money and then robbed me blind when I was in the bathroom and took off. There hadn't been any sisterly hugs offered, either, or touching of any kind. Not a hand on an arm. Nothing. Her personal space made mine look normal.

I'd only seen her a couple of times since . . . and

on those occasions, I gave her money for a hotel. I was nothing if not a fast learner. Still, in the end, she was my sister. My last family, no matter how sociopathic. And she was a sincere sociopath, through and through. What to do about that when it slammed up against sibling loyalty, I didn't have a goddamn idea, not one.

Attached to the photo was a stapled police report. I didn't bother to read it, letting it all flutter down to fall half in, half out of the door. Balanced on the threshold, it rapidly turned to a soggy mess. "It's a mug shot, big deal," I said, bored. "She practically sends them out as Christmas cards."

"Well, maybe that's true." He bent, picked up the papers, and tried to shake them out. "But has she ever been arrested for assault with a deadly weapon before . . . on a police officer? Or been nine months' pregnant while she sits and waits for trial? Georgia has a three-strikes law, Mr. Eye. Glory has two other violent felonies on her record in addition to this one. She has the potential to go away for life without parole."

For a split second, I thought that might be the best place for her, but then there was the baby. And the guilt. If I'd found her sooner rather than her finding me, maybe she wouldn't be this way. Or at least not this bad. I'd done all I could, but all I could had fallen damn fucking short.

"What about the father?" I asked without emotion.

"Apparently, on that subject your sister isn't talking."

Or didn't know. The baby would go to Family Services. What wouldn't happen is giving it to me, a self-employed, unsocial psychic. I was nothing but a con man from their point of view, a single male ripoff artist, not precisely parent material. They wouldn't be flashing their panties in joy to give the child to me, only relative or not. I wasn't saying that the kid might not be better off adopted by a nice, carefully screened couple than being raised by Glory or me. Unfortunately, my sister's life had shown that careful and screening didn't always go hand in hand when it came to Family Services. They had taken a stubborn, wild, and defiant little girl and given her to people who had done . . . things to her. Those things had turned her into something predatory and treacherous to the world around her. They'd taken a wolf out of the wild and turned it into a man-eater.

I hadn't been able to save her then, and it was too late to save her now, but maybe I could keep her out of jail. As for the baby . . . I grimaced to myself. Something would have to be done. If only I could buy the time to do it. I wasn't surprised that Glory hadn't called me for help. She had the unshakable conviction that she could control any situation, and until now, she'd been right. Given enough time, that still might hold true, but if so, it would probably involve a hospital guard beaten half to death with a metal bedpan during a faked labor. Something to be avoided if possible. Life and the things she'd done would catch up with Glory eventually, but it wouldn't be now, not if I had anything to say about it.

"You telling me you can do something about this?" I said, my voice dangerously flat.

"Not me, but the people I work for, yes."

"So you're not really an academic, private or otherwise then." A not-so-big surprise. My lips curled coldly. "You only play one on TV." I'd known the ID in his wallet was fake. If my memories hadn't told me, then the suspicious niggle in the back of my brain would have. I knew a liar when I saw one, no matter how practiced.

"You think I'm a blackmailer." He folded the papers, tucked them into his jacket pocket, and set his jaw. "I guess you have every right."

I thought I saw a flash of self-contempt in his odd eyes. His conscience was evidently pricking him as he rammed that knife into my back. What a good guy. Yeah, right.

"Extortion." I remained in the doorway to block his way and enjoyed the tiny revenge of his continued soaking. "Manipulating the judicial system— all this over something that is mostly smoke and mirrors, Chang? I'd think you'd have better sense."

"Oh, I have sense. I have all the sense you could want and then some." The regret disappeared, to be replaced by an unshakable and ruthless determination. "People are dying, Mr. Eye. I have no idea if you can help us stop that or not. But if you can, you *will,* and I'll do whatever it takes to make that happen."

"Ah, it's all in the name of truth, justice, and the usual crap, is it?" I leaned forward and said without emotion, "You're a real humanitarian, there ... Hector."

Sometimes you don't have to be psychic; you only have to follow your instincts. I watched as his jaw tightened in surprise. How's it feel, you son of a bitch? I thought savagely. Surrendering to the inevitable, I turned away from the door and headed for the fridge, knowing he'd follow me. Thanks to Glory, he had his foot in the door and there was no getting him out now. After retrieving a beer, I said impassively, "Charlie said I'd like you. Guess what? He was wrong." I still remembered it clearly. Charlie wanting to be my friend, wanting to make a family out of the three of us when I got out of the home. Hector didn't seem to be as kindhearted as his brother.

"And Hector, psychics, *real* psychics, don't like liars. It means you're trying to deceive us and insult us all in one."

I popped the tab on the beer and took a swallow. "Don't sit on the couch. You'll ruin it. And if you're looking for a towel, you're not going to get it."

"How did you read me? You never touched me," he asked grimly.

"Read you? Christ. How many half-Japanese

guys with pale blue eyes are running around Georgia? And drop the fake Chinese name. First time you run into someone who speaks Chinese, you'll embarrass the shit out of yourself." I took another swallow. "It was obvious the second you walked into my office that you're Charlie's brother, but without his personality."

Hector ignored the snipe, standing unmoving with the door at his back. "You remember Charlie?" he asked neutrally.

I shrugged. There was no percentage in lying, and hell, hadn't he filled the daily quota already? "I remember." Staring down at the can, I could see the distant shimmer of golden liquid. I remembered Charlie, all right. A few months of rooming together, studying together, eating together, and every moment of it, I'd spent denying that he was my friend. I'd say I'd been a real asshole, but that would imply a change had taken place, wouldn't it? "Enough to recognize his brother when I see him. His lying, blackmailing brother. Charlie must be so proud."

"Charlie's dead."

Two words. Only two.

Then again, wasn't pink shoe just two words? Sky falls. World ends. Amazing what you could do with a mere two words.

Not once had I ever thought I'd see Charlie again. Not once had I entertained the notion of looking him up. That would've been breaking my own rules, rules that had been in place since I was fourteen, and I didn't do that. Abby had broken a rule for me, but I wouldn't have done it. I would never have taken that step. I'd had a family, then lost it. I wasn't going down that path again. I wasn't running to another abandoned well or a drowned sister, not for the rest of my unnatural life. I'd known Charlie wasn't for me, as a friend or a brother, simply because no one could be. But I had liked knowing that he was out there somewhere. An insatiable appetite for knowledge, a heart wholly undamaged by life, and a crooked smile under a crooked nose, that was Charlie, and a Charlie Allgood in the world could only be a positive thing.

Now . . . now it was a darker place. Shadowed.

In some ways, a lot less worthwhile.

I closed my eyes and drained the rest of the beer. I'll call you, he'd said stubbornly. So just take the damn calls. And he had called. I'd been long gone, over the fence and down the road, but I didn't need to have been there to know that. He'd called. Unlike his brother, Charlie hadn't lied to me. Not once. Sorry, I thought silently. Sorry, geek boy. Just . . . so goddamn sorry.

"I'm not much of a memorial for him, is that what you're thinking?" Hector's emotionless voice hit the stillness like a bomb.

I ignored his question, although he was right. It probably was what I would've thought, but right now, I wasn't thinking much of anything . . . at all.

Opening my eyes, I looked blankly at the can in my hand, the thin metal dimpled from my tight grip. "Do I need a jacket, or is this something we can do here?"

There was a moment of silence, and then he said quietly, "Pack a suitcase. I don't know when you'll be back."

And just like that, all my plans, all my rules—my whole damn life—went right out the window.

6

We dropped Houdini off at the vet's. Hector, other-wise known as the blackmailing son of a bitch, said I could bring him if I wanted. Yeah, well, I didn't want, thanks so much. God knows where I was going to end up in this shit-fest, but I did know where Houdini would. Safe with Abby. I told the vet I'd had a family emergency, if you could call it that, and could she board Hou for the next few days until Abby came home. I left a corresponding mes-sage on Abby's answering machine. She knew the only family I had left could cause a five-alarm emer-gency without breaking a sweat if she wanted and wouldn't be unduly worried if I was gone for a while trying to sort it out. She'd take care of Houdini as long as he needed it.

I had a feeling that might be a long, long time.

"For a psychic, you're not especially curious, are you?" There was an edge to the question. It was the real Hector now, in glorious living color. Impatient and used to being in control, a real alpha bastard through and through. No wonder he'd had trouble pulling off the easygoing professor routine. And that short haircut—not a cop, I'd been right there. Cops didn't blackmail . . . well, not usually. No, not a cop, but something similar. Add that fake ID he'd been sporting, definite government involvement. And in Hector's case, probably military.

As if it mattered one way or the other. I was still screwed. Grimly, I continued to count the rain-drops on the passenger-side window. It was a habit I'd never really broken. Ceiling tiles, driveway pebbles, the polka dots on my fifth-grade teacher's dress, drops of water on a dark car window, whatever it took to let your mind wander. To disengage.

"When you're All Knowing and All Seeing, who gives a shit about curiosity?" I commented without interest. In the gleam of a passing streetlight, I saw my reflection in the glass, but it was Glory's face that stared back. The same pale skin, the same red hair, although mine was several shades darker. I didn't grin, but Glory did, delighted by the trouble she'd caused me. And wasn't that my baby sis all over.

He snorted, tapping fingers against the steering wheel. "Charlie talked about you, you know. That's how I found you. How I even knew you existed."

Damn it, Charlie, I thought, I liked you whether I wanted to admit it or not, but would it have killed you to keep your mouth shut about me? An internal stab reminded me with relentless fervor that if he hadn't revealed me, something else would have eventually. Pushing it down, Glory, Charlie, all of it, I focused on the window again.

Two, six, eight . . .

"He told me years ago what you could do. At least, what the other kids said you could do," he amended. "You weren't one for showing off, apparently, because he didn't see anything firsthand."

Pushing. He was pushing, because you couldn't tell me good old Hector was one for idle chitchat, just shooting the breeze. Whatever this son of a bitch wanted, he didn't even want to wait until we reached our destination to start prying it out of me. A liar, a blackmailer, and now let's add rude as hell to his résumé. No, Charlie really had missed the mark on that one. I didn't like Hector one goddamn bit. "How long?" I asked, eyes still on the window.

"How long?" he repeated. "How long what . . . oh." His jaw worked. "Ten months. He's been gone ten months."

I knew from experience what ten months was. It was the blink of an eye and forever all rolled into one soul-killing whole. Giving up on the rain-splattered window, I folded my arms and watched the windshield wipers instead. Hypnotic, the back and forth of it. Dependable, reassuring. So very unlike life itself.

"You know, you don't much seem like a believer," I pointed out, changing the subject. I had no idea where we were going or how long it would take to get there. Maybe I shouldn't be wasting time sulking and instead try to gather some information of my own. I'd like to survive this not-so-little fuckup if I could, and "forewarned is forearmed." Just because I'd gotten that out of a fortune cookie didn't make it any less valid.

"Charlie is . . ." I cleared a suddenly thick throat. Damn humidity. "He was an open-minded kid. I imagine he was the same as an adult. But you?" I didn't bother to look at him. My assessment was already done. "That shit I just don't buy."

"Really?" It was an abrupt, humorless laugh. Harsh and bleak. "Well, Charlie always did have a way of changing my mind." Apparently, both the pushing and the conversation were over with for the moment, as with a savage twist of his wrist, he turned on the radio. Country and western filled the car, and I slid down in the seat with a silent groan. Oh, hell no. Blackmailed, all but kidnapped, and now subjected to audio torture.

As some of my more full-of-shit colleagues would say, some days it doesn't just pay to leave the astral plane.

Sometime later, a hand on my shoulder shook me back from a light doze to consciousness. Rubbing my eyes, I grimaced at the taste of stale beer in my mouth and checked my watch. Two and a half hours. We were still in Georgia, then. Nice to know. "We there yet, O fearless leader?" I sniped.

"We're here," he confirmed, opening the door and climbing out. I followed, more stiffly, and took a look around. The rain had stopped. It allowed me to see my accommodations in excruciating detail. There were several low concrete buildings, blazing bright security lights, and more concertina wire than Gitmo. Oh, joy. Opening the door to the back-seat, I retrieved my duffel bag and grunted. "Which way?"

"You're one cool son of a bitch, I have to give you that," Hector said with the faintest thread of reluc-tant admiration. "Either that, or you're too stupid to live. I haven't calculated the odds between the two yet."

He expected questions. He expected demands. Expected the flailing of a drowning man. But I'd learned long ago that when life dumped you in the riptide, you had to ride it out. Tread water until you saw an opportunity; float, keep your eyes open, and wait. Sometimes it was all you could do. I was barely wet. Struggling now would only sink me for good.

"Calculate." I lifted my eyebrows and added a sarcastic smirk. "Maybe you're more like Charlie than I guessed, Doc. Maybe that haircut isn't as military as I thought." I shot a pointed look at the twelve-foot fence that surrounded us. "Yeah, maybe." I threw the strap over my shoulder. "Point out home sweet home for me, would ya? Wait, bet-ter make that cell sweet cell."

Not waiting for an answer, I began to trudge to-ward the cluster of buildings.

"I didn't have a choice." The words that came from behind shocked their author almost more than me, I guessed. He bent to explain himself, in an attitude that fit Hector like an ill-fitting shoe. Could be there really was more of Charlie in him than I expected. "People . . ."

"Are dying," I finished for him, still walking. "So I heard." It might be the truth. At this point, who knew? What I did know was that Hector had lied to me in the beginning. Why should I believe he wasn't lying now? "So I heard. And from such an honest guy, too."

I had a way of ending conversations myself. Hector moved past me, spine stiff, and led the way to one of the buildings on the right. He may have been several feet in front of me, but I didn't delude myself into thinking he wasn't aware of my location at every moment. In other words, decking him with my duffel bag and making a run for the fences was pretty much the fantasy realm of action movies. Even if it weren't, there was still Glory to consider. Glory and the baby. My sister—she'd shoplift anything that wasn't nailed down, but apparently she'd missed the birth-control aisle.

"Here we are." There was the turn of two keys, and a heavy slab of a door was opened as teeth were bared in a humorless grin, paying me back. "Cell sweet cell."

A hall bathed in subdued light ran for about twenty-five feet, then branched off in both directions. Doors with small glass and chicken-wire windows were evenly spaced on both sides. "Any of my respected associates here? Bunkmates?"

"No. All turned out to be more reasonable than you." The pale eyes were fixed on me coolly. "Imagine that." Unlocking a door on the left, he continued brusquely, "Seven A.M. wake-up call. Be ready by seven thirty. It's going to be a long day."

Long day. Right now, that was the least of my concerns. I stared past him into the room. It was small and military bare. One narrow bed, a small desk with a chair, and a wall-mounted lamp. There wasn't room for anything else. Although the walls weren't pink, I could still taste the chalk and sweat of Cane Lake. It purged the aftertaste of the beer and roiled sickly on the back of my tongue. Not the state home, but it may as well have been. I was a prisoner again. Trapped yet one more damn time.

"There's a bathroom and shower through the far door." The eyes were still on me. Assessing now. Measuring. "You will be locked in. I can't do anything about that. Project regulations."

"My sister would be enough to keep me here," I responded tightly, shifting my weight. "You don't need a goddamn lock."

"Regulations," he repeated, unmoved.

Taking a breath, I held it for a second, then blew it out. "Yeah, regulations," I said colorlessly. I hefted the duffel bag and walked through the doorway. I tossed the bag onto the bed with every expectation of hearing the door slam behind me. When it didn't, I looked over my shoulder to see Charlie's brother watching me. Not John Chang, not Hector the blackmailer, but the brother Charlie had talked about with pride more than ten years ago.

"I remember what it was like." The keys dangled in his hand, catching the dim light. "Being a 'guest' of the state." His lips twisted, and he ran a hand over his short hair as he said with a tone brittle as old glass, "I guess we all do." The hand dropped to the door handle. "Call if you need anything. Someone is on duty at all times."

He paused, then added without emotion, "Welcome to Summerland." He gave the name a special emphasis, but by the time my eyes went to the buttonless and featureless phone on the desk and back again, he was gone. The lock engaged with a metallic click, and I was alone.

In a cage.

I shook it off. It wasn't my first cage. I'd gotten out of that one, and I would get out of this one. I just had to bide my time. Play the cards I was dealt. Live by all those useless clichés that never helped a damn when they were actually applied to you. Leaning over the desk, I switched on the lamp. The puddle of light was anemic at best, especially compared with the pitiless glare of the overhead fluorescent light. I hit the switch by the door, and the buzzing white light flickered then went dark. Sometimes the dark was better . . . or the near dark, anyway. I returned to the desk and sat down. Resting my hand flat on the surface, I considered. Time to take the gloves off.

Literally.

7

Morning came. That was the best you could say about it. It came. The phone rang twice promptly at seven and then went silent. I didn't bother to pick it up. There wasn't anyone I particularly cared to talk to right now, and I doubted whoever was at the other end would take an order for eggs over easy. I swung my legs over the edge of the bed and sat for a moment with aching head in hands. I'd taken the gloves off, all right . . . for all the good it did. The room was as empty and sterile as the surface of the moon. The cheap furniture was all new, as were the sheets and blanket. The same thin, scratchy wool that I'd slept under at Cane Lake. It made me wonder: Was there, like, one guy who had the market cornered? Was he standing on a street corner hawking his wares? "Institutional blankets! Get your institutional blankets here!" Intimidate children and freeze the asses off adults, what a bargain.

As for the room, I'd gotten exactly jack shit off of it. Even the walls themselves had nothing to tell me. As far as I could tell, I was the first person to have slept here. My buddy Hector Allgood really wasn't taking any chances. But why? He wanted to use me, use what I could do, yet he was damn sure doing his best to keep me from it. Between trying to puzzle that out and the hangover from trying to suck information out of a place where it simply didn't exist, the headache was a solid weight behind my eyes. Grimacing, I stood and headed to the bathroom. Maybe I'd luck out and my gracious hosts would've left me a bottle of aspirin.

As with the eggs over easy, it just wasn't happening.

After a quick lukewarm shower—damn military—I dressed in a pair of old jeans and a faded green pullover. I left the black at home. I wasn't looking to impress anyone here, wasn't trying to put on a show. As a matter of fact, the less impressive I was, the happier I would be. Hell, if I could get them to buy the fact I was a fake, maybe they'd put my ass on a bus and send me home. Allgood had me backed into a corner thanks to Glory; I had no choice but to cooperate. But there was cooperation, and then there was cooperation. So what if Charlie had passed on a few rumors? Like Hector had said, he hadn't seen anything firsthand. So then, why couldn't I be just a con man, one exceptionally lucky and talented con man? Staring at myself in the bathroom mirror as I pulled wet hair back into a ponytail, I gave a snort. What the hell. It couldn't hurt to try.

When the rattle of a key in a lock came at the door, I was more than ready to go. A concrete shoe box wasn't my idea of plush accommodations, and I wanted out. Now. There was a chance I could be going somewhere worse, but right then, it didn't matter. I just wanted out. Sitting at the desk, I straddled the chair, propped an elbow on the back, and rested chin in newly gloved hand. I was casual, relaxed, cool . . . and the walls were not closing in. Just as they had not been closing in all night. As for the door, the door that was still stubbornly closed, it would open. Any time now. The lock made a grudging, reluctant sound. Yeah, any time. Any goddamn time. The metal slab finally swung open, which was nice. Yeah, very nice. Nice that I didn't have to get up and give it a vicious kick.

"About time." I grunted. "You have my paper and Belgian waffles?"

The man in the doorway ignored me, replaced the keys on his belt, and jerked his head toward the hall. "Let's go."

It wasn't Hector, who obviously had better things to do with his time, but the guy was military all the same. And this time, I had a uniform to back it up. Army green. Blackmailing more victims before nine A.M. than most people blackmail all day. Wouldn't their mamas be proud? Standing, I stretched and then swiveled to reach for my duffel bag. "Leave it," came the order. With a low forehead, a heavily acne-scarred jaw of pure granite, and the flat black eyes of a cottonmouth, GI Joe made Hector look like a damn teddy bear.

"That mean I'll be spending another night here in the Taj Mahal?" I asked, not bothering to hide my displeasure.

Cottonmouths aren't like rattlers. There's no spine-chilling sound of Satan's castanets to warn you what's coming your way. There's only the bunch and flash of pure muscle before the pain of liquid lightning spreading through your screaming flesh. You might see the cold gleam of the corpse-white that lines its mouth before the fangs bury themselves in you, but often you don't. It's simply too goddamn fast. A human cottonmouth wasn't much different. I'd started to turn away from my bag and back toward Hector's replacement when the fist hit the side of my neck and jaw. It wasn't a punch, although it had sucker written all over it. It was a clubbing blow, meant to take me down to the floor. And take me down it did.

I caught myself on my knees and managed to snag the chair with one hand. The combination of the two kept me upright, barely. I shook my head as black spots spread like oil across my vision. My left ear rang unpleasantly as the heat began to spread and my skin began to tingle and tighten. Sucking in a breath, I waited for my vision to clear. As a replacement for caffeine, this was not the morning picker-upper I was looking for, but I had no one to blame but myself. Well, okay, I could blame the subhuman piece of shit in a uniform, too, but there was no getting around the fact that I should've been ready for him. Cane Lake had taught me never to turn my back on anyone, especially an employee of our beloved government. Thinking those lessons didn't apply in the adult world was a mistake I couldn't afford to make, not again.

"Let's go, asshole," was the bored echo.

I had to give him points; he was nothing if not consistent. Counting myself lucky that he hadn't planted a boot in the small of my back while I was vulnerable, I climbed back to my feet. The dancing black blobs were dissipating almost as quickly as the burning of my face was building. That was going to be a nasty one. Cautiously, I pressed fingers to my jaw and worked it back and forth. Not broken, but chewing wasn't going to be a friend of mine any time soon. Worse yet, the bastard was wearing gloves—Hector's doing no doubt. Thanks to the sanctity of the almighty experiment, I hadn't even gotten the quickest of readings off the punch.

"Good one." I gave him a grin, hard and bright. It hurt, but damned if I'd let him see that. "You related to my step-daddy?"

I could see the coiling consideration behind the black glass of his dead gaze. Was it worth being a few minutes late to give me another mind-your-manners? In the end, we must have been on a tight schedule, because he took a handful of my shirt and shoved me toward the door. I let him. If Glory hadn't been an issue, maybe I could've given him something to think about. I didn't delude myself into thinking I could take him in a fair fight. He outweighed me by a good fifty pounds of pure muscle, not to mention that *I* hadn't been trained by the Army to kill smart-ass red-haired psychics with my bare hands. Nope, a fair fight was out. But then again, who ever said I fought fair? GI Joe was on my list. It might take me a while to get around to him, but I would.

Grocery lists I lost; my shit list was forever.

Outside and trudging through ankle-deep soup, I ended up three buildings over with a headache, a jaw ache, and an utterly trashed pair of formerly black sneakers. Stained and heavy with good, honest red Georgia mud, they were promptly toed off when I passed through the door. By the time I reached Hector, I was one pissed-off prisoner in socked feet. Cooperate? Right, you son of a bitch. You think I'm psychic? Then you just fucking *try* to prove it.

The room was big and in some ways the very picture of a lecture hall, or so I imagined. I'd never gone to college. How many times had Boyd sneered at the thought of that? More than I could count. Ending up on my own, I could've gone. I had the money eventually, but by that time, I was in my mid-twenties, and those kids . . . Jesus, they seemed so young. So damn young, like a different species. Dump a sharp-toothed alley cat like me in the midst of those sleek, pampered pets, I couldn't see it. Maybe once white trash wasn't always white trash. But a freak is ever a freak, and freaks don't play well with the normal kiddies. It didn't make that much of a difference in the end. An undernourished sex life left plenty of time for reading. Who knew blue balls would make for a self-educated man?

Allgood and four technicians in white lab coats were conferring around a table loaded down with machinery, some of which looked oddly familiar. I couldn't put my finger on what exactly had cranked up that uneasy feeling tickling the back of my brain, but something had. With my less-than-loyal and unmuzzled guard dog at my back, I moved down the shallow tile steps to the front row of seats and sat down. At least there was no fold-out desk or number two pencils. Without looking up, Hector dismissed my new best friend. Seconds later, he straightened, took me in, and ordered dispassionately, "Sergeant, stop." Only a sergeant? I was surprised that his cream hadn't risen a little further to the top. An amoral, fun-loving sadist like him should be a general by now.

Suddenly, Hector was looming over me with assessing eyes—Charlie's eyes—studying my face. "What happened?"

Although the question was directed at me, Sergeant Sunshine decided to provide an answer. "He tried to make a run for it. I had to clock him one."

"Is that so?" This time, Hector made sure I was involved in the conversation. "Mr. Eye, is that what happened?"

Snorting, I stretched my legs out and raised my eyebrows. "Oh, yeah," I commented sardonically. "I was halfway over the fence before your boy caught me. I was like a frigging gazelle in that mud."

"And the hell with your sister," he said quietly.

I tapped a socked toe against the floor and responded with a yawn that automatically had my hand wanting to cradle my screaming jaw. I fisted it and held back. Never let anyone see a weakness: Cane Lake 101.

"That's right. The hell with Glory."

I didn't bother to tell the truth; I didn't bother to lie. Why? What would be the point? What did it matter? It wasn't up to me who Allgood would believe. People typically made up their minds without any messy facts or, God forbid, the actual truth. Trying to tell my side of it wouldn't accomplish much more than making my jaw hurt worse.

"I see." Hector started up the stairs. "Borelli, come with me."

Allgood wasn't wearing a uniform, but he obviously ranked higher than the sergeant, as Borelli turned smartly and followed him. It was nearly twenty minutes before Hector returned, alone. He had a bottle of water with him and a small container of Tylenol. He handed them to me, sat in the seat next to mine, and asked, "Do you need medical attention?"

I popped the top on the Tylenol and gave him a curious sideways glance. "No. I've had worse. Sergeant Sunshine hits like a girl."

He looked like he wanted to give a snort of his own, then he offered matter-of-factly, "Well, he'll have time to grow into a woman now. He's in lockup, and there his ass will stay until I say differently. I don't tolerate abuse from my men."

"Yeah, it's only the upstanding blackmail you go for." Ignoring the water, I dry-swallowed a nonrecommended dose of the painkiller. "When do we get this show on the road?"

"And he only punched you the once? What restraint." He rubbed a hand over a suddenly tired face. Judging by the lines in his face, Hector had skipped more than last night's sleep. He looked years older than his age, with a weariness that only comes from many sleepless nights. "It won't be long. Leave your gloves on. I want the results of this experiment to be immaculate. We don't have time for anything less, not now." Allgood was wearing a lab coat, too, and I was beginning to think he came by it honestly.

"What are you, Allgood?" I demanded abruptly. "A scientist? A soldier? What the hell are you?"

"Why can't I be both?" he responded with faint amusement. He stood, fished around in one coat pocket, and tossed me two pudding cups and a plastic spoon. "Here, breakfast. It's all we have time for." Then he added with mocking humor, "And it's soft."

So much for sympathy. I gave an internal grumble. My stomach echoed that grumble, and I peeled the plastic film from the top of the first cup and went to work. Chocolate caramel. Not bad. By the time I polished both of them off, my "peers" had arrived. In one big group, they must've been bused in. Bright-eyed and chipper, I'd have bet they all had more than a pudding cup for breakfast. And if I thought their eyes were bright, I only had to take a good look at their clothes. Jesus Christ. I slumped down lower in the chair.

My people, joy.

Yeah, I'd admit to playing to the crowd. It was part of the gig. But there was a line I drew. These guys played cat's cradle with that line, and they did it while wearing velvet robes and rhinestone-studded turbans. Although, to be completely honest, there were a few who went in the other direction. They dressed like college professors or *Matrix* extras. Dark suits, turtlenecks, a discreet diamond-accented watch. Hell, one guy even had a TV show. It was local to New York, but I caught it occasionally on cable and laughed myself sick. New York . . . Allgood had indeed cast his net far and wide. I wondered what story he'd told them—the same one he'd tried to spin in my office? A nice, safe, academic study of psychic phenomena? Didn't those guys *see* the fence, the guards? I snorted into my empty pudding cup. Psychic, my ass. They didn't even qualify as mildly observant.

"Jackson, sugar, is that you?"

I rolled my eyes upward to see a familiar face. "Madame," I said easily. "I'm surprised to see you here. Funny how fast five to ten flies."

The round face hardened as mascara-ringed eyes narrowed to venomous slits. "Always the sweet talker, aren't you, Eye?"

I raised the unopened water bottle in her direction. "A toast. Accused but never convicted. You give us all something to shoot for, Joyce."

Joyce Ann Tingle, otherwise known as Madame Maya Eilish, was self-proclaimed queen of Atlanta. Hell, she all but ruled the tristate area. She was as adept at dodging charges as she was at robbing her clients blind. Not content simply to deal the cards or gaze blankly into a crystal ball, she sold spells and curse removals. Two thousand was the going rate for the latter. Pretty good money to wave a chicken feather in your general direction. And then there was the rumor that she'd had a rival's shop burned down—while he was in it. A canny businesswoman, indeed. A seared lump in the burn unit doesn't provide much in the way of competition.

With a sweep of silk muumuu, she waddled off and left me to my devices. Here was hoping I had an untorched shop left to go home to . . . that is, if I survived this. The rest of the "psychics" milled about before finally settling into chairs scattered throughout the room. Before us, they were assembling cubicles; back to back, there were eight total.

Apparently, this was going to be the assembly line of paranormal testing. In and out and moving on to the next self-made Nostradamus. And that was precisely how it went. Four at a time, the guinea pigs were shuffled down one at a time to individual carpeted boxes, where whitecoats waited for them in opposite cubicles. The shared wall prevented any visual cues to the psychics, and from the flat drone of the voices asking the questions, audio cues weren't exactly flying fast and loose, either. With nothing but the backs of interchangeable inquisitioners to look at and unable to make out their low mutter, I let my lids fall and indulged in a short snooze. It didn't seem long, but when a hand at my shoulder shook me awake, more than two-thirds of the clairvoyant crowd was gone. Lucky them.

"Your turn."

I looked up at Hector and pasted a grin on my aching face. "Ready to be dazzled?" I hoped it would be by my amazing talent for utter and complete bullshit. Lying to prove I *wasn't* psychic—it had to be a first in this group.

Raising eyebrows, he gave the deadpan answer, "Always." When I was up and moving, he added, "Third cubicle, take a seat."

As I walked, I pictured how it would go in my head, how I hoped it would. I wasn't smug or stupid enough to think it was going to be a piece of cake. Allgood was many things, a son of a bitch chief among them, but gullible he was not. I had one chance, and it was a damn slim one. Then I saw what waited for me in the cubicle, and that chance instantly evaporated. The equipment that had looked so familiar . . . up close, it clicked. I recognized it from countless TV shows and movies. It was a lie detector. A damn lie detector. I froze with one hand resting on the back of the cheap plastic chair. Was I screwed? Let us count the ways.

"Sit down, Mr. Eye. I'll hook you up personally." At my elbow, my own private shark watched with an inscrutable gaze.

Outmaneuvered, I wasn't used to it, and I didn't like it. Then again, I doubted Hector much cared what I did or did not like. I felt my eyes go flat and distant, and then . . . I sat. What else was left to me? I was painted into a corner there was no getting out of. At his order, I took my gloves off while he pulled on his own pair, latex surgical ones. My movement revealed the tattoo on my palm. Allgood noticed it instantly. "Unusual." He leaned in for a closer look. "Appropriate, though, for the All Seeing Eye."

It was a tattoo of a wide-open eye taking up nearly the entire surface of the palm. I flexed my hand and said mockingly, "It's cheaper than a billboard."

"There's no denying that. You seem to have advertising down to an art." He shook his head and Velcroed a probe to my index finger. "Is there a reason it's blue?"

Yeah, there was a reason. And that very reason

meant the question wasn't my favorite one. It was the kind that Abby had long learned to avoid and that Glory had already lived through the answer to. Tess was gone, but I carried her with me every day, etched on my skin. But I wasn't hooked up to the polygraph yet, was I? Charlie's brother could choke on his idle curiosity.

"No. No reason. And also, *Hector,* none of your goddamn business."

"Fair enough," he said, without offense. He looped a blood-pressure cuff around my upper arm and finally finished up with a strap around my chest. Pulse, blood pressure, and respiration, pinned down six ways from Sunday. It was common knowledge that this type of thing wasn't foolproof, and an amoral bastard like me had no qualms about lying, but I'd seen enough of Allgood already to know he'd make the damn machine all but sit up and sing. Thanks, Glory, I thought with resignation. Now both of us are out of luck.

When Allgood finished with me, he said aloud, "Begin."

From the other side, my unseen questioner started. He went through a list of basic questions, the usual drill for setting up a baseline of responses, I was guessing. Is your name blah blah? Do you have a sister named . . . on and on. At least they weren't too personal. They could've been much worse. Hector was bound to know my past. He was a man who did his homework, and it was all in the public domain. Certainly it was to someone as connected as he seemed to be, and maybe to just about anyone else. After all, the shooting had been declared self-defense. It was part of my Child Protective Services record, not a criminal one that would've been sealed when I turned eighteen.

And then there were the newspapers. They'd had a field day. It was front-page news: *White Trash Massacre!* That'd been the local down-home paper. They didn't hold much to journalistic ethics.

They even took pictures of the bloody porch of the house after the bodies were removed.

Bastards.

When my base reactions were captured, the real questions began. "I'm holding up a card," came the first. "Is it blue?"

Je-sus. Trapped *and* subjected to this deadly dull crap. Not a fate worse than death but close. Damn close. "I don't know," I said flatly.

"Yes-or-no answers, Mr. Eye," Allgood corrected firmly at my shoulder.

"It's not a yes-or-no question," I shot back, irritated. Too bad it wouldn't keep on in this vein, but Hector knew about my gloves. Knew about me. He wouldn't be fooled.

"Then how about we rephrase," he said, taking over for the moment. "Do you know the color of the card?"

"No." Smooth and unbroken, the line recorded my truth.

"Would you know the color of any of the cards your tester held up?"

As it stood now? "No." Indifferently, I ran a short thumbnail along the fake wood beneath my hands.

"Then let's try something different." Allgood moved around to the other side of the testing area. When he returned, he had a watch in his hand. It was older, the metal worn and brimming with all sorts of goodies. Fatalistically, I watched as Hector let it fall into the palm of my hand. There was no way out of it now.

"Let's start with his name." Folding his arms, he put a foot on the metal frame of my chair and moved it and me a few inches so he could see my face . . . my eyes. I had the feeling Allgood's instincts were as reliable as any lie detector. "Is it Marcus?"

And here we were.

"You know what? You have me." Now, there was a truth you didn't need a machine to register. He did have me, and I might as well face up to it. Between Glory, the machine, and Hector's innate savvy, I didn't have any recourse. No fucking recourse at all. "You own my balls, and there's not a damn thing I can do about it, so why don't we speed this up." I tossed the watch up, caught it, then slapped it down. "His name is Thomas Jerome Hickman. He went to Columbia University. He has a master's in psychology, a wife named Beverly, a leaky toilet, an overweight cat called Alexander the Great with a leaky bladder to match, a mortgage that is eating him alive, and, oh . . ." I smiled, a dark and curdled motion. "He's wearing a pair of women's underwear. Yellow panties with pink rosebuds. Big-girl undies, size fourteen. Too much sitting behind a desk, eh, Tommy?"

Hearing the faint sound of choking from behind the partition, it was almost worth it. Yeah, almost.

"Sir." The voice wasn't so blandly vanilla now. "That is absolutely not true, I swear. I can show you." There was more choking, this time more pronounced. "I mean . . . no. Let me . . ."

I took pity, more on myself than on the invisible jackass. "Tighty whiteys," I admitted with a snort. "But the rest is true."

"It looks like Charlie was right about you." Hector shook his head ruefully. There was still a healthy dose of skepticism in his eyes, but it was colored by a reluctant amazement. It was one thing to be open-minded, more for your brother than for yourself, but it was another altogether to actually see proof before your eyes. "I should've known. Charlie was right about everything." The cautious wonder disappeared so quickly it should've qualified as a magic trick. "Ordinarily."

And just like that, the almost-human Hector was gone, replaced once again by the embodiment of a true military man. Stiff upper lip, an even stiffer spine, and eyes empty and neutral. "Make yourself comfortable, Mr. Eye. You have a long day ahead of you."

He wasn't lying. For hours, I read person after person, all in lab coats and all with the most boring personal objects money could buy. Watches or wedding rings were the usual currency passed my way. Not one yo-yo or good-luck charm or whimsical key chain. Nope, it was a singularly mundane crowd here at Alcatraz. No flash, no pizzazz, no sense of personal style, not an ounce of showmanship. Abby would've been appalled and certain it was nothing a few sequins and rhinestones couldn't have fixed. Sparkling lab coats for one and all. Step right up.

Hopelessly bland my testers may have been, but to give credit where it's due, they were fairly quick-witted . . . once they finally got in gear. Almost immediately, they wanted to know why I couldn't simply read people instead of their belongings. And thanks to the polygraph and the silently looming presence of Allgood, I was forced to admit that I could. Hell, it wouldn't have made any sense if I couldn't have. But the difference between reading a person and reading something that belonged to him was the difference between IMAX and a nineteen-inch television. It was simply too much. Coming at you from all sides with a voice louder than an arsonist God at the burning bush. It soaked every molecule, pounded every neuron in your brain. There was no distance, no taking a breather. Every time I took someone's hand, it was a guaranteed skull-crushing headache and the taste of blood and tin in my mouth. Believe it or not, that wasn't my idea of a good time.

Not that my new pals would've given a shit. So why bother to tell them? Like a trained monkey, I did what I was told. Read objects, read people, and finally laughed grimly when they wanted to know if I could "see" the future, move things with my mind, or, even better, start fires.

"Jesus," I said with some disdain. "You guys watched too much *X-Files* in your day. Read too many trashy books. Even I don't believe in that crap."

"What about life after death?"

With head resting in my hands and a death grip on my skull, I looked up at Hector's studiously blank face. Charlie was gone, and I knew what he wanted to hear. Maybe I would've been kinder if I weren't being blackmailed. Maybe I wouldn't, as I'd faced the truth about Tess long ago. I didn't know for sure. But I did know that at this moment, I didn't feel kind. My head hurt, my jaw hurt, I was tired and hungry, and I was mad. Yeah, I was pissed as hell, and that did not lead to the path of gentle kindness.

"Grow up, Hector," I drawled. "There's no great beyond. No fluffy clouds and halos. No tunnel with a big family reunion at the end. Not once have I ever picked up anything beyond the death of someone when touching an object. Gone is gone. Dead is dead." I closed my eyes as the headache swelled, and as I so often did, I saw a lonely pink shoe. The clearest memory of my life, so bright and diamond-sharp that I almost believed I could put out a hand and pick it up. I never tried. I'd already done that once, and from that moment, nothing had ever been completely right or good in my life again.

"Dead is dead," I repeated with a tightness that thrummed behind my voice like an overly taut guitar string.

I wouldn't have been too surprised if Allgood had hauled off and popped me one or at the very least walked away. It was his brother I was talking about. Then again, he'd already locked up the one guy who'd beat him to the punch, so to speak. It was my second guess that hit the jackpot. He did walk away, but not before startling me with a hand that rested for the briefest of moments on my shoulder. He knew about Tess and the others. He could guess I'd give anything to believe different . . . but it wasn't different. I was literal proof of that.

"Not always," he countered with a trace of bleakness he either couldn't hide or didn't try to. Then he did walk away to herd the last of the "psychics" out. Hours had passed, although it seemed like days, and it didn't look like anyone else had made the cut. Didn't I feel special? Shit.

I dropped my gaze back to the desk surface and tried to ignore Hickman's endless chatter at my elbow. Good old TJ Hickman had finally come from around the partition. And as always, I was dead on the money. If he had worn women's panties, they would've been big-girl for sure. Pear-shaped, stammering, and cheerfully harmless as a puppy, he regarded me with moon-pie eyes. Round and wide, they had the recaptured belief in Santa Claus, the Easter Bunny, and Merlin's magic all swimming around in there. I'd seen it before. Show people something slightly askew from their normal world, and they'd use it as an excuse to put a bright and shiny glow on their whole damn life. It turned them into kids again. Why, I didn't know. What kind of miracle was it that I knew his wife made a buckwheat and soy casserole that kept him constipated for days and that he had a box of Twinkies hidden in his garage? Or that his ever-loving mama had sent him to a fat camp every summer he was in high school? Dull, boring, and kind of pitiful, yes. Miracle? No.

"Tylenol," I muttered between clenched teeth, ruthlessly interrupting his words raining like bright coins.

"Oh. You have a headache?" The stuttering kid on Christmas morning disappeared under the thirty-five-year-old professional. "Is that often a side effect of what you do? How intense a headache do you get? Do you have visual disturbances with them?"

I ignored the questions and repeated with a limp snarl, "Tylenol. I could spell it, but I'd think a guy with a master's could figure it out on his own."

The wide mouth snapped shut, and hazel eyes blinked. Nodding, he disappeared in search of the almighty painkiller. Hickman had about as much spine as your average garden slug. Pleasant, good-hearted, but he was there for reasons that trumped his academic background. It was a trait similar in all the lab coats I'd read today. Placid, fearful of authority, and unlikely to stick their noses where they might be chopped off.

In other words, like me, they didn't know shit.

Division of labor, they called it. I'd picked that out of one of the many brains I'd stirred through. There was an operation already running, Project Summerland. They were to screen for any possible psychic talent for the project, and that was all they knew. Sum total of their nonknowledge. And while some were more curious than others, no one had poked around to see what they could find out. They accepted the sketchy information they were given and did what they were told. Not a single trouble-maker in the lot. I'd bet my ass Hector had hand-picked every last damn one of them. Of course, this would be the same Hector who hadn't let me read him as the day had dragged on. Everyone else had been fair game but not Allgood. Not the only person in the room who actually seemed to know what was going on. Wouldn't want to throw me a crumb, now, would he?

By the time Allgood returned, I was in the process of popping three more painkillers. He glanced at my still-unopened bottle of water. "You are a glutton for punishment, aren't you?"

"I'm here, aren't I?" I put the heels of my hands over my eyes and rubbed.

"Yes, and I realize exactly how much choice you've had in that." He looked as tired as I felt. "Come on, Eye. I'll take you to medical, then to get something to eat."

I dropped my hands and shook my head. "No. I already said I don't need a doctor." And neither did I need to end the day by being poked and prodded by some sadist with icy hands.

"Hickman said you have a headache." He picked up the bottle of water and rolled it between his hands. "It's obvious that it's from what you've been doing today."

"Yeah, couldn't have been that punch to the jaw," I said with an antagonistic grunt.

"Very well." He sighed as he tossed the bottle to a lab coat walking by. "Then you'll have the EEG and a CAT scan tomorrow. Now, let's see what fine cuisine they're serving in the mess."

I'd imagined the tests would come headache or no. Map the brain, map the ability. Map me. I rubbed my eyes again and rose to my feet. "As long as you don't make me read the pork and beans," I grunted as I slipped my gloves back on.

The cafeteria, luckily enough, was in the same building. No slogging through mud was required, which was good, considering I'd long lost track of my shoes. The place was empty except for a few chattering whitecoats and two soldiers off in a corner. It was stuffed cabbage roll night, apparently, and I passed over it in favor of sticky macaroni and cheese, greens, runny instant mashed potatoes, and a glass of chocolate milk. Unfortunately, there was no beer on tap. Just my luck. I was hungry enough that I could actually eat the swill, and I did, shoveling it down with need if not enthusiasm.

"Not a big cabbage roll fan?" Allgood sat down opposite me as the table rocked on one uneven leg from the added weight of his tray.

"Vegetarian," I said succinctly. The piece of white bread I'd been given on the side was rock-hard, but I slathered it with butter and ate it anyway. It wasn't any worse than Cane Lake food. Wasn't any better, either, but it wasn't worse.

"Does that have anything to do with your . . ." He fished a small bottle from his pocket, poured a shot of foamy white liquid, and chugged it before finishing. "Talent?"

Quick. Always so quick. Like his brother had been. With the edge of my appetite less sharp, I began to shove piles of food back and forth with my fork. It was an old habit, one that had gotten my ears boxed but good in the Boyd days. After all, one shouldn't waste the precious food that his lazy ass had nothing to do with putting on the table.

"It's not like people," I offered absently. "I don't get clear memories, just fuzzy flashes. Nuzzling for milk, the falling rain on your back, the smell of wet hay." I looked away from the ground beef on his plate. "The feel of a steel bolt punching through your skull."

There was silence, then the sound of porcelain scraping the surface of the table as Allgood pushed his plate away. "What do you sense when you drink that?"

I looked up to see him indicate my glass of milk and almost smiled despite myself. "Warm sun and sweet grass."

If I had a bad day, which, now that I ran my own life, was a helluva lot less than the old days, I sat on the floor with Houdini, placed a hand on his broad head, and soaked up endless doggy wonder. A full stomach, a well-chewed toy, a soft couch—through a dog's eyes, that was a true glory that couldn't be matched, the only heaven in existence. I missed the furball, missed him like crazy. I turned my attention back to my food and quickly cleaned the plate. I didn't waste any more words on Allgood. He was the reason I was missing my dog, my carefully constructed life.

Either sensing my mood, which wasn't hard to do, or too tired to make further conversation, he left me alone as I finished eating. Then we were off to retrieve my muddy shoes and make our way back through the swamp to my luxurious suite. If possible, it seemed smaller than it had before. A shoe box to cram me into as if I were a crow with a broken wing.

I just wasn't sure if I was going to be nursed back to health or buried in the backyard.

"How's your head?"

I sat on the bed and skinned off my shirt. "Fine," I said shortly.

"Jaw?"

He did go on and on about the suddenly precarious state of my health. If I was a cat, he'd already be digging a hole in the backyard for my ass.

"You know," I offered matter-of-factly, "the concern would be a helluva lot more sincere if you weren't the cause of all this. Wonder what Charlie would say about how you're treating his old roommate." I didn't say "friend." I wasn't that much of a hypocrite, not even to drive home the sharpest of points.

And sharp it was. Allgood's knuckles tightened to the whiteness of bone on the doorknob. "Who knows?" he said in a voice empty and cold. "Perhaps you'll get to ask him." The door closed between us, and I was left to ponder the implications of that.

Could be it was the backyard for me after all.

8

The next day was spent with Dr. Mengele—at least, that's what I expected, a military doctor with cold hands and frozen heart. When you're the power-less guinea pig caught up in an experiment you can't yet fathom, you don't hold out much hope that the guy who sticks you with the needles is going to pet you first. I was wrong, on one count, anyway. Dr. M. Guerrera had warm hands, even through a snug set of latex gloves. She also had dove-gray eyes and a gentle curve of mouth, nude of lipstick or gloss. Black hair was caught back in a tight braid that fell nearly to her waist. It wasn't the blue-black of Allgood's but was streaked with a rich rust brown. Her skin was the same color as those streaks, only several shades lighter. She reminded me of my kindergarten teacher all those years ago. Miss Bethany had made us cupcakes, given us hugs, and matter-of-factly wiped up the blood that gushed from noses busted by monkey bars or play-ground brawls. Warmth and competence. Just what you want in a doctor.

Yeah, I'd have come over all fuzzy if not for the whole prisoner-against-my-will situation. Call me difficult, if you want. Smiling nurturer versus heartless jackbooted monster, it didn't matter. She was still the enemy. And I'd be willing to bet it'd be a cold day in hell before a lollipop would follow any of what they planned to do to me.

Hector had roused me at eight A.M. and marched me straight to their medical facility. There was no stop at the cafeteria. Some of the tests would require a contrast agent injected intravenously, he informed me. Wouldn't want to vomit chunks of leathery eggs or hunks of processed cheese should I have an anaphylactic reaction to that, now, would we? If I had good aim, damn straight I would want that. I would stuff down second helpings if that would contribute to the cause. But, as always, good old Hector was less than the picture of indulgent cooperation.

The facility itself was well equipped, even to the eyes of a typical layperson . . . me. The room was big enough for ten beds with space left over. I balked in the doorway at the sight of gleaming metal, starched sheets, and the sharp, tongue-coating smell of disinfectant. I'd never had a good experience in a place with those particular things, and I didn't expect this time to be any different. Granny Rosemary had died in a place like this. She'd been Glory's and my best hope—our only hope—of staying out of the system. But of course, she'd died because, hell, where would the punch line be without that, right?

At Mom and Tess's funeral, she'd sat down in one of those cheap plastic folding chairs and never got back up again. Purple with flecks of foam on her lips, she'd been hauled away in an ambulance. She'd lingered for a day or two, but I never got my hopes up. By then, I'd gotten the message but good. You only had to pound it into my brain so many times before I made the connection. Hope was the candy in the pervert's pocket, the stereotypical soap in the prison shower, the cheese in the trap. And life . . . well, life was what happened when you leaned in for a look.

"Mr. Eye." Hector's voice was patient in my ear but unyielding. "The tests are painless, I promise you."

I was fairly certain I'd already driven my point home to my warden on the whole trust issue, and on top of that, my jaw hurt more than it had yesterday. In other words, talking was both pointless and painful at the moment. I settled on giving a scornfully disbelieving grunt, squaring my shoulders, and walking into the room. In short order, I was given scrubs to change into, after which an excruciatingly detailed medical history was taken, covering me and every relative I knew of. Then again, a medical history was *attempted* might be a better way of putting it.

I knew nothing about my real father. I hadn't

known him. He'd left town not long after he'd gotten my mom pregnant with me. I knew his name, and that was about it. Did he have diabetes or heart disease? Prostate cancer? Hypertension? Was he an all-powerful psychic with erectile dysfunction? Damned if I knew or cared.

Dressed in the pale blue scrubs given to me by a cute nurse who reminded me of Abby, I sat on the edge of one bed, with one hand holding ice at my jaw and gloves still firmly in place. Every answer I gave was clipped, short, and a little thick from my swollen jaw. Hector's stone face had tightened perceptibly that morning when he'd opened the door to my room, and he'd immediately offered me more Tylenol. Apparently, I was a little less pretty than I'd started out yesterday. Dr. Guerrera had taken one look at me and disappeared into a back room, to return with an ice pack. I'd given serious consideration to ignoring it but decided in the end to let stubbornness take a backseat to pain this one time.

"I'll get an X-ray of your jaw, Mr. Eye," Dr. Guerrera told me as she finished up the history and put away the clipboard. "It would have been better if you'd been brought in yesterday." The glance she gave Hector was pointed and cool.

He could've explained that he'd offered and I'd refused, but Allgood didn't cut himself any slack. For a blackmailer, he set remarkably high standards for himself. "I dropped the ball, Meleah. I apologize."

She sighed and shook her head as she gathered supplies at my elbow. "I'd thought better of the men assigned here. Who was the Neanderthal goon who did this?" Her latex-covered fingers touched my jaw gently, running from my chin to just under my ear.

"Sergeant Borelli, and he's now out of the equation," Allgood said flatly. He'd lost the lab coat from yesterday and was dressed in a simple black shirt and slacks. Somehow he managed to make it look like a uniform, starched and immaculate.

"Borelli." She winced and frowned. "Yes, I suppose if anyone were to assault someone, it would be him. He doesn't precisely spread goodwill and charm wherever he goes, does he?"

"He spread plenty on me," I muttered.

Meleah Guerrera lowered her gaze, and Hector, if anything, looked more grim. His man, his fuckup, I could read it clearly behind pale eyes.

"Have you gotten Glory out of jail yet?" I asked abruptly.

"We're working on it." Allgood exhaled. "But even when we do, she'll be in our custody until we're finished with you, Eye. She'll be treated well, certainly better than in prison, and when you've done your part for us, she'll be released. Free and clear."

A sharp-toothed vixen dumped back into the henhouse. But what could I do? She was my sister. She was all the family I had; bad genes and sociopathic tendencies didn't change that. She was . . .

damn it, she was all that was left of the old Jackson. He'd died at age fourteen, somewhere between that old well and a shotgun. He was dead and gone, but sometimes when I heard Glory's voice on the phone, all sugar over a layer of pure self-interest, it made me remember. Starry nights, peanut butter sandwiches, and the laughter of two little girls. If she were gone, if that were gone, it would be like those things, bright and hopeful, had never been. I didn't want to admit that.

Pushing the unpleasant and futile thoughts to the back of my mind, I gave a hard-edged smile. "Eye? Come on, Hector. After all you've done for me, you should call me Jack." I dropped the dripping ice pack carelessly onto the bed and added matter-of-factly, "Your brother did."

He didn't like that any more than he'd liked any of my other digs, but that didn't matter, because Hector was a professional. Unlike Borelli, I sincerely doubted you would ever see him lose his temper. He was the embodiment of unbreakable control, with all his emotions—the fine and the not so fine—locked in a triple-chained suspended box that even the real Houdini, not my dog, would've scratched his head over.

"Very well, Jack," he said with a metallic calm that thinned only slightly over my name. "Let's get on with the tests, shall we?"

Dr. Guerrera called for Eden, who turned out to be the Abby-nurse, to start an IV in the back of my

hand with quick and painless efficiency before lead-
ing me to an X-ray machine. I folded my arms and
shook my head at the paper that mostly covered the
table, *mostly* being the key word. "Unless this thing
is fresh out of the factory, I need a sheet. An unused
sheet." I couldn't touch any part of it with my bare
skin. At first consideration, it didn't seem like it
would be too bad. The majority of the people who
had lain there wouldn't have stayed long enough to
leave much of an impression. It would be the quick-
silver of minnows in a rushing stream. Splinters of
memories, here and gone. But there was always an
exception.

Death was a big goddamn exception. People
tended to die on medical equipment. A peaceful
slipping away wasn't so bad, a momentary tightening in my lungs, a coldness that numbed hands and
feet. A heart attack? Crushing trauma? A burst
blood vessel in the brain? Those were . . . disagree-
able. Dis-fucking-agreeable. It had happened to me
once. A fender bender had caused me to end up in
the ER. I'd been woozy, concussed, and sloppy.
One full-blown seizure later, when transferred to a
gurney, it was ingrained in me never to be that careless again.

Dr. Guerrera turned and tilted her head curiously at Hector. He nodded immediately. "Do it,
Meleah. We've actually found the genuine article. If
he says he needs it, then he does."

She seemed doubtful; a scientific heart beat

under the stethoscope that rested on her chest, but she retrieved a sheet from a shelf full of linens and spread it. "Have a seat, Mr. Eye. We can do your jaw while you're sitting up." It would've seemed odd to see a doctor personally performing tests like X-rays, but I was guessing the fewer people they had involved with their project, the happier they were. One doctor, one nurse who was drawing blood from me at the same time I was getting my jaw X-rayed. Who they all were, of course, was still a mystery. There was obvious military involvement, yet Dr. Guerrera didn't appear to be military, and neither had the scientists performing yesterday's tests. Hector, on the other hand, he had definitely been military at some point in his life, but he didn't seem to be now.

Summerland.

Allgood had said, "Welcome to Summerland." I wasn't an idiot, and although I had nothing but scorn for my colleagues and the history of paranormal phenomena in general, I *was* familiar with it. I knew of Summerland. It was a name given to the land of the dead, heaven, the afterlife, whatever the hell you wanted to call the crutch you used. It was spawned in the late 1800s by a fraud of truly great proportions, the Joyce Ann Tingle of her time. I had to wonder in what capacity they were using it here. Since they were bringing "psychics" in so late in the game and because, according to Hector, people were dying, I had to think it was less about the paranormal and more about the death. And wasn't that a fun thought.

Yeah, not so much.

My jaw wasn't broken. That was the bright point of my day. The tests, more scans than your average grocery cashier saw in a week, lasted until mid-afternoon. In between them, the nurse, Eden, kept up a constant chatter. I didn't mind. It was what reminded me of Abby, not her looks. Abby had the short platinum curls and pale brown eyes. Eden had a polished bob of chestnut hair, eyes the color of a country pond, dark green and still. She also had small winged fairy earrings that swung cheerfully. That whimsical touch and the talking, and she and Abby may as well have been twins separated at birth.

"A real psychic. I can't believe they found one, and you even look like one." She used her gloved hands to peel off the round EKG pads from my chest. It seemed my heart was fine. "Or maybe you make yourself look like one because you are one. Part psychic, part actor." She smiled, her teeth small, white, and even. "I wonder if I brought my Silly-cat in . . . I call her Silly, short for Priscilla. I inherited her from my mom who had a huge thing for Elvis. But if I snuck her in, could you tell me what she's thinking? Or why she pees in my boyfriend's shoe instead of the litter box?"

She *was* an Abby clone. It was the only explanation.

"I can tell you what she's thinking right now, no touching necessary," I drawled. "She's thinking if she were three times her size, she would eat you." Funny, yes, and every cat person asked it sooner or later, but funny or not, it was the truth. Every cat that was awake when I'd smoothed its fur with a bare hand thought that. Every cat I touched that was asleep dreamed that. Not that animals thought like people. As I'd told Hector, it was more emotions. But their emotions were so much stronger than ours that it was, in a way, a method of thinking. It was no less an expressed intelligence than what we worked with—only different.

She frowned. "Silly-cat loves me. Don't tease like that, or I'll be afraid she'll smother me in my sleep. She's fat as a biscuit."

"Eden, enough," Meleah warned in a low voice. "If Thackery heard you, he'd fire you on the spot."

Eden shook her head and gathered up all the plastic-wrap trash that medical tests produce. "That one. He has one mood. Bad. If you ask me, he needs to get laid in the worst way." She laughed. "Of course, if he was psychic, his dowsing rod wouldn't find a thing. If he even has one. He probably had it removed so's not to distract him from his almighty science." She gave me a wink and walked off to dispose of her armful of waste. Definitely Abby all over.

Meleah—Dr. Guerrera—must've notified Hector that all the prodding in the world that could be done on a live person had been performed. He showed up just as Eden walked away. And about time. By then, I was hungry enough to eat whatever was slopped on my tray in the cafeteria, and it was a good thing, too.

I poked dubiously at the shriveled brown lump on my plate that was masquerading as a baked potato. Fluorescent orange goop cascaded over the sides of it and pooled into a sticky puddle. It looked more like a biohazard than the questionable source of nutrition it was. Hell, at least it was soft. Theoretically. I started in on it.

"And here we are again." Hector contemplated the limp tuna fish sandwich before him. "Meleah will have all the scans read by the morning."

"Whoopee," I responded. "I'll tell all my friends."

"Aren't you at all interested to know if what you do is detectable by medical means? How the structures of your brain might differ from others'?"

It seemed Hector and Charlie did have something in common, an insatiable curiosity. Charlie's had been blazing bright and out in the open. His brother kept his far more tightly under wraps, but it was there. Almost reluctant, mostly hidden, but there.

I countered his question with one of my own. "So, Hector," I said, imbuing his name with mock camaraderie, "what are you a doctor of? Or was that a lie, too?"

"No," he said evenly. "I have a doctorate in quantum physics, as well as one in applied mathematics. Charlie was a neurobiologist but also had a doctorate in engineering." He tilted his head slightly, watching for a reaction ... any reaction. "Not that you're remotely curious about that, either, I'm sure."

He didn't get a reaction from me, but I couldn't deny to myself that there was a fleeting sense of warmth within. Neurobiologist and engineer. Good for Charlie. I never had a doubt that he'd be something impressive, because Charlie himself was an impressive man. Even at the age of seventeen, he'd been a man, and one hell of one to boot. The potato, thick and cloying with cheese, stuck in my throat, and I chased it down with milk. Plain, no chocolate today.

"And did the Army put your overachieving ass through college, Dr. Allgood?"

"Very good. One would almost think you were psychic, Jack." He used the name I'd facetiously requested with false courtesy and checked his watch. "Nearly done? We have an appointment with the project leader."

"He's not going to poke and prod me, too, is he?" I picked up a few packets of crackers and put them in my pocket. One thing you learn when you're a hungry kid on the run: you see food, you take it. If you weren't hungry then, you'd be hungry later. It was a habit I'd never been able to shake. "Because that's getting old fast. Of course, that's only the guinea pig's point of view, which I'm sure amounts to jack shit."

"I don't think you have to worry." He stood. "Dr. Thackery considers his time too valuable to be spent running tests that mundane. He has people who do it for him." It was said so very mildly that I was immediately suspicious.

"So, there's a tall dark asshole in my future, eh?" I raised my eyebrows and added, "Besides you, I mean."

"Actually, he's blond." He left the rest conspicuously unaddressed, pushed his chair under the table, and gestured. "After you."

We walked to another one of the buildings in the compound—the largest one. The moment I passed through the door, I could hear the hum. I could feel it, too. It was everywhere—in the air, under my feet, throbbing behind my eyes. It wasn't loud, but it was inescapable and annoying as—

"Shit." I closed my eyes and ground the heel of my hand into my forehead.

Allgood turned from speaking in low tones to the guard at the door. "What . . . oh, the vibrations. It does take some getting used to, but eventually you learn to tune it out."

Here was hoping I wasn't around long enough to pick up that particular skill. "Jesus." I gave up trying to rub the sound out of my head and set my teeth against yet another incipient headache. I opened my eyes when I felt something nudge my gloved hand. A familiar red and white bottle of painkillers was resting in my palm.

"Keep it," he said with genuine apology. "We don't exactly seem good for your health." Hector was either softening up or he was more like Charlie than I wanted to admit.

I shook the bottle lightly and decided to hold off for the moment. If today were anything like yesterday, I would need them more later on. I followed silently as he led me down a hall and into a large, open lab area. The far wall was glass from ceiling to floor, and behind it squatted a mammoth machine, oval-shaped. It was encased in smooth white metal and almost looked vaguely medical in nature, but I had my doubts. Some fancy new X-ray machine wasn't enough to justify the military presence or the blackmailing of an obscure psychic.

"Is this the one?"

The voice came from the side, and I turned to see a man approaching, followed by two more. The one in the lead had a laptop computer under one arm and a brusquely impatient expression. It sat with ease on his face, which was all sharp angles and planes. His hair, a little spiky and long from inattention, was blond streaked with gray. He had ferociously intelligent brown eyes behind silver-framed glasses and a pugnacious jaw. "Finally," he muttered under his breath, not waiting for confirmation as to my "oneness." He pushed up the sleeve of his lab coat to check his watch and shot Hector a barbed glance. "We're behind schedule. Did you give him a tour first? Dinner and a show?"

Tall dark asshole versus short blond asshole. The reality was no improvement over the prediction.

"That's precisely what I did, Julian. I'm sorry, did you want an invitation?" Hector answered smoothly, with a deliberate insult behind the first name. He was talking to a man who, unlike Hector, would shove his academic degrees down your throat in the first moment.

Eyes narrowed behind clear lenses. "It's approximately forty-two hours until the next ether-rip, Dr. Allgood. Do you want to engage in this sparkling repartee or do something more useful with our time? Perhaps something along the lines of saving a few lives or so. Your decision entirely, of course. Shall the rest of us go for coffee and croissants while you think it over?"

Damn. I felt my status as ruling smart-mouthed bastard slip a fraction. I was curious about the phrase ether-rip, but I could wait to ask Hector later about that. I certainly wasn't asking this guy. He was one razor-edged, cold son of a bitch; working with him was probably hell on earth. I didn't have it in me to feel sorry for Hector, but surprisingly, I could feel sorry for Charlie's brother. Hector was the one who had coerced me into being here; Charlie's brother was the one who'd fed me before tossing me to the wolf in the lab coat. That meant, of course, the emotion passed, and I went back to feeling sorry for the one who really deserved it. Me.

Hector stretched out a hand and reappropriated the bottle in mine. Shaking out two capsules for himself, he said flatly, "Jackson, this is Dr. Julian Thackery. His entourage is Dr. Sloane and Dr. Fujiwara. Thackery, this is our ace in the hole, Jackson Eye. Or he will be, assuming we don't starve him to death." It was the barest minimum of an explanation and apparently all he was going to give.

Dr. Sloane had eyes that might as well come from a sci-fi cyborg—glass balls empty and hollow except for the cold fire of science. Dr. Fujiwara's were human and mildly sympathetic, as if he were a researcher who knew that giving cute white mice cancer was necessary, but he regretted it. Did it all the same, though. *C'est la vie* or *c'est la morte*. Which was worse? Not to have a conscience or to ignore the one you had?

Thackery exhaled and pulled off his glasses to pinch the bridge of his nose with two fingers. "We're wasting time we don't have. Is it any wonder nerves are running high, including mine?" He replaced his glasses and added briskly, "Now, let's see what your pet psychic can do." A whole three seconds of forced humanity, and Dr. Dick was back.

Thackery moved off to a long table that was parked against one wall. Allgood and the other doctors followed, and after a beat, so did I. There were more whitecoats milling about, men and women.

All of them seemed to share the same sense of urgency. Some stared at computer monitors, while others clustered by what looked like a clear Plexiglas partition. As I watched, a map was projected from within. Brilliant colors and exquisitely sharp details bloomed. Several locations were marked with a bloodred ring. One such circle was chosen and expanded into an aerial view of a lone house.

"Jackson."

I turned away from the oddly ominous sight and joined the two at the table. As I was sitting, Thackery had picked up a file and was thumbing through it swiftly. It was my file, judging by his next comment. "Psychometry." He frowned and tapped his fingers on the table as he read. "That's all you can do?" Sloane and Fujiwara, positioned behind him, exchanged a glance.

"The things I can do are limited only by my imagination and the distance between my foot and your ass," I replied matter-of-factly, as I slouched in the chair and held out a hand to Hector for the bottle. I'd made an about-face on my earlier decision. There was no time like the present.

Before Thackery could articulate his offense—and, trust me, you don't turn that particular purple color if you're not offended—Hector spoke up. "Considering that until yesterday, we didn't have proof that psychic phenomena actually existed, Thackery, I believe we're ahead of the game."

"Allgood, we're not even *in* the game," he shot

back, slapping the file shut. "And I think we know who we have to thank for that. Charles moved too fast with the project. You know it. I know it. The entire team knows it."

The patches of skin over Hector's cheekbones whitened. "Is this something you truly want to start, Dr. Thackery?" he asked, voice empty of the emotion clearly seen in the blanching of his skin and the setting of his jaw.

Yeah, this place ran like a well-oiled machine. I'd be out of here in no time. "Can we get this show on the road?" I demanded before the next volley. "I'm not exactly getting paid for this, you know, and as much as I love pro bono work, I have a dog to feed."

"You are getting paid," Hector corrected, his jaw relaxing minutely. "It probably won't be your standard two hundred dollars an hour, but you'll be compensated."

I blinked. I liked to think . . . no, I *knew* that I could correctly read most people and situations down to their foundations and below, but I had to give it to Allgood. He took me by surprise; I had not seen that coming. Not a hint. I recovered enough to curl my lip in disdain. "It's hard to make a living as a blackmailer if you pay your victims, Dr. Allgood."

There was a knowing glint in his eye that indicated that I hadn't fooled him with the weak sarcasm, but Hector only slipped a hand into his pants pocket and pulled out a plastic cuff. It was of a size to fit a man's wrist, but it was nothing like a hospital bracelet. This was actually solid, about three inches wide, and looked as if it would be heavy. "I think, Jackson, it's time to show Dr. Thackery what you can do." He slid the ring across the table toward me. "I need this man's location. Where he is at this moment."

Thackery leaned back, folded arms across his chest, and watched me with the cool skepticism of Dr. Frankenstein presented with a cocker spaniel's brain. Sure, it was a brain, but it wasn't quite what he'd sent out for. And he had his doubts that it would be especially useful.

I ignored him and peeled off a glove. Any questions I might've had, whether the man they wanted me to find was an industrial spy or something similar, would be answered the second I touched the cuff. There was no need to voice them. I was almost eager in reaching for it. I was tired of being in the dark. Normally, I wouldn't have given a shit what they were up to in this muddy prison, but being that it was affecting me rather personally, I wanted to know. Despite Hector's occasional outburst of humanity, no one was going to watch my ass for me; I had to do what I could for myself. This piece of white plastic might be a start for that. Discarding my glove casually to the side, I picked up the bracelet.

The next thing I knew, someone was picking me up.

The hands had turned me over onto my side as I vomited miserably. Through bleary eyes, I could see it spread over ugly green tile. The floor—I was on the floor, and I hurt. The back of my head was aching fiercely, as were my forehead and my neck—hell, my whole body. As the heaving stopped, I could feel a warm rush of liquid at my hairline over my left eyebrow as someone snapped fiercely, "Where is Dr. Guerrera? Where the hell is Meleah?" Hector's voice. Hector's concern. Hector's goddamn *fault*.

"You son of a bitch," I slurred through lips that felt numb, then swallowed against another rise of bile. "Charlie."

"I know, Jackson. I'm sorry. God, I'm sorry." I felt my head lifted carefully as something soft was placed beneath it. It was a towel, brand new and telling me nothing. Thank God. "Someone give me some rubber gloves," he rapped out, and seconds later, I could feel cool latex fingers pull my own glove onto my limp hand. Still lying on my side, I tried to focus as Hector swam into view. He tossed another towel over the vomit and knelt beside me. There was a folded washcloth in his hand, and he pressed it against my forehead. "Tell me if you get anything off this, and I'll get another one, but we need to stop the bleeding."

I must have looked as confused as my sluggish mind felt, and he added, "You hit your head on the table when you fell." He hesitated. "You had a seizure." Judging by the gray cast to his face, it must have been a bad one. A real doozy. Maybe I'd get a bonus for the show. Watch the psychic as he flops like a fish out of water, pukes like a frat boy, and hopefully doesn't piss himself. Good clean family fun; come one, come all.

I closed my eyes and muttered thickly, "Bastard. You knew."

"No." That was the esteemed Dr. Thackery pitching in. From the sound of it, he was behind me, probably giving a wide berth to the vomit. He didn't strike me as having a God-like compassion for his fellow man. Like old times. He was another Lewis Sugarman out of Cane Lake. He had more regard for keeping his shoes clean. "Charles died painlessly. There was no reason for us to suspect you would react this way. I'm sure you perform . . . what is the terminology? Readings. Yes, you perform readings with the objects of the dead all the time." There's nothing quite like someone making supercilious excuses for their behavior while you're lying near a pool of your own sick.

"Painless." I choked out a laugh, stark and humorless. Rolling onto my back, I folded my arms tightly across my chest. It was an instinctive gesture I thought I'd outgrown. Don't touch. It was from the early Cane Lake days when I'd had less control over my so-called gift. I closed my eyes as Charlie's last moments squeezed my brain in a fistlike vise. "Wasn't painless." In fact, it was as far from painless as you could possibly get. The seizure I'd once suffered at the hospital had been caused by touching the metal railing of the gurney I had been lying on. I'd picked up the death of a man who'd been shot numerous times in the torso with a semiautomatic. Acid had boiled free from a perforated stomach to burn everything in its path. Tattered lungs had filled with suffocating blood. Bones had been shattered, tearing the flesh around them with calcium shrapnel. He'd bled and cried for his mother and screamed and screamed and screamed.

Apparently, so had I. Charlie's death had been right up there with that. I'd touched that curved piece of plastic and felt it all. Normally, an object has to be with someone a long time to build up their personal signature, to contain a summary of their life. But there are exceptions. A violent death is the one that tops the list. I didn't know exactly how Charlie had died, because he himself hadn't known, but I felt it . . . every god-awful, agonizing second.

"What are you saying?" Hector's voice was hoarse, but his hand retained firm pressure on my forehead.

Despite his efforts, I still could feel the blood trickling back into my hair. He had known but couldn't resist one last test. Never mind if he and the others genuinely, if stupidly, had assumed that Charlie had gone easily into that good night. Hector had played his game without thinking that he hadn't known, couldn't know what Charlie had actually felt, and I was the one who'd gotten burned.

He also didn't know the worst. Charlie hadn't known exactly *how* it had been done, but he'd known *what* had been done.

He'd been murdered.

"Nothing. I'm not saying a damn thing."

And I didn't. From that moment on, I didn't say another word. Charlie had known that someone had killed him, but he didn't know who, and then he didn't know anything but pain. That meant I didn't know, either, and I wasn't about to let a murderer catch on and put me next on his list. I'd say things had gone from sugar to shit in no time, but there hadn't been any sugar to begin with. From the frying pan into the fire, maybe. Charlie, damn it, what the hell did you get your old roommate into?

Meleah Guerrera showed up with a couple of medical technicians, and I was put into a cervical collar, strapped to a backboard, and lifted to be whisked off to medical. The gurney, liberally covered with fresh sheets that no one had died on, bounced out of the building and over mud that had dried to uncomfortable peaks and gullies. The sky was that unlikely Georgia summer blue, scorched to a pale denim by the blazing sun, and I watched it with unblinking eyes until we entered the comparative cool gloom of the building I'd left only ten minutes before. Allgood and Thackery followed, engaged in a low-voiced, heated exchange. If I'd

tried, I might have made out what they were saying. I didn't try. I had enough to think about.

Charlie was the kind of person who, if given the
opportunity, would have changed the world. Unfortunately, his opportunity ran out too soon, but
he had been well on his way. He had big plans, great
plans, and those plans had killed him. But if they
hadn't, what he would've accomplished . . . Charlie
always was a dreamer. Eminently practical, blaz-
ingly intelligent, but he'd never been content to
keep his eyes fixed on the ground. Charlie wanted
to fly—in ways man had yet to accomplish. He'd apparently had a bigger budget than Icarus, though
he'd ended up the same damn way . . . even if someone had helped him out with a big shove.

I'd missed him before. Yeah, I'd deny it to anyone, including myself, but I had. And now . . . I
knew him. Knew every moment of Charlie's life as
if I'd lived it with him, side by side. His twin, his
constant shadow. I saw myself through his eyes—
sullen, smart-assed, and so transparently vulnerable
it made a young, bighearted Charlie ache. I saw
Hector as a child—responsible, straitlaced, and
with braces so bright they could strike you blind. I
celebrated every birthday and holiday. I was there
when Charlie proposed to Meleah and she gently,
wisely turned him down. When he got drunk with
his brother over it, I tasted the beer on my tongue.
And when he finally admitted to himself with a rueful laugh that it was for the best, that he was already

married to his work, I felt his relief and acceptance. I thought I'd missed Charlie before, now and again. God, I hadn't had a clue.

I tried to push it aside to focus on the fact that not once did he have an enemy that he knew of. Everyone liked Charlie.

So who had killed him?

"Jackson, I need you to answer my questions. I need to evaluate you."

I blinked and opened my eyes. I hadn't realized that I'd closed them, lost in Charlie's memories. Meleah was leaning over me, concern in her now wholly familiar gray eyes. Around her neck on a chain hung a ring. Silver, it was inscribed with a simple flowing pattern. I lifted a hand to capture it, the metal bright against the black silk. "You told Charlie you lost it."

Her mouth opened and closed before she took the ring carefully from my hand. "I did. I found it a month after he died. It was in my car under the seat."

"Smells like lemons." I closed my eyes again. Her car had smelled like lemons every time Charlie rode in it. And although he hadn't much liked lemony things—hated lemon meringue pie, found lemonade too tart—he'd liked the smell. Liked it because it was a Meleah smell. I found myself liking it for the same reason, which wasn't good. I needed a little distance in time and space from all the "Charlie" whirling around in me. His death/murder had been enough to sear the details of his life into me with more force than usual. It had happened before, and there was only one cure for it.

"I need to sleep." I crossed my arms across my chest and tucked my hands protectively into my armpits. "Now."

"I'm sorry, Mr. Eye, but you've had a seizure, struck your head. We need to do X-rays and an EEG at the very least." She said more, but I missed it. I didn't need permission to sleep; I was only giving fair warning. I couldn't have stayed awake if I'd wanted to. The only way to deal with such an abrupt and bruising onslaught of knowledge was to shut down temporarily. I'd learned that the hard way over the years. My body was calling the shots here, not me. I closed my eyes, and less than a second later, I was gone. Gone but not alone.

Charlie was with me.

9

When I woke up, it was to blue skies, green trees, and mellow sunlight drifting through a window. I blinked blurry eyes, and the warm image resolved itself into a mural painted on the wall. What a rip-off. Of course, classified was classified, but on the other hand, we wouldn't want bed-bound patients to go stark raving mad, either. So let's *paint* a window on the wall with a happy little outdoors scene. That's as good, right?

Yeah, I was all sorts of cheered. I shifted my gaze from a fat blue butterfly and a positively obese puff-chested robin to look at the room around me. I was still in the infirmary. A curtain pulled around my bed gave me the illusion of privacy without the actual benefits. There was the pull and tug of sticky pads and wires on my bare chest; apparently, I was hooked up to a heart monitor. In case I tried checking out of life early before they'd wrung me dry of whatever made me useful to them, the doc could pop in with a shot of adrenaline to get the old pump going. How'd that old Eagles song go? *"You can*

check out anytime you like, but you can never leave"?
Hell, I couldn't do either.

I sat up a few inches and took in more. The bed-
rails were padded with blankets and tape. I wasn't
sure if that was to protect my mind or my skull. A
stray touch or seizures. Or both. I was covered with
a sheet, and when I peered under it, I could see
scrub pants and socked feet. At least I didn't see the
ultimate indignity: a catheter. It would have been
hard to look into those calm gray eyes of Meleah
again after that. I stripped the glove off my hand
and raised it to touch a sore spot at my hairline. I
could feel a low ridge of stitches. Didn't seem like
many. My hand moved to the back of my head, and
I winced as I traced a large bump. Sighing, I combed
a hand through tangled hair. Not a good day for
yours truly. If it was still day. I looked back at the
"window." With that as the only thing to go by, who
knew?

"You're awake, Mr. Eye."

A face peered around the curtain, and a smile
bloomed across it as if I was Christmas and Easter
and every birthday combined into one. It was
Abby-nurse Eden. She came in and took my hand,
the one that was still covered with a glove, as naturally as if she were my mother or sister sitting a bedside vigil. "You can't read people through gloves,
right? I'm not hurting you, am I?"

I shook my head slightly, not trusting my dry
throat for speech yet.

"I'm so relieved you're all right." She tightened her grip reassuringly. "Some people here . . ." She scowled—Florence Nightingale outraged. "They aren't careful with people. Only their precious *things*. Scientific bullshit." Coloring as she said "bullshit." Judging by the tiny cross hanging around her neck, she was a good Christian or Catholic girl, and cursing wasn't her thing. "As if any machine could be worth a human being. They make me ashamed to be the smallest part of this stupid project and ashamed of the people in it. They honestly do."

Her green eyes solemn, she squeezed my hand again. "I thought being a psychic was like a miracle. So amazing and wonderful. A gift from God. But I think I was wrong. It's not, is it?"

"A gift?" This time I answered, my voice as hoarse as I expected. I wished for some water. "Not so much."

I tried to ease my hand back. Except for Abby and Houdini, I wasn't used to all this touching. Sincere and well meant or not. But she didn't release her grip. Abby would've approved.

"Well, don't you worry, sweetie." She was my age, thirty, or a few years younger and calling me sweetie as if I were five. "God might test you, but he rewards you, too. There's always a balance. For the burden you carry now, you'll have equal joy. That's a promise. Have faith that you have good things coming to you. And if you need to talk while you're here, I'm your nurse. *Your* advocate. My duty is to you first before anyone else, even your doctor. I'll do anything to help you. I mean that." Her green eyes were determined enough to show that when she was on your side, she was totally on your side, and ruthless in her credo and devotion if she had to be.

"Eden? Is he awake?" A ringless hand pushed the curtain back, and Meleah stepped through. It was hard to think of her as Dr. Guerrera now. Not when Charlie and I could remember her sitting on a lawn with a lap full of yapping puppies or stringing lights on a Christmas tree in an old, snug T-shirt and cheery pink pajama pants with a hole in the knee. And then there was another picture of her, watercolor soft, curled naked in simple cotton sheets the color of buttercups. She was round and full, with a crescent-shaped scar dark on her copper-colored hip.

"Just now, Dr. Guerrera." Eden let go of my hand and patted it, just like my grandmother had always done. "I'll see if I can find him something to eat." Then she was gone, and I was alone with Meleah.

"How are you feeling?"

I thought about it for a moment, cataloguing my aches and pains. "Like shit," I said honestly.

"That's probably to be expected, considering what you've been through." She picked up a clipboard that had been hanging off the foot of my bed and began jotting things down. "Could you be a shade more specific? It might make the difference between Tylenol and brain surgery." There was a hint of a smile on her lips.

With that motivation, I became a little more verbal. "My head hurts, and I'm stiff pretty much all over."

She nodded. "That's to be expected. You gave your head a good knock, front and back, and you're bound to have muscle soreness from the seizure. I'll give you a mild painkiller and a muscle relaxant. You'll feel better." Finishing with my chart, she added soberly, "I'll tell Hector you're awake. He's been worried."

"I'll bet." The words didn't have the same acid burn that they would've before I'd touched that bracelet. It was harder to hate him when I'd seen him grow up through Charlie's eyes. Harder but not impossible. "You can tell him his guinea pig is alive and kicking. He'll be thrilled." More resigned than cutting, but at the moment, off-balance and out of sorts in my body, it was the best I could do.

She sighed and ran absent fingers along the long braid that trailed across her breast. "He's a good man, like Charlie was. A good man in an extremely bad situation. I wish you could see that."

I could see that, if I looked through Charlie's eyes. But I could look through my eyes, too. The picture there was different. Sharper-edged, less forgiving. Like me. And oddly enough, despite having read Charlie now, having collected his life . . . I still didn't know what Hector and Thackery wanted with me.

What Charlie and his project—and it had been his brainchild—had been trying to achieve had a superficial resemblance to a psychic event . . . or in my book, so-called event. But that was it, superficial. It was science, crazy and out there but science nonetheless. What the hell could I do to further the project now that Charlie was gone? And someone had obviously gone to a lot of trouble to make sure it hadn't worked to begin with. Murder in this kind of closed-doors facility was a high-risk investment and definitely a lot of trouble.

"I see all sorts of things," I replied matter-of-factly as I slipped my glove back on. "When Hector gets over here, maybe he can explain to me what some of those things are." Hector couldn't have killed Charlie, I was pretty sure of that. Blackmail for a higher cause, one I still didn't know about, yes, but murder his own brother? Hard to believe. Then again, I'd seen worse come in and out of my shop, and you'd never suspect it from their smiles or sweet little-old-lady faces.

"Beyond stubborn, the both of you." She shook her head. "I'll have Eden bring you the pills with breakfast if you're feeling up for it."

That answered one question. I'd been out of it for nearly twenty-four hours. More than half the time Thackery said they had left. I was surprised that guy wasn't in here slapping my face ruthlessly until I woke up. Hector did what had to be done, in his mind, without hesitation, but he did have regrets. The esteemed Dr. Thackery wouldn't waste a second on regret and probably wouldn't actually recognize the emotion if it bit him in his cold, uptight ass.

"Breakfast will be . . ." I checked with my stomach. Dubious, but game. "Okay . . . I think."

Fifteen minutes later, Hector showed up with it himself. The tray held a banana, a sealed container of blueberry yogurt, a carton of milk, and a bowl of oatmeal. "Eden called the cafeteria for this. She said to keep it simple and easily digestible. This is the best I could do," he said quietly.

I watched as he set the tray on the wheeled table beside the bed and expertly pulled the table over my lap. He was back in his lab coat and was sporting sleepless lines and bloodshot eyes. "What, Hector?" I asked. "Long night? Too bad. I slept like a baby." I opened the milk. "Or someone who was put in a coma by an asshole. Take your pick." Considering that Hector, as far as I could tell, didn't know that his brother had died in agony, much less had been murdered, I wasn't being fair. I felt a pang over that before I remembered where being fair had gotten me in life.

Here.

Hector was more than aware of who said asshole was, but he didn't bother to put up a defense. Pulling up a chair, he sat heavily, much of his natural grace in abeyance. "I thought I'd killed you, Jackson," he said wearily. "Believe it or not, there's not much you can say to make me feel worse. I'm right there in the moment: Callous Bastard of the Year."

And there came that taste of Charlie. A shuffling of pages, a fanning of faded photographs. Hector joining the Army to pay for his college so Charlie wouldn't be put in the position of being financially responsible for his younger brother. Because of that, Charlie had been able to work his own way through school along with quite a few scholarships and grants. MIT wasn't cheap even with those things. What Hector had done had made it possible for Charlie, made it possible for them both.

Grumbling silently at myself, I felt the dark-edged emotions lighten some. I fought it, but you can't escape knowledge, not really, even when it's not your own. Ripping the foil off the yogurt, I said almost under my breath, "Maybe you'll get a plaque in the mail."

He blinked, confused at a comment that was far less razor-edged than what he expected. "Maybe. So . . . how are you doing?"

I took a few spoonfuls of the yogurt and gave it a moment. When my stomach accepted it without incident, I moved on to the oatmeal. "Didn't you ask the doc?" I asked with a knowing quirk of my eyebrow. Of course, he had. He might have all the regrets in the world, but he still needed me for some reason. There wasn't anything about my health that he wasn't going to know.

"Yes, I did," he responded, leaning back in the

chair and washing a hand over his tired face. He kept his eyes on me, though, somber. Sincere. "But now I'm asking you, and I don't just mean physically."

Ah. Talking about your innermost crap. First Eden, now Hector. Like the few times Abby showed up with the chick-flick movies and forced me and Houdini to suffer through the talk, talk, talk that fixed everyone's problems, enriched their lives, and closed the hole in the ozone layer, all while she snuffled with her own box of Kleenex. What fun. Yeah, right . . . maybe later.

"Charlie was your brother, Hector, not mine. He was my roommate for a while and a nice kid, but that was a lifetime ago. A memory." The banana was a little soft, but I ate it anyway. Concentrating on it was easier than concentrating on other things.

"A memory," he repeated, then dropped the hammer. "Fine, I'll accept that's what he was before, but what is he now?"

Christ. He had to go there, didn't he? He couldn't let me enjoy the goddamn banana, he had to push it. I pushed the table and tray away, swung my legs over the side of the bed, and stood. "Where's the bathroom?"

Eyes narrowed on me. "You're stalling."

"I've been in this bed almost twenty-four hours, and you think I'm stalling?" I folded my arms. "Hey, if it's proof you want, pick a spot. I'm up for a challenge. I think I've got enough to spell my name *and* yours."

He snorted. "I stand corrected. It's down about fifteen feet and on your right."

He was right, of course. I was stalling, but that didn't make the need any less pressing. By the time I came back, I was feeling slightly more relaxed. The fact that I'd actually been able to walk there and back without anyone holding my hand or standing guard helped more than I would've guessed. Naturally, there would be someone outside the infirmary door to make sure I didn't make a break for it, but I still wasn't going to take that tiny bit of freedom for granted.

By the time I sat on the edge of the bed and folded my arms, I was more than ready to work toward having all my freedom back. "Okay, Hector. Let's get down to business. I know what Charlie was doing. I know about the experiment, and I know that he died during it." *Died* being the cleanest, safest word for what had happened. "Now for what I don't know. What do you need me for?"

"You saw it all, then? You saw the experiment . . . you know what he was trying to do? You understand it?"

I shifted my shoulders. "Eh. Think of it like reading the blurb on the back of a book. I get the general outline. I know what Charlie was trying to do, but I don't really understand anything. I don't get the how, and I definitely don't get the why. I'm not really up on my quantum physics and whatnot." I shook my head and said dryly, "Astral projection.

What will you wacky scientists come up with next?"
Because basically, that had been Charlie's goal, the
project's goal: the dissociation of awareness from
human form. Charlie had wanted to be able to
come and go from his body like it was a summer-
house at the beach. Wacky wasn't quite the word.

"The military uses for it would be immense, I'm
sure you're aware." He reached into his pocket and
pulled out the bracelet that had taken me down so
swiftly. I gave it an uneasy look as he turned it over
in his hands. "But to Charlie, it was simply the pure
love of doing what was thought to be impossible.
To be able to travel instantly or nearly so. To perhaps see things no one had seen before. To be spirit
outside of flesh."

Good old Charlie, smart as hell but obviously
crazy as a bedbug. "Yeah, okay, whatever . . . but it
didn't work out for him, did it?" I pointed out.

"No." He studied the bracelet, then put it away.
"There were successes of a sort, with computer
models and animal experimentation."

I didn't ask them how they knew if Rover was
taking a walk on the astral side or not. I already
knew . . . almost. I saw it through Charlie's eyes.
Something about brain waves and measuring the
ambient energy patterns in the air. I didn't actually
understand it or have anywhere close to a complete
cataloguing of the information. It was more like
hearing the occasional phrase, in Charlie's voice,
drift through my head. Bits and pieces that made up

an elaborate painting. I might not see or understand every stroke of the masterpiece, but I could see the picture.

"So it worked fine with Rover but not for Charlie. Anyone know why?" I met his eyes squarely. I knew why, but Hector didn't . . . I hoped. Even if I knew for sure, spreading that knowledge couldn't help my situation. It could only hurt it. What would a murderer do if he thought a psychic knew the motive for his murder and was only a mandatory project-personnel reading away from figuring out his identity? Nothing good.

"No." He cleared a suddenly constricted throat. "There were no malfunctions found. No energy spikes. No reason for Charlie to die. We didn't even know it was . . . painful until you told us. We thought his heart simply stopped while he was in a state very similar to a deep sleep."

It wasn't a moment I wanted to relive even in passing, and I went on quickly. "We still haven't gotten around to why I'm here. What the hell do you possibly think I can do for your project?"

"We need you to find Charles."

I turned my head to see my best pal Dr. Thackery standing by the curtain. He looked marginally more rested than Hector but not by much. He'd had a late night, too, apparently, but I would've been willing to bet the long-gone homestead that it wasn't spent worrying about me.

"*What?*" I asked in disbelief.

"We want you to find Charles," he repeated, "by reading him."

All right, what was this? What the hell was this? "You want me to find what? His *ghost*?" I asked derisively. "I can't read a ghost. Mainly because I don't *believe* in ghosts."

He stepped further into the room, face as bland as my morning oatmeal. "Charles isn't a ghost . . . precisely. How shall I put this so you might grasp it?" he pondered in a tone so supercilious that I wanted to beat him on the head with my oatmeal bowl. "Charles is no longer living, true, but he's not dead. Well, not *entirely* dead." A long finger tapped his chin as he finished absently. "Not yet."

Hector's jaw muscles bunched at the casual dismissal of his brother's life, but he said nothing.

All right, this was about as weird as it got, and coming from a homegrown Georgia psychic, that was saying something. "Hector," I demanded, "what is this bullshit this guy is flinging? What's he saying about Charlie?" I might not completely trust Allgood, but I damn sure trusted him more than Thackery. If I'd died on that cold bastard's immaculate lab floor, his first thought would've been for the project, his second for calling the janitor to clean up my remains. Hector was far from perfect, but he was worlds away a better man than that. And right now, except for Eden's sympathy and duty, he was the only one remotely on my side.

"He's right," he said thickly. "Charlie's not gone.

Not completely. His body died, but not before the experiment succeeded. Apparently, he was passing into a state of astral projection just as his heart stopped. Meleah couldn't . . . we couldn't revive him. There was nothing for him to return to."

"And he's just floating out there?" This was nuts. Flat-out nuts.

"We're not sure what he's doing or even how aware he is, but he's there." Hector stood, stripped off his lab coat, and hung it over the back of his chair. "The machine activated. It flooded Charlie's body with alpha-wave ions to trigger an OOB. It worked just as it had once before. He'd made it once before."

OOB being an out-of-body experience. But this particular time, unlike the first, he hadn't made it back.

"How do you know he actually made it the first time?" I asked skeptically.

"It's possible to read a very unique energy signal after the OOB is initiated. Plus, we wrote a word on a piece of paper on a desk five offices down when Charlie was already in the machine. When Charlie came back, he knew the word. He'd traveled down there and read it. Only five rooms, but we thought we'd start small."

I could see movement in his lab-coat pocket. He was running a thumb over the bracelet.

"The second time we read the same signal as Charlie went out, but when he died, it dissipated.

We thought he was gone, but ..." Hector paused. "It turned out we were wrong. Unfortunately, it was weeks before we realized this, and during that time ... people died."

People were dying. That was the justification he'd used for the blackmail. People were dying. Now I was apparently about to find out why.

"What does one have to do with the other?" I asked with wariness. I had the sudden feeling that maybe I didn't really want to know the connection. Considering the blackmail, my seizure on a cold lab floor, and Charlie's murder, I couldn't see any way the information could be classified as good, hopeful, or even remotely entertaining.

"People died," I echoed. "Why?"

"There is no why," he countered immediately. "Charlie wouldn't be part of what was happening if he could stop it. He wouldn't be able to stand it if he knew what he'd caused. Charlie . . ." His throat worked. "Charlie was a good man."

At that, Thackery obviously made the decision that if the story was going to be told, he'd have to tell it. "Charles is trying to get back, but he has no place to return to. His body is no longer viable. But more than not having a destination, he also has no road, no pathway. There is no door, which was his body, for him to enter our layer of time and space, so he's trying to *make* one. And that . . . that is not working out well for anyone." He pursed his lips. "To say the least. We're up to seven dead now. I hesitate to guess where the body count might eventually top out. It doesn't bode well for the experiment or our careers."

"Yes, our *careers* should always be foremost in our minds," Hector said acidly. "You son of a bitch."

"If the government pulls our plug along with our futures, Dr. Allgood, then there will be no way to stop, or help, Charles. Is that what you want?"

"No," Hector shot back harshly. "That's not what I want, Thackery. So just shut the hell up and get on with it."

Dissension in the ranks. Ordinarily, I might have exploited it. But now, with all I knew and Charlie's memories, memories of a better man than I was, lurking in the back of my mind, I couldn't force myself to do it.

"Wait, just *how* is Charlie causing people to die?" I aimed the question at Hector, but it was Thackery who answered.

"It's complicated." He frowned. "It seems that the normal ether that forms the backdrop to our existence functions as a mirror. Energy, events, nearly everything bounces off of it . . . is reflected. However, in incidences of extreme violence, mental or physical, the ether can be frayed. Raveled like old cloth. If it frays enough, instead of mirroring an image, it imprints one. Records it, basically. This is what gives you your stereotypical 'ghost.' It's simply a recording."

"Yeah, that's fucking fascinating," I interjected,

"but I'm still waiting to hear what it has to do with Charlie."

The skin next to Thackery's mouth whitened, but he deigned to explain. "The reason is twofold. First, these areas are weakened. Apparently, Charles senses this, and these are the places through which he's trying to find his way back. Second, when this happens, the ether begins to rip. And when it does, those so-called recordings go from passive to active."

Confused, I turned to Hector. "Plain talk, Hector. Tell me."

Expression weary, he sighed and folded his arms. "Lizzie Borden took an axe and gave her father forty whacks, right?"

Okay. Simple enough. "Gotcha."

"Suppose you went to her house and saw something. Maybe she was in the bedroom doing away with her mother or in the parlor with her father. You might actually see that if the place fit all the requirements of a true recording, but you would only see it. But if Charlie tries to come through . . ." He shifted his shoulders in discomfort but went on. "That recording goes from television to virtual reality. You wouldn't be watching Lizzie. You would be the violence trigger. You would *be* Lizzie, or someone else in the house would. Charlie rips the ether, twists it. Your normal rules of physics and metaphysics go tumbling out the window, and the recording shifts to not-so-glorious three-D."

"Normal and metaphysics, not sure I've heard

those two in the same sentence before." The floor was cold, even through the socks considerately left on my feet. Now it seemed even colder. "You're saying that Charlie has tried to come home via a few haunted houses and caused past murders to be reenacted? That's . . . hell, that's crazy."

"I know," he said simply. "Here." He lifted his lab coat and pulled a rolled-up folder out of an inner pocket.

And what he gave me made for interesting reading, if you were into slasher gore, which I wasn't. Three houses, the sites of past brutal murders, were hit with copycat killings all within the past eight months. Two cases had been murder-suicides, and in the third, the poor bastard responsible for the new killings was rotting in a mental institute, claiming he'd been possessed. I wondered if the "almighty project" had any plans to help him out in the same fashion as Glory. Why did I have my doubts?

All three of the original murders had taken place before 1950 and had been brutal as hell. Their encores weren't any less bloody. There were pictures. I closed the folder, dropped it onto the bed, and restrained the desire to rub my hand on my scrub pants. Gloves or not, those glossy papers had felt dirty to the touch.

"And you want me to find Charlie before he causes something like this again?" I shook my head, noticing that Thackery had disappeared while I had been looking at the files. "I can't do that. Charlie's not here. Wherever he is . . . whatever he is, I'm all about reality, okay? I know that sounds pretty fucking ridiculous, considering what I do, but hell . . ." I rubbed my forehead. The headache had subsided minutely, but it remained. "There it is."

"He might not be here now." Going by the brackets of pain beside his mouth, Hector's own headache wasn't much better than mine. "But he will be trying again, and soon. When he comes through, you should know. We can pinpoint the time extrapolated from his past visits to predict future ones to nearly the hour. You could take something of his then, read it, and get a lock on his location." He must have seen my automatic shudder of revulsion at the statement. "Something old," he hastily revised. "Not the transplanar-interlink cuff. Something older wouldn't have Charlie's death imprinted on it, would it?"

As much as I wanted to lie, I didn't. Why? Because Charlie would've thought less of me. And while up to yesterday that wouldn't have affected me in the slightest, it did now. It was as if he stood at my shoulder, his pale eyes bright and expectant, thinking only the best of me, thinking I was still a scared kid who'd do anything to prove that I wasn't. He would fade; the Charlie presence/feeling would slowly melt away. I'd come across this in the past. Not often, thank God. But it had happened, and the odd sensation of *knowing* someone, of sharing their memories along with your own, didn't last. A silent

Charlie wouldn't judge me forever. He wouldn't try to make me a better person for too much longer. And I wouldn't have to see his brother or his lover Meleah through his eyes anymore, either.

That was one reason not to lie. The other reason was Glory. I was still her ticket to ride. Lastly, the one that really tipped the scales? It wouldn't have done me any good. Hector wouldn't have believed it. An easy out like that for me—he wouldn't have bought it for a second. I gave a silent noncommittal shrug.

Hector took it for what it was. The tight stretch of his mouth relaxed slightly. "You can also help us map which places could be genuine targets for Charlie to try to come through. Most locations we can verify ourselves through old police reports and newspapers, but there are older houses where the information is sketchy. We were hoping you could perform readings on those to see if they had violent histories that might have imprinted on the ether."

He was right. Georgia was full of them. Supposedly haunted plantations restored to their former glory, others that were no more than tumbled stones and bones. "What about battlefields?" I asked. Georgia was full of them, too. I knew the location of every major one and avoided them like the plague if possible. You would think Atlanta itself would be unbearable, what with the burning and sacking and all, but so many people had lived there since then, it was like thousands upon thousands of woolen blankets muffling the long-ago terror. If you kept your gloves on, cities were fine. A stretch of field soaked by blood—that was a different story. If I tripped and fell out there, if I touched bare skin to the ground, I'd never get back up again.

"No. A battlefield is too large. For Charlie to come through, he needs a smaller, hence very concentrated area of violence. One as massive as the Battle of Chickamauga or Kennesaw Mountain would likely splinter him into multiple threads of energy. Virtually destroy him. On an instinctual level, he must know that. He hasn't tried a single one of them."

I folded my hands across my stomach. I was stuck. Well and truly stuck. But the sooner this whole Charlie fuckup was resolved, the sooner I could get on with my life. And I really wanted it back, my life. As for Charlie's murder, Christ, I had to think about that. Getting involved in that could get me killed just as quickly as Charlie had died. And justice, that was only a word . . . wasn't it?

"So." I exhaled. "How do we get started?"

I can't say the tired face of Hector brightened; there wasn't much in his own life that was too goddamn bright at the moment. But he did look relieved.

"We take a field trip," he answered, standing. "I'll grab you some clothes."

Field trips. They hadn't been all that much fun in school.

I was betting the same held true now.

10

"If we do find Charlie, or wherever Charlie's trying to get through . . ." Could this be more bizarre? And if I, the resident psychic, thought it was bizarre, then bizarre wasn't even the word. "What do you plan on doing? I mean, seriously, Hector, that movie wasn't real, you know. No such thing as proton packs. So who you gonna call?"

Behind the wheel of the generic Ford, Hector snorted, and it was despite himself, I knew. Dead brother aside, the guy was one serious and somber son of a bitch. I'd have labeled him responsible and deadly dull if it weren't for the occasional flicker of wry humor I saw behind the stoicism. And if not for pieces of Charlie whispering in the back of my thoughts, telling me what Hector had gotten up to in his younger days. Taking out the entire back of their parents' house with a microwave jury-rigged for a moon flight? Hell, that was truly inspired, if unintentional, destruction right there.

"I don't think it'll come to that," he said dryly. "The team has been working on a way to pull Charlie entirely back to this plane. It's what he's attempting now but can't accomplish. He needs more power. If we can feed it to him on his precise personal energy signature, if we can do that for him, he'll come through and . . ." His mouth flattened, and the glint of amusement was gone. "Dissipate," he finished abruptly. "This level of physical existence can't support him."

I propped an elbow on the window frame and watched as a blur of black, white, and green passed by. Cows and fields. Wouldn't life be easier if that's all there was to it? Cows and fields. "And then he'll go on to a better place."

"I thought you didn't believe in anything like that." He turned the wheel, and we jounced down a rutted dirt road. "That you thought we simply stopped existing."

"Who's to say not being isn't better than all this?" I could see a house through the trees, flashes of faded rose brick. "One long nap. Maybe you haven't taken a really great nap, Allgood, but I have. I'll take that over fluffy clouds and annoying harp music anytime, thanks."

He didn't call me on a philosophy that wasn't precisely dripping with sunshine and roses. After all, he had a file on my past—on Tess, my mother, that nightmare bastard Boyd. What I'd done. He knew I came by my beliefs honestly. He knew what had made me.

Or unmade me, depending on your point of view.

"This it?" I went on. I rolled down the window, and the cloying smell of honeysuckle drenched the hot air that flooded the car.

"The first," Hector confirmed. "File's on top."

I fished the folder up off the floorboards and paged through it. I was sure I looked ludicrous, thumbing the pages with black gloves that didn't exactly go with the jeans and green long-sleeved T-shirt I'd packed. That was the thing about the gloves; they went with the whole All Seeing Eye gig but not so much with the casual look of a good old Southern boy. Forgetting about my ego for a moment, I scanned the pages. The house was dated back to the late seventeen hundreds. A man, Jeremiah Farrell, had built it for his wife, Felicity. They'd lived there and multiplied. Damn, and *had* they multiplied. Thirteen kids in thirteen years. Apparently, they'd also been a robust family, and infant mortality just passed them by. By year fourteen, Mrs. Farrell had either had enough or had flat-out lost her mind. There wasn't any postpartum depression back in those days; there was only crazy. And sometimes there was pure homicidal mania.

Felicity killed them all. Every last one. But unlike Lizzie, she didn't stick to an axe. Her husband was a hunting man, as all men were back in the day. She hacked and shot and bludgeoned until the wooden floors coursed with blood, a blood that never came clean. To this day, the floors shone ruby in the light.

Or so the story went.

It was a legend that had lived for hundreds of years. Trouble was, it couldn't be backed up by any records. There had been a Jeremiah and Felicity Farrell, and they had had several children. That had been confirmed by an old church registry. There could've been a murder . . . or seven or ten. Or they could've moved back to the Old Country or out West. It was all lost in the mists of time. Until me.

Great.

We pulled up to the house . . . or what was left of it. The porch was a sagging disaster area, and the windows and front door were boarded up. I climbed out of the car and glanced askance at the moldering ruin. "Not exactly on the tour of historic houses, I take it."

"Not quite. They're working on it, I hear." As Hector strode through the knee-high weeds, I heard the rustle of a snake heading for the high ground. "Preserving history is an admirable goal."

"Yeah? I don't see any historical society lining up to support my ass, and I'm all about history." I looked up at the second story, which was covered by a creeping wall of poison ivy. "And I'm much better-looking than this heap."

"A great opportunity missed on their part, I'm sure." He went to the trunk and pulled out a crowbar. "Give me a few minutes, and I'll have us inside."

Ah, that would be *hell* no.

"I am not going in there, Hector. No way, no

how." I made my way through the weeds to the porch and pulled off a glove. "If fourteen murders actually took place here, I'll just have to touch a wall to know. I don't need to be feeling around for phantom blood on the floor. Jesus. You want to see another seizure?"

"I stand corrected." After leaning the crowbar against the car, he followed me. I'd started to climb up onto the porch, but after a good look at the gaping holes and the warped wood, I headed for the side of the house. It was doubtful the wooden front structure was original to the home, anyway.

Clenching my bare hand into a fist for a moment, I sucked in a deep breath. "Okay. If I look like I'm swallowing my tongue, do me a favor and shove me away from the wall. You know, if you're not too busy taking notes."

"I have a near-photographic memory," he countered impassively. "I'll transcribe them later."

"Smart-ass," I muttered. Then, giving up on stalling any further, I stretched out my hand hesitantly, Charlie's excruciating death still firmly in mind, and touched warm brick.

I saw it.

I saw it all.

Every year. Every day. Every moment.

Love. Hate. Hunger. Warmth. Laughter. Tears. Loss. Abandonment.

Blood.

Death.

But no more so than usual in a house that had lived so long. I dropped my hand and pulled my glove back on. "The only thing Felicity Farrell killed was her husband's sex drive when she threatened to treat his dick like a chicken neck and give it the chop. And after thirteen kids, who could blame the woman?"

"No violence, then?"

"Not the kind you're talking about. A few fights. Someone's granny fell down the stairs and broke her neck, but no murders. Although Lily Ann's dog ate her sister's rabbit. I guess the rabbit might call that murder." I swatted at a deerfly buzzing about my head. "So, one down, how many to go?"

"Too many." Hector grunted and wiped the sweat from his forehead. Sweat. The man was actually human after all. Someone write that down. Oh, wait, Hector had a near-photographic memory. He could simply remind me later. I ducked the fly again and headed back to the car.

"When do we stop for lunch?" I called over my shoulder. "I'm starving. Not that the yogurt wasn't a filling breakfast—you really know how to keep your psychics happy."

"I believe I liked it better when you were sullen and silent." Hector moved past me and got behind the wheel.

"As opposed to?" I drawled, slamming the car door shut after I slid into the passenger seat.

"Sullen and sarcastic."

• • •

Lunch was a long time coming. We went through two more ancient houses and a feed store and finally ended up at a cave. The houses had come up dry, and the feed store had been host to one murder, though not the massacre legend had painted. And apparently, that was not enough violence to make it a target for Charlie. The cave, Hector promised, was the last one before we ate, and I was holding him to it. No food, no mojo.

"We're here."

I wasn't dozing, not really, but the voice was jarring nonetheless. Too many winding Georgia roads, too much hot sun through the windows. I last remembered a spill of rotten fruit along an orchard we'd passed. Red, gold, and brown, the peaches had rolled free of a wicker basket. As pictures went, it was sad in a way, wistful, but it was beautiful, too.

"Where's here?" I muttered, rubbing tired eyes. "The hole in the ground?"

"Yes, Carlson Caverns. Sawney Beane's American summer home." Hector stared through the windshield, and his mouth twitched minutely, which I'd come to recognize as his version of a scowl. "Tourists. Look at all the tourists."

It was more than a few. There were dozens of people milling about the gravel parking lot in front of the path that, per the huge sign, led to the cavern.

"What are you, a vacation Grinch?" I yawned. "And who the hell is Sawney Beane?" The name actually sounded vaguely familiar, but I was tired and starving and not in the mood to chase the thought around my weary brain.

He checked his watch, decided the tourists weren't going to dematerialize to suit him, and turned to address my question. "He was head of a legendary family of cannibals. The Beane clan supposedly lived in a Scottish cave in the fourteenth or fifteenth century. Sawney and his highly incestuous family killed thousands of innocent travelers, dragged their bodies back to their cave, hung them on hooks, and ate them." His pale eyes considered me. "Did I already say supposedly?"

"Yeah, you did."

Note to self: avoid Scotland. Avoid it like the fucking plague. The hell with supposedly; better safe than sorry was my rule.

"You're not telling me this place is the equivalent? Because, Allgood, guess what? I really don't want to hear that." I made no move to get out of the car, although I sincerely doubted that Georgian cannibals had once roamed the area. I was simply tired and cranky as hell. Rubbing dry, tired eyes, I grabbed the last folder and opened it. After scanning the two pages, I thought about fighting the impulse to roll my eyes. I didn't fight it long or hard. "I can't believe we dragged our asses all the way here for this crap. It's right up there with the Headless Horseman or, hell, the Great Pumpkin."

"I never figured you for a Charlie Brown fan, Jackson."

"Oh, shut up, would ya?" I complained, my drawl thicker with weariness. "Bottom line is you don't need a psychic to vet this one. It's pure bullshit. Historical bullshit, maybe, but still bullshit. Not to mention a total waste of my time." As the entire damn day had been. "I'm beat." I pulled the lever on the side of the seat and dropped it into the reclining position. "Bring me back a rock. I'll read it, and then we can finally grab some lunch."

A large hand reached across me, opened the door, and gave me a firm shove out. I didn't fall on my ass; the force of the push had been very carefully calculated on Hector's part in consideration of the fact that I'd just that morning crawled out of a hospital bed. The effort didn't stop me from giving him a poisonous glare.

"Is that your way of saying 'or we could walk to the cave'?"

"You *are* a psychic, aren't you?" Hector closed his door, checked his watch again, and added, "Let's go buy a ticket."

The tickets were ten bucks apiece. Ten bucks to see a muddy, frigid hole in the ground. Needless to say, I didn't pay. There was a tour guide, potbellied in shorts, a Carlson Caverns T-shirt, and tube socks. With a booming voice that issued out of a gingery beard, he led the way into the cave. "Carlson Caverns was first discovered in 1771 by an expedition led by..."

I tuned him out. I wasn't particularly interested in who had been the first unfortunate bastard to trip and fall through the cave entrance while screaming like a banshee. I was interested in lunch, sleep, a whole lot less of Hector, and that was it. And sun... sun would be good. Forget that I'd just been cursing the hot, sweaty grip of it. Standing in a nature-formed grave freezing my ass off made me appreciate a heat that baked you to the bones. Sighing, I shifted from foot to foot and folded my arms against the chill. A little boy standing at his mother's side looked over at me. About seven, with a baseball cap and a backpack, he grinned cheerfully. An all-American boy, missing front tooth, freckles, skinned knee—and then he flipped me off.

All-American, all right.

Snorting, I looked over at Hector. "I'm starving. Let's get this over with."

I stripped off a glove, bent down, and picked up a rock. Freezing. Bored. Paid ten bucks for this? Tourist thoughts, and unsurprising ones at that. I dropped it, took a few steps, and picked up another one. Same thing. I wandered a little farther out toward a side tunnel off the main cavern. Mr. Carlson himself was finally getting to the legend as I walked.

"And in 1864, a Confederate Army deserter holed up here to hide from his unit. Hart Renfrow.

Apparently, ole Hart wasn't right in the head to begin with, because he lived in this Georgia tomb for seven years, just sure as can be that his fellow soldiers were still looking for him, waiting to string him up. And when winters got hard and game was scarce . . ." Out of the corner of my eye, I saw the guide's mock leer highlighted by a flashlight under the chin. Je-*sus*. I was glad the ten bucks hadn't come out of my pocket.

"Yes, ladies and gentlemen, when game was scarce, *he ate people*." His voice sank to a horrified whisper. "Crept over to the outskirts of Carlson City and stole them. Women and children, mainly, but the occasional man. In those days, they thought bears or wolves had gotten the missing, but you and I and Hart Renfrow, we know better."

He went on, but I'd heard more than enough. What a colossal waste of time. Hector had followed me, and I glared at him over my shoulder as I reached for the stone wall of the tunnel for the last check I was going to bother to make.

"Milk shake and fries, you got it? And I want a huge-ass hot fudge sund—"

The world went away. This world. But there were always other worlds, weren't there? This one had the stench of boiling flesh hovering on a winter chill, half-skinned naked women hanging from racks lashed together from tree limbs, and bones littering the floor to crunch with every step. Yes, every slow and sure step you took as you prowled closer to the five-year-old girl hiding under her mother's body. She was screaming for her daddy over and over and over. Screaming and screaming and—

The sun.

I blinked. Blue sky and sun and a warmth that could melt any chill, even that of Carlson Caverns, an atypically bitter Georgia winter, and Hart Renfrow.

"Hunhh," I mumbled less than coherently. There was more heat under me, intense and so goddamn wonderful I could've lain on top of it for the rest of my damn life.

"You with me, Jackson?"

I turned my head slowly to take in Hector's wary expression. Was I with him? Was I here? Good question.

"She wanted her daddy," I said blankly as I looked away back to the sky. "Renfrow thought she tasted good. Tender. Went way too fast, though. The little ones always do . . . always did." It was like a nightmare now that contact was broken, but not a fresh one—an old one from years and years past. Thank God, except I'd never thank anyone who'd made me see what I had seen.

I sat up to see that I'd been lying on the hood of Hector's car, just your average overloaded psychic taking in the sun.

Hector wasn't looking wary any longer, he was looking flat-out worried as hell. Worried about my mental health or about my ability to do the job—it didn't matter which. In the end, they were one and the same.

"Get a T-shirt, Allgood." I rubbed my mouth, hoping there was no drool. "What you're looking for doesn't get more righteous than this." Not when you were trolling for massacres, serial killings, and explosions of violence.

"Yes, the eyes rolling back in your head and the *Exorcist* whispering before I dragged you out gave that away." He held out a hand to help me down. My glove had been replaced, but I still ignored the offer and slid down on my own. My knees wobbled a bit as I hit the ground, but I locked them in place and managed to stay upright.

"Whispering?" I repeated cautiously. "Me? What was I saying?"

He pulled the car keys from his pocket and looked at them with far more focus than they required. "Little girl." He shook his head and squared his shoulders. "You were saying, little girl. Come here, little girl. Come here, sugar and spice and everything nice. Come here. And you sounded . . . hungry."

I looked back toward the entrance of the cave, past the curious stares of tourists waiting for the next tour, past cars, and beyond the modern world. "He was," I said simply. "Always hungry. No matter how much he ate, how many he ate. He was always hungry." I turned my back to it, physically and mentally, to grimace faintly. "Me, on the other hand, I think we can forget lunch."

As it turned out, my body didn't agree with that notion. I'd been working it steadily today, and psychic exertion was considerably more draining than the physical kind. By the time we reached the diner, I was sweating buckets, and it wasn't from the heat. Clammy and soaked with cold sweat, I knew my blood sugar had taken a serious dive, and I ripped into the complimentary crackers the second we hit the table. Annie's Big Fat Fannie was a barbecue joint, but there was enough in the way of side orders there for a vegetarian to get by. Potato salad, macaroni salad, cole slaw, a cheese sandwich, fried biscuits with apple butter, strawberry-rhubarb pie, and pint jars of sweet tea garnished with a frozen slice of peach. As for Annie's generous fannie, the woman was damn proud of it. Good for her.

She was a whirlwind in the tiny restaurant, bustling from table to table in jeans and a sparkly halter top about thirty years too young for her. She treated the three waitresses like daughters, scolding and praising in one breath. Greeting regulars with hoots of joy and hugs and greeting strangers just the same, she was nothing but grins and sass and good heart. One regular in dirty clothes with a permanent alcohol glaze in his eye was given free food and a hug the same as everyone else. The world needed more Annies.

"You boys doing okay?" She beamed as she wrapped an arm around Hector's shoulders and squeezed before leaning on the edge of the table. Waist-length platinum-blond hair was teased into a stiff, hairspray-coated, billowing cloud, turning her into a Rapunzel of the Bible Belt. As for her fannie, I wouldn't say it was fat, but if you were an ass man, there was more than enough to catch your eye. Earlier, I'd seen her catch a few country boys gawking from the counter. She'd turned to slap it briskly in their direction. She'd laughed. "Double helpings, boys, and more than pups the likes of you can handle."

"Doing good, Miss Annie," I said politely, sliding a look toward Hector as I wondered how to insinuate that he was a fan of the fannie. From the stone-faced glare I received in return, it was plain to see that he was doing a little mind reading of his own. Letting the opportunity at humiliation go, I added, "Best fried biscuits in Georgia."

"Damn straight there." She beamed even brighter behind thick pancake makeup and bright green eye shadow. And before I could anticipate it, she wrapped her hand around my bare wrist as it rested on the table. "What's with the gloves, cutie-pie? You look like O. J. Simpson."

"Um. Poison ivy." I gave her a plastic smile. "Nasty case. Don't want to give it to anybody."

"You poor thing. You have the calamine? Nothing works like the calamine, except for an oatmeal bath." She let go of my wrist to give me the same hug she'd given Hector. "You be sure to do that tonight before bed. Coat up good with oatmeal. It'll do right by you, you'll see." And then she was gone, and my hand flashed out to yank Hector's plate of barbecue away before he could take a bite.

"What are you doing?" he asked, baffled, already reaching out to pull it back.

"You don't want to eat it," I said darkly. "Trust me."

He let his hand drop and said cautiously, "Do I even want to know why?"

"Probably not." Annie was over at the counter with an arm around each of those blushing boys and laughing like a loon. It seemed that our good-hearted hostess didn't like the dogs that ran in the neighborhood. Loud, digging in the garbage, giving those stupid dog grins when she chased them with a broom. No, Miss Annie didn't like that at all. And if the little shits were stupid enough to come up to you when one hand was filled with food and the other held your old butcher knife, well, it couldn't be a sin to do what had to be done, right? Worthless creatures. Even God made a mistake once in a while. And waste not, want not.

"Let's just say Miss Annie is the reason they don't need an animal shelter in these parts."

I made my way methodically through the side orders in front of me, only because I doubted I would've been able to get up from the table under my own power if I hadn't. My appetite had taken some serious blows today, no way around it.

Hector, meanwhile, let it alone—the situation, the barbecue, and everything else on his plate—as he turned green. Normal people. They were so damn lucky. I remembered what it was like before I was fourteen, before Tess's shoe. Ignorance was bliss—one of the oldest clichés around, and it had every right to be. Nothing was more true. Finally, Hector chanced one biscuit, saying wearily, "We're done for the day. And tomorrow . . ." He turned his glass jar of tea one way, then the other. "Tomorrow, if our calculations are correct, Charlie will try to come through, somewhere."

I wondered if it was still Charlie, the way he had been. Intelligence, emotion, memory—was that what was trying to return home, or was it a blind amorphous urge and nothing more? Just a leftover instinct with nothing behind it?

"How will that go?" I asked with reluctant curiosity.

"We'll have teams at the most logical locations. The ones authenticated and with the highest violence quotient. The higher the latter, the more extensive the 'fraying.' The teams will move in if a violence cycle begins to repeat and, hopefully, prevent any further deaths. You'll have a few of Charlie's things and see if you can pinpoint it when he does come through. If you can get the location the moment he appears, that team can move in immediately, and we can rush the equipment in." He exhaled, one corner of his mouth twisting. "Piece of cake, right?"

Since he didn't believe it, either, I wasn't going to make the effort. "Why doesn't every team have its own Charlie-busting device? It'd make things a helluva lot easier."

"It cost three and a half million to build the one we have, and we're not exactly high on any politician's funding list."

Good reason.

Back at headquarters . . . I'd always wanted to say that as a kid. That's the way it had always gone in the superhero cartoons or the buddy cop shows. Back at headquarters was where you figured out what you'd learned, regrouped, then went out to kick ass.

At that moment, I couldn't have kicked anyone's ass unless they were under four and in the middle of naptime. I eased onto the narrow bed, bit back a groan, and lay back to stare at the ceiling. Meleah had said that I'd have residual muscle soreness from the seizure. She knew her stuff, unfortunately, Meleah did. Meleah, not Dr. Guerrera . . . and that's why I ignored Hector's offer.

"You can stay in the infirmary, Jackson," he repeated. "There's plenty of empty beds, not to mention painkillers and muscle relaxants at your fingertips."

When you move like an eighty-year-old man, apparently people will notice. And while the infirmary was a slightly nicer cage, it was still a cage. I could deal with that, at least for a while, but I didn't want to deal with seeing Meleah with too-familiar eyes and wondering where Charlie began and I ended.

"I'll be okay." I covered my eyes against the buzzing light with a forearm. "Turn that out before you lock me in, would you? It's like a laser beam from hell."

"I'm not locking you in."

I moved my arm enough to give him a disbelieving glance. "You're kidding, right?"

"No. Fuck regulations." Hector showing he was the big dog and Thackery could kiss his ass. "I think your clearance level has gone about as high as it could go now." His pale eyes were tainted with exhaustion, like dirty ice. "I'm through being an asshole because circumstances dictate it. Charlie wouldn't be happy with me, and I'm not too happy with myself." He moved to the door and opened it. "You'll stay because we can help your sister and because you want to help Charlie, whether you admit that or not." He shook his head. "Even to yourself. I'll send Eden with some pills. See you at five."

Five A.M.? I groaned mentally as he shut the door. It was easier to focus on that than on the grab bag of goodies he'd thrown in my lap. My cage door was open. Of course, Glory was the real cage; they had never needed a locked door to keep me here. But . . . I looked at it—gray, metal, ugly, and unlocked— and suddenly, I could breathe. The claustrophobia was still there, but knowing that I could open the door anytime lifted it enough to let me breathe without feeling as if I were strangling.

As for the other things, Hector giving me his trust and being so sure that I would've stayed regardless if only to help Charlie—as if he thought he knew me now. Knew who I was on the inside. He ignored my snark and was acting more like his brother. Too damn perceptive. I wasn't comfortable with that. I'd let Abby in. I didn't think I had room for any others.

Once I was loaded up with Tylenol, muscle relaxants, and more of Eden's sympathetic pats and anger at my condition, the night passed in a blink, and I was faced with the ugly reality of too-damn-early. There was the smell of eggs and toast under my nose, and I pried up eyelids with a mind of their own and fifty pounds of concrete on their side. At least, it felt that way. I did get them open, though, to see the blurry vision of gray scrambled eggs and limp soggy toast.

"This is a joke," I mumbled thickly. "A bad joke. Go away."

"It's not much to look at, Mr. Eye, I know, but I did bring a cinnamon roll and coffee from the outside world. I hope that will make up for our cafeteria's failings."

My eyes widened to fully alert. I'd assumed it was Hector. I must've been stupid with sleep; Hector had never smelled like that. She smelled like oranges and cinnamon. When Charlie's memory didn't pop up to comment on the change from lemon, I decided either the scent was new or Charlie was beginning to fade. It didn't matter which, because either one was a good way to start the day. I'd liked Charlie, but it was time for him to go. I couldn't be his tombstone, eulogy, and life's history all rolled into one forever.

I sat up and reached immediately for my gloves. After pulling them on, I shoved my hair back and snapped a rubber band around it. "I'll take the roll and coffee, thanks."

She aimed gray eyes at the eggs and gave a philosophical sigh. "I'd throw them to the crows, but they won't touch them, either." She deposited the tray on the desk and handed me a paper bag fragrant with the smells of butter, icing, and dark roast.

"I didn't know doctors made house calls anymore, much less with cinnamon rolls." And a damn fine cinnamon roll it was, too. It was the size of a saucer and dripping with all the things that made life worthwhile—sugar, butter, grease. I had to take my gloves back off to eat it, and it was more than worth the trouble.

"Yes, well, most doctors don't tend to patients who are being held against their will." Her lips tightened. "Who are being blackmailed."

Maybe, like Eden, she was on my side, too. Charlie had nothing to contradict absolute integrity in her. Then again, Charlie had been too good for his own good. And good people are gullible.

"True." My eyes narrowed as I wiped sticky fingers on a napkin from the bag. "And you think a roll and coffee makes up for that?" She was an amazing woman, and I didn't need Charlie to tell me so, but that didn't let her off the hook for all this.

"No," she responded quietly. "I'm not sure anything would." Laying warm fingers on my arm, she added, "I am sorry. I know it counts for very little, but I am."

Behind the words, I saw her. Five years old and standing by the window where the cage hung. Her *abuela* kept two doves, gray and white with soft pink eyes. They watched the sky through silver bars, and that wasn't right. No one should be in a cage. Everyone should know freedom. *Libertad.* Everyone should know the sky. And so she'd opened the window and then the door to the cage, and off they flew, without hesitation. As if they'd been waiting for this moment all their short lives. Meleah had waved in joy until she couldn't see them anymore. Waved and waved.

I looked blankly at her hand on my arm. "Don't."

She removed it instantly, mortified, I could tell by the flush under warm amber skin. "I'm sorry. I forgot. It is inexcusable of me." Because a good doctor didn't forget that one patient was a diabetic, and she didn't forget that another was psychic.

"It's okay." I took another bite of the roll. "It's not

an easy thing to remember." I smiled, ready for a little harmless payback and because, hell, I was curious. "Did your granny bust your ass for letting her birds go?" I raised a hand for a short wave, a simple one-two bend of the fingers. "*Libertad, pequeñas palomas.*"

Freedom, little doves.

Her mouth opened slightly, and the flush faded. Then, amazingly, she smiled back, her gray eyes warm. "She scolded me quite fiercely, but it was worth it. Of course, the silly birds came back the next day looking for supper." She gave a gentle shrug. "I did what I could."

Which is what she was doing now. For Charlie. He was in a cage, the same as I was, the same as the birds, but the door to it was much more difficult to open than when she'd been five. Maybe if we were lucky, both Charlie and I would get our *libertad*.

Maybe.

I finished up the roll and the coffee just as Hector came through the door. "It's a party," I drawled, toasting him with an empty paper cup. "BYOCB, though. Bring your own cinnamon bun."

Hector was not amused. Tense and on edge behind his usual stone mask, no amusement to be found. "Get dressed, Jackson. We have to get set up at our location."

"Not the cavern, right?" I demanded with a little tension of my own. I'd had enough of that place—more than enough. Charlie could come through there wearing bells and whistles and dancing a god-damn jig, I didn't care. I was *not* going to be there.

"No. I made sure we pulled another site. The last thing I want, Eye, is you gnawing on my shinbone."

Well, I stood corrected. There was a little humor in Allgood after all. Desperate and dark battlefield humor but humor all the same. "Stringy as hell," I said, wrinkling my upper lip. "I wouldn't waste my time."

Meleah's smile widened then faded. "Hector? You'll let me know when something happens, yes? Thackery certainly will not."

"Of course." He rested a hand on her shoulder and squeezed lightly. "You're as much a part of this as anyone, no matter what that bastard says."

Thackery apparently knew everything about winning friends and influencing people—and had tossed that knowledge into the toilet and flushed repeatedly. I definitely wouldn't be sorry to see the last of that bastard. If I had to take bets on who might murder Charlie, although I was very carefully *not* thinking about that, he'd top the list.

Meleah, though, and even blackmailing Hector—they weren't that bad. Good people in a bad situation, I was forced to admit, as much as I didn't want to. I didn't want to be sympathetic to their situation and them, I just wanted out. Wasn't that right? I told myself. Wasn't it? As Meleah left, she raised her own coffee cup to me. "*A la libertad,*" she said solemnly. "To liberty."

Here was hoping it was that easy, I thought as she closed the door behind her.

Hector eyed me, assessing, but said nothing—at least, not about Meleah. "Get dressed," he repeated. "We don't have all day."

"That statement has Mom written all over it." I tossed my cup into the garbage can. "You want to remind me to use the bathroom before we go? Maybe tell me to wear clean underwear, too, while you're at it."

This time, he said nothing at all, the pale eyes narrowed to slits.

"Okay, okay," I said. "Sheesh. Do I have time for a shower?"

"No."

"Great," I mumbled as I stripped and changed into jeans and a long-sleeved T-shirt. "If Charlie does show up, he'll be promptly driven away by my funky stench. There's a ghostbusting tool Murray and Aykroyd never tried."

"Actually, you smell like a giant cinnamon bun. Very manly. Now, get your goddamn ass in gear." There was humor in the words, but his eyes didn't show it. Why would they? Today was the day he was hoping to take what was left of his brother and end it permanently. It had to be done, but that didn't mean it hurt any less.

I finished tying my sneakers, put on my gloves, and stood. "Okay. Let's go save Charlie."

It wasn't as cool as, say, let's go kick some noncorporeal ass, but it was far more true. We might be ending Charlie, but we would be saving him, too, because Hector was right. Charlie would far rather be gone than continue hurting people. The nonexistence of the grave would be vastly preferable. Then again, Charlie believed in life after death . . . real life, not the lab-created kind. Funny how someone so brilliant could be so damn naive. And may a heavenly choir of angels sing you to sleep.

Shit.

Our location turned out to be an old mill. Lassie could've told us those were never good places to hang out. Trouble was bound to pop up—it was the law.

It *was* nice, though. Weeping willows bowing over a chuckling creek. The silver wood and stone of the mill was like a pool of moonlight at odds with the bright morning sun. I tossed a rock into the water with my left hand. In my right, I held Charlie's key chain. When the time came, I'd strip my glove off and try to track Charlie, try to get the jump on him by at least a few seconds, give the team at the chosen location a heads-up.

Our location didn't have the big guns this time. The equipment had been taken to the place with the highest body count: the cavern. It was considered the most likely place with the highest amount of "fraying." When I asked Hector why he hadn't gone there with that team, he hadn't responded, unless you consider jaw clenching a response. Thackery. The son of a bitch had a lot of power, maybe enough to get Hector thrown off the project. It was the only thing that explained Hector's presence behind me at the stream and made Thackery seem more suspicious—keeping Charlie's brother at arm's length from Charlie was what a murderer would do.

"It's time," he said quietly. "Ten minutes until ETE." I looked over my shoulder and raised my eyebrows questioningly. "Sorry. Estimated time of ether-disruption."

"Scientists." I snorted. "Geeks."

"Supergeek, actually, and proud of it," he corrected, and tapped his watch. "Jackson . . ."

No more putting it off. Taking a deep breath, I transferred the keys to my other hand, stripped off the right glove, and then cradled the hunk of metal again, this time against bare skin. The mill was already verified; now it was time to read Charlie. There were the usual bits and pieces of him floating about in the keys. Driving for groceries. Taking Meleah's puppies to the vet for shots. Cruising in the rain with Elvis wailing about wild horses and hound dogs. The flotsam and jetsam of daily life. The normal results of a reading. Unconsciously, I relaxed and enjoyed the warm weight of a puppy in my lap and the sounds of the King shaking the speakers.

Then it started.

At first, it was almost indistinguishable from the backdrop of the memories. It was just another emotion. Lost. I'm lost. It was so faint and muted that I expected to see Charlie pull a map from the glove compartment. Just a mild annoyance. Maybe he'd stop at a gas station and ask for directions.

It was because I forgot. For a moment, I forgot what had happened the day before at the caverns. The talent was banged up a bit thanks to reliving Charlie's death, bent but not broken. Emotions were hazy TV viewing instead of living 3-D, and Charlie wasn't feeling the kind of lost that a map could do a damn thing about.

Trees. Water.

How do I get in?

Where's the door?

Where's the door?

Where is me?

Where, where, where, where, where, where . . .

"Shit," I muttered, shoving the keys into my pocket and looking around wildly. As if I'd be able to see anything.

"What?" Hector demanded.

"He's here," I said instantly. "He's looking for a way in. He's lost. He's looking for a way home. He's looking *here.*"

Hector was on his cell phone immediately, but the caverns were easily an hour away. They'd never get there in time. I started toward the mill at a run to warn the others. We had a team of six: Hector, me, and four others. And one of us was about to get real ornery real quick.

The mill didn't have the history Carlson Caverns did, but it wasn't all kittens and frigging rainbows, either. Hundreds of years before the phrase "going postal" was around, there'd been a similar one in these parts: "gristed." Or, to be more precise, "done got himself gristed." This one hadn't been a legend needing my confirmation. This had been in the papers of the day. One of the mill workers, I had no idea what his name had been, had flat lost his mind, tossed his coworkers off the roof, then chopped up their bodies with an axe and fed the pieces down the hopper to be milled, a.k.a. gristed. By the time someone found out what had happened, whatshisname—really, what the hell *was* his name?—was chopping off pieces of himself to feed to the hungry mill.

There were no axes here, though. That was a good thing. It's hard to chop up people without the proper tools, any homicidal maniac could tell you that. Reasonable, logical, but it didn't stop the screaming from starting.

I hesitated for a split second, then ran on. How bad could it be? Three of them were scientists loaded down with their geeky equipment. The remaining guy was a soldier, but he was unarmed as a safety measure. Everyone was. Not even a penknife among us.

And yet the screaming went on.

As I continued toward the mill, I could hear the grass-muffled pounding of Allgood's feet behind me. He pulled even with me as the first person was thrown off the roof. I skidded to a stop and could feel my jaw slacken as the man tumbled through the air, white-coated arms windmilling and mouth stretched wide in a scream. He hit the ground with a highly unpleasant thump and a bounce. He was still twitching, though, when he came to rest; the fall was only a little more than two stories. I liked to think that was an excuse for what I said next, but it probably wasn't.

"Geeks falling out of the sky. If that's not a sign of the Apocalypse, I don't know what is," I said, awed.

Hector swore and ran into the mill. I didn't follow, not yet. Instead, I shaded my eyes and peered at the roof, because a little information goes a long way toward not having to realize firsthand that you can't fly. I didn't know for sure who was up there— I tended to label the scientists as geeks one, two, and three and the soldier as goon one. Geeks and goons didn't need names—or so I'd thought. This was geek number two on the roof and unfortunate geek number three on the ground. The guy on the roof doing the tossing, his name was . . . Damn. His name was . . . Bob, I pried out of my brain, triumphant.

"Uh, hey, Bob," I called up. "Can you just, I don't know, not throw anyone else off the roof for a minute and listen up?"

A cloud crossed the sun, blocking the glare, and I could suddenly see him perfectly. Raging eyes, saliva cascading over his chin, and his mouth twisted in a hoarse scream. Because he was the one screaming. Without a second's pause, it went on and on and on. It was the kind that rips throats to bloody shreds and minds to the very same. The worst part was that I didn't know if it came from Bob himself or the recording playing in him. It reminded me of an old commercial: *Is it live or is it Memorex?*

But he didn't stop or listen. He bent and dragged another form into sight. The goon. I could see blood in the blond hair. Bob hadn't been able to find an axe, but he'd found something to use to whack his coworkers over the head. A length of wood, maybe. It seemed that when the recording loop within him couldn't reenact the event exactly, it stuck with the spirit of it: death. Lots and lots of death.

Bob grunted as he moved the soldier over the peak of the roof. Grunted, screamed, grunted, screamed some more. Insanity incarnate. I'd only seen one thing in my life more disturbing than this.

A well and a drowned little girl.

Tasting bile, I tried to hold on to the casual tone. "Bob . . ." No. That wasn't who he was now. Jim, Joshua . . . what the *fuck* had been that guy's name in the file I'd skimmed?

"Jacob!" I said triumphantly. "Jacob, I know you can hear me. I need you to listen to me, okay?"

Jacob Messersmith was long dead and had nothing to do with this current mess, but a certain pattern etched into the fabric of reality didn't know that. The energy, alien and trespassing, flowed along that pattern like water filling an empty riverbed—it brought to the pattern a very limited facsimile of life. An imitation of it. But imitations don't always know that about themselves. Computer programs are a good example. Jacob didn't know that he didn't exist, and Jacob recognized his name.

The screaming stopped. He stared at me, his hands tangled in the dark green T-shirt of the soldier, one heave away from moving forward with his task. "Jacob." He said it in a voice thick and gravelly. It sounded as if his throat was choked with stones and blood, and it was as far from human as you could get. "Ja-cob."

But that made sense, because he wasn't human, was he? He wasn't even a he. *It* was nothing . . . nothing that *thought* it was something.

"Jacob, you look like you're having a bad day. Want to talk about it?" That was me, a shrink to a paranormal rerun. It didn't get much more screwed up than that. I wasn't even sure I could talk to a pattern. Did it have enough information imprinted in those violent moments to be able to respond beyond killing? Was there an imprint of Jacob's mindset, his emotions and thoughts? Or only his actions?

"Jacob," I repeated when the doughy face stared down at me blankly. "What's going on? What'd these guys do to piss you off?"

"Jacob." There was blood on his lips—from the

screaming, I thought. "Jacob." The limp form of the soldier bobbled in his grip. "*Gott. Gott* tells Jacob. *Gott erklärte mir*. God tells me. They are against me. They plot. They would murder. They are demons. God tells Jacob to be his right hand. To smite the fallen ones."

Great—not just an animate pattern but an animate, *schizophrenic* pattern. I had no hopes of reasoning with him. How do you reason with a DVR player? I could only hope to distract him, to make the disk skip, so to speak, to give Hector—

And there he was. On the roof behind Jacob-Bob. He'd left the scientist part behind, and now he was all soldier, loose and tense all in one.

"Jacob," I called again hurriedly. "Demons. Tell me about the demons."

"The fallen ones. *Gott* says smite the fallen ones," he mumbled, the blood streaking his chin as he hefted the unconscious soldier. "*Gott* took their demon wings. They can no longer fly. They can only fall." And with a horrible smile, he started to toss the soldier.

But Hector got there first. With an arm around Bob's windpipe, he choked him out, quickly and ruthlessly. With his other hand, he caught the soldier before he tumbled over the edge of the roof. Which was good for me. It saved the awkward decision of do you try to catch the poor bastard or do your damnedest to avoid being hit by his falling body. Instead, I was able to check the guy already on the ground. Both of his legs were bent at brutally ugly angles, but he was still breathing, and, considering, that definitely put him in the "came out ahead" column for the day.

Then I went into the mill to look for geek number one. I found him in seconds. The blood on Jacob's mouth hadn't been from the screaming after all.

Christ.

It took several minutes for us to get the geek and the goon off the roof, our feet slipping and sliding on dangerously decayed wood. As we grunted and yanked at the limp bodies, Hector said, "Charlie?"

"Jesus, I've been busy, okay?" I muttered, but I dug my still-naked hand in my pocket and closed them around metal. Dogs, Elvis, rain . . .

Nothing else.

"He's gone," I answered. "Sorry." And I was.

Although, truthfully, the rest of us seemed to do much better when Charlie wasn't around.

11

"Do you drink?"

Hector stood in the doorway of my "room" with a six-pack in his hand. "I wasn't sure if it would affect your . . ." He circled a finger to finish the sentence.

"My mojo? My happy hoodoo?" I indicated the desk chair. "Screw it, and bring it on. Tonight I'd drink paint thinner if it was in a nice enough bottle." I did have the occasional beer while Houdini snuffled around my feet for a sip. It didn't affect my abilities. I could drink myself deaf, dumb, and blind, and it still wouldn't have mattered. I'd done it once or twice before, when I was young, stupid, and a little less able to deal. All it did was make the psychic movie a little fuzzy around the edges. It didn't dull it enough to make drinking a hobby or a necessity. And I wasn't going to be like those drunken losers who'd hung around the house when I was a kid. The old man included. Mom had tried, but if there was an asshole in the tristate area, she'd fall head over heels for the bastard.

But there are always exceptions, and with what I'd seen today, I was all about exceptions. I accepted an already opened beer from Hector as he twisted off the cap to his own. "Isn't drinking on duty against the rules?" I took a cool swallow.

"That's the advantage of being ex-military. If I get caught, the worse they can do is fire me." He took a long swallow of his own before rubbing his forehead with the heel of his hand. "So . . . what did we learn today?"

"That reruns are for shit." And that I missed my dog, my home, my nonhomicidal secretary. Abby had never once tried to throw anyone off a roof for God. Okay, there was the Bible-thumper or two who regularly vandalized my poster. Jacob gave me bad ideas. It would be ironic, considering this situation: toss a man *of* God off a roof because absolutely no one told you to. I was sure God's hand would ease him to the ground as gently as a feather.

"And that Charlie isn't necessarily going to be drawn to the places with the most violence. Maybe he can sense things only so far, geographically speaking. Maybe he's just drifting here and there, and wherever he happens to pass . . ." I shrugged and took another drink.

"Does he know?" The question was as abrupt as Hector's thumb was methodical in peeling off his bottle label. "Does Charlie know what he's doing? Does he know what's happening?"

I could finish the rest of that without his words.

Because he couldn't. Charlie couldn't know, because Charlie wouldn't cause death and terror. His brother wouldn't believe that of him. Couldn't. And Hector was right.

"No." I shook my head. "He doesn't know. I'm not sure he even knows he's Charlie anymore. All he knows is being lost. He's lost, and he can't find his way, but I'm not sure there's any reason behind what he does. Where he goes. What spot he chooses. There's just lost and a sense of banging futilely at a closed door." I rested the bottle against my knee. "I'm sure you see the downside to that."

"We can't predict where he'll go. We can't have the equipment waiting. If . . . when we finally catch him, it will be a matter of sheer luck." Hector leaned back in his chair. It wasn't relaxation, which I wasn't sure the man was capable of, it was exhaustion. "But the timing is still within parameters. We can't predict where, but we can predict when. And now we know: evacuate all possible locations for the ETE except one. Eventually we'll catch him."

"And the people who live there or are plodding through their favorite cannibal vacation spot?" I raised eyebrows in question.

"Chlorine leak. Anthrax scare. Terrorists." He shifted his shoulders and gave a humorless smile. "We have a thousand of them."

"I thought *I* was supposed to be the con man." My lips twitched despite myself. Maybe I was getting Stockholm syndrome or maybe just a good buzz. Either way, I felt for Hector. Every which way you looked at it, his pooch was screwed but good. It wasn't only Charlie's memories that had me seeing that. For the first time, I let myself see it, too. I let myself feel an empathy that I didn't try to shove down. I was getting soft in my old age.

"Actually, Eye, you're one of the more honest men I've met."

A compliment. If this was a made-for-TV movie, I would've been touched . . . right up to the moment he added, "You're too much of a lazy son of a bitch to bother to lie."

I actually grinned this time. I wholeheartedly blamed the alcohol for that. Or it could've been the relief that *I* hadn't been thrown off a roof. Take your pick.

"Who's the psychic around here, anyway?" I finished off the beer. "And I'm not that lazy. You saw my house. Neat enough. God knows I don't have a housekeeper touching my things"—contaminating my things—"and Houdini still can't figure out how to use a mop."

"You're right. And from the intel I gathered on you, you work seven days a week. That's not the sign of a lazy man." He opened another beer. "So then you're simply a son of a bitch. A hardworking bastard of the highest order."

"I'd argue, but I worked too hard to be a bastard to give up the title now." I held out a hand for the next Bud. It went down as smoothly as the first.

"Since I'm obviously in this for the goddamn long haul, why don't you tell me about Thackery? He doesn't seem to be in this for the betterment of humanity. Flying around the universe seeing pretty lights sounds enlightening and all, but where's the money in it? Where's the glory? Thackery seems the type to want both of those things."

"Therein lies the military involvement." Hector's pale eyes were tired. I wasn't sure if it was that or the alcohol that made him more forthcoming. Or maybe he thought I deserved to know. Having observed him for the past few days, I was thinking it was the latter. He was very much like his brother. "Imagine the benefit if you could go anywhere, see anything, but no one could see or detect you. In the seventies, the CIA had remote viewers working for them with some success. Imagine what they could do if astral projection was available. An operative could travel along the ether, like a skater on a sheet of ice. There would be no secrets any longer . . . not to our side, anyway."

I'd suspected that was what was going on, but it didn't stop the sour curdle of my stomach. "Yeah, funny how I'm never on 'our' side. In school or now, I'm an outsider, always will be." That was the thing about sides. The one in the know, the one with power, it tended to get smaller and smaller, and more and more of us got tossed over the line to the unpopular side. The loser side. The side that ended up looking up at the bottom of a boot on its way down.

"He made a mistake." Hector looked blindly at his empty bottle. "Charlie always trusted people. He brought me into the project halfway through, and by then . . ." He exhaled. "It was too late. The money was spent. The deal was done."

"Signed in blood on the dotted line." I shook my head. "Charlie was always too good for his own good."

"I know." He sat still for another moment, then carefully set his bottle on the desk. "But he took care of me, and now it's time for me to do the same for him."

Even if the only thing left of Charlie was a feeling of being lost. One emotion out of hundreds, an unconscious trace of a human being, but it didn't matter to Hector. He wasn't letting down Charlie, or even a piece of Charlie—he was that kind of brother. I knew, because I tried to be that kind of brother. Which was why I was there to begin with.

Glory. The baby. Shit. I sighed, and the strong consideration of one more beer became a done deal. You could bet my sister wouldn't be the slightest bit grateful for what I was doing for her, only take it as her due. But Charlie . . . Charlie would be proud as hell of his little brother, Hector, although it was hard to imagine Hector as anyone's little anything.

"When's the next ETE?"

"Two days."

"We checking out any more locations before

then?" I took another glum swallow at the thought of how festive that would be.

"You'd be amazed at the number of massacres, spree murders, and serial killings that have taken place or are rumored to have taken place in Georgia." He opened another beer for himself.

"Not so much, no." After what I'd seen peering into people's heads throughout my illustrious career, surprise wasn't something I had left in me. The sweetest little grandma you could imagine had secrets. They never thought about that when they came to see me. It was as if they thought I was a guided missile. They pointed, and I went. They didn't consider that I saw it all. I saw where they lost their keys, ring, necklace, wallet, where Aunt Susie's junior-high baby had ended up after adoption, that Mama was in the freezer while her Social Security checks kept coming. They thought I saw what they wanted me to see, but they were wrong. If they knew, safe to say I wouldn't have any customers. Not a one.

And then there was my own personal massacre.

Hector, again, didn't have to be psychic to know what I was thinking. "Charlie knew," he said with cautious sympathy. You couldn't be sure how killers would take to talking about the blood on their hands. "He didn't have your records like I do, but he didn't need them. Charlie had his heart and his faith in people, in you. All the rumors he heard at that state-run piece-of-shit hellhole, he knew better." Apparently, Charlie had talked his brother's damn ear off about me back then and not just about the psychic stuff. But Charlie had thought we were friends.

Hell, I was an idiot for taking this long to figure out that he'd been right.

"He knew you did the only thing you could, even if he didn't know the details." The details that Hector, courtesy of my files, did know.

I looked into the mellow gold of the beer held fast in the bottle. It was better than thinking of the color of well water. Well water isn't that nice to look at, not the kind that came out of abandoned wells. That water is dark and full of things you don't want to know about. Bones and the sludge that once made up the mice and rabbits that accidentally fell in and began to decompose. Tess hadn't accidentally fallen in. She'd been put there, and there she had drowned. I had never stopped wondering about that. How it had felt when she'd screamed and flailed, sinking and popping up, over and over, because even at five, Tess could swim like a fish. But with the well opening fifteen feet above and no way out, no one can tread water forever—not even a little girl who couldn't fathom that her mommy or her big brother wouldn't come save her. That they couldn't somehow *know* when she needed them the most.

In her last, lost, drowned breath, she'd thought we'd come. That we'd know to come save her.

But I hadn't known, not until I picked up her shoe, not until it was too late. I thought that was probably the only thing that kept me sane, that my first psychic connection started with Tess's last breath, Tess's death—not during it. If I'd had to feel every second of my little sister's terror and suffocation, I doubted there'd be a Jackson Lee around anymore, unless he was in a mental institute with dead eyes and drool on his chin.

I'd looked down into the well, still holding that pink shoe, and seen the back of Tess's head, her strawberry blond hair drifting, her hands riding pale on top of the water. I couldn't reach her. The water was too far down, and I knew she was gone. That didn't matter, though. If there'd been any way physically that I could've touched her, I would've pulled her out. I never would've left her like that. I would've held her, cradled her in the grass, and let the hot sun warm her. I would've told her I was there. Repeated it endlessly. I was there for her now. I'd always be there for her. That's what I would've said, stupidly, pointlessly. Sometimes there's nothing else to do except the stupid and pointless, because it's for you. Only you. The dead can't feel you hold them, and they can't hear your lies.

But I didn't have that option. I couldn't reach Tess, so I ran home, frantic to beat my other sister there. Glory would be getting off the bus from school soon, and Boyd would do to her what he'd done to Tess. I'd thought he wouldn't touch them.

He hit me time and time again, but they were girls, fragile and breakable. I thought he would never touch them, but look how wrong I'd been. I beat Glory home; she'd dawdled at a friend's house. Lucky, that. So goddamn lucky. I didn't beat my mom. I wasn't sure she'd understood anything I'd said. I didn't remember saying anything, but I must have, as my throat was sore for days. I'd screamed with enough rage and pain that it should've brought down the fucking sky.

My mom, meek and ground down from years of that pig's abuse, hadn't once lifted a finger to stop Boyd from what he did to me. I'd tried not to hate her for it, but deep down, I did. I shouldn't have, she was a victim like me, but it's hard to argue with hate. I forgave her that day—that's what I told myself, the day she finally found her line in the sand. Whatever I'd told her about Tess was enough to carve a line as deep as the Grand Canyon.

She went after Boyd with a butcher knife.

He'd called me a liar, her a crazy bitch, then he'd taken the knife away from her and killed her with it. He'd put it through her throat, and she'd bled to death in less than three minutes. Which I knew because it had taken me less than a minute to get Boyd's shotgun from his bedroom closet and blow his brains out. I'd felt his hot breath panting on my neck, heard him stumble, fall, and then stagger back up as he tried to beat me there to do the same to me. Too late. Sitting in a recliner all day wasn't good practice for killing an agile teenager. It was only good enough for dying.

With Boyd's bone, blood, and gray matter splattered on the wall, I held my mom's hand. She tried to say something, but with that much metal through your throat, no matter how much you want to, you won't get a word out. I told her it was okay. That we'd all be okay now. Of course, it was a lie, the same one I would've told Tess's body. Nothing was okay. Nothing would be okay again, but you don't tell dying people the truth. Even at fourteen, I knew that. In my mom's last moment of existence, I gave her the only thing I could: peace.

A priest and a psychic will tell you the same on your deathbed, but only the psychic will know it's a lie.

I didn't want the beer anymore. I handed it to Hector. "Then Charlie and my file would've told you why I'm the only psychic who'll tell you there's no life after death. Because if there was, that would mean there was a God, and trust me, there's no God, no matter what your nurse Eden thinks." No God would've stood aside and let Tess and my mom die that way. Car wrecks, cancer, heart attacks, those things I could reconcile with a God, but what had taken place on that blood-soaked screaming night-terror of a day? Never. That couldn't be justified or explained. It simply couldn't.

There was no God, no heaven, but hell could be found on your doorstep when you least expected it.

I'd lied all those years ago to my mom as she slipped away, and I hoped I'd done it well, but I'd never learned how to lie to myself. It would've made life easier if I had.

Hector dropped the beer into the garbage can before sweeping the other empties in. "I hope you're wrong, and not just for Charlie's sake. I'd like to think your stepfather has an eternity of hellfire to burn in and a devil inserting a pitchfork up his ass for every second of it."

The comment actually had the corners of my mouth curling. "Hector Allgood, the man with the unexpected silver lining."

Hector, who thought I was an honest man. Hector, who I saw as Charlie had seen him . . . and as I'd seen him over the past two days. Hector, a man in a corner but trying to do the right thing: save what was left of his brother and save innocent lives. Hector, a man who despite a near lifetime of caution had earned my trust when I thought I had none left to give.

A man who deserved the truth.

I said it abruptly, without softening the blow. I knew from personal experience that there was nothing that would make it easier to hear. Easier to live with.

"Charlie was murdered."

12

As bombshells went, it wasn't what I expected. Hector didn't move other than his eyes narrowing. There was rage there, searing and hot, but pain, too. The kick-in-the-gut kind, an agony that sucked the oxygen from your lungs and the hope from your soul. Then he blinked, and it faded.

"I know."

It was my turn to blink. "You know?"

"I helped Charlie build the transplanar interface." At my blank look, he elaborated. "That machine that looks like a giant CAT scanner. It, linked to the cuff, is what initiates the OOB. Bottom line, I'm not the engineer Charlie was, but I was still there every step of the way. I couldn't make the leaps of intuition a brilliant engineer like him could, but I could follow the basics, and I know the machine didn't malfunction. It wasn't Charlie's mistake. Charlie didn't make mistakes, not when it came to science." His hand balled into a fist—unconsciously, I thought. "Someone killed him, either to stop the project or to steal it."

In his mind, that could be the only reason. His brother wouldn't have had any enemies—none that didn't covet his work. And hell, as cynical as I was about the human race in general, I wasn't sure Hector was wrong about this or about Charlie.

"And you didn't think dropping a psychic into the aftermath would be like tossing me into a shark tank with a hungry great white or onto the front yard of a Colombian drug lord with 'snitch' written on my forehead?" I demanded. "Line up the personnel in the project, and in a half hour I can tell you who the murderer is—and the murderer knows it. *That's* why I didn't say anything until now. Christ, I'm surprised there wasn't cyanide in the crappy cafeteria food you served me. My life isn't worth a dime now. What the hell, Hector?"

He shifted uncomfortably before saying, "It's not like I expected to find a real psychic. It was a last-ditch effort based on an experiment Charlie planned but hadn't gotten around to yet. I had all the faith in the world in my brother, but I admit"—he gave a wistful smile that sat oddly on his roughly carved face—"I thought it was his scientific Santa Claus."

"Santa Claus?"

"Every scientist has one. The theory you want to believe but you know either isn't real or is beyond your ability to prove." He shrugged. "It was Charlie's one fault: he was never wrong. Never. There were times I was jealous. I'd feel guilty for saying it, but hell, Charlie would laugh."

"Good. You can save that guilt for me, then."
There was one beer left on the desk. I went for it
without offering it to Hector first. *Faint of heart ne'er
won fair beer.*

He returned to the subject of my future survival.
"I've assured everyone that there will be no readings on anyone, that I take violations of project
members' privacy very seriously. Most don't believe you're psychic anyway, and whoever killed
Charlie doesn't know I suspect murder. You're as
safe as I can make you."

"Which would be not very." I opened the beer
and took two deep draughts. "You don't know murderers."

"And you do?"

"I've been in the business, really in the business,
for twelve years. I know murderers. I know the
ones who know what they are. And I know the
ones who think leaving senile Grandpa Eddie
under a tree in the woods in two feet of snow wearing nothing but his underwear is just a mercy. 'Oh,
Officer, he wanders off all the time. I'm so scared
for him. I've been praying and praying.' Whether
it's for fun or for convenience, killing to both kinds
is like a good beer. One is never enough." I shook
my half-empty bottle to demonstrate. "And when
one of them has a lot to lose, paranoia is like air to
them."

He took the hint of my wagging bottle and
reached behind him for the bag to pull two more

out. Now that was magic. Screw being a psychic. He handed me the second-to-last one, and took the last for himself. "Why would a murderer come to you to begin with?"

"They're stupid, or they're nonbelievers there with their boyfriends, girlfriends, wives, husbands. Mostly they're stupid."

"Unfortunately, whoever killed Charlie isn't stupid. Chances are, he's one of the most intelligent men in the country. Which is why this." Hector had come into the room wearing a lightweight black jacket. He stood, stripped it off, and tossed it onto the desk. Then he pulled out the gun he'd had tucked into his waistband at the small of his back. He held it out to me, butt first. "Wear the jacket. Keep it hidden. If someone makes a move . . ." He gave a grim flash of teeth. "Just make sure you put a hole in the right person."

I made no move to take the gun, an automatic—ironically, the twin to the fake one I kept under my desk. "I don't like guns."

"You probably wouldn't like a geek, as you label us, putting you down like a rabid dog. Only in a far more inventive and painful way. Take it."

"Let me rephrase. I won't use a gun." Not again. No matter how deserving of a bullet someone might be.

He frowned. "This could be your life. I'll do everything I can, but someone got to Charlie. They might be able to get to you. I'm going to get the bastard, don't doubt that. Get him and make him pay, but until then, don't you want to live?"

"What I want is to stay sane." I cut my finger on a letter opener once, badly enough to gush blood and require a few stitches. When I smelled the blood, tasted it when I automatically put my finger into my mouth to suck it clean, I saw it all again. I lived it again. Screaming. Blood. Brains. Gobbets of fat spilling on the floor. A genuine posttraumatic flashback—so the used college psych textbook from my shelf said. If a little blood did that, what would shooting a man do?

Nothing good.

"Give me a stun gun or a Taser. Or I'll keep this." I hoisted the bottle in my hand and finished it off. "I'm good at improvising. But no guns. I guess an ex-soldier like you can't understand that."

"There's no such thing as an ex-soldier, and no one who understands it better." He returned the gun and shrugged back into the jacket, hiding it from sight. "I'd put someone outside your door, but I don't know who I can trust now that I know you're the real thing. I can't be sure if they're my men or someone else's."

"I hope Thackery is on your list."

"Just because he's a sociopath and an asshole? Or does a good imitation of both?" He moved to the door.

"Sarcasm is the lowest form of humor. I know. People tell me that all the time."

"Working with you makes it self-defense," he said. "So, tomorrow at eight?"

Bemused, I leaned back on the bed, resting on my elbows. Good old Hector had asked this time. He hadn't told me; he'd asked. Charlie would've been proud. That wasn't my usual sarcasm, either. He honestly would've been. He'd raised Hector up right. The man had manners when he wasn't too full of darkness over his brother to remember them, which put him one up on me. I'd never learned to have them at all.

Manners or not, eight was eight. "Nine," I countered. I thought about adding that Meleah could bring me breakfast again, but Hector's manners might end there. Charlie and Meleah had ended their relationship before he died, but I doubt that mattered to his brother. It shouldn't have mattered to me, either, but it would have if I let it. I didn't. It was another thing that floated through my Charlie memories, fading but still there. He wanted Meleah for Hector. He'd figured out that Meleah realized she had chosen the wrong brother, and Charlie being Charlie, he'd planned on making that right.

But then he died, and nothing can be made right by a dead man.

"Eight it is," Hector said, ignoring my counter-offer. Ex-military trumped manners every time.

It was eight in the morning when we left, but this time it wasn't just Hector and me. That son of a bitch Thackery came along for the ride. Not in the same car, of course. He didn't want to be contaminated by something science couldn't measure. Or he was the murderer and playing it safe. He had Dr. Fujiwara with him. Fujiwara, whose eyes were sadder than previously. After my seizure, I'd gone from a sympathetic little lab mouse to a damaged one. He looked down the one time I met his gaze, but not before I saw the lines of pained regret creasing his forehead.

In contrast, Thackery's expression was one of unconcealed disdain. His desire to have space between him and me went beyond the possibility of being a murderer. He was actually repulsed by me personally. It wasn't hard to see in his stony regard and the tight line of his lips. Contamination, a freak, right in his clean hall of science. Maybe you could back my freakdom up with theories, and as science progressed, maybe evidence and proof that could be measured by a machine would rain down from the sky, but I was still a person, not a process. An *unpredictable* person, and Dr. Thackery didn't like unpredictable, I was sure. It didn't fit into his narrow, tight world—his results-driven, money-driven world. If only I'd been a process, if only I'd fit into a computer program or a test tube, I was sure I'd have been all puppies and sunshine to him.

It was fine by me having him follow in a car behind us. That early in the morning, I didn't want to see anything, and definitely not Thackery's rigidly disapproving face. Hector had the sense not to talk to me until I'd put away two coffees. Cafeteria coffee, utter crap, but with enough caffeine to have my fingers tingling under the gloves and a few words spilling from my lips in a cranky mutter. "Where?"

Well, one word. I was a man who got to the point. It was one of my better qualities.

"A take on Lizzie Borden. A son beat his parents to death with a chunk of firewood in 1853. And to commemorate the occasion, they turned the place into a bed-and-breakfast. Have a few cold chills with your honeymoon. The proprietor says it's a popular spot."

"Ain't that grand? Nice to know my faith in humanity is right where it should be—the basement." Outside, it was drizzling. Sun hot enough to sear and a sticky rain the next day. That was Georgia for you. "Seems high-profile enough to have had the newspapers cover it. You shouldn't need me. Reliving murders isn't like cable, okay? It doesn't make for a good morning. In fact, it makes for a pretty shitty one."

"Have my coffee. I don't think yours has kicked in yet." Hector turned on the wipers. "The mother and father disappeared. When he was sober, Seth Miles stated that his parents ran off and left him with a worthless farm and a stack of unpaid bills. When he was drunk, he said he killed them. Their bodies were never found, and nothing was ever proven. Suspected, yes. But a drunken confession and no bodies didn't make it to court back then. It is possible his parents left Miles. He was an alcoholic troublemaker most of his life and a drain on their resources."

"And if wishes were horses, it wouldn't be rain falling from the sky right now. It'd be a storm of horseshit." I took his coffee and gave a tired, mulish stare out the windshield. Being used as a Geiger counter for terror and death managed to erase a fraction of the beer-buzz camaraderie of the night before.

"I'm sorry, Jackson." He did sound sorry, but that helped me exactly zero. "But you're the only one who can do this. Of all your colleagues, you were the only genuine article. You're rare." I thought I sensed a fleeting regret. "Which isn't so great for you, I know, but the sooner this is over, the sooner you can get on with your life, you and your sister."

Hector didn't mention getting on with *his* life. It would be hard to think about if I were in his shoes. He'd spent so much time running around trying to free Charlie that he probably hadn't had time to genuinely come to grips with his brother's death. Near death. Whatever the hell it was. He had that ahead of him; he wasn't a fool, he knew that. It wasn't precisely something to look forward to.

Been there, repressed that.

The Miles farm was long gone. The neighborhoods that now covered it were older. Early nineteen hundreds, houses with character and so much gingerbread trim that I expected to see Hansel and Gretel any minute—I hoped not pursued by a man with a hunk of firewood and a crazed, wild light in his eye.

Although the farm was gone, the main house remained. With a quaintly old-fashioned sign surrounded by masses of daisies, the Miles Massacre House was still open to all. It was actually called the Peach Tree Inn, but where was the truth in advertising in that? We pulled into the circular drive of the rambling farmhouse, followed closely by the car carrying Thackery, Fujiwara, and the military driver requisitioned from the motor pool. The military might have Thackery by the short hairs, but I didn't think the asshole knew it. Or if he did know it, he thought he could twist it to his advantage. The man had ego, you had to give him that.

"You think Thack and his pet, Fujiwara, booked the honeymoon suite here?" I drawled.

As expected, I was ignored. I climbed out of the car and squashed a daisy. Frowning, I stepped back and watched as the flower slowly wavered back upright. Tess had liked daisies. Didn't all little girls? I carefully circumvented the billowing drifts of white and yellow and headed for the porch stairs. Another wraparound porch typical of the South, it was sprinkled with wicker furniture, mainly rockers, and pot after pot of blooming flowers. Poppies, roses, brown-eyed Susans, and more daisies.

It was remarkably cheerful for a supposed house

of death. Didn't mean a thing. I'd once touched the wedding ring of a perpetually smiling grandma. She had smothered two of her babies fifty-some years before, and she'd never felt one moment of regret. The sweet hid the poisonous all the time—in nature and in people. Why should buildings be any different?

"You said you don't actually have to go into the buildings?" Thackery's voice came from behind. "That's what Allgood's report stated. You can do your little tricks from right here, then."

The man knew I was the genuine article—he had proof—but it didn't stop the thick coating of disdain over his words. If he was capable of emotions other than arrogance and contempt, I'd yet to see that. It put my cocky sarcasm in the shade. I might have to try a little harder.

I bared my teeth in a humorless grin. "Care to shake? I'll bet you have all sorts of skeletons rattling around. Got a little too friendly with the family goat when you were a kid? Let's have a look."

Most likely a murderer, and I was pushing him. Sometimes I just couldn't help myself.

Cold eyes took me in and dismissed me. "Do your job, Eye."

Yeah, do my job. Thanks to my third-strike baby sister, that's what I was getting paid for.

"I'm Miz Susannah. This is my place. Can I help you gentlemen? You boys need some rooms?"

A curious voice came from behind the screen

door. There was also a mop of tightly curled silver hair, amber-brown eyes magnified by thick glasses, skin as dark as aged mahogany, and a smile as cheerful as an entire field of those front-yard daisies.

"Ma'am." Hector moved in to distract her while I stripped off my glove and put a casual hand against the wood of the house. It was painted a brilliant blue, the pure color of a summer sky. It was the color of a kid's playhouse, not what you would put on a real house, but it worked. It was nice. It made me think of a childhood I'd never had—candy apples and fresh white sheets drying in a spring breeze, barking dogs and sleeping cats, lemonade and new clothes for school. The American dream. I hadn't had it, but it was right there. Year after year, happy people came and went, and the house was always that candy apple, sweet on sweet with every bite.

Until I took a bite of 1853.

It hadn't been a chunk of firewood. It had been an axe handle. But it had done the job. First, dear old Dad. Dear old tightfisted Dad who never gave a nickel when a penny would do. And Mother, who whined and whined until you thought you'd go deaf from her pathetic bleats. She was the one who'd gone deaf, though—deaf, dumb, and blind, and no whining bitch deserved it more. The satisfaction that had come from beating her gray head over and over and over—

With the taste of a savage contentment not my

own still in my mouth, I pulled my hand back and put my glove back on with quick, methodical movements. "Bingo. Can we go now?"

Fujiwara's soft, faintly accented voice asked politely, "You actually did see it? You know it was murder even though no bodies were recovered?"

"I saw it. And you people didn't include what kind of farm it was in the file. It was a pig farm. He fed Mom and Pop to the pigs. Twenty minutes later, they were being digested. The perfect crime." I amended, "For a drunken idiot."

Miz Susannah remained behind her screen door, her mouth a perfect Ω, showing a good dental plan and sturdy dental adhesive. Then she croaked like an unsettled crow, "You . . . you boys want some lemonade . . . and cookies?" She started to close the main door. "For the road?"

Fujiwara brightened. "I would very much like some lemonade."

Thackery gave him a withering glare, then turned to clatter down the porch stairs and back to the second car.

"No lemonade for you, Fuji," I said sympathetically, because I wouldn't have minded some lemonade and cookies, either. But when I turned back to see what my chances were, Miz Susannah seemed to have had enough of our weirdness and slammed the thick wooden door behind the screen. I heard a bolt slide into place.

Making friends wherever we went.

13

Two days, ten misses, and one hit later, I was standing at Job's Quarry, my hand wrapped around Charlie's keys.

It was Job as in the biblical Job. The preacher had been Brother Job, and the town was the Trials as in the trials of Job. 1840. It hadn't been much of a town or much of a cult. Ten gullible families and a scattering of tents that would do them until cabins could be built. But purification came first. You had to prove yourself righteous enough to receive God's word through Brother Job and to live in the Trials under the same prosperity the original Job had come to know once God and Satan had stopped dicking around with his life, killing his family, and giving him boils and leprosy to see just how far faith would go.

Show me a horror movie that equals that, and I'll pay you fifty bucks.

Ten families plus Brother Job's disciples came to about eighty people raising the canvas town of the Trials. At the end, there was only one to abandon it.

Job left the bloated, floating bodies of the faithful—and they were faithful, suicidally faithful—and wandered through the woods, shouting to heaven of his trust in the Almighty. He stayed faithful, too, despite the loss of all of his followers, despite the hunger, the coming winter chill. The walking, raving embodiment of faith . . . right up to when he ended up as a bear's last snack before hibernation. When those jaws fastened around his neck, ripping and crushing, that faith vanished like a magician's rabbit.

The Lord giveth, the Lord taketh away.

Then again, who's to say the hungry bear didn't get *its* prayer answered?

I stopped staring at the blazing orange water and turned my head to see Fujiwara eating a sausage-and-biscuit sandwich he must've brought from the cafeteria. "They put blood in their biscuits."

He gaped at me. "Ex-excuse me?"

"Job's followers. As the wine was the blood of Jesus, Job followed in his footsteps and sliced his arm every morning when the women made biscuits. Drip drip." I smiled cheerfully. "Smart for a psycho. He combined the blood and body, wine and host into one. Thrifty bastard."

Fuji dropped the sandwich onto the ground and hurried to Thackery's side thirty feet down the quarry beach. The machine to enhance Charlie's energy and pull him through the ether to dissipate was still at what they considered the best bet: Cannibal Caverns. But Thackery wanted to see me at work if, by random chance, Charlie tried to come through here. At least, that's what he said, but I saw something needful behind his blank face. There was something more to wanting to watch me work, not that Thackery was sharing the why of it. I'd find out sooner or later, one way or the other.

"Why did you do that to Fuji? He's harmless." The question broke into my thoughts and held exasperation, if not much surprise.

"Because, Hector, he feels sorry for me being dragged into this by blackmail but has his nose up Thackery's ass anyway. He doesn't have a brother to free, like you. He *does* have a shred of conscience but no excuse for ignoring it. Besides, and this goes for all of you, if you're going to benefit from what I can do, you should get to experience some of the downside. Although, trust me, hearing about it sure as hell isn't the same as living it." I gave Hector a sideways glance. "If I could give this *gift* to you and spend the rest of my life digging ditches, then maybe I would get a little God in my life, because it'd be a damn miracle."

"You might get part of your wish." Hector folded his arms as he kept his eyes on the still water. "This is one of the few sites rumored to show a genuine ether recording of the event. People throughout the years claimed to have seen Brother Job at work, always as the sun sets."

"Yeah?" That had been when the baptisms took

place. "Seeing it isn't the same as feeling it, but I'll cross my fingers and take what I can get."

In the very next moment, get it I did.

And a lot more.

I heard one of the soldiers, unarmed as they'd been at the mill, for all the good that had done, yell in shock and fear or a damn good imitation of both. He was standing on the high rock wall on the other side of the quarry, opposite where we stood seventy-five feet down on the narrow strip of gravel and red mud beach. I looked where he was pointing, to see a white blur under the water glowing with the fire of a descending sun. I crouched and put my one ungloved hand fisted around Charlie's keys against the ground. The blur rose, and the body of a woman surfaced. Her arms were spread, hovering on the top of the water like the wings of a bird. Her hair was black, I knew, although I couldn't see it. It was covered by a white scarf. A woman's hair is the jewel of God. Let no man but her husband see it.

"Rachel Adams. She was fifteen." I knew I said it because I felt my lips move, but I didn't hear the words. She drowned. Brother Job baptized his followers until their life and their sins fled their bodies. And if God deemed them worthy, he would return that life to them and send the sins to hell. Funny, no one proved quite good enough for God to step in. Job was mighty disappointed. *Mighty* disappointed, as he and his disciples held the men and women of the Trials under the quarry water. Even more disappointed when he himself held the head of his last disciple under and that man proved too sinful to return as well.

Another body floated up, dark pants, white shirt, open eyes reflecting the bleeding rays of the sun.

"Adam Jacobson. Nineteen years."

Then another.

"Joseph Bevins. Eight."

Another.

"Mary Bevins. Five." She held a doll, a rag doll in a pink dress.

There was more shouting, men who'd seen war horrified by the virtual photo of a long-dead little girl. Only an image out of death's memory album revealed for a moment, and their brains short-circuited.

Walk a mile in my shoes? They couldn't walk even a second.

"Mary Bevins. Five," I repeated, my eyes fixed on the small spot of pink. "Lungs filling with water as she screamed for her mommy."

Pink doll. Pink shoe. A wide quarry or a narrow well, was there any difference?

Mary Bevins. Mary, Mary, quite contrary, until Brother Job said nursery rhymes were the work of the devil. Mary, Mary, whose mommy was right there, her hand with Brother Job's, holding her little girl under the water for God.

Mary and Tess. Five years old, screaming to be saved, but no one listened.

The pink patch bobbed in the water. It wasn't the dress on a doll. It was a shoe, a pink shoe. Tessie's shoe. The floating form wasn't a little girl named Mary. It was my sister. It was Tess, and this time I wouldn't be too late. I lunged into the water after her. I took two long steps and dove into the water. I was with Tess in seconds. I wrapped an arm around her to lift her up, lift her to the air, lift her to life.

My arm passed through her. I tried again with both arms and the same result. I was there, right there, and again I couldn't save her. Just as I couldn't all those years ago.

Another set of arms wrapped around me this time, the grip solid and unbreakable.

"It's not her, Jackson. It's not Tess."

I was being yanked back through the water as I fought.

"Shit, I'm a goddamn idiot," Hector swore savagely at himself. "There was no way I shouldn't have known this could happen."

Not Tess.

It couldn't be Tess.

Tess was gone.

I wasn't reliving the life of Job. I was reliving my own.

The dying rays of the sun shifted, and I saw my sister change into a girl with soaked brown curls and wide-open gray eyes before she disappeared, leaving only the waves I'd made in her wake. All of the bodies disappeared with her, and that's when the yelling turned to screaming. And the screaming turned to gurgling and praises to God on high.

"God accepts your soul and returns it to thee."

It echoed over and over again from four different throats as the last ray of sun disappeared under a velvet purple bank of clouds.

"God accepts your soul and returns it to thee."

"God accepts your soul and returns it to thee."

The echo of four became one wailed litany. "Godacceptsyoursoulandreturnsittothee."

God hadn't planned on returning those souls to anyone, but it was a little late for that warning.

I spit water and said hoarsely, "Charlie." I'd dropped his keys in the water, but I didn't need a reading from them to know what the hell was happening. No one did. We had ten men: Hector, me, Thackery, Fuji, and six soldiers. Brother Job had his disciples to help him conduct the baptisms. Three soldiers were doing their best to drown the other three, and Fujiwara was up to his chest in the water, both arms beneath the surface to his shoulders, and Thackery was nowhere in sight.

And right then, I began to wonder why only those who committed violence and not the victims had their personalities imprinted to be replayed when triggered by Charlie's attempts to return. Thackery had said that violence frayed the ether. Why that and not fear and terror? Thanks to Boyd, I'd experienced all three, and fear and terror felt just as powerful as dealing out aggression. But I wasn't an asshole with a giant brain and a degree in physics like Thackery, so I guessed I'd never know.

"Jackson . . ."

And maybe I should stop wondering and help save some people from following the fate of the cult of Job. I couldn't save Tess. Tess wasn't there. She was long gone, but I could save someone else.

We were in the shallows of the water, and I shook Hector off. "I'm okay. I just . . . I'm okay now, all right?" I didn't wait to see if he believed me or not. I went back into the water, heading for the nearest soldier holding his thrashing comrade under for the glory of God. Hector hadn't come across with a Taser yet, but he had slipped me a nicely illegal pair of gloves before we'd left that morning. These did more than protect me from psychic images. They had lead weights sewn into the knuckles, and they gave a punch an extra snap—which I delivered to the back of the soldier's neck.

He went limp. I caught his shirt with my other bare hand—reading nothing of consequence—and kept him from sinking while his unwilling come-to-Jesus participant erupted out of the water, coughing and wheezing. He was still expelling quarry water, and his eyes suddenly took on a fanatical glow as he tackled me and the unconscious soldier. "God . . . accepts—" was all he managed to choke out before the three of us ended up buried in what could have been our unpleasantly wet grave.

I fought my way back up into the air, dragging

the guy with me with one hand and swinging the other in a fist. The blow took the other soldier directly under the chin as he surfaced. He promptly toppled back under the water again, and soon I was pulling two dead-weight, but alive, goons out of the water to dump them on the shore.

Hector was taking out the soldier who'd dived off the rock wall to play disciple. He choked him out the same as he had the man at the mill. "You have a hell of a punch," he told me as he took his opponent out. "Why didn't you try it on me?"

"Because you were behind me, and you pour your breakfast milk over steroids instead of Cheerios." And because I'd realized in time that he'd been pulling me away from an illusion in the water that wasn't my sister and wasn't my past. I moved to the next zealously chanting soldier surrounded by roiling water. Fuji was closer, but if he succeeded in drowning Thackery, I wasn't going to be crying any tears. Thackery was most likely a murderer, and if he died at the hands of the echo of another murderer, that was poetic justice at its best.

"I lift weights. I don't take steroids." He threw the soldier he had knocked out into the arms of the half-drowned one. "You have two couches. One for you and one for your dog. That doesn't shout 'exercise fiend.' Hell, if you walked that dog a block, you'd both be winded."

It was strange to be snarking with someone while trying to keep a long-past massacre from taking lives in the here and now. Although not as strange as you'd think. It was a tough thing to do, face someone who's screaming about God, temporarily insane, and trying to drown whoever he can get his hands on. I lived every day in other people's pasts and secrets, and even I found this pretty damn creepy. A little sarcasm was a welcome distraction from the weirdness factor.

As I handled the last soldier with another punch, putting my new glove through its paces, I retorted, "I run ten miles every day!" When it wasn't too hot, and it was always too hot. "I'm a natural athlete!" Close enough. I did run and swim, but at the Y, where they had air-conditioning. I was built lean, and I was in shape enough to take care of myself. I hadn't forgotten my teenage years and that someday I might need that skill again.

"Ask your guys when they wake up if they don't feel like they got a natural ass kicking. Cane Lake lessons stick with you. Even Charlie swung one helluva mean book bag," I added, giving over the unconscious man to the one who came up out of the water. He coughed up water, caught his baptizer, and didn't take over the role as the other soldier I saved had done. Hector's hadn't, either. That meant something.

I looked up at the sky, twilight now, as if I could see Charlie and his book bag, but of course, I couldn't. And without the lost keys, I couldn't feel him, either. But there wouldn't have been anything to feel, anyway. As the soldiers and Hector started to pry Fuji off a submerged Thackery, the small scientist's eyes cleared from fanatical to frantic. Along with stuttered fervent apologies, that told me what I needed to know. Charlie was gone, as was the repeating, gibbering chorus that had been the mirror's reflection of Job and his disciples.

Thackery, unfortunately, was still here and alive—vomiting water and glaring at Fujiwara as if he'd throw him onto the nearest French Revolution cart headed to the guillotine. Fuji's stuttered apologies went straight to plain incoherent stuttering. I couldn't make out a single word. The other men, the baptizers and the baptized, recovered and slowly dried in a Georgia heat that the coming night wouldn't begin to tame. Most of them sat with their heads in their hands. I didn't know if it was from the sensation of a rerun of dead killers in their heads, almost being drowned by their brother soldiers, or the sight of Job's victims back for a reunion tour.

I should've been at least somewhat happy. I mean, welcome, guys, to just a small part of my world. Feel what I feel every damn day.

I wasn't happy, though. Six formerly tough-looking guys now seemed to want nothing more than to be anywhere but here. As far as I knew, they'd been in battle, seen friends die, but that living hell was something they were prepared for. What the sun had set on today had shown them a layer to this life that they knew nothing about and didn't *want* to know anything about. And this had been a recording. If ghosts really had existed, who knew what knots would've been tied in their brains? Then again, the scientists had told them what to expect, I was guessing. Or at least, Hector would have—the possibility of the visual recording.

Seeing that, knowing that it wasn't ghosts, it wasn't life after death, it was only a fluke of physics, it could be that some of them were less upset by what they'd seen and more shaken by a loss of some religious faith.

One person, not surprisingly, wasn't shaken at all. He was adjusting perfectly fine to visions of dead bodies and almost being drowned by his employee. Not only was he fine, but he had a *theory*. That gleam I'd noticed in his eye earlier was now the brilliant glint of a cold operating light bouncing from a surgeon's scalpel. "It's you, Eye. You and Hector combined, perhaps." Thackery became caught up in coughing, but lungs sloshing with water couldn't stop the bastard for long. It seemed nothing could. "You're providing a focus for Charles. Considering our location"—he gestured at the water—"you could say you're the next best thing to a scientific fishing lure." He said it so smugly that I wished Fujiwara had more upper-body strength or Hector had been slower in pulling him off his boss.

Hector studied Thackery with interest, not much hope, but he was listening. "How did you come to that conclusion?" His dark hair blended into the night, but his pale eyes were visible and challenging.

"First, he's your brother. That is one tie to this plane, blood or genetics. It doesn't matter. Second, there's Eye." He addressed me without even waiting for me to bow and kiss his ring. He had to be in the midst of a scientific orgasm.

He ran a hand over his light hair and shook the water from his fingers. "You say your psychic ability only lets you feel people when you touch an object that belonged to them. You touch Charles's keys, and you can sense him trying to get through. I think Charles, changed as he is now—the fragment that is left of him—is feeling you as well. This is the second time Charles has shown up at your and Hector's location, a location of lesser violence in comparison with the others available. A less likely location. Less ether-fraying. This could mean no more random guessing. No more aiming for what we think is the highest violence quotient. With the two of you and the machine at the next appearance at any location on the list, we could put an end to Charles once and for all."

"I know you meant 'set him free,' not the asshole thing you actually uttered," I said flatly. I didn't like the way Thackery talked about Charlie. I knew Hector had to like it even less. I didn't believe we'd be setting Charlie free to a better place, but I did believe we could let him dissolve into nonexistence.

That had to be better than what he was going through now.

Lost.

Everyone had to remember when they were little, and I mean really little, that being lost was the worst feeling in the world. Pure terror. I wouldn't want to sentence anyone to an eternity of that, certainly not someone who'd once forced his friendship on me when I denied that I wanted it. I'd lied, and he'd known it. I owed Charlie, and I was committed to paying that debt.

"I'll stick with scientific terminology and ending what fragments of the failed experiment that was Charles and now happens to be killing people fit better than—"

He didn't get a chance to finish his fancy scientific sentence before a fist hit his nose, which flattened in an explosion of blood.

Thackery was knocked onto his back and was now coughing up both blood and water. Hector unballed his fist and said calmly, "See? No steroids, or I would've killed him instead of only breaking his nose."

"You know, Hector," I commented, "you're beginning to grow on me. Now, let me kick him in the ribs, and let's call this fucked-up day over."

I didn't get to kick Thackery. Hector wouldn't let me, which was pretty unfair, considering he'd given the man the nose of a twenty-year veteran prizefighter.

We all ended up in the infirmary. Some for near drownings, some from being knocked unconscious with a blow from an illegal sap glove in the back of the neck or in the jaw, one with a broken nose, and one from good old-fashioned near hysteria.

Hector hadn't gotten hurt or swallowed any quarry water, but he hung around at Meleah's order. She called it a request, but I knew an order when I heard one. He leaned against a wall, arms folded, bored with Thackery's blood-bubbled threats of getting him thrown off the project. Fujiwara was the opposite. He had gone from babbling to silently shaking like a Chihuahua in a meat freezer. The natural nurturer Eden clucked over him, rubbed his back, and promised that Thackery would understand that he hadn't tried to drown him on purpose . . . not his purpose, anyway. I thought they were going to have to give in finally and sedate the guy, but he eventually calmed down enough to wrap a blanket around himself and shuffle out of the infirmary to head back to his room.

I was waiting in line for an X-ray. Meleah wouldn't take my word that I hadn't inhaled any fluid when I'd been struggling with the soldier underwater. Aside from Thackery's fury and Eden's reassurances, delivered personally to each patient in the room, no one was doing much talking. The soldiers were as pale and shadow-eyed as they'd been at the quarry. I remembered the feeling from long ago, when I first started seeing into the past: if you don't talk about it, if you don't think about it, it won't be true.

Too bad it didn't work.

Hector was either nursing a satisfaction over taking Thackery down or contemplating Thackery's theory. As for me? I'd like to claim that what had happened at the quarry was the same old same old. Nothing new. I'd been in my natural environment, unfazed as a pig in shit. A good old Georgia psychic boy who went through this every day—minus the actual hands-on violence.

Yeah, I could claim it all I wanted, but it would be bullshit. It was Tess. Long-dead Mary Bevins hadn't been my sister, but she'd done a good job of stirring up memories out of a murky past I'd done my best to bury.

After my X-ray, read and approved, I went the way of Fujiwara and the soldiers and walked out the door. I was the third-to-last to go. Thackery was staying to have his nose set, and Hector stayed to tell Meleah what had happened; at least, that was my guess. He'd promised to keep her up to date on Charlie. A strong woman like her wasn't about to let him off the hook.

"You all right, Jackson?"

I didn't pause at Hector's question as I passed him. "I'm always all right, Allgood. Haven't you seen that yet?" I kept walking, and he was polite enough not to call me a liar. He *did* call me a liar later and one cursed son of a bitch when my room exploded. I didn't blame him.

Since Hector had issued the order that I had the run of the lesser-classified areas of the base—housing, cafeteria, infirmary—I was able to go alone from one building and slog solo over the now-dried peaks and valleys of red mud to the housing unit that held my room. I wanted to shower the mineral smell of quarry water off of me and sleep for about twelve hours.

The quarry scent did stay with you, enough so that I almost missed the other smell as I pushed the door to my room open. This was a smell familiar to everyone, but in particular, it was a smell for which I had a hair trigger buried in my subconscious.

The door was already swinging open when I threw myself back and down the hall. The explosion didn't completely blow the door off the hinges, but it drenched it and the floor and the walls outside it in flames and the reek of gasoline. The air was superheated. It felt as if it was searing my lungs as I pushed my way to crawl farther down the hall away from the fire. Alarms were blaring, help would be coming, but I'd always believed the universe helps those who help themselves, and I kept slithering along the dingy tile. I snatched a desperate look behind me as I moved faster. The fire crept after me, but not as quickly as I expected.

When I thought I was far enough away from the

inferno, if not the heat, I rolled over and tried to stand. I made it, but I didn't know I would have if a hand hadn't helped me halfway up.

"Damn it, Jackson, you call this all right? I know you don't believe in an afterlife, you cursed son of a bitch, but why are you in such a hurry to prove it to yourself?" Hector kept me upright while giving me hell.

"Someone tried to kill me. I *know* you're not blaming *me*," I accused. "Especially when I told you this could happen. Murderers *don't like* psychics. If I'm cursed, you did the cursing when you brought me here."

A crew was trying to put out the fire, but they weren't having any luck with their extinguishers. Instead of being put out, it was spreading like the breath of a dragon. "It's napalm!" one guy shouted. "Goddamn napalm! Get the Halon extinguishers!"

Their voices were muffled by the masks they wore, but Hector heard enough to push me into motion. "Move it. Napalm puts out enough carbon monoxide to gas an entire kennel." As we ran, he asked, "Not that I don't think it a good thing, but why aren't you dead? Napalm isn't a natural inhabitant of Georgia. It's not like a black widow that creeps under your door. How are you not a barbecued corpse?"

"Joyce Ann Tingle, better known as Madame Maya Eilish." I was panting as we turned a corner into fresher air. "One of the psychics you tested.

She burns down rivals' shops, and she doesn't care if they're in them when she does. Any psychic in Atlanta would turn and run at the whiff of gasoline at their door, same as me." I leaned against the wall. "They said napalm. I know this used to be a military base, but there can't be napalm just lying around."

"Probably homemade. Gasoline, Styrofoam, and soap, and you're done." He fished a ring of several keys out of his pocket. "Here. Go straight down this hall, then take a left, and it's the fifth room on the right. Lock yourself in until I knock on the door. I'm going back to see if they've got it under control yet and can tell when it was put in place. Probably hopeless, but . . ." He shrugged. It was more of a guilty twitch, actually. He was getting good at the guilt. Good enough that I controlled a smart-ass remark, took the keys, and went.

It was nearly an hour later when there was a tired pounding at the door and Hector's voice. I unlocked and opened the door and immediately demanded, "What's up with the *Brady Bunch* room?"

The room he'd sent me to had two sets of bunk beds in it. They took up enough of the small space that two people standing at the same time was tight quarters. Very tight, and we authentic psychics liked our personal space.

"Someone tried to kill you. I thought you'd want a friend to watch your back." Hector sat down heavily on one of the lower beds.

"I already have friends. Two. That's enough." I still stood, arms folded, doing my damnedest not to look defensive. Two real friends was more than most people had. People had acquaintances— other people they had little in common with and even less emotion for—but since the majority of people didn't want to be alone, they called these half-strangers friends. It was easier to cope with life if they had that one word. Fake it, because otherwise they couldn't take it.

That was final proof that real ghosts didn't exist: Charlie didn't appear to call me on my bullshit.

"One of your friends is a dog," Hector pointed out. Damn it, there was no better friend than a dog. "But if you don't think you need friends," he continued, "you certainly need a babysitter—one with a black belt and a gun."

"And whose fault is that, me needing a bodyguard?" I paused. "You have a black belt, and all you did to Thackery was break his nose?"

"Unlike whoever blew up your room, I'm not a murderer, and, no, I don't have a black belt. I have the unarmed combat training the Army gave me. If a black belt had been floating around there, we'd improvise and use it to strangle you. It's more efficient. Now, sit down. I'm too tired to strain my neck looking up at you all night."

I grumbled under my breath but sat on the opposite bed. I pulled the rubber band out of my hair and scrubbed my scalp with gloved fingers. My hair, my clothes, my skin, it all still smelled of quarry water. I hadn't taken advantage of the tiny shower in the equally tiny bathroom. Not yet. Hector had said it: someone had tried to kill me. If *Psycho* and Anthony Perkins had taught us anything, it was that someone else always had a key to your room, and naked in a shower is no kind of defensive position. That didn't make me a coward. It made me practical, with a good base knowledge of classic horror cinema.

"Find anything out about the fire?" I asked.

He shook his head. "Definitely homemade napalm. The instructions on how to make it are all over the Internet, but the heat of the fire was so intense that it melted the triggering mechanism, although it could've been a simple one, for just opening the door a few inches to set it off. Or it could've been a complicated one. There's no way to know now if it was set up before we left or quickly jury-rigged after we came back."

"So it could've been anybody?"

"Except for the guy who punched you the first day. Sergeant Borelli. He's still in lockup, but other than him, yes, anyone that has access to the base. A little over a hundred. Even Cafeteria Carl is on the list. He could've done it on a break between scooping up mashed potatoes. Homemade napalm probably tastes better than the food he serves." He dropped his head in his hands, looking the same as the soldiers had at the quarry. "God help me. I sound like you now."

"Nice to know something good has come out of my all-knowing, all-seeing presence." I grinned despite myself, but the smile fell away with my next question. "Why is there a murder to cover up at all? Why would someone want to kill Charlie?"

"I don't think it was about Charlie. I think . . . no, I'm certain it was about taking down the project, or stealing it, or both. Thackery always thought he should be the lead on this. If he was and it was successful, he could write his own ticket for the rest of his life. And to be open-minded, there is always espionage, foreign and domestic. The project could be sold for billions, especially to an unfriendly country who'd like very much to get a behind-the-scenes look at every secret we have."

"I still put my money on Thackery." I got back up and started opening the drawers to the one bureau. There were sweats, jeans, and long-sleeved T-shirts, all new with the price tags still on them. It seemed like Hector had been planning on watching my back even before the fire, and I'd been there long enough to be running out of clean clothes—burned-to-a-crisp clothes now. Hector would know that I wouldn't want anyone touching my clothes to run them through whatever industrial mill of a laundry they had there.

Except Thackery. I'd give a great deal to get a look into his inner self, to see if murder lurked there or just general jackassery.

"How'd you know my size in jeans?" I asked suspiciously. The sweats and shirts would be easy enough at a glance, but jeans?

Hector lifted his head to give me his own version of a grin, small but real. "Eden picked them up for me. Apparently, she has the dimensions of your ass down to the millimeter. Must've done a lot of mental measuring."

"Who can blame her? Best damn ass in the psychic community. Ask anyone." I grabbed a pair of sweats. "I'm taking a shower. Think about how you're going to steal something of Thackery's. An ink pen won't do it unless he's had it several years."

I took my shower, and a crazed killer didn't try to stab me, which I took as a good sign but not a sign that *Psycho* was wrong. After all, someone had tried to burn me alive. Even Alfred Hitchcock hadn't gone that far. I tried to save some hot water for Hector, whose day had been as long as mine. It wasn't easy, considering the water had never been hot to begin with, tepid at best. I came out and crawled into the lower bunk I'd been sitting on. Hector headed for the bathroom. If the water was cold and he yelped, I didn't hear it. I was already asleep.

14

"I wasn't able to lift anything for you to read from Thackery in the lab earlier."

I snorted and pointed at Hector with a fork. "You're big, but you wouldn't have lasted a day on the street."

"Maybe not, but I pull my weight in other ways. I have decided to pull those strings and let your sister out of jail early. Blackmail never sat easy with me before, and it sits even less so now that someone tried to kill you. Your life is at risk, and I won't force you into this if you could die as a result. I'd prefer you were here of your own free will."

Mornings . . . they didn't bring bluebirds in this place, but they brought surprises.

Not that it was that much of a surprise. It'd only been a matter of time. Hector out of the goodness of his heart was going to let my baby sister go. *That* was a good one.

I finished chewing the soggy toast and said, "Glory escaped, didn't she?" I reached for the cardboard carton of OJ on the breakfast tray. "She hurt anyone? Correction: how badly did she hurt them?"

Sheepish was a good look for Hector. I liked it. "She took down one guard and one policeman. They're in stable condition. She did some serious, ah, testicular damage to them both with the guard's baton and then drove off from the hospital in the police car. Disappeared off the face of the earth, a nine-months-pregnant John Dillinger."

"Faked labor pains, right?" I shook my head at my own stupidity. "I should've told you to stuff her file up your ass when you showed up at my door. I knew she'd get out sooner or later. She doesn't need my help. She hasn't in a long time."

"But you still gave it." Hector was eating his own breakfast, eggs and toast. He hadn't eaten meat since the barbecue-joint incident. Wise choice.

I shrugged. "She's my sister." And that, as far as I was concerned, said it all. I was done with my OJ, so I took his. It was what he got for being a crappy liar. "So out of the goodness of your heart, not to mention your loss of blackmail material, I can now take that free will, get up, walk the hell out of this bucket of crazy you have going on, and save my life in the process?"

He gave me what normal people consider a penetrating, assessing look. But then again, normal people spend their entire lives blindfolded. They only find the truth by accidentally running into it face-first. As he looked for the selflessness deep in my soul, most likely getting eye strain in the process, I didn't wait on his answer. Holding out my hand, I ordered, "Your car keys. Sorry about no 'please,' but I'll throw in a really hearty 'thank you.'"

"After all you've seen, what you know has happened and will keep happening, you could actually go?" The doubt and disappointment were palpable. Then it was only disappointment as I half-stood, leaned over the table, and fished in his lab-coat pocket for his keys.

"Let's see. People are going ghost-psychotic, and, yeah, I know there's no such thing as ghosts, but it's a good phrase for what's happening. They're throwing people off roofs, gnawing bites out of their legs, trying to drown people in God's name, and none of that was even personal. Then someone tried to burn me alive. *Alive*. That *is* personal, and it's only going to get more personal until I'm dead." I found the keys and held them aloft, jingling them in triumph. "Hear that? That's the governor calling to pardon my nearly fried ass out of the electric chair."

Hector—being Hector—didn't give up. "You'd leave Charlie the way he is? You'd take the chance people might die?"

"Sooner or later, you'll happen to have your fancy million-dollar Charlie lifeboat in the same location he pops up in. There are only so many local massacre sites, and I've helped you map all the questionable ones. And I haven't stopped anyone from almost dying. You've done most of that yourself. Now, where's your car parked?"

"Fine." His lips tightened. "I won't make you stay."

"But *I* will."

A hand grabbed my shoulder, squeezed it painfully tight, and pushed me back down. Good old sociopathic Thackery—I'd seen him across the cafeteria from the moment we sat down.

"Allgood, if you can't deliver what the project requires, I will. We carry dual responsibility here, which means dual authority." The grip tightened. "If it takes guards to keep you here, Mr. Eye, I know we have a sergeant locked up who'd enjoy some face time with you."

I gave him a shove away. "I don't do my best readings with a broken jaw."

"All we need you to do now is Charlie detection and acting as a lure. You can do that with several broken bones, jaw included. Think about that."

With those friendly words, the dick was gone. I waited a beat and tossed Hector's keys back to him before flourishing another set with a smug grin. "And *that*, Dr. Allgood, is how you steal an object to read."

We went back to our room where we'd slept and Hector had played Secret Service. He'd ruled out an empty lab as too dangerous. Thackery was everywhere in the science division, overseeing all, stealing every ounce of credit he could, and stripping away any presence of self-esteem down to the bone, then sucking the marrow as an afternoon snack.

"No, tell me what you really think about the guy, Hector." I grinned as I sat on the mattress and studied the key chain on Thackery's keys. It was a small, squat metal rocket with "Fat Man" hand-painted on the side. Figured.

Oppenheimer, Father of the Atomic Bomb, had once quoted "I am become Death, the destroyer of worlds." He'd had concerns over what he'd helped birth into an unsuspecting world. Thackery was no Oppenheimer. Thackery was all about patents and royalties and the hell with the consequences.

"How about I tell you instead what I think about you and your show at breakfast?" He wanted to be pissed, but I, who myself was all about self-survival and cynicism, was putting my life on the line for him and his brother. It left him without a leg to stand on and hesitant about using the other one to insert a boot up my ass. Despite what he'd said in the cafeteria, I hadn't done what he'd expected. I hadn't done what I'd expected, either.

Argh, I *couldn't* be changing. If life had taught me one thing, it was that change was rarely for the better.

"Never mind that. Why don't you tell me why you're staying? It's definitely not in your best interest."

"Don't look a gift horse in the mouth. As for the show, the Art of the Con," I offered cheerfully, in spite of my inner perplexity at straying outside the Jackson norm of looking out for my own ass and my own ass only. Ignored it and went with the good mood, because putting one over on Thackery just automatically summoned one. "Misdirection, misdirection, misdirection. Oh, and dumb marks and clueless eyewitnesses."

The clueless eyewitness didn't care much for that, either, but gave it up with a disgruntled exhalation. I laid the keys down on the bed and peeled off my glove, letting my tattoo show. "I picked pockets before I was a psychic. It's like riding a bicycle. Larcenous fingers never forget. And I faked years of psychic shit before I gave in and started using the real deal. You don't have to have special talents to steal from or manipulate people to get things done. You only need flexible morals and an extra-small in off-the-rack consciences."

"You didn't use your psychic ability when you worked the carnival as a teenager?" When I shook my head, Hector asked in the simple confusion any normal person would use, "Why?"

"Because it's not fun." I hovered my hand over the keys. "It's never fun." It sucked is what it did. It sucked long and hard, but I muscled through because it was how I made my money and it was who I was. I hadn't wanted to believe that for a long time, but in the end . . . it was me.

I closed my hand around the keys and felt the flood.

I didn't *let* it through. I had no choice. I touched, and it came, sure as death and taxes. I knew one much better than the other, but that's why God made accountants.

I tightened my fist around the metal as wave after wave crashed over me. I could feel my body temperature dropping like a rock.

Great.

Fan-fucking-tastic.

I'd mentally called Thackery a sociopath more than once, but I hadn't meant it. True sociopaths are rare. Assholes are common. I'd thought Thackery was more likely the second. I was wrong.

Stepping into the mind of a true sociopath was like locking yourself in a walk-in freezer, alone. All the warmth was immediately drained out of you. There was no physical reason it should happen—sociopaths weren't walking Popsicles—but it happened just the same. And then there was the aloneness. There was no one else in the world but you. No one in the room, no one in the building, no one in the state ... the country ... across the ocean. Not a single speck of life anywhere, not even bacteria. You might as well be on the surface of the moon.

That *was* being a sociopath. The sole creature in their universe. People, animals—they weren't the same as you. They weren't alive. They didn't have meaning beyond that of game pieces on a board. Usually less meaning than that, more like stupid, clunky furniture you had to rearrange to get a certain result. Boring, all that manipulation. So damn boring. Sometimes the result could be entertaining, depending on how you were hardwired. Some so-ciopaths killed, and some didn't. It wasn't that the ones who didn't kill had a problem with it—other than risk. Manipulation was boring, but prison was even more so.

Thackery was smart. Little Julian hadn't cut up Fluffy and Fido behind the shed. No, little Julian went to an advanced school and took many per-fectly reputable biology and anatomy classes where you obtained your own cat for dissection from the local shelter.

Teenage Julian hadn't strangled coeds at his col-lege. He paid hookers, who took a little extra money for a lot of extra abuse.

Grown-up Julian hadn't killed his widowed fa-ther for a hefty inheritance. He simply hadn't re-minded the forgetful man to take his heart medicine and made a bet with himself how many months it would take.

And Dr. Thackery hadn't killed Charlie . . .

I hadn't killed Charles Allgood, because I'd known there was a spy in the program who would do it for me. I'd seen subtle alien fingerprints in the computer codes. Witnessed the tiniest of glitches barely perceptible to me, much less the peons around me, and I told no one. I thought, "What would I do as a spy out to sabotage and steal a program?" and I'd been correct. Disrupt the equip-ment and kill the test subject. Now I was calculating that I was smart enough to identify the spy in time to fix blame, save the program, and become Charles's successor.

There was the remaining Allgood to think about—and then the unbelievably improbable discovery of a real psychic. Someone who could find the spy before I did and snatch the spoils. I had to rethink my lifetime rule of doing the one thing that could potentially destroy my life. And it came down to the question: did the risk outweigh the benefit? I hadn't been certain.

But then, as they most often did for me, things began to fall into place. I hadn't targeted the spy yet, but the spy had targeted the worst problem for both of us.

Jackson Lee Eye.

And if I was very fortunate, Allgood, in a doomed attempt to save a scientifically perverse life, would be disposed of as well. Because that was Dr. Hector Allgood down to his DNA.

A "good man."

A Boy Scout.

An idiot.

"Jackson, you're turning blue, for Christ's sake. Are you all right?"

I dropped the keys and gazed blankly at an unfamiliar hand, bloodless and white, with blue, cold-pinched fingers. Allgood was calling me by that troublemaker's name. It was insulting, demeaning, debasing. I wasn't a mutant. I was genetically perfect. "Shut up," *I ground out, fighting a tense jaw and numb lips.* "And do *not* call me that."

"Damn it. I can do nothing but fuck up with this shit. It's a wonder Charlie lived as long as he did with my ass around." *A hand circled my arm.* "We need to go to the infirmary. It's where we should've done this to begin with."

I looked away from my hand to my legs. Wrong clothes. Wrong body. What had happened? I didn't panic. People like me did not panic. We took advantage of every situation. We were the puppet masters, control-ling every movement of the deaf, dumb, and blind wood under our fingertips. We . . .

We . . .

My brain wrenched, and the colors in the room changed. No one saw colors exactly the same as the next person. No one saw the world the same as the next person. I inhaled air that felt almost searing to frozen lungs; pushed Thackery, his memories, and his thoughts to the side; and came home.

"It's okay." I resisted Hector's grip, grateful for the thousandth time in my life that I wore nothing but long sleeves. I wasn't ready for another reading yet, especially an accidental one. And I didn't want to spend any more time in the infirmary. I was there so often now it may as well have been a Starbucks. "I kicked Thackery's ass to the mental curb. I'm me again."

"What happened? That can't be how every read-ing goes for you. You wouldn't survive it." Hector was unconvinced about my claims to health, mental and otherwise, because he pulled the blanket off the top bunk and dumped it in my lap. "And wrap up. You look like a guy on an Arctic expedition who for-got his igloo key. Hell, I can even see your breath."

I put my glove back on a chilled and shaking hand before cocooning myself. "Goddamn sociopaths. It happens every time. Lucky I don't run into more than one or two every couple of years. And no, ninety-nine point nine percent of my readings don't go like that. Thackery has an extremely strong personality and mind. Both are highly fucked up, yeah, but they're strong." Getting rid of Thackery's keys had been more help than the blanket, but between the two, I did begin to warm up.

"Sociopath?" he said sharply. "He did kill Charlie, then?"

"No. Not exactly, but he let it happen. I guess it depends on how good your lawyer is as to whether that's murder or not." In my book, it was. He didn't have absolute concrete knowledge that Charlie would die, but he had a good idea and hope in that black vacuum where a soul should've been. I used to play fast and loose with most of the moral code, but when it came to murder, no one was more black-and-white than I was. Losing my family in butchery and blood had made certain of that.

"How about we get the hell out of here? Out of this whole place. This is only the second time I've been in this room, and I'm already sick of it. It's a combination of a *Brady Bunch* camp and a maximum-security cell." I stood and dropped the blanket. The summer heat would do a better job of baking my bones, driving away the lingering cold. "I'll tell you the whole thing."

"Considering, that's not a lot to ask for. There's a Denny's a half hour away."

"Denny's. You really know how to reward your friendly local psychic." But it didn't stop me from quickly reaching for the doorknob at the thought of some temporary freedom.

Hector beat me to it. "Bodyguard, remember?"

"If you think you're fireproof, go ahead." There was no smell of gasoline. I still needled him. I enjoyed having someone new to mock. Abby gave as good as she got, and Houdini's dog brain didn't quite grasp sarcasm.

Outside, for once, I didn't complain about the searing sun or the heat. I enjoyed it. It helped chase the rest of Thackery back into that dark walk-in freezer where he belonged. I was bemused to see Hector get down on the red dirt and edge under his car before checking the engine.

"Homemade napalm is one thing. A car bomb is a damn sight more advanced than that."

"There are many kinds of industrial spies, Eye. Some are as intelligent as the scientists they steal from. It's not beyond possibility if we have one—"

"You *do*," I interrupted.

"Right, then they may be smart enough to start in the amateur realm, having us looking for amateur work should their first attempt fail." He brushed red dust from his pants and shirt. "But I'm smart, too. Charlie always said that the Boy Scouts stole 'always be prepared' from me."

"You boys care for some company?"

We both turned to see Meleah, an uncertain smile on the smooth oval of her face. Hector, for a moment, appeared as uncertain. He'd taken in more than he'd ever planned in the past few days. Where I was learning to trust, he was learning to distrust. A dead brother, backstabbing colleagues, unknown assassins—it would take the faith of any good man.

His eyes flicked to me, the man he'd known for a week, over a woman he'd known for years. Disillusion, whether it came to you as a child or as a grown man, it was a life-changing blow either way. I gave him the barest of nods. Meleah had touched me accidentally. I'd already read her. There was nothing bad there. She was that endless Christmas morning of lights, the curve and gleam of ornaments, the rich taste of eggnog, and the sweet smell of puppy breath from the soft ball of sleeping fur curled up in her lap. I often did my best to wipe my mind of all of my readings, but once in a while, I found a memory worth keeping. This was one of them. And if Hector ever pulled his head out of his ass, he could have Christmases like that for the rest of his life.

"I'm not the safest person to be around right now, but if you like living life on the edge . . ." I got into the car, leaving the door open. "But you'd better ask Hector. He's willing to throw himself between me and certain death, but he might not want you to do the same." I closed the door and let them sort it out.

The end result was that Meleah ended up in a booth at Denny's, tapping her fingers on a greasy menu with a confident smile now replacing her hesitant one. Hector didn't look happy. It could've been from wanting to protect Meleah or dread at hearing how Thackery had played a part in Charlie's death. Could be both. I didn't guess. There was nothing I could do about either one. I concentrated on telling the story, resulting in no one looking happy, and making my way through my vegetarian scramble. I didn't mind eating breakfast twice. I had nothing bad to say about cheese.

"Thackery let Charlie die?" Meleah didn't touch her food, while I managed bites between words. She was a doctor. She'd seen death before, but there wasn't a doctor alive who'd seen as much as I had. Everyone I read had known someone who had died, and on average, I read ten people a day. The Black Death could've lurked inside my skull by this point. You got used to it, or you went crazy.

I got used to it.

Shrugging again on the subject, I gave her an answer similar to the one I'd given Hector. "He was about eighty percent sure it would happen, so it depends on how you look at it. A normal nonpsycho wouldn't have automatically thought an industrial spy would rig the machine to kill Charlie. A normal person would just assume they'd screw up the machine so it didn't work at all. But Thackery is thinking from the view of a sociopath, and I'd say your spy is a fellow sociopath to do what he did. So Thackery *did* know, better than anyone else would have. To me, it's murder. To someone else, I don't know."

"I know," Hector said grimly. He hadn't bothered to order anything to eat. "He saw someone about to push Charlie off a cliff and just let them. He's a murderer. The trouble is, we have another, more proactive murderer out there and no idea who they are. And they're brilliant. We never did find out who caused the transplanar to malfunction. We can't find anything wrong with it—besides that it killed my brother—not in the programming and nothing suspicious on the security footage."

That was odd, but I was a psychic, not an expert in industrial espionage.

I gave them the rest of it: the fact that Thackery was repeating his sociopathic ways with Hector and me. Someone wanted to push us over that same cliff, and he was pleased as hell to let them do it.

"Couldn't you read everyone at the facility to find the spy?" Meleah asked.

I gave an internal twitch. "And how many people do you have staffing the base?"

"Approximately one hundred and twenty or so," she answered. "Is that too many?"

After one of nature's nightmares like Thackery,

even one more today would be too many. "I can do a max of twenty a day, but I don't know how many days I could keep that up. Two. Maybe three. Ten is a better number. That's doable, and I don't need to sleep fifteen hours after. But it doesn't matter how many I can read, right, Hector?"

Hector had taken the bill, folding it neatly. "He's right, Meleah. Our assassin isn't going to take a chance on Jackson taking a look inside him. He'd cut his losses and destroy the entire base whether he had all the transplanar designs or not. Self-survival over a paycheck."

After the meal, Hector paid. I didn't offer to chip in. I wasn't being blackmailed anymore, but I liked to think that a history of it meant free meals for the duration. Outside, we had walked to the corner of the building when Hector stopped us, his hand held up by his shoulder. He'd wanted to park out front where he could keep an eye on the car from one of the plate-glass windows, but no spaces had been available.

"Let me take a look first."

"I've never seen a spy or assassin blow anyone up at a Denny's in the movies," I said dryly.

"How many actual spies and assassins have you done readings on?" Meleah took up for Hector. He might not have to take his head out of his ass after all. Meleah could grab a handy crowbar and do it for him.

"You've got me there," I admitted. "Sociopaths, yes. Spies and paid assassins, no."

As Hector took a step around the corner, I leaned out for a look myself. Hector stopped after the one step and crouched down low, tilting his head to scan the undercarriage of the car. It was four spaces down, but the cars that had been parked between the corner and our ride were now gone. Hector had a clear range of vision. From the stiffening of his shoulders, I could tell he didn't like what he saw.

I didn't wait for him to straighten or yell a warning. I grabbed the back of his shirt and yanked him back around the corner just as the car exploded. One second I was standing, and the next I was flat, half on concrete, half in cedar chips that nestled scrubby bushes struggling against the wicked summer. There was nothing but ringing in my ears, although I knew everyone in the restaurant would be screaming. Everyone alive. I rolled over, window glass cascading off of me, and saw flames above the roof. An explosion that big, the car bumper only a few feet from the building, anyone sitting on the other side of that wall would be lucky to be breathing. Or unlucky, depending on their condition.

From the corner of my eye, I saw Hector. He was trying to sit up. Meleah had been behind me. I turned my head to see her echoing Hector's motions. Good for them both. I was staying flat until I was sure my head was still attached to my body. Then again, whoever had planted that bomb was here. Or close. They'd seen Hector spot it and stop. They'd chosen to go ahead and blow it by remote control, hoping at least to get one of us. If Charlie's brother was gone, Thackery would be in complete control and have me thrown off base before they'd finished picking up all of Hector's pieces. I'd be alive, but I wouldn't be a threat anymore, not to Thackery or the spy. A win-win for both bad sides.

I remembered being a kid—little, maybe five— and I'd thought in those days that there was a good side and a bad side. Then I grew up and learned that there can be multiple bad sides and sometimes not a single good one to fight them all. But that was not the case here. Hector had dragged me into this, yet he was the good side with more on his plate than he could handle.

I sat up, my gloves protecting me from the glass on the shattered windows that littered the concrete. A moment later, I crouched and was on my feet. I was swaying, mildly nauseated, deaf as a fence post, but it didn't stop me from thinking.

When you were watching your prey, waiting to flip a switch, press a button, or dial a number on a cell phone to set things in motion, a bomb was a trick. A simple trick but a trick all the same. You didn't want to be detected ahead of time, and you didn't want to be seen. What to do? Denny's was in a row of three restaurants, and beyond that was nothing for miles. Someone sitting in a car by themselves, not in the restaurant eating, that was noticeable. So what did you do? What someone like me would do. What an ex–con man would do.

Misdirection. Misdirection. Misdirection.

I ran to the far edge of the parking lot. The restaurants were spaced far enough apart to get a view of their fronts and sides and a partial view of the backs. Denny's was at the end, with Hector's car burning between it and the next eatery. That next one in the middle was an Italian place, and beyond that was a steak place. I saw running people who were screaming in all of the parking lots. I couldn't hear them, but their mouths were open wide with terror. Screaming was a logical guess. I didn't see anyone sitting in a car alone. I did see a refrigerated meat truck parked in front of the steak joint. Steak places did need steak, but you delivered your frozen dead cow through the back. You didn't ruin the customer's appetite by carrying it through the front door. But the back of the meat lover's delight didn't have a view of the Denny's side lot. That was blocked by the middle restaurant.

As misdirections went, it was pretty shitty, but out in the middle of nowhere as we were, options were limited, and sometimes the best of us have to make do with less than the best of plans.

I started running again, this time through the next parking lot and headed for the one where the meat truck sat. I doubted that the windows had been tinted in the cab when the truck was stolen, but they were now. I saw a shade, the horror-movie creepy-phantom kind, move inside as the window began to roll down. Ghosts I didn't have to worry about. This son of a bitch, he was the deadly one.

Already through the next parking lot, I was on the verge of passing over a concrete curb to enter the one with the truck. I was close when I saw the gun, but not too close to imagine a bullet exiting the back of my head in a spray of blood and brains. I should've dropped to the ground behind a car. It was the smart, staying-alive-to-bitch-another-day thing to do—except . . .

Except I was fucking *pissed*.

This shit had killed Charlie, someone I'd liked no matter how much I denied it. He'd tried to kill me with napalm and then a goddamn bomb. In the boondocks of Georgia—a *bomb*. Who does that?

Someone whose ass I was going to kick to the state line and back before doing worse. I didn't like guns, I hadn't since I'd held one for the first and last time at the age of fourteen, but there were other ways to get things done. And as we said in these parts, sometimes a man just needs killing. This son of a bitch fit the bill.

I crouched but kept running—right until the asphalt parking lot came up to slam me in the face. Or it would have, if I hadn't gotten my hands under me in time to avoid a broken nose. I did get some road rash on my chin from the feel of it and the breath knocked out of me as at least two hundred pounds landed on my back. I did discover that some of my hearing was back as I heard shots fired from about thirty feet in front of me and more from about three feet above my ear.

With the hearing in one ear gone again, I depended on the other to hear a truck's engine revving, the screech of metal hitting metal, and the roar of an engine fading.

"Shit." It wasn't me who said it. I didn't have enough breath in my crushed lungs to say anything, but I wholeheartedly shared the sentiment. King Kong rolled off of me and took a fistful of my shirt to pull me up to my knees and yank me around to face him. "Idiot. Are you dead? You damn well should be."

I wheezed until I had enough air to snap back. "I had a plan."

Hector, gun still in his other hand, gave me a light shake. "And what *was* your plan, Jackson, that was going to save you from running straight at a gun? I'm dying to know."

"Ducking." I glared and pushed his hand off. All that anger and adrenaline and nothing I could do with it. It was a little different from using my fake Glock to scare off junkies out to rob my shop. I'd been lucky. None of them had had guns yet, only knives. A fake gun and Houdini were more than enough to take care of them. This time, I had faced a gun, a real one, and my only disappointment in what I'd done was that Hector had been able to catch me. My stepfather had tried to kill me when I was fourteen, and this asshole was trying to kill me now. Enough. I'd had enough.

"Motherf—" Hector cut himself off. He'd cursed more today than I'd heard in the entire week or so that I'd known him—even when a cannibal was throwing his colleagues off a mill roof. His post-Army discipline was failing him. "I blackmail you, almost get you killed, then drive you over the edge to suicidal. Why not? It's what I deserve. I'm going straight to hell. No doubt about it."

He stood and turned to a heavyset older man who'd been running to his car, keys out. Unfortunately for him, it was his car next to which Hector had tackled me.

"We need to borrow your car." Hector didn't point the gun at the guy. First, Hector didn't have that in him. Carjacking and giving the man a heart attack were a step beyond blackmail. Second, he didn't need to point his gun. The guy had taken one look at it down by Hector's leg, seen me on my knees, and threw the keys and waddled off as fast as he could.

"Get up. We still have a chance to catch the bastard without getting shot in the process."

He clicked open the lock and climbed behind the wheel. I managed to get into the passenger seat while getting the rest of my breath back. There was the slam of one of the backseat doors, and Meleah had joined us. As Hector started the car and tore out of the parking lot, she fastened her seatbelt before reaching forward to pinch the back of my arm.

"Are you suicidal?" she demanded.

"What's with you two? I *had* a plan. Jesus."

We hit the ramp and two seconds later the interstate. "Yes, he had a plan," Hector said darkly. "Ask him about his well-thought-out, completely non-suicidal plan."

"You were a helluva lot nicer to me when you were blackmailing me." I searched the road ahead of us for sight of the truck.

"That was before you broke me. Charlie lived with you for months and still remembered you as a friend twelve years later. I'm with you one week, and you make me question my own sanity. Damn, there it is!"

And there it was—miles ahead but within reach. Refrigerator trucks didn't have the speed of a plush, fast Lexus. Within thirty seconds, we were almost on it. With less than half a mile before we'd be technically tailgating it, Hector pulled his gun back out of his jacket pocket. I should've noticed the faint sag of the material. I liked to think I had my powers of observation left over from the days when I only read people's faces and body movements, but either I was fooling myself or my skills were blunted instead of sharpened by knowing that there was a killer out there. Not a good showing for a former con man.

"What are you going to do with that? Shoot through the metal panels or pull up beside the truck and shoot over my head again?" I asked, not yet willing to forgive the scathing dismissal of my ducking plan.

"It's not a that. It's a Beretta 92F, identical to the M9 I carried in the Army. It's dependable. I like dependable in situations like this. And I'm going to try for the tires." Hector sounded as if I had insulted his best friend.

"Does that work in real life?" Meleah asked. I heard the tinkle of glass she shook off her shirt and out of her russet-streaked hair.

"You're handling the bomb thing like a pro," I commented. Unlike the searing anger that had pumped through me. I hadn't liked bullying directed at me when I was a kid, when I was at Cane Lake, and I liked it less now. I wished I had a baseball bat instead of a pissant pair of weighted gloves for when we caught up to the son of a bitch. "You're like every doctor I've read. You have repression down to an art form." It was true. They all had boxes in their subconscious, and the face of every patient who died on them went into that box. It made sense. How else would you move on to your next one if the memories of the deceased ones stayed with you every minute of every day?

"I'll break a few things later when I have more time. Now I'm more worried about catching the man who killed Charlie. Hector, can you actually shoot out the tires of the truck?"

"With my knowledge of physics, you'd think it would be easy—it's not. If this doesn't work, I'll ram it."

That had me clicking my own seatbelt into place.

Ramming didn't seem a better plan than ducking, the hypocrite. A Lexus was sturdy, but a refrigerator truck made it look like a Tonka toy in comparison.

Before I could point that out to Hector, he leaned forward over the wheel with his eyes narrowed. "Now, what is that?"

Our semi-stolen, semi-borrowed car was eating up the road, and we were only eight or so car lengths behind the truck. I saw what Hector was referring to. There was a black line across both lanes of traffic—it almost looked metallic. The cars in the slow lane were passing over it as the truck blew past them in the fast lane. Whatever it was, it looked and seemed harmless. It did nothing to the cars or the truck. I didn't know anything about physics or the ease of shooting tires out of a speeding truck, but I did know one thing: if it looks or seems harmless, it never is.

"Son of a bitch." I grabbed Hector's shoulder. "Stop! Don't drive over it!"

Too late, though. We were going too fast, and by the time I said "Don't," I heard the blowout of all four tires. The car skidded off the road, hit a ditch, and flipped over onto the roof. There was the peculiar crunch of safety glass fracturing but not shattering, held in one gluey whole, and the crump of metal buckling against unforgiving earth. I couldn't breathe for a moment, the seatbelt had tightened around my chest, I was hanging upside down, and I was choking from the force of the air bag that had hit me and the billowing clouds of dust that came with it. But I did abruptly remember. I knew what that strip of metal was, and I hadn't seen it in the mind of one of my clients. It wasn't the lingering image of one of my readings. No, I'd seen it on TV while slouching on the couch, drinking a beer, and sharing a cheese pizza with Houdini.

I'd seen it on an episode of goddamn *Cops*.

15

"Remotely deployable spike strips," I repeated, sitting on the bank of the deep ditch and rubbing my chest. A seatbelt can save your life, but it hurts like a bitch. "Don't tell me you didn't use them in the Army."

"I spent most of my time in military intelligence as a glorified gofer. I had the Mensa-level IQ, but I didn't have Stanford and Cal Tech on my curriculum vitae yet. I enlisted to pay for that, but yes, we have spike strips, just not 'remotely deployable spike strips.'"

The thing had been flat and smooth until we drove over it and the guy in the truck triggered the spikes to open. He had planned his escape in case the explosion didn't work. This guy was good, sneaky, and better at distractions than the former con man I was.

"It's the Army. The food could double as concrete for housing developments. The remote ones are news to me." Hector had ripped free a strip of his sleeve and was wiping a trickle of blood from

Meleah's forehead. It wasn't from the wreck; her seatbelt example saved us all. No, her blood was from the flying glass in the explosion. Although Meleah was better trained to take care of it herself, Hector was finally stepping up to the plate. Meleah might not need that crowbar after all.

Not that newfound love was going to do him any good. Police sirens were wailing like an F8 tornado warning, and the flashing lights were moving fast toward us. We would be off to jail and facing everyone's dream come true: a body-cavity search and a neckless cell mate wrapped in three hundred pounds of steroid-rage-enhanced muscle.

"You had to steal a car," I grumbled. "I hope they find Jimmy Hoffa up there when they snap on the gloves and bend you over at the station."

"You misjudge the situation. Our project is funded by the government—the kind of government the majority of the country knows nothing about—the ones who do know are living in a bunker with tinfoil hats."

He'd made a call before wiping at the blood on Meleah's copper-brown skin. Maybe he was calling in the *X-Files* guys to back us up, vouch for us. I crossed my fingers. I could take care of myself, but I'd rather not have to bruise my foot or both fists doing it. I'd spent my teenage years kicking ass to survive. I didn't miss it. Sometimes it was necessary, but I'd take cheese pizza with my dog over inflicting blood and broken bones. Maybe I'd gotten lazy when I hit the big three-O, or I'd simply had enough violence in my life.

"Fine. You get us out of this, and I'll tell you what women really think about men. Not *Cosmo* shit, either. The real deal. It'll help your dating life"—I finished under my breath—"or ruin it completely."

Meleah heard the last part. The woman had the ears of a bat. "Shhh," she said with annoyance. "It would give him a stroke. Men aren't meant to know. You're not meant to know."

"And don't you think I wish I didn't? It's a burden no guy should have to bear or live up to." A state police car braked beside us. It hadn't come to a complete halt before one cop had jumped out, screaming with gun pointed. "Ah, shit."

Hector started to stand up and reason with him. Mensa, my ass. The one person you don't ever try to reason with is a state cop on an adrenaline high. He spends most of his day giving tickets and reading gun magazines. When something exciting comes along—like a Denny's explosion and people fleeing the scene in a carjacked Lexus—he or she is going to make the most of it. Not obeying commands while trying to talk your way out of it—especially while stepping *toward* the cop—that's only going to get you pepper-sprayed, Tasered, or shot.

I snagged Hector's arm and pulled him down beside me.

"Monkey see, monkey do." I grunted at him. I rolled on my stomach in the dirt and laced my fingers at the small of my back. Meleah was doing the same. Luckily, Hector's gun had flown out the window, ripped from his hand, when the car started to roll, or Hector would already be pepper-sprayed, Tasered, *and* shot.

Hector landed in the dirt and copied my position. "It'll be all right. I made the call. They'll pull us out."

I was roughly handcuffed. "I hope so. Since it was self-defense, my juvenile files aren't sealed. All I need is some DA trying to get reelected changing his mind, deciding I was a fourteen-year-old Bundy at the start to my life of crime. I've been to jail before, Hector." Only for a day, only before it was all sorted out and I had a cell to myself, but a day even in a podunk country jail makes an impression on a kid. I dreamed of iron bars for weeks afterward. What my life would've been like if they hadn't believed me and the evidence. "I didn't much like it."

Fortunately, Hector's government muscle came through after we were fingerprinted but before we made it to the mug shots. Ten minutes later, men in dark suits and sunglasses came in, flashed badges, and ushered the three of us to a black car out front. We left mystified and furious cops in our wake, which almost made the whole day worthwhile. Before I'd found the carnival and lived on the streets picking pockets, I'd had to bust my ass to outrun a cop or three. They couldn't just let a kid make a living.

"Don't say a word until we get back," Hector said at my ear in a whisper so low, lips barely moving, that the Men in Black didn't notice. It looked like, same as always, the right hand didn't know what the left was doing—even in secret government organizations. I had a feeling that when all was said and done and this entire project was finally written up, the amazing All Seeing Eye, psychic Jackson Lee, was not going to be featured anywhere.

Thank God.

On the other hand, there were bound to be many uses the government could find for a psychic, enough uses to last until I was old and gray, then dust in the ground. If that happened, I would've been better off staying in jail.

Once we were back at the base, we were dropped off without a word. Meleah headed back to the infirmary, Hector and I to the main science building. Thackery was waiting for us. He appeared unhappy and, well, *thwarted,* rather like a zoo veterinarian who'd just lost his shoulder-length rubber glove, speculum, and favorite watch inside a pregnant elephant.

"What now?" he demanded. "First your psychic's room is napalmed, and then the car he was riding in was apparently blown up. Are you sure he's a psychic and not a sadomasochistic pyromaniac instead?"

That's why he was feeling frustrated. He was disappointed that I hadn't been *in* the car when it had exploded. "I'm psychic enough to know you did double the dissections of the other students in your anatomy class because you just loved picking out cats at the pound and cutting them up. And no matter what you told the teacher, it damn sure had nothing to do with extra credit."

He stared at me, the color leeching out of his eyes to match the chunk of ice that masqueraded as his brain. He was a Bundy, a Dahmer, a Gacy who hadn't crossed the line to killing people—letting it happen, yes, but not doing it with his own hands. But someone knowing what he was, *exactly* what he was, down to his last sociopathic cell—it could push him over that edge. At least when it came to me. But I was tired of tiptoeing around this shit. In the week and a half since I'd been there, nothing had been done. Not one damn thing. Charlie hadn't been saved. A spy hadn't been caught. The only thing that had been accomplished was that I got to take a tour of several very nasty places and "see" many even nastier murders take place. If I had to take a tour, I'd have chosen a goddamn cruise, not this. The sooner we could wrap this up, the sooner people would stop dying, and the sooner I could go home.

If that took pushing, I was read to push my guts out.

I knew Hector agreed, because he followed right along. "We know there's an industrial spy here. We know they killed Charlie. And Dr. Thackery . . ." He leaned forward until he was nose-to-nose with the smaller man and bared his teeth in what would pass as a smile if he were a crocodile. "We know you knew about the spy and didn't tell a goddamn soul. That makes you responsible for my brother's death in my eyes, if not the law's. So I'd advise you get behind the team on this one while I decide just what I'm going to do about that." He moved in even closer, causing Thackery to take a step back. "About you and Charlie. Start thinking *hard* about who the spy could be. Start *now*. I'll be back soon to see what you've come up with. Jackson, come with me. I need to go to the armory to get another *gun*."

Thackery didn't move as we passed him. He had to be calculating whether the gun was for him. At least, I hoped he was, the prick. Hector was striding down the hall at an angry and fast speed, but running at the Y seemed to have helped, and I kept pace easily enough.

"You know you made a lifelong enemy there," he said.

I shrugged philosophically. "An enemy is just a friend you were smart enough to stab in the back first before he got you. Besides, you were on his list before me. In fact, I imagine everyone he has ever met is on the Thackery shit list. We're nothing special."

"Special enough to be at the top." He stopped. "The armory's around the corner. This isn't a military operation, Jackson. We have military support around if we need it, and we damn sure have needed it, but bottom line: Thackery and I are in charge here." And whoever had sent the black car was in charge of them. "That means I can check out as many handguns as I can carry. We're in trouble, me, you—so this time, let me get you a damn gun. I understand because of your stepfather why you don't want one, and you might not have to use it. I'll do my best to make sure you don't have to use it. But we need to be armed if worse comes to worse."

A gun.

Boyd, the lazy, rattlesnake-mean, abusive shit. Until I was fourteen, I had one mental picture of him, only the one: him sitting in the filthy, beat-up recliner and drinking beer until he was drooling drunk.

From fourteen on, that picture would be replaced by him lying in the small, cramped hall of the house. He filled it, actually, from wall to wall, the fat slob and his beer gut. Not that beer was what came out of it when I hit him with the first shotgun blast. Instead, handfuls of fat that looked like masses of yellow grapes. Loops of intestine like you'd see out of fresh roadkill, only bigger and more. It hadn't stopped him, though. He'd kept staggering toward me until I'd pumped the shotgun a second time and put another load in his head. He'd been close enough to me then that they had to bury him without a face. There was no covering up that crater with a dab of mortician putty.

And the smell. I'd never forgotten the smell of cordite, blood, and leaking guts.

The bedroom where he kept the shotgun didn't have a window. I had to climb over his body to get to the phone to call the police. I tried not to step in . . . him. But he was everywhere. Covering the entire floor and some of the walls. There was no way around it. I left a sneaker trail of blood and other things as I ran to the kitchen and the phone. Footprints of what used to be Boyd. Sometimes now, sixteen years later, when I put on my shoes, I checked the soles for Boyd—

"Jackson? Did you hear me?"

"No guns," I answered, resolute.

"Damn it, it could save your life." He ran a frustrated hand over his short hair, still neat and in place despite the explosion and the wreck. Not like Charlie's hair. That boy could have walked out of a barber, and in two seconds people would think he'd been in a windstorm.

"It could," I admitted.

"Then *take* one."

"No guns," I repeated, and for a moment, I thought he was going to smash his fist into the wall as he rolled up his fingers tightly.

"Taking one could save your life. Not taking one could cost you your life. That bastard out there could kill you. You could die, you asshole."

Die because Hector had pulled me into this and now was dealing with the consequences, guilt being the biggest one right now.

"I could." I shoved my hands into my pockets.

"Yeah, I could die, and I will before I touch a gun again. Sorry, Allgood. That's just the way it is. Next time you go after a psychic, you should check out their phobias first. Get me a baseball bat, and I'll beat the son of a bitch's head flat enough that you could serve it up as a pancake. But no guns."

Hector swung his balled-up fist, but not at the wall. He swung it at me. I slithered to one side, did a leg sweep, and dumped him on his ass. I meant it. I'd been taught to take care of myself. Cane Lake for dangerous teens, a little Krav Maga at the Jewish Community Center for dangerous adults. Hector had to know some Krav Maga moves himself from Army training, but at the moment, he was feeling too pissed, too guilty, and too out of control to see them coming from a psychic he assumed sat on his butt all day telling people where Great-aunt Edna Mae's lost will was.

"A sock stuffed with your mess hall's mashed potatoes?" I suggested helpfully. "One hit with that, and I guarantee brain damage."

He lay flat, unmoving, and closed his eyes. I let him gather the edges of his control and glue them back together in silence. Hector had had a difficult couple of months. His brother died, a brother he'd loved; I still felt from reading his keys how much Charlie had loved his younger brother. The hero worship he'd seen in Hector's eyes when they were kids and the respect and affection when they were adults. Then had come the massacres, forcing

Hector—who Charlie had known down to his bones was one of the most honest and honorable men around—to resort to something as dirty as blackmail. Now that blackmail was looking more and more likely to get its victim, me, killed. And Hector would hold himself as responsible as if he'd flipped the switch on the detonator with his own hand.

All in all, I figured Hector deserved some stress relief. If that meant letting him throw a punch, what the hell? I'd let him. It didn't mean I'd take it, but he could swing all he wanted.

Finally, he opened his eyes and shifted them to where I leaned against the fungus-colored wall, arms folded, getting some rest of my own. It was barely past noon, and it had already been a long day. "Sorry," he said, the traditional Hector Allgood calm back in his voice.

"Yeah, that was pretty sorry. There are five-year-old girls at the Jewish Center who would've broken your elbow and your knee, and then crushed your larynx with that kind of swing." Dark eyebrows knit ominously, and I let him off the hook. "Fine. You're forgiven. You were only trying to break my nose out of concern for my life. I get it. It's a little fucked up, but I get it." I held out a gloved hand.

He hesitated, then took it, and I helped heave him to his feet. "Why don't you go? Leave? I told you the blackmail's off. Someone's trying to kill you. There's no reason for you to stay and risk your life."

"Would Charlie leave?" I asked. I wasn't actually curious. I already knew the answer.

"No, but—" He clamped his mouth shut before the rest of the sentence could escape.

"But I'm not Charlie. I'm a selfish, money-hungry, antisocial asshole who doesn't give a damn about anything or anyone but myself? Is that what you were going to say?" I wasn't angry. It was mostly true . . . or it had been true.

"It was," he admitted. "But that's wrong. That's not you. It takes a lot of digging to get to the real Jackson, but you're not selfish, and you do give a damn. In this situation, more than you should. Still, you did get one thing right." His lips quirked. "You *are* an asshole."

"Born and bred." I grinned as we began to walk on toward the armory.

"So," he said after a pause, "are you going to tell me or not?"

"Tell you what?"

"You said if I managed to get us out of jail, you'd tell me what women really think about men. I've been thinking I might be able to use the help." He didn't squirm like a thirteen-year-old kid with a crush, at least not on the outside. But on the inside? I knew he did. Meleah had him hooked but good.

"Right. I did say that." I shook my head dubiously. "Are you sure you want to know? I mean really, one-hundred-percent positive?"

This time, the punch connected, but it was a

light one and aimed at my shoulder. I took the sting as a yes.

"All right. Your funeral. Women are smart, and they know men are dogs, which we are. But they also think that there are a few special exceptions out there who put love before sex straight out of the gate. They think when they meet one of these great guys, he'll be so fascinated by their mind and personality, their hopes and interests, that it'll be months before he even thinks of looking at their ass. They believe this guy will love them from the beginning—before sex ever enters the picture."

"No."

"Oh, and to this Prince Charming, cellulite is invisible." I slapped him on the back.

"*No*. You're lying. They have to know that's only movies, TV shows, books—fantasy wish fulfillment. That's ludicrous. You're kidding me, Jackson, aren't you?"

I could smell the desperation in the air. Like several of my clients, he was getting a truth he didn't want.

I slapped him again, this time with more sympathy. "Welcome to my world. We're an alien species compared with women, and they know it. But they want to believe you're the *good* alien among all the other horny ones ravaging the world. Luckily, Meleah is one of the rare women who can handle the truth. So when she catches you checking out her ass in whatever hot dress she wears on your first date, she'll just laugh, roll up the menu, and smack you

on the muzzle with it. She'll accept your doggy nature, you lucky bastard. And don't tell me you don't
know what I'm talking about with Meleah. You
know. She knows. Even Charlie knew and was
about to send her flowers and sign your name to
them right before he . . ." I stopped.

"Before he ran out of time," Hector finished quietly.

Shit. Now I was the one who was sorry. I didn't
think I ever said I was sorry to anyone except Abby,
who would pinch my ribs ferociously if I didn't.
Since the day of the pink shoe, I thought the universe and everyone in it owed me and owed me big.
No one deserved a sorry from me. Instead, I gave
Hector the best I could: an excuse. "I'm usually
smoother as the All Seeing Eye. Maybe if I put the
black back on."

He halted by the armory and knocked on the
wire mesh. As the metal rattled, he answered the un-
said sorry instead of my defense. "Don't be. It's
something about Charlie I didn't know, a piece of
him I didn't have. That's a gift." He cleared his throat,
and his eyes lightened. "And you didn't even charge
me for it. Charlie was right. You make a good friend."

I snorted. "I haven't come close to totaling the
bill for this entire fuckup yet. Just you wait." Then
the mesh slid up, and I could see an entire wall covered with guns. I immediately stepped back but almost as immediately spotted something I liked.

Liked a lot.

16

Thackery didn't have an office. None of the scientists did. They had workstations and metal stools. No lumbar support in hell. Ergonomics didn't rear its comfort conscious head here, not for the peons. But as one of the head honchos, Thackery did have a desk and a real chair.

Hector, too—one that he and Charlie had shared and which had a bag of Milky Ways in the bottom drawer. Charlie loved them. He'd bought that bag at a Walmart a week before he died, along with shampoo, an ugly-as-hell knockoff Hawaiian shirt, a Stephen King book, a box of cereal—the small box. He'd wanted the bigger box, but they were out, and...

I rubbed my forehead with the heel of my hand, the slide of the leather glove breaking the train of thought. Charlie should've faded more by now. A death reading takes a few days to turn loose of me, but it'd been more than a week. There was a great deal more of Charlie left in my mind than there should be.

Maybe it was because he wasn't gone, not completely.

Whatever the reason, it was giving me a headache, and I reached into my pocket for the Tylenol. I carried the bottle with me everywhere now. This place was not conducive to a pain-free existence. I popped two pills for the headache, glumly knowing it wouldn't help any with facing Thackery's winning personality.

"Have you been thinking, Thackery? About our mutual problem?" Hector asked flatly as we approached the man's desk. He had his lab coat back on, but it didn't do much to hide the new shoulder holster and gun beneath it. "Thinking as if your life depended on it, because it just may."

Thackery's glare was coldly emotionless. Everything about the man was cold. Sociopaths—I couldn't understand how evolution had screwed up so badly to toss out this mutation once in a while. Even having one as a sister, I couldn't understand it. Glory had always been careful not to touch me once we'd reconnected. At first, I thought it was because I'd let her down, hadn't found her, hadn't saved her from being put through who knew what. But after a total of two conversations with her, I'd known—anyone with a shred of conscience would've seen—there was a different reason. Glory didn't touch, as Glory had nothing to give. She could only take. She wouldn't hug a *chair*, would she? To her and Thackery, that's what people were.

Things. But she was my sister, and I'd put Band-
Aids on her thin, bruised, mosquito-bitten legs
from the time she could first walk. I couldn't make
myself forget that. And I couldn't blame her for the
mess I was in. She'd gotten me into it, but I was the
one who refused to walk away. This wasn't about
her. This was about me. Glory might not be completely human, but I was.

Thackery opened his desk drawer. Hector's
shoulder shifted, and his hand moved inside his
coat to rest on the grip of his gun.

"It's not a weapon. It's a list," Thackery said stiffly.
"Of everyone I believe to have the scientific and
mental capacity to sabotage the transplanar with a
method we can't detect."

"Be careful," I warned dryly. "Better put on some
gloves. The paper's probably coated with poison.
No, wait. He's touching it with bare skin. You should
be fine."

Hector took it, and I scanned it along with him.
Not that it did me any good. The only name out of
the eight that I recognized on it was Sloane, who I
remembered thinking looked like a dick when I met
him. A dick and a protégé of Thackery's. I'd looked
into Sloane's eyes as he stood behind Thackery like
a faithful lackey and seen nothing but science, not a
hint of a soul.

"No Fuji?"

"The man urinates himself during performance
reviews. He lacks, to put it bluntly, the balls to even

entertain the idea of jaywalking, much less killing." Thackery was scornful. Lacking the ability to murder to improve your career path wasn't a quality he admired.

"Too bad those ghost balls at the quarry didn't last a little longer. Cyanotic blue is a good look for you," I drawled. I flat-out gave up on not saying "ghosts." They weren't ghosts, yeah, but the phrase "reenacted episodes of ether-recorded violence" was straining my tongue. "Hector, point out the other seven geeks on the list, and I'll give you a lesson in picking pockets. Thanks to reading Thackery, I won't be able to read anyone else today, but I should be able to read them tomorrow."

"That was an inexcusable breach of my privacy," he accused.

"But letting Charlie die when you might've been able to save him, that's nothing, is it? No big deal. I know what you are, Thackery. A mistake of nature. A walking, talking brain full of bad wiring. So guess what? I don't give a *shit* about your privacy. Hell, I should be compensated for having to wade through the filth that's in your mind." Hector had his hand on my shoulder and was easing me back.

Once we were across the room and out of earshot, I said quietly, "He's a killer, Hector. He didn't use his own hands this time, but he has the taste now. He's seen how easy it can be. Sooner or later, there'll be another Charlie, and that time he'll be personally responsible."

"No, he won't. I'll make certain of that." Hector didn't say how he'd make certain, and I didn't ask. I didn't care. Thackery was a copperhead, poisonous as they came. There was one thing to do when it came to those.

My only thoughts were that I hoped that Hector didn't get caught and that if he needed it, I had a brand-new shovel at my house.

I'd successfully obtained personal objects from six people on the list with none of them the wiser. I hadn't been able to get to Sloane, who regarded me as the equivalent of a homeless vampire. Whenever I drifted close with a made-up question about the project, his face tightened as if he'd smelled an entire Dumpster full of garbage, and he hurried off as quickly as possible. He did his best not to make it appear that I was the issue, always implying there was an "urgent" matter for him to take care of, but I thought another word for this was "convenient." Then there was a Dr. Kessler, who hadn't shown up for work today. He'd called in sick. Also "convenient." I wondered if he'd spent the night before stealing a refrigerated meat truck.

Fujiwara, on the other hand, kept trailing me around, apologizing in a guilt-laden tone for his actions at Job's Quarry. I had no idea why. It wasn't me he'd tried to drown. Finally, I told him the only apology I wanted was for his not finishing the job of sending Thackery's sopping-wet ass on to the glory of God and to leave me alone already. He did, more morose than ever. I was glad he wasn't on the list and I didn't have to read him. I'd need to grab a phone book and dial the first six numbers of the suicide hotline first. That was one depressed, pathetic guy.

Once again, I was back in the cafeteria. It was beginning to feel like my vacation home. Hector, with all of my stolen trinkets stuffed into a plastic bag inside his lab coat, was eating lunch with Meleah. I'd practically had to boot his ass over to her. They could use some quality alone time, and Hector couldn't see her ass under her lab coat, making it a good chance that he wouldn't screw up this pseudo-date or get smacked on the nose with a plastic spoon.

"How you doing, sweetie? They treating you with more respect now? Treating you like a person and not one of their little mechanical toys?" Eden placed her tray opposite mine and sat down. Today she had tiny sea horses dangling from her lobes. Each one had a rhinestone so minute that when it glittered, they winked at me.

"Hector's come around. He's not as bad as I thought." I quickly added, "But don't tell him I said that. He's too used to being an alpha dog. Having something to hang over his head is good for keeping his ego in check."

She gave a smile that was all dimples and a very slight overbite. On her, it worked. It gave her an elfin air, not that I believed in elves any more than I did in ghosts. "He's a puppy dog. He has a big bark, but he'd much rather cuddle in your lap and get a good scratching behind his ear."

I tried to picture Hector curled in anyone's lap—except mine—his six-foot-plus tall body in a ball with his head tilted to reveal the soft spot behind the ear for a nice rub. A few of my brain cells imploded, and I buried that image in my mental box of things never to be remembered again, adding a few extra loops of subconscious chain around it. "I'll take your word for it, Ms. . . ."

"Eden. I told you to call me Eden, and I meant it." She reached over and pinched my sleeved arm precisely as Abby would've done. "Now I'm going to say grace before I eat. You don't have to say it with me."

"Good," I drawled. "I wasn't planning on it." Praying to an empty sky was time wasted that I could use for shoveling food into my mouth.

She pinched me again. "Though you could at least stop eating for two seconds out of respect for my beliefs."

"You could not pray to someone every bit as fake as Santa Claus out of respect for my beliefs, too, but I don't see you doing that." I took another bite, but I couldn't help a small grin as I chewed. She was bubbly, feisty, smart, and protective. Teasing her made me nostalgic. If I lived through this, I'd have to tell Abby all about her long-lost twin.

She frowned. "I hope Saint Peter paddles your sassy butt when you get to the gates. You deserve at least that." Then she zipped through grace at a record speed before I could insert any more taunts. She picked up her fork, then put it back down with a sigh of exasperation. "Lord love a duck. I almost forgot."

Lord love a duck. I hadn't heard that one since before my grandma died, and I'd not yet learned why the Lord loved ducks more than the rest of his so-called children, but what's life without mystery? As I watched, she pulled a clear plastic bag out of her lab-coat pocket, using her napkin to lift it. "I didn't think me handling it for a few minutes would hurt you much, but I didn't want to take a chance. Not like these other vultures with no care for anything but their own tail feathers." She glared at Thackery, who was far across the room, eating his own lunch. A Japanese bento box. No cafeteria swill for his refined palate.

"Take two a day," she ordered, pushing the bag full of giant red pills over to me before putting the napkin in her lap and starting on her macaroni casserole.

I picked them up with a gloved hand, although she was right. She wouldn't have touched the bag long enough to leave a land mine of memories behind. It was safe. "What are these? Suppositories for elephants? They're bigger than my pinkie."

"Vitamins. And they are not bigger than your

pinkie, you baby, but I'll bet they're bigger than something else." She lifted both delicate eyebrows in challenge, birds taking flight. Laughing birds. "And I take them every day without fail. You need to as well." Laughter gone, the order was given with all the solemnity and stern demeanor of the entire medical field behind her.

"I've been eating this food for months," she continued, "and I was weak as a day-old kitten until I started taking them. Without these vitamins, I'd have died of scurvy or malnutrition a long time ago." She used the fork to stretch the cheese from the macaroni high in the air—a good seven inches before it snapped. "Jackson, sugar, do you think that came out of a real live cow? It's probably glue that the Chinese had left over from a factory or two. They mixed in some food coloring, and when it turns us into mutant lactose-loving zombies, the FDA will say how awfully sorry they are they didn't catch it sooner." She sniffed suspiciously but took a bite anyway.

"Mutant lactose-loving zombies?" There I was, smiling again. "You watch a lot of horror movies, I'm guessing."

"Only the cheesy ones." She laughed, and I almost laughed with her—as bad as the joke was. And it was extremely bad. Some people have an infectious laugh, and she was one of them. I only managed to stop myself and save my reputation as bitter, cynical psychic of the year by stuffing a bite of my own macaroni into my mouth and chewing.

"It's silly, I know," she admitted, cheeks flushed with humor, "but in this life, sometimes silly is the only life preserver you have. You have to grab on until the big waves pass and you can make it to the shore."

Her eyes were among the most happy and the most peaceful I'd seen. Either she'd never seen a truly big wave or she handled it much better than the rest of us. She checked her watch. "Oh, I can't believe it. I only had twenty minutes for lunch, and I spent ten standing in line. I have to go." She patted my hand, completely ignoring the leather between our skin. "Now, take your vitamins. You'll feel better, I promise you. Otherwise, you'll wither up to a husk like the ones I'd see in the garden spider's web when I was little."

In seconds, she'd taken her tray and dumped it and was out the door with healthy brown hair streaming behind like the tail of a running horse. An old guy at the gas station when I was ten used to tell me stories about cowboys riding tornadoes. Cyclone rangers, he called them. That was Eden, rushing from place to place so fast she'd have to be hitching a ride on a cyclone to get there.

"It looks like I wasn't the only one with a lunch date." Hector sat beside me, pale eyes far too pleased and smug. "And if ever there was someone who needed to be laid, it's you. It's difficult to be bitter when you're a fulfilled man. And it's difficult to get someone to go out with you when you're a sarcastic, snapping one. Eden's manna from heaven for you—and her name fits."

He was trying to return the favor I'd done him with Meleah. It didn't stop me from scowling. This wasn't junior high. Not only that, but Hector had no idea what sore point he was poking with his nosy finger.

"Allgood, let me give you a few seconds of my sex life. This is the play-by-play." I leaned close, cupped my hands around his ear, and whispered—but it was a loud whisper and penetrating. Inescapable. The way it was in my mind. *"Did I wear clean underwear? Did he wear clean underwear? I remember that guy with the skid marks. God, that was horrible. What was his name again? Great! This guy's are clean. Oh, Christ. What's his name again? I'm terrible with names. Mmm. He's not as big as I thought he'd . . . ohhh, he's a grower, not a shower. Very nice. Names I forget, but I never forget a big dick. He's a good kisser, although a little more tongue wouldn't hurt. I wonder if he'll be inspired to use that tongue downtown. Men are so selfish about that. What? He wants me on top? Nooo. I hate the way my breasts look when I'm on top. Maybe I should get a boob job. They'd stay plenty perky then. What does a boob job run these days? Crap, I'm losing my concentration. Ahhh, there it is. This is sooo good. This is so what I needed after my tests came back clean from the clinic. No HPV will set you free! No HPV will set you free!"*

I dropped my hands and returned to my macaroni. "That's the first five minutes. Now, how long could you keep it up with that in your head the entire time?"

"If she has that much attention available for an internal monologue, I don't think you're doing it correctly. Perhaps a book or an instructional DVD . . ."

"I liked you better before you developed a sense of humor," I growled.

He took in a breath, held it, and did his best to aim for serious. I rated it two stars out of five. "Have you ever thought if you picked a different type of woman, took the relationship slowly, that her thoughts might be more encourag—ah . . . all right, let's be honest, not so bad? Yes, let's go with not so bad. Aiming too high before you're ready can ruin your confidence."

"Of course, I've thought about different types of women. I'm not an idiot, but there's a bottom line you haven't thought of." Recklessly ignoring the fact that I shouldn't read anyone else today, not after what Thackery's reading had done to me, I took off my glove and held my hand out, palm up. The tattooed blue eye stared gravely up at Hector in invitation. "Go on, Hector. Take it. Take it, and tell me there isn't at least one thing you've done or one thing you've thought in your life that you don't want anyone to know. Ever. Not Charlie. Not Meleah. No one. Because it was wrong, maybe it was worse than wrong. And chances are, you being you, that you only thought it, didn't act on it. But you still don't want anyone to know, do you? Despite the fact that all people have those thoughts."

I kept my hand between us. "Go on, Hector. Prove to me that I can have a normal life. That I can have a real relationship with no secrets. That I wouldn't have to lie to her about what I know about her innermost thoughts. That eventually when she found out the truth, she'd be able to cope with the fact that I knew what shamed her most. Tell me it wouldn't be the end."

Hector studied my hand, lost in the blue of the nonblinking eye, but he didn't take it. His own hand started to rise, but it made it no more than an inch off his leg before it returned. "I feel like an asshole."

I put my glove back on. "People are people, Hector. If my clients knew that every aspect of their life belonged to me with one reading, I wouldn't have any clients. Don't be too hard on yourself. I wouldn't let a psychic read me, no fucking way, no fucking how."

"That doesn't change the fact that I feel like a coward. I use you to do what I wouldn't want done to me. It's not only cowardly, it's the definition of a hypocrite."

He was such the martyr. Giving up on the macaroni, I said, "Fine, then. That's an easy fix." I had my glove back off and my fingers looped around Hector's thick wrist in a second flat. He started to jerk away but stopped. Hector had misjudged himself, and now he was proving it. He wasn't a coward or a hypocrite. After not quite a minute, I let go.

"Your version of Cane Lake wasn't any better than mine," I commented. "The day Charlie got you out of there was the best day of your life." A day when everything was chased with sun and the claws of confinement turned loose of the grip it had on his mind and heart. It was like in *The Wizard of Oz* when everything turned from black-and-white to a thousand shades of brilliant color. "Charlie was your hero. He always had been, but when he stood waiting for you at the curb, he was like God to you. Someone who would never let you down, someone who would never leave you behind. You had him on that pedestal but good and a gallon of Super Glue to keep him there."

He made a sound in his throat, choked, thick, angry. I exhaled, uncomfortable. This wasn't what I did. I didn't counsel. I found things, people, pets, told the histories of quaint old objects. I left this part of readings strictly alone. Until now. "Everyone hates them, Hector, the people who die on you. Every single one of us. It doesn't matter if they died of an incurable disease, had an unexpected heart attack, were hit by a car, drowned, or even were murdered. It doesn't matter. You still hate them, and you hate yourself because you know it's not their fault— which makes you resent them more and makes you feel more of a selfish, worthless monster in your own mind. As deep, dark secrets go, Allgood, every-

one in the world has that on their list." The headache of a second reading too soon pounded behind
my eyes, and I dug for the Tylenol again. "It passes.
And I don't have to tell you that from other readings. I can tell you from personal experience."

I picked up the plastic bottle of water and washed
down the pills. I thought about Eden's vitamins but
decided I'd take scurvy over the chance of choking
on one of those horse pills and having Hector give
me the Heimlich. "I forgave my mom for dying. I
even forgave her for letting Boyd smack me around.
I forgave her for not leaving him and maybe keeping Tess and herself alive. I forgave my grandma for
having a heart attack and leaving Glory to the system and me to Cane Lake. And eventually, I forgave
myself for hating them to begin with. Give yourself
a break. It'll get better, and Charlie wouldn't hold it
against you."

"How long?" he asked grimly. "How long does it
take? Until it gets better?"

"How long did it take when your parents died?"

"That long, then." He wasn't happy. The truth
rarely makes people happy.

"The more you hate means the more you loved.
It's no consolation, but it's true." I hoped a different
truth would help. "I was surprised to find *that* your
deepest, darkest. Pissing your bed until you were
eight, that would've been my best guess."

There I was with more help. That was the kind of
guy I was. I gave and I gave and I gave.

"It's hereditary and linked to somnambulism—sleepwalking, you jackass." He might not have been consoled, but he was distracted. That was the next best thing. "And I was seven and a half."

I slapped his back. "Sure thing, Hector Peegood. Kids can be cruel with those elementary-school nicknames, can't they?"

"I can't believe I'm trying to save your life," he snapped.

"I can't believe my life needs saving because of you," I shot back.

He covered his eyes before running the same hand through his hair instead of over it, and this time, it *was* Charlie hair, sticking straight up. He deflated slightly. "Charlie honestly wouldn't think less of me?"

"Nope. He might think you're an idiot and put Super Glue on your desk chair as a lesson about pedestals, but he wouldn't think less of you," I said honestly. I'd been less honest about my mother. I hadn't forgiven her yet for not leaving Boyd. Tess could've lived if she had. I wasn't confident I could ever forgive that. I could forgive the slaps and busted lips my stepfather had given me, but not Tess. I couldn't forgive that my mother had been part of losing Tess. But there's the truth, and then there's too much truth. I gave Hector his truth. Mine was my burden alone.

"One more day, then." I changed the subject. "Two days since the quarry and one more day until Charlie tries to come through again?"

"One more day," he confirmed. "And then we set Charlie free."

Into the freedom of nonexistence. The blackness of the void. The nothingness from where we came. That was another truth Hector had no need to have repeated at the moment. There were times when the truth was worse than any lie.

Like now.

17

The next day, I was back in the infirmary with a wet washcloth over my eyes and a nice plastic puke basin on the bedside table just in case. "You said on an average day, you read ten people without a problem. Kessler's still MIA, and Sloane is avoiding everyone now, not just you. That made it only six. What the hell is wrong with you?"

I moved the washcloth a bare inch to glare at Hector with one eye. "Is that a concerned 'What the hell is wrong with you' or a where-do-I-find-parts-for-a-malfunctioning-psychic 'What the hell is wrong with you'?" He knew perfectly well what was wrong—he simply didn't want to admit it.

"Can't it be both?" He sighed and settled deeper into the plastic chair that should've had his name painted on it by now, as often as I ended up here.

"No." I gritted my teeth with both pain and annoyance and slid the washcloth back into place.

"All right. It's the first. And I feel guilty. Since Charlie's accident, I've felt nothing but guilt. Then you show up, the answer to it all, but I don't get any answers—only more guilt," he said, as I kept my eyes closed against the headache and let the heat of three warmed blankets soak into me.

I heard him blow out a frustrated breath before adding, "Two more sociopaths and one psychopath? Are you positive?"

"Scientists who want to work on a project that could lead to U.S. dominance of the entire world's intelligence community. That reads like a job application for some kid's comic-book supervillain. Did you think you weren't going to get some bad apples? I'm kinda surprised there are any *good* apples. Didn't you have some sort of psychological testing done on the applicants?" Now my jaw was locking up more from the irritation than the pain.

"They are all highly respected in their fields, all with PhDs and some with multiple PhDs."

He sounded defensive. Good. He should.

"Because, Hector, the men who invented the hydrogen bomb only had their GEDs, and look what a great idea for the world that turned out to be. Now turn over any rock, and you'll find a terrorist trying to make his own little radioactive toy, and every dictator has a backyard full of nukes. No one was looking at the big picture in that bunker." I sat up and tossed the cloth. It wasn't helping. "I'm glad I wasn't alive then to read any of them. My brain probably would've melted and leaked out of my ears." I pushed the blankets aside, too. The coldness of the sociopaths had mostly faded. What was left was bone-deep, where artificial heat couldn't touch.

"It doesn't matter, anyway. Your three, four counting Thackery, need to be locked away and their brains donated to science to see where nature went wrong, but they didn't kill Charlie any more than Thackery did. *Why* they didn't do it, I don't know, but they didn't. Biding their time, maybe. You'll have to ask them. Although Morganstern has killed two hookers so far, and he has no intentions of stopping." That had been something I hadn't enjoyed seeing through his eyes at all. A bullet in his head would do the world a favor.

"Now," I went on, chilled and fed up with evolution's mistakes, "I need to go outside and get into the sun. My bones feel like they're made of dry ice."

He cleared it with Meleah, and soon we were trudging through dried red mud that crumbled under our feet, taking in the scenery of squat, ugly buildings, a fifteen-foot-tall chain-link fence, and the razor wire that looped along the top. It wasn't a Hawaiian villa with your own private beach, but it had the sun. I'd make do. I'd thought life had finished teaching me about making do. Nope. Life never tired of making you its bitch.

"You're out of here after tomorrow," Hector said abruptly. He'd taken off his lab coat, not caring who saw the holster and gun he wore. Or maybe it wasn't that he didn't care. Hector was smart. He wanted whoever was out there to know he was ready. "Once we save Charlie, put him at peace, you're going home. We'll still try to fix the project, get Summerland up and running again before the spy makes off with all the schematics and computer codes, but you don't need to risk your life for our work. And despite the fact that I'm putting him in the ground when all is said and done, Thackery will have a good shot at finding this guy. He's not psychic, but he can think like the son of a bitch. He's already shown us that."

The blistering summer sun felt good, so much so that I wasn't sweating a drop under my long-sleeved black shirt. My psychic gear. Yeah, like the rockers say, I was back in black—my head in the game. Jackson had left the stage, and the All Seeing Eye had taken his place. That had to be why I felt less than relieved at this talk of my departure—leaving a job undone wasn't my way. I used to con, lie, and steal, but now I earned every penny I made. Plus, I didn't like murderers of the innocent. Charlie had been a grown adult, but in his way, he was as innocent as they came. It had to be a combination of the two, because I should've been saying, "Praise Jesus, and I won't let the razor wire hit me in the ass on my way out."

What would be the point of me staying? I knew there was no justice. There was revenge. Yeah, that son of a bitch Boyd had seen that up close and personal, but there was no justice. It wasn't my place, regardless, to help out Hector with either concept.

His project, his exceedingly bad apples, and none of it my problem. Hell, I was a saint for sticking around to pull Charlie home. Mother Teresa herself would've lent me her spare habit and rosary.

But . . .

No. No buts. I did not want to be thinking this. It wasn't about what I liked or didn't like. This was not who I was. I had a bottom line, and my bottom line was survival. It always had been. Tomorrow night, I was taking a car—after Hector searched it for bombs—and my ass was out of there. Homeward bound. Nothing was changing that.

Not to forget that the bastard spy had tried to kill me twice. That wasn't the sort of thing I let people get away with. My stepfather would stand up and shout, "Testify!" to that, were he not a decomposing pile in an unmarked pauper's grave.

Well, unmarked by stone. When I was eighteen, I'd tagged it. I'd been drunk, and I had pissed about a gallon on it. Thanks for the memories, Dad.

This unknown son of a bitch had killed Charlie and tried to do the same to me. It didn't seem right that I wouldn't be there to kick him in the head one or five times as a great big fucking thank-you for playing.

It didn't make a difference. I had a whole day to make that decision. Resort to common sense, stick with my commitment to keep my ass in one piece, get back to the Jackson born in blood and the warm embrace of the emotionally sterile state institute. At least, that guy I knew. This new guy was nuts, reckless, and far too concerned with things that weren't his business.

I'd just completed that thought when the things that weren't my business shot me in the back.

Lying flat in the same red earth that the county had buried Boyd in, logic told me that I'd fallen. My mind told me that the ground had reared up and smacked me in the face. "Jackson!" Hector's hand was on my shoulder, squeezing hard.

I coughed and pushed out the words, "Nothing . . . you . . . can . . . do. Go . . . get . . . the . . . dick."

He hesitated, then there was the sound of his feet pounding against the dirt as he ran. I continued to stay flat, both to be less of a target and because breathing was agony. I didn't want to imagine what trying to move would be like. The only part of me that disagreed was my fingers digging into the dirt as the pain crushed my ribs in a massive fist. It ebbed and flowed, the fiery, stabbing ache, and finally focused on the left side of my back.

"Jackson?" Hector was back. Already? It couldn't have been more than minutes, although the agony in my back was saying bullshit to that—it felt more like seconds in recovery time. Unfortunately, Hector didn't sound as if he was waving a flag of victory. I felt his hand below my scapula, his fingers probing. "Okay. I got it. The son of a bitch nailed you right over the heart."

"The same son of a bitch who, I take it, got away."
The pain was the same, but I no longer felt as if my lungs had taken the weekend off. Breathing was easier and talking doable. I appreciated that, because I had something to say. "I asked you for a bulletproof vest. I felt the *bullet* fine. I didn't feel the damn *proof* in it at all." I pushed up on my hands and knees and groaned at the spike of pain. "Ah, shit. What's it made out of? Your grandma's leftover yarn? Christ."

He hooked his arm under my right one and helped me stagger to my feet before juggling the blob of metal in the palm of his other hand. "It's a big enough round. Nine-millimeter, same as I use. Without the Kevlar, it wouldn't have just hit your heart; it would've exploded it."

"I told you the vest was a better choice for me than a gun." I winced as I tried to straighten. "But I still think someone at the nursing home crocheted the damn thing. It feels like my rib is broken."

"I'm sure it is." There wasn't much sympathy in the pronouncement. I could've used more—a whole lot more. "But a cracked or broken rib is a hundred percent better than dead," he finished matter-of-factly.

"And you didn't catch the bastard?" I could be wrong. Ghosts could exist. This guy appeared and disappeared at will like one.

"I didn't even *see* him, and this isn't a sniper's bullet by any stretch of the imagination. He had to be close." Once I could stand semi-upright and take a step without the threat of being shoved into a Notre Dame bell tower, he let go of my arm.

"I swear, Allgood, if you had been behind me instead of beside me, I'd say you were the shooter. This guy's goddamn invisible." I swore out loud and proud with every step I took. I knew . . . *knew* I could feel the broken edges of a rib grating against each other.

"You've already read me. You know I'm noble and true. Red, white, and blue. Practically Superman, I'm so damn heroic, but apparently, I couldn't find a killer if you dropped me onto death row at a supermax prison," he said bitterly.

"I'm lacking in social skills except when it comes to flattering my older female clients, but I have a feeling I should say something here. Something to comfort you in your time of emotional upheaval . . ." I took one more step, blasphemed against God, his son, and the Virgin Mary as my rib howled again. "Here it is: fuck your emotional upheaval. Be a man, for God's sake. At least *your* ass wasn't shot."

Strangely enough, that did the trick.

As Meleah was looking over my X-ray, after giving me a high enough dose of painkillers to have me seeing the world in a new and improved way, Hector was having the base searched. Not for a nine-millimeter—the base was full of them. Anyone who was carrying a gun was carrying a nine-millimeter. Instead, he was having the base searched for Dr. Sloane, and he'd sent two soldiers to Dr. Kessler's house to bring him in. There was no more pickpocketing, and, while Hector knew I couldn't do any more readings today—not after the axis of evil I'd already come across—he said he was fine with locking the two scientists up overnight for peace of mind. And if they wanted to trade their chances of being part of a potentially Nobel Prize–winning experiment to press kidnapping charges, he'd like to live long enough to see that day.

Hector, the bitterness faded and his mood improved by my newly enhanced social skills, returned and stood patiently at the foot of my gurney—at least, patiently until I asked Meleah why she wasn't wrapping my ribs and followed it with the advice that if she caught Hector staring at her ass, she should take it for the compliment it was.

"We don't wrap broken ribs these days. You read too many old private-detective novels. Move slowly and carefully, and it'll heal fine on its own." She glanced at Hector, whose face struggled to pick one emotion from the flood that crossed it. I thought he settled on resignation. "He's quite the romantic, isn't he, Hector?"

"He's something, all right. There's no getting around that." He frowned, but it didn't stick. Sighing, he snorted with visible amusement—or invisible amusement and blatant exasperation. He had the face of an Everest cliff, all granite and ice. It made it hard to tell. Normally, I could read people's expressions like a mood ring, but not Allgood. He was a challenge. "Just how much pain medicine did you give him?"

"Too much, probably. But considering his reaction to the readings earlier and being shot, along with the bruising and broken rib, I thought he deserved the happy maximum."

"You hear that, Jackson?" He gave a stinging flick of his finger to my sock-covered toe. "You feeling happy?"

"Happy," I repeated agreeably. "You can shoot me every day if you give me a barrel of these pills to take home."

"I don't think that'll be an issue. By now, the shooter's found out that you're still alive, which means he knows about the Kevlar. If he shoots you again, he'll go for the head. All the happy pills in the world won't help you there." He gave my lower leg a brisk pat and me a large, wolfish grin.

"You're being shitty, aren't you?" In all honesty, the pills did make it difficult to tell.

"Yes, I am." He patted me again.

"Was it the thing I said about Meleah's ass?"

"You got it in one."

"Fine. See if I use my social skills to help the romantically challenged again." I yawned, feeling the room swing up and down, then back and forth. It was a nice sensation, the world as my personal hammock. I liked it. "You know, Meleah, you should take sympathy on the man. He hasn't been laid in eleven months, two weeks, four days, and . . ." I checked my watch, willing the blurry numbers to coalesce. I stopped when a grip fastened around my ankle and tightened. "Hey." I gave Hector a poisonous glare. "If I wasn't doped up to my eyeballs, that might hurt."

"Trust me, there's no 'might' to it." But he let go. "Time to get serious, Jackson. I know you haven't felt this good since you were Mr. December on the Hot Psychics of Atlanta calendar, but I need you to tell me if you're up for this tomorrow. It's a long drive to the caverns, and I can't have you high as a kite if something goes wrong—such as the recording kicking in before we've zeroed in on Charlie."

That was a mental picture that sent the happy packing as fast as a Republican senator who'd knocked up his mistress. Charlie trying to fight through the ether was, as far as I could tell, seconds away from being simultaneous with the cycle of violence spinning into play mode. I thought about it, which wasn't easy, as my thoughts were distracted more than once by the narcotic haze. Eventually, I locked it down and ran a hand over my face. "I won't be able to wrestle any of your soldier goons like I did at the quarry. I won't even be able to take Fujiwara or any of the other geeks, if it comes to that. But I will be able to tell you if—when—Charlie is coming. That'll give you and your

Charlie-busting machine two or three seconds to go to work."

Then it hit me what he'd said—the location. It was astounding how fast that drugged-up contented feeling vanished.

"The caverns? The cannibal caverns? God, why there? Thackery said Charlie was drawn to you as his brother and me as a psychic link much more than the level of violence imprinted on the ether. Couldn't you have picked someplace less dangerous? Someplace where we won't be trying to eat each other?"

And where I didn't hear little girls crying for their mommy before they were hung up on hooks, lambs to be gutted and drained.

Tender honey chile. Like fresh churned butter, melt on your tongue so tender . . .

"Ah, Jesus." I closed my eyes, but it wasn't enough. I clapped my hand across them, squeezing from temple to temple, trying not to see the curve of metal, the crimson waterfall, the trailing brown waves of hair. "Go away, Hector. Go the fuck away, and don't come back until it's time to go tomorrow."

He didn't. He explained instead. I wasn't interested. "We decided it would be best if all elements were optimal. You, me, and the highest level of violence—to be on the safe side. To make certain this time is the last time."

Certain? Nothing was ever certain. PhDs, my ass. They were all idiots. Every single one of them.

And I was nothing more than a piece of their Charlie-busting machine. Something to be used, and the hell with the consequences to me in the process. I was an idiot, too, to have ever thought differently.

"Go away," I repeated flatly.

This time, he did, his footsteps followed by the lighter ones of Meleah, and I was left alone with thoughts. Many thoughts.

None of which was mine.

18

"I brought you a change of clothes. You can shower here in the infirmary instead of going back to our room. It's probably safer, limiting your exposure to other personnel as much as we can." Hector put a meticulously folded pair of jeans and black shirt on the foot of my bed.

I ignored him and took another bite of the pancakes Eden had brought me. Homemade blackberry ones with real maple syrup, not those hockey pucks from the cafeteria. As far as I had determined, she was the single saving grace to this particularly heinous pit of hell. She'd come in the middle of the night with more pain medicine, this time an injection. When I'd asked her when she slept, she'd winked and replied, "When I don't have special patients. And you've been through enough here, Jackson Lee, that you're labeled permanently special on my list." She'd patted my arm with her hand, safely covered with a latex glove. "Now, roll over to your side. This goes in your hip."

"Dr. Guerrera only gave me pills before. Why the

needle?" But I'd already been rolling. Pill or injection, the previous pain medicine had worn off, and my rib had been more than ready for more.

"This has something extra to help you sleep. Don't think I hadn't noticed you weren't doing any of that." She'd gone for stern, but the sympathy had washed that away.

I'd returned immediately to lying on my back. "I don't need that. I don't need to sleep." I hadn't wanted to sleep; that had been closer to the truth. The whispers, the screams, the sounds of chewing, the wicked curve of a hook—they were all more clear when I was asleep.

The sternness had returned, along with a finger shaking the likes of which I hadn't seen since my granny Rosemary. "I hear you have a big day tomorrow. Riding out to one of those creepy sites." She'd made a face. "Doing more of your psychic readings. You need your sleep."

"I'm not doing any more readings. I'm going to help with Charlie tomorrow and then be home, *my* home, before midnight. No more readings and not another night spent in this hellhole. Dr. Allgood is on his own from now on." Like I should've realized that I'd been all along.

"I don't blame you one tiny bit. These people have all the compassion of a toad, and I've been thinking long and hard about finding another job with people who care, not people who care who they can use." She'd tilted her head. "Well, you'll get plenty of sleep tomorrow night, then, and sleep through the next day if you have any sense. You're positive you don't want the shot?"

More than. She'd shaken her head. "You're a stubborn one, but I'll miss you, Mr. All Seeing Eye." She'd given me an impish smile and apparently had gone home, slept three hours, and then was up making me the best good-bye pancakes I'd ever eaten.

And which I continued to eat while Allgood went on to annoy me further. I didn't appreciate reminders of my first episode of gullibility since I was six or seven. "I had three guards on the infirmary door last night. I know you didn't want to hear it at the time, but I didn't want you to think I'd leave you without backup until we get you out of here."

I didn't say anything as I wiped syrup off my hands and put my gloves back on.

"You didn't think that, did you?" he demanded.

I took the clothes and stood. "No. I thought about how men were stringy, women were better, but little girls tasted best of all. I thought about how my hooks needed sharpening as they were beginning to blunt on bone. I thought about how once it seemed the winter would never end. But that was when I was hungry. Now my stomach was full, and I hoped the snow never stopped falling." I headed for the shower room.

"We're not going there," Hector said, his voice harsh and guttural. There was a tinge of green to his face from my recital of cannibal Renfrow's thoughts. Hundreds of years old, but to some people, people like me, they were as clear and sharp as the day his blackened, corrupted brain had spat them out. "I've already told Thackery and the others. They didn't like it, but *they* didn't see you there, and none of us can see what you saw. Going back there might be the most logical choice, but it's not the most humane one. If I can keep my soul intact through all this, I will." He exhaled. "We're going to a low-risk site. One at the bottom of the list. It's a simple family dispute over a fifty-fifty split of a farm in a will. One brother whacked the other over the head with an axe handle. It's still a murder, has to be, but it's nothing close to what had happened at the caverns."

I kept walking. He started to grab my arm as I passed but aborted the motion almost before it began. "I apologize for considering anything else." The formality of a good man who was finding out that pedestals weren't healthy things—not for your brother and not for yourself, especially when you tumbled off of yours. "Desperation is no excuse for becoming like the rest of them. I'm sorry, Jackson."

I paused at the door and took the biggest leap of faith of my life. I let myself trust him again, and this time not because of Charlie but because of Hector himself. Abby had told me hundreds of times that people can't live without trust. They can exist, but they can't live. I was beginning to see that she was right. Hector had messed up, more than once, but he'd also risked his life to save mine—and more than once on that, too. He wasn't perfect, but I wasn't any kind of fool in believing I was, either.

I gave a single nod. "All right." It wasn't apology accepted, but it was the closest I could come to it. I went on into the shower and closed the door behind me.

Fifteen minutes later, I was out, changed with the shirt over a new Kevlar vest. Hector had said next time it would be a head shot, but it hadn't stopped him from doing what he could in case I was lucky and a head shot wasn't practical for my invisible stalker. And wasn't that some kind of luck? Hoping someone would shoot you in the chest instead of the head. With my damp hair pulled back tightly into a ponytail and with gloves on, I opened the door to see that Meleah had shown up. She was standing next to Hector. Moral support.

"Have you two made up?" she asked.

"Yes, ma'am, we're just peachy. Bestest friends." I dumped my dirty clothes onto the bed. "Hector's going to braid my hair, and then he's going to show me his new dollhouse." All right—trust with a shaky foundation and a razor-sharp defense mechanism, but a modicum of trust was better than none at all. Hector would have to accept it for what it was: the best I could do right now.

"I suppose that means yes." She smiled. "Are we ready for this, then? To set Charlie free?"

"You're going?" I asked, admitting to myself that

it wasn't the worst idea I'd heard as Meleah made the argument aloud.

"Every time you and Hector are together at one of these sites, someone is thrown off a roof or nearly drowned," she noted pointedly. "I think a doctor is mandatory for this trip. And . . ." She touched the ring hanging on a chain around her neck. "I'd like a chance to say good-bye—to my best friend. My family."

I understood that. I'd have given anything to say good-bye to Tess.

Once the van was loaded, it was Fujiwara driving. It was a good idea to bring him along. If you wanted anyone caught up in a violence cycle and trying to kill you, it was Fuji. He wasn't very good at it. That upped everyone's chances of survival considerably.

Thackery was in the front passenger seat. That I didn't care for much. The sociopath who had let Charlie die through indifference and ambition wasn't someone I wanted watching my back. But Hector had said, lack of conscience aside, that next to him, Thackery was the best scientist, and he'd rather have him in sight than lurking back at the base unsupervised, doing God knows what. Psychic reading wasn't any kind of proof that Hector could take to his government oversight contact, and Hector did have his own eventual plans for Thackery that government oversight had no part of.

That left three soldiers in the first bench seat,

Meleah and me in the second seat, and Hector in the back with the Charlie buster, or what he called the Transplanar Energy Reintegration and Stabilization Device. I used the name to distract myself from the sharp ache of my rib. No happy pills today for the psychic who needed to stay sharp and focused.

"Someone has a thesaurus fetish, and it is out of control," I drawled. "They need help. Professional mental help that can probably only be found in Germany in some experimental psychiatric study run by Freud's cryogenically frozen brain in a jar."

"I named it," Thackery said stiffly from up front.

"So surprised. It would take a narcissistic egomaniac to come up with a name so boringly geeky that they wouldn't even use it on a *Star Trek* episode. Hell, I'm astounded you didn't name it after yourself. Wait." I groaned. "You did, didn't you? The Thackery Transplanar Energy Reintegration and Stabilization Device. God, what a dick. You should patent it as a sleep aid, too, because that's what it'll induce halfway through actually saying it."

Hector was running last-minute diagnostics time and time again on the Charlie buster as the van sped along the road. Whether the machine worked or not and dissipated what was left of Charlie or failed and left Charlie still roaming to activate brutal aggression sprees, Hector wasn't going to have a good day either way. That he was able to give an amused snort at my taunting of Thackery was my good-bye to him, like Eden having said good-bye to me with pancakes. We all had our talents, and we all used them in different ways. Who wouldn't think the bite of sarcasm wasn't as tasty as that of blackberry pancakes?

Although we were no longer going to the caverns, and Thackery had bitched a solid hour about that, the drive was every bit as long as Fujiwara had told us. With the van's tinted windows, the scenery was all shadows. The radio was silent, as was everyone else. The soldiers weren't big talkers, and Hector and Meleah were distracted by hopes and fears that were one and the same thing. I took the opportunity to nap off and on, making up for a sleepless night and getting some respite from the pain that Tylenol did nothing to dull. It was a damn shame they couldn't make a narcotic that kept you happy, pain-free, but without the fuzziness.

I dreamed of Charlie and those pink walls of Cane Lake. The pink that had been the final straw. The color that had reminded me too much of my lost sister's shoe. I remembered lying to Charlie about taking his calls. When I woke up with a crick in my neck, I realized that I hadn't lied. I was going to be there to take Charlie's call, his last one. I hoped that made up for all the other unanswered ones.

The van was bumping over what felt like a dirt road. That was standard for a Georgia farm. Hector had said one brother had beaten the other over the head with an axe handle for the privilege of gaining twice the acreage, so it had probably been a while ago, a hundred years, give or take. These days, everyone had a thirty-eight shoved in a drawer somewhere, nice and convenient when arguments became a little too hairy. Hell, if you wanted to drive on up to Tennessee, they had some places that would let you carry guns in a bar, because nothing mixed like alcohol and bullets. And nothing cured a hangover when you didn't have a head left to host it.

A Georgia farm, I thought, as we hit another bump that had my rib groaning. They'd been lucky with that list of theirs. What if someone had razed one of those massacre houses and built a mall over it? Would there still be a recording? Would an employee suddenly go berserk at the Gap and start beating customers over the head with a mannequin arm since axe handles weren't available?

The van stopped, and Fujiwara announced almost cheerfully, "We're here!" Fuji cheerful while sitting next to the testicle-withering Thackery— what had happened there?

Thackery looked out of his window. "Someone killed his brother over *that* land? He should've stored that homicidal fury up for something more valuable," he stated disparagingly. I couldn't see jack from where I was sitting, but if a sociopath, who would gut you like a fish for cutting him off in traffic, didn't think it was worth killing over, chances were it really wasn't.

Thackery checked his watch. "Wait, we're only an hour before ETE."

Okay, this one I remembered. Estimated time of ether-disruption. I was pretty proud of myself on that one, proud enough not to notice Fuji's reaction—or lack of one—to Thackery's temper tantrum.

"An *hour,* Dr. Fujiwara. You underestimated travel time by *two hours.* That is completely inexcusable."

I heard Fuji's door open, some low words, almost whispered, then the door shut, but I didn't make out what he said. Truthfully, I didn't try. Unless he was telling Thackery to stick his head up his ass, something poor Fuji lacked the balls to think, much less do, I wasn't interested. I remained uninterested for several more seconds until Thackery's harsh inhalation exploded out into a shocked snarl. "What do you mean, ten minutes, you spineless, brain-damaged *nobody*? What the hell is going on here?"

Ten minutes. We only had ten minutes with a machine that had taken twenty minutes to load into the van? Ten minutes and a Fujiwara who was suddenly unafraid of his boss, when before his eyes came close to rolling back in his head with very obvious fear whenever the man entered a room? Very obvious, when at times "very" can mean "too" and "too" can mean "not at all."

"Shit," I said, leaning past Meleah, pushing the sliding door open, and jumping out.

I hadn't seen it coming, not for one second.

But now I knew it all.

Thackery was right. This place wasn't worth fighting about, much less killing over. It wasn't a farmhouse. It was a four-room shack. Weathered wood eaten down to almost nothing by termites, it was small, cramped, and leaning drunkenly on its foundation. The windows were cracked and completely covered in red dust. The grass surrounding it was parched brown—hadn't seen a sprinkler or a hose in its life. Year after year of thirsty lives. Inside, the kitchen had once had linoleum, green and orange, curling at the edges. The living room had had remnant carpet, brown as mud, a recliner patched with duct tape, and an orange couch with torn cushions where a boy had slept at night. A narrow hallway with a wood floor slick from use led to two bedrooms—one for the man and woman and one for the two little girls. Although that could've changed as the swing had. The splintered porch swing those girls had sat on, rusty chains creaking loudly with every pump of their legs, was gone. One thing wouldn't have changed, though. If it had been at night, if the stars had been out . . .

They would've been the same stars I'd watched from this yard as a kid, eating a peanut butter sandwich and dreaming of mansions, fast cars, pretty girls, paying for my sisters to go to college and away from here—fantasies of a life to come.

But it wasn't night. It was—I yanked desperately

at my sleeve—it was one fifteen. Ten minutes, Fuji-wara had told Thackery. Ten minutes. He was right. That's when it had happened—at one twenty-five. That's when everyone died, including a Jackson who had dreamed childish dreams. Birthed in his place had been a bloodied one who knew that not having dreams meant you couldn't lose them.

"You son of a bitch!" Fujiwara was at the front of the van, and I ran to take him down hard. I felt the impact of the two of us hitting the ground vibrate through me. I knew he felt it that much more. Red and black flickers of rage ringing my vision, I rammed my fist into his face, feeling the crunch as I shattered his cheekbone. It wasn't enough. I couldn't begin to imagine what would be. I hit him, and then again. "What have you done, you bastard? What the hell have you *done*?"

Hector's hands on my shoulders, trying to pull me off. His grip was firm, but his voice was shaken. He recognized the house from the files, because this file had interested him most of all. My file. The nightmare of someone you knew versus the night-mare of people from a hundred years ago—which would stick with you more?

"Christ, Jackson, stop. Let me hit him. I can hurt him in ways that will still let him talk. We need him to talk. To tell us why here."

Hector wanted to hurt him? Fine by me. As long as someone was doing it, I didn't care who that someone was. But talk? The time for talking had been over the second I'd left the van, from the moment I'd actually seen where we were.

He had managed to remove me from the scientist, whose face I'd left a bloody ruin.

"*Talk?*" I snapped. "There's nothing to talk about. And why here is easy. This jackass"—I kicked the fallen man hard in the ribs—"has sabotaged me. You think I can do a reading on Charlie here? You think I can do *any* kind of reading at all?" I rubbed at my eyes with the glove-covered heels of my hand, growled, and kicked the fallen man again. This time, he curled up into a ball with a groan. Good. Great. I hoped I broke every fucking rib he had.

Grabbing on to what calm I could, I added, "If he's sabotaged me, he's probably sabotaged your machine, too. I won't be able to do a reading to lure Charlie here, and even if I could, this goddamn spy has no doubt made sure you couldn't do anything about it." He'd taken down their project, and now he was making certain that they didn't get it back up.

The three soldiers were out of the van, confused but awaiting orders. Thackery, who conveniently liked to give orders, gave them one. They restrained Fujiwara with plastic ties around his wrists and ankles and left him lying in the dirt.

Hector looked at his own watch and came to the obvious conclusion that he didn't have time to question Fujiwara. "Let's get the machine out. Now!" he directed, and the soldiers moved with him to the back of the van. The four of them began to lift and move the machine considerably faster and with somewhat less care than they'd loaded it. "I ran the damn diagnostics five times. It was green to go every time. I didn't find anything wrong."

"Like . . . you found . . . nothing wrong . . . with the . . . transplanar." Fujiwara grinned, a scarlet bubble popping from his split lips. "And who . . . designed the . . . diagnostics for the . . . reintegrator?"

I didn't need Hector's grim expression or an Alex Trebek guest shot to let me know that had been Fujiwara's department.

"It doesn't matter," Hector insisted. "He could be lying. He's lied all along, and we've never suspected him. He's made three attempts on your life, and we didn't see a glimpse of him once. He's playing all of this like one big game, and this could be a bluff. It would be in line with everything he's done so far. Jackson, he can only sabotage you if you let him. Take Meleah's ring."

With Charlie's keys lost in Job's Quarry, the plan had been for me to use the engagement band he'd given Meleah, the one he'd insisted she keep despite her refusal of him. It had belonged to his mother, and he had known Meleah would end up wearing it one day when Hector and the truth finally came to a meeting of the minds. Charlie had carried that ring with him all the years after his parents had died until he'd given it to Meleah. There was more than enough of him imprinted in the metal for a reading.

If I would do one. But I wouldn't. Not here. Not in this hour of all hours. I couldn't open myself at all for fear of what might slip in—memories that had nothing to do with Charlie. I'd already lived that blood-soaked, cordite-burnt day through my own eyes. I wasn't going to relive it through the eyes of my mother as she drowned in her own blood or through those of that bastard Boyd, whose thick fingers had reached for me as I turned with the shotgun and blew off his face.

And, God, never, *never* through the eyes of Tess, whose lungs had filled with water when her arms and legs couldn't keep her afloat any longer. My baby sister, who I knew had thought with her last breath that her big brother would find her. Save her. Her big brother, who never let her down, not one time in five unbelievably short years.

Not one time . . . until the very first and last time.

"What's happening? What is so wrong with this place?" Meleah was confused as she pulled the chain over her neck and tried to press the ring into my hand. I jerked my hand back and let the ring fall to the ground.

"It's home," I said bleakly. Hector had told Meleah about my file, my past, because she knew—I saw it in her eyes.

Stricken, then determined, she looked from me to the house and back. "No. It can't be here. You can't do it here." She crouched and reclaimed the ring. "Jackson is right, Hector. We can't ask him to do this. No one can ask him to do this."

"How did Fujiwara know?" I demanded, as Hector and the others—Thackery, who had a career on the line if not a soul, joining in, too—struggled and sweated in the god-awful heat with a machine that had to weigh more than six hundred unwieldy pounds. "About this place? Is it on your list? In your Big Book of Bloody Massacres?" I'd trusted him, not once but twice, and how stupid had I been to go down this treacherous and broken road again?

"Jackson, God, no." Hector's hair was soaked, his breath heavy with exertion. But that's all it was heavy with. I didn't hear any guilt. Although I'd not looked at Fujiwara twice, had I? When it came to industrial espionage and a rampant run of socio-paths, ex–con man or not, I was out of my depth. In all of this, I doubted once that I'd actually grasped what was happening around me. "All the places on the list are at least fifty years old. The more time that has passed, the more time the ether has to fray. But it doesn't matter. Even if it didn't work that way, I wouldn't have let them put your house on the list. I wouldn't do that to Charlie's friend, and I sure as hell wouldn't do that to *my* friend."

That word, that goddamn word that came so fucking easily to him.

I looked back at the house where Boyd had taken it all from me: my mother, my sister, my innocence, an innocence I hadn't then realized I had. He had taken my whole life, past, present, and future. He'd taken it all, every breath, every step, every decision, until my dying day. I was who I was, every cell in me, because of him. He had made me more than my mother's womb ever had.

Because I had let him.

But now, maybe I could unmake some of that. I couldn't change the past he had gobbled up, but there was a chance I could rip the present and the future out of his long-dead hands. I couldn't do it for myself, and I was an unparalleled expert at doing things for me and only me, yet I could do it for Charlie. I could do it for that homely kid who'd refused to take no for an answer and helped me when I'd needed help the most. I'd thought I'd been surviving Cane Lake no problem. I'd been wrong. I hadn't been surviving it; I'd been becoming numb. If Charlie hadn't been there, poking and prodding, waking me up, showing me there was a life outside the fence, I'd have stayed. Boyd had made me, all right, but add two more years of Cane Lake on top of that, and I wouldn't have an Abby hovering around the edges of my life. I wouldn't have Houdini. I wouldn't have enough to offer even a dog, and they only gave—they didn't take.

One person I hadn't managed to push away and a dog. Some people wouldn't consider that much of a life, but compared with what it would've been without Charlie's influence on me, it was a miracle of one. Whether he knew it or not, Charlie was giving me a chance at another miracle, if I would take it. I could pay him back and put this all behind me in one fell swoop.

I closed my eyes. The heat from above became somehow hotter. I was an ant, and someone had shoved a magnifying glass between the sun and me. Is that you up there playing around, Boyd? No. There's no up there. If there was, there'd be a down there, and that's where your wide ass would be burning for eternity.

There was no hell for Boyd, I knew that. It was all right. There was another way to banish him from existence . . . by banishing him from my life.

I opened my eyes, took off my glove, and held my hand out to Meleah. "Give me the ring. Give me Charlie."

"Jackson," she started, already shaking her head.

"It's all right. Just . . . don't let me trip over my own two feet and touch anything else." I tried for a smile. It didn't feel particularly encouraging. She must have seen something, however, as she carefully placed the ring and chain on my palm. It was cool, a circle of relief on hot skin.

"Four minutes." Hector's countdown was followed by the thud of six hundred pounds hitting the ground. A few seconds later, there was a hum that vibrated up and down my spine as heavy and pulsating as a hive of enraged hornets. "Machine is up and good to go."

He hoped. I wasn't as sure. Fujiwara hadn't needed to bluff before. He'd been what I didn't believe existed: a ghost. We hadn't suspected him, seen him, or found any evidence at all that it had been him. I'd felt sorry for the son of a bitch, having to endure Thackery's rages. He'd fooled us all, seemingly without effort. I had the feeling he was somehow doing the same now.

I closed my hand around the ring. It wasn't as if I opened myself up to Charlie. It wasn't as if I'd opened myself up to anyone since this had first begun sixteen years ago, when I'd picked up Tessa's pink shoe. What I had didn't come with an off switch, or hell, I'd have taken a simple mute. But right now, there was only the taste of old memories, nothing new.

My eyes drifted to Fujiwara. Flat on his stomach with his hands cuffed at the small of his back, he had his head turned to one side, and although the blood remained a steady run from his nose, he was still grinning. His teeth were red, but the smile was as happy as they came. For a man in a shitload of trouble, he didn't seem to feel that he'd done anything but come out on top.

"Why'd he let himself get caught?" I asked abruptly, turning to Hector. "You said it before: we never caught a glimpse of him. Now he just gives himself away. Why? There has to be a reason."

"Three minutes," Thackery snapped before Hector could reply. "We don't have time to delve into the mind of this insane piece of garbage now."

All of the things Fujiwara had managed to accomplish without detection before, that didn't say insanity to me. It said he was smart, smarter than all of us standing there. He'd let us know who he really was for a purpose, and it wasn't aimed at simply throwing me off. If that's all he wanted, he would've made another try at killing me—fourth time's the charm.

Something was off. I'd known with the car bomb at the restaurant that he was as good as the best of con men when it came to distraction. That, though . . . that had been nothing.

This . . . this was a true marvel of distraction.

But what was it misdirecting us from? Where was the hand in the pocket, lifting the wallet? What was the trick?

"Jackson, two minutes. I hate saying it, but Thackery's right. We're out of time."

I focused on Hector. He stared back, unhappy but resolute. Thackery and he were both right, but not in the way they thought they were.

"I think we are. In more ways than one," I said. It was too late. Whatever Fujiwara was doing in addition to stopping the project from cleaning up the mess, the mess being Charlie, there was nothing we could do about it now. He'd either failed and we were about to save Charlie, or he'd succeeded and I was about to relive a waking nightmare.

Without the shotgun, without the knife, how bad could it actually be? I closed my eyes and tightened the fist I'd made around the ring, the metal digging into my flesh.

Bad enough.

I opened my eyes and shifted my attention back toward the house. There wasn't a single tree around it. It would've been better if there were, a merciful blot of shade instead of the bleached-bone heap that hunched under a ruthless sun. All of its sins were bare for anyone who cared to look . . . and for those of us who wished to hell we didn't have to.

Two minutes may as well have been two seconds, and then, as before, I felt Charlie try to come home.

Lost. Where did everyone go? Where did the world go? Where's the door? Where's the door? Where . . . where . . . where . . .

"He's here," I rapped out. "Charlie's here. Whatever the hell you're going to do, do it now!"

I'd done my part. My massacre might not have aged like a fine wine, but Charlie had sniffed my psychic curse out. It had brought him here. It was time to see if Fujiwara was bluffing or not. The squat piece of technology built to save and destroy Charlie all in one went from ominous buzzing to the eager whine of a chain saw biting into wood. The air suddenly felt heavy, and not from the heat. It felt as if gravity had doubled. There was a metallic taste on the back of my tongue. It wasn't the copper of blood. It tasted more like nickel or silver, close to the taste of the dime I'd swallowed when I was four, and for a moment, the white-hot light of the sun was tinted with green. Green, but not a shade of green I'd seen before or knew existed.

As my stomach clenched at the unnatural glare, Hector shouted, "It's locked! Some kind of energy loop. It's feeding on itself. Go! Everyone, run!"

I made a grab for Meleah's arm, but she was already gone, headed for what to her eyes would be the nearest shelter. Thackery, Hector, and the soldiers followed her. The house. Run? Not there. Any direction was better than that one. Hector stopped on the sagging boards of the porch as he saw me standing, unmoving. "Jackson, come on!"

"Hector, don't. Not the house. Charlie's here, and you know what happens next. Get out of there!" I didn't care if the Charlie buster was the equivalent of ten sticks of dynamite. I didn't care that no one had weapons to use in this reenactment. That house and what was coming were the greater threat, hands down, at least to me. We'd made the wrong call, all of us, and I didn't want to be around when the piper came calling to wad up that bill and shove it down our throats. I ran toward the field on the left, away from the house, away from the machine that was now screaming, darkening the air further with a color so destructively deviant and *wrong* that my eyes could barely see it.

When the explosion came a fraction of a second later, being thrown to the ground with vicious force was actually a relief. Simultaneously, the sun, air, and gravity had returned to normal. I blinked up at the sky. I was flat on my back, which was a mass of pain—the one rib being joined by the rest. I'd hit on my stomach but rolled a few times, how many I hadn't counted, to end up on my back. The machine wasn't screaming anymore. It was a blackened mass sending smoke that tasted of acid billowing high into the blue.

Question answered. Fujiwara didn't bluff.

19

I felt the tickle of grass on my skin. I hadn't lost the ring, but the bare skin of my hand was resting on the ground. I jerked it up, holding my breath. No. Jesus, no. No screaming, no feeling of blood rising to gush out of your throat, no water sucking you down to endless suffocation.

I exhaled when none of that appeared. That day must be trapped in the house . . . and the well. I pulled my other glove out of my pocket, put it on, and shoved the ring in its place. I didn't need it any longer. I already knew Charlie was here. Worse, with Fujiwara's sabotage, I knew what that meant.

As I pushed myself up on my elbows, my entire body ached. Despite that, nothing else seemed to be broken. I was lucky. I hadn't been close to the reintegrator. The soldiers had been, though. Like all the goons on the project, their job was to protect the geeks. They had been bringing up the rear, holding back enough to guard Hector and Thackery's flank. Now they were down and unmoving in the brown grass. One was breathing; the other two weren't. Neither was Fujiwara, who had a foot-wide piece of metal protruding from his chest, that crimson grin now carved permanently on his face.

I didn't see Hector. He'd heard my warning. He would've gone after Meleah to try to get her out of the house through the back. They hadn't made it. I knew even before the screaming I'd been relieved not to have filling my head suddenly ripped through the air. It was a woman's scream but not one of fear. It was pure rage—"My baby! You drowned my baby!"—it was the words of my mother. This was what she had screamed at Boyd as she went after him with the butcher knife. Her words but not her voice. It was Meleah.

The show had started, I thought numbly. I didn't move. There were no weapons, I repeated to myself. No gun and knife, and the soldiers weren't armed— protocol for any reenactment mission. Nothing that bad could happen. I thought it again and one more time before I swore. I heaved myself to my feet and went step by slow step toward the last place I wanted to be.

"Boyd, you motherfucker, don't! Don't! No, Mom! No!" Hector's shout and a cry of anguish from the past that I didn't remember. Had that been me? I recalled every detail—why didn't I remember that?

I ran. The past was horrific and littered with bodies, but this was the present. There were people I knew here and now, living people. And maybe this time I could do something to keep them that way. I hit the porch and was through the door as the line of scarlet on Meleah's brown skin begin to spill blood. Thackery had slashed her, but he hadn't put the knife through her throat as Boyd had done to my mother. Meleah was strong and athletic, not the beaten-down, worn wisp of a woman my mom had been. Meleah had moved quickly enough to escape the knife . . . almost.

Knife. What was a knife doing here in an abandoned shell of a home? There was nothing. No furniture, no appliances, not a single discarded flea-market fake painting on the wall. How could there be a knife like the bright and shiny new one in Thackery's hand? Now Hector was turning and running down the narrow hall toward the back bedroom . . . where the shotgun had been. If the knife had been replaced, I had every expectation that the shotgun had been, too. Fujiwara's manipulation from beyond the grave.

Sometimes things are so wrong and so bad that your brain refuses to deal with them in the here and now. You can almost feel the pop-and-sizzle of the short-circuiting brain cells before numbness covers your mind in an insulating blanket. That blanket let you step away and see things clearly—see what has to be done. This had happened before. It had let me react, not freeze up in the face of death. Had allowed me to see that someone had to die, and un-

less I wanted it to be me, then I'd better find a way
to stop it.

There was no pop-and-sizzle this time. There
was only reality, hypermagnified. The universe only
gave you one psychotic split per slaughter. This second time around, I was on my own. I dealt with it. I
didn't have much choice, and I already had one run-
through. What was an encore performance? A
piece of cake, right?

Right.

As Thackery followed Hector at a run down the
hall, I gripped Meleah's arms as she staggered back
against the stained plasterboard and helped her
slide down to a sitting position. Peeling back her
hand, blood under her immaculately short polished
nails and in every crease of her knuckles, I faced the
slash that ran across the front of her throat. It was
bleeding, but it wasn't the waterfall spill I'd unconsciously expected. It wasn't deep enough for arter-
ies to have been cut. It wasn't precisely superficial,
but she wouldn't bleed to death.

I didn't think.

She wouldn't die.

I hoped.

I ripped the pristine white sleeve of her lab
coat—professional always, even on field trips to
hell. She was a good match for Hector. Would that
they both lived long enough to find that out. I
wrapped the sleeve around her throat and tied it
snugly enough to help with the bleeding but not

enough to cut off her air. "Put your hand back up." I pulled it up for her and pressed it to the quickly staining cloth. "It'll help."

Her eyes met mine as her hand automatically stayed where I'd placed it. "He drowned my baby," she whispered. "Jack." My mom had been the only one to call me Jack, like the girls had been the only ones to call me Jackie. "He killed our Tess."

"I know . . . Mom." I swallowed. A recording, only a recording with more depth and scope than any duplication should have. "I know. Stay here. I'll get Boyd. I promise."

I ran a soothing hand along her hair and then stood from my crouch to run down the hall after Thackery and Hector. Thackery had kept hold of the knife, something Boyd hadn't done, since he'd left it buried in my mother's throat. He had something else that my stepfather had lacked. Boyd had just been a fat, lazy bastard who had no hope of out-running a fourteen-year-old. Thackery was a whip-pet of a man. Lithe and fast.

But Hector was no skinny teenager, either. His body was honed and hardened by military ser-vice. He could outrun the runt that I'd been. Thackery was quicker than Boyd. Hector was quicker than me.

He'd already fired the shotgun. I'd already been throwing myself onto Thackery, knocking him and the knife down, where they could do no more dam-age. Unfortunately, in Hector's eyes—*my* eyes from sixteen years ago—the damage had already been done. His hands had already found the shotgun in the closet, and his finger had already pulled the trigger. I wished I'd been slower. Thackery didn't need saving. I was another matter. The buckshot mainly hit my chest and was stopped by the Kevlar. Some of it hit a few inches under my left arm, an area unprotected by the vest. Only part of the load but enough to blow me off Thackery and land me on my back. People say it feels as if you were kicked by a mule. People, they always goddamn lie.

The pain spiked sharp and hot, and blood coated my gloved hand when I touched the multiple punctures through cloth and flesh. I looked up from my hand to Hector. He didn't see me. One shot. It had taken two to put Boyd down. As Thackery growled and propelled himself up from the floor, blade in hand arcing straight for Hector's chest, Hector fired the second shot, right into Thackery's face—Boyd's face—the same as I had done.

And if there was balance in the world, any at all, that's where it would've stopped, the killing. Hector would go to Meleah's side and tell his mom that everything was fine. Everything would be all right.

The world laughed at that one.

Whoever had left the shotgun hadn't only loaded it, they'd also left extra ammunition. Thackery was gone, a faceless corpse lying across my legs in a hallway I used to slide down in socked feet. But I was still alive—in serious, nerve-shredding pain but alive. That made me another Boyd to take care of. Hector disappeared into the back bedroom and returned to load the shotgun with two more shells by the time I managed to use a handful of Thackery's lab coat to pull myself up into a sitting position. I ignored the gray haze that blurred my vision. "Hector," I said hoarsely, but he wasn't Hector now. "*Jackson*, it's over. You killed him. You killed Boyd. He's dead."

The shotgun stayed trained on me, and Hector's pale eyes didn't blink. They were empty. That didn't mean he hadn't heard me. If I could've seen into my own eyes when I'd put Boyd down, I wouldn't have seen much of anyone home then, either.

"Jackson," I emphasized again. The guy at the mill had heard me, or at least I'd pushed the recording into a minor detour. "Jackson, your mom is hurt. She needs you."

This time, Hector did blink, and his lips peeled back from his teeth. "You stabbed her. You murdering bastard. She's dying. You've killed her. You killed Tess. No more killing. Not by you."

I saw them simultaneously: his finger tightening on the trigger . . .

And the shoe.

It was at his feet, halfway between him and Thackery's shattered skull. It gleamed bright and pink as the day Mom had bought it and as the day I'd found it in the grass. One small pink shoe. Tess's shoe . . . although she'd been buried in them both.

Her pride and joy, her favorite possessions. How could she be buried in anything else?

This was dying, I guessed. Not your whole life running like an overly long James Cameron movie. No, just small moments. Small shots of the things that had derailed your life altogether. It made sense. It made you glad to go. You could finally see the whole screwed-up mess put to rest, because there'd never been any real hope of turning it around with one selfless act. That was movie shit, and movie shit was just that. Pure, unadulterated, get-your-hopes-up and pull-the-rug-out-from-under-you-every-time shit.

"Go on then, Jackson," I said quietly, my eyes still on the impossible shoe. "Boyd has to go, and you know it. Pull the trigger. Hector, if you remember this, it's not your fault. Some things have to play out. You can't stop a recording in the middle. It has to play out until the end. Things just work that way."

I didn't look up to watch him pull the trigger. If he did remember this, I didn't want that to be one of his memories. Nightmares cut at you a shade less in the dark of the night if you don't have to see them looking back at you.

But instead of the shotgun blast that I couldn't possibly hear until after it tore off my head, I heard something else. Something as impossible as the shoe.

"Boys are so stupid."

I lifted my gaze—not by too much, I didn't have

to—and saw her standing behind Hector. She had small fingers hooked into his pocket as she peeked around his hip. The strawberry blond hair was in a bow. Green, to clash completely with the shoe. Tess had always had her own unique style.

"Jack Sprat, I'm awfully busy now." There was the same overly dramatic sigh I remembered. Her face brightened. "You found my shoe!"

"I did." My lips were completely numb. I didn't feel them move. "I wish I could've kept it before, but I thought you'd want it more." Hector hadn't pulled the trigger, or he had and here was the afterlife I'd always denied. I didn't like being wrong. I hated worse to admit it. But now, if this was what happened when you died, I didn't mind being a blind idiot. "Where were you all those years? Why didn't you come see me?"

She cocked her head and smiled, happy as she'd ever been . . . always been. Every minute of every day. "I came all the time. Except not so much since, um, December? Other than that, I visited you tons and tons. But you couldn't see me or hear me. You never pay attention." She stomped her socked foot playfully, and suddenly, the pink shoe was back on her foot as she stepped out to stand beside a frozen Hector. He was breathing, I could see that, and maybe that meant I wasn't dead after all. Why would I stick around to watch the man breathe?

"I *knew* you'd need help. And if you wouldn't listen, then I'd have to smack you one and make you listen." I felt good and solidly smacked, that was true. She reached up and pinched Hector's side. "Wake up, Hector. Put the bad gun down and wake up."

Hector jumped, as if he'd received a small electric shock. "What . . . ?" He looked at the shotgun in his hand and hurriedly eased back on the trigger before placing the weapon on the floor. "Jackson." He was pale under his darker skin. "I shot you. God, I *shot* you." Thackery he paid no attention to. After all, in his mind, Thackery had been a done deal, anyway.

Tess shook her head, hair swinging and fierce with exasperation. "Boys. Boys can't do anything right."

Hector's head jerked around and then angled down. I was certain my file had pictures. He knew who he was seeing, what he was seeing, even if I was having trouble wrapping a mind suddenly made of mush around it all. "Tess?"

"You hurt Jackie, but I guess it's not your fault. I thought doctors were supposed to be smart and have suckers. Grape suckers are the best." She turned an expectant gaze on him, only to sigh again, this time in disappointment, when his mouth opened without sound and no suckers came out of his pocket. "I think you need to go back to doctor school, but I have a present for you, anyway."

She held her hand up imperiously for such a small thing, a small thing who hadn't even been made of flesh and blood for a long time. I could see that now. A stray beam of sun had struggled through the bedroom window to find its way to and then through her. She wasn't transparent. She was luminous and delicate, made of the wings of butterflies.

"Charlie." She wriggled her fingers impatiently. "Chaaaarlie, I have to go. I'm late. It's my birthday party. Hurry up."

Her hand disappeared in a ripple of air and returned holding on to a much larger one. The rest of the body stepped through a larger ripple, and I saw the messy hair and big nose I hadn't forgotten. They were as homely as ever, and Charlie's smile was as wide and pleased. "You found me."

"Everything that's lost is found sooner or later," she said solemnly. I saw her hand tighten around his to squeeze reassuringly. "It's time to go home, Charlie. You'll love it. It's everything and everything and everything."

He nodded. "I can't wait to see." He was so close to Hector that their shoulders rested against each other's, and Charlie bumped his harder, judging by the sudden tilt to Hector's stance. An older brother's affection. Pale blue eyes to pale blue eyes, he added warmly, "You did good, little brother."

"Charlie." Hector said it with the purest of belief and relief.

"You found the one guy who could help you save me. I owe you big." Then Charlie turned his gaze to me. "I knew you'd answer my call. Just like you promised at Cane Lake."

"One helluva long-distance charge," I managed, my tongue as numb as my face and lips. I wasn't Hector. I had nothing this trusting or this deserving in me. No faith. This couldn't be real. As much as I wanted it to be, it was the denial of what I'd believed for almost my entire life. How could I believe it? All of it?

A kiss brushed across my cheek, and I turned with what had to be half-crazed eyes to look into those of my sister, still five years old, still beautiful.

"You won't forget this, Jackie. You'll try, because you're a boy, and boys are stubborn. But I won't let you. No way you'll be able to ignore me now." She smiled again, a little sadder, the kind of sad that broke me with her next words. "It wasn't your fault you didn't save me. We all take turns. It wasn't yours. But it's my turn to save you now. And I will."

They were gone, the two of them, as if they hadn't been there to begin with. Couldn't have been there, and my thoughts clamped onto that firmly, because that made sense. Impossible shoes, impossible sisters, they don't happen. Hallucinations from blood loss, that happened. Some damned ether disruption went screwy and messed with your mind, that happened, too. But the long lost? They don't come back, and they don't speak to you. They don't absolve you of things that can't be absolved.

"You're already doing it, aren't you, you stubborn bastard?" No matter what he said, Hector sounded unnerved. Amazed, too, but he'd definitely had his world tilted on its axis. "Going straight into denial of a full-blown miracle."

"You shot me. That means you don't get any say into what I do or don't do. And there are no miracles. It's not like the Vatican is behind funding your project." I lifted an arm, swallowed bile that scorched my throat at the pain the movement caused, and demanded, "Help me up. We need to check on Meleah."

He was already as pale as he could get, but I saw the apprehension etch its way into his face.

"She's going to be all right." I thought she was, and right now, that was the best to be hoped for. "She was quicker." I didn't want to finish the rest of that sentence, and I didn't. "I think it looks worse than it is."

I was on my feet, thanks mainly to Hector hoisting me up with one hand while the other held the shotgun. I hadn't seen him bend over to pick it back up. I knew I hadn't, but there it was. I could've missed it.

I knew I hadn't. But I could have. It didn't have to be Tess who put it in his hand. And why would she? Why would he need it now? He wouldn't. I held tight to the last thought, because denial needed help now and again. Back where I'd left her, Meleah remained sitting on the floor. She managed a smile at our appearance. "Hector. Jackson." The cloth around her throat and under her hand was only half scarlet. The bleeding had slowed. I'd been right. She would be all right. Hector, her, me—we were going to walk away from this, unlikely as that would've seemed minutes ago.

Which proved once and for all that I was limited to reading objects, places, and people. While bullshit illusions were wide open, the future was closed to me. I'd always been grateful for that.

Until now.

Stepping through the open front doorway, as cheerful and smiling as always in the face of adversity and carefully designed plans gone wrong, Eden glowed with the same inner joy she'd never failed to show. She stopped when she saw the two of us, standing upright.

"This is inconvenient," she noted, not dressed in nursing scrubs anymore, frowning a little. "All good boys and girls should be dead now. I did expect maybe Thackery would've survived, being the obnoxious ass that he is. I was rather looking forward to finishing him off as a loose end."

Eden. My nurse advocate. On my side against all others who would use me without regard, when really, all along, her own regard had been as predatory as a silent fin slicing through the water. And considerate enough to wear latex gloves always around me, to save me from an unwanted reading. Too bad I hadn't seen that a reading was more unwanted by her than by me. Eden, who came bearing the gift of an injection of painkiller and sedative in the middle of the night.

"What was in the shot you brought me last night like a good little Florence Nightingale?" I asked, propping myself against the nearest wall, the easier to ride out the waves of pain radiating from the buried shotgun pellets.

She smiled, the dimple flashing beside her mouth like the morning star. "An overdose of Flecainide. A therapeutic dose is just the trick for an arrhythmia. Too much stops the heart altogether. It's what I gave Dr. Allgood, along with the sedative he normally received in his preexperiment physical. Fifteen minutes later, he's in the transplanar, and in fifteen more minutes, he's dead. It's a good drug for falling through the cracks of a toxicology report." She flashed the same smile at Hector. "You wondered why you couldn't find what was wrong with your little toy. That's because nothing was. Charlie was a dead man before he climbed into it."

Her gun, the same nine-millimeter Hector carried on base, was trained on him. He was the only one of us armed. And wasn't that lucky? The shotgun in his hand, the one I hadn't seen him pick up, the one that if he'd thought about it, he wouldn't want to pick up again after turning Thackery's face to hamburger with one barrel and taking me down with the other one.

"But you didn't want the shot, Jackson, and as you were so certain you were leaving today and no more readings were in the works, I backed down. No one likes a pushy nurse. And I'd had my three other shots at you. It seemed only fair." In keeping with her bouncy Eden persona, she was wearing whimsical fairy earrings. I didn't want to die *period,* but I really didn't want to die at the hands of someone wearing fairy anything. "It was fine with me if you escaped with your life. I only kill people who are in the way. I get paid for my work. I'm not into extra credit. I don't even mind all that much about Fujiwara. He was a good partner, but with this job, I have enough to retire, and with his share, I might get two villas instead of one."

"You killed Charlie." Hector sorted through it all to home in on what had started it all. The project breakdown, giving Fujiwara enough time to gather all of the data about it. She couldn't have foreseen what would happen with Charlie, who wasn't quite as dead as she'd hoped, but what a lucky break for her. Charlie had caused more confusion and crippled the project even further. Until I came along, everything was as sweet as those blackberry pancakes she'd made me. And even then, I hadn't been a threat to her or Fujiwara, who deserved an Oscar for his acting skills. But Eden was as competent a killer as she was a nurse. No sense in taking chances. It was only after three failed attempts outside the infirmary that she was willing to risk taking a run at me inside it. I imagined that if she'd gone through with it, she'd already be in another country by now with the information Fujiwara had gathered. This plan—my house equipped with the weapons of the past—was nice for cleaning up a few loose ends like Hector and Thackery, who might eventually have figured things out about Fujiwara, but it hadn't been strictly necessary.

But some killers embraced the better-safe-than-sorry standard.

And so did some scientists.

Hector wasn't waiting for more talking—if there was going to be more, which I highly doubted. Eden was happily polite in her murdering ways, but she was one for getting things done. The shotgun in Hector's hand, put there by Tess I now knew, wasn't pointed at Eden, not specifically. The muzzle was tipping halfway between waist high and the floor as he faced her. It wasn't a chest shot, but right then, any shot would do, and he took it.

The roar of the gun firing came at the same time as she disappeared, lunging to one side. Standing as she had been in the doorway, that put her outside and out of view, either with shattered legs or unhurt but not nearly as cheerful as before. Hector started for the door, pumping the shotgun as he went. I was right behind him, a little slower, as he'd already used it on me, and the pain of that didn't fade like a scraped knee. It only grew more white-hot with every passing minute.

That didn't stop me from grabbing a handful of his shirt and yanking him off his feet as I dove toward the floor. The faint shadow of the gun I'd seen through a window filmed in red dirt turned into an explosion of glass and three bullets that passed over our bodies to embed themselves in the wall. Hector growled and this time was at the door long before me, out into the sun and gone. I did follow, but I couldn't catch up. Shot once today, shot once the day before with a broken rib to show for it, it took the marathon out of my running. But I kept moving doggedly through the grass growing taller into fields I still recognized from sixteen years ago, following a path I'd once run as the colors of the day all faded to black and white behind the horrible truth I'd known.

It was in that tall grass that I found Hector, down and swearing, with a bullet hole through his upper leg. "Go after her," he gritted between his teeth. "She missed the femoral artery, but she hit the damn bone. It's broken. Don't let her get away, Jackson. Not after all she's done." He held the shotgun up to me.

She'd killed Charlie. She'd arranged for Meleah to have her throat sliced, me to relive something no one should relive, and my friend to be shot. No, she wasn't fucking getting away from any of that.

I started after her, and Hector snapped, "No, you son of a bitch. You take the damn gun. Take it, or she will kill you, do you understand that?"

I shook my head. Everything in my life had changed or was trying to change since Hector had shown up, but this never would. "I don't need a gun." And for some reason, I believed it. Hector yelled that I was a "Suicidal bastard!" but I honestly believed it. I didn't need a gun for Eden. It was crazy, completely insane, I knew that, but it wasn't suicidal, because I knew. I just knew. Eden would be taken care of, no gun needed.

I was still running, my hand covering the slow bleeding where the Kevlar had failed me, when I saw her far ahead. Her hair was the brilliant shine of chestnut streaked with red and gold under the sun, and she ran like a gazelle. I didn't say anything, but she must have heard me stumbling through the grass. Her head turned to take me in. I couldn't see the green of her eyes, she was too far off, but I could see her smile. All triumph. Still running, she brought her gun up and over her shoulder to aim dead on me. I could feel the weight of it as heavily as the sun's heat that pressed down. Eden's smile widened.

And then she was gone.

I slowed down to a walk then. I hurt, and with every breath, my broken rib stabbed at the surrounding flesh. There was no hurry, anyway. I knew where Eden was, and she wasn't going anywhere.

When I finally reached the well, it was quiet. Not a bird flew in the sky. The incessant hum of insects had turned to the quiet of a church. I looked down into the dark water that was a bare glitter and gleam thirty feet below and saw nothing else. No pale smear of a hand raised up. No body floating on the surface. Eden had gone to the depths . . . of a well that had been plugged with concrete by the county sixteen years ago after a young girl named Tess had drowned there. There was no concrete now and no sign that there had ever been.

Wasn't that a mystery?

Her nine-millimeter was balanced on the edge of the stone, deadly as a water moccasin. I nudged it with my foot and dumped it into the well. With the distant splash, I murmured, "You forgot something." Then I walked away and back to Hector. When he asked about Eden, I shrugged and answered.

"She wasn't much of a swimmer."

20

A month later, I was doing my version of cooking: microwaving four cheese pizzas, one after the other. While some things changed in life, the combination of me and an oven remained a catastrophe of nuclear proportions. I also had bowls of chips and dip and a case of beer in the refrigerator. Abby had promised to bring cheesecake for dessert. Houdini was intrigued by the smell of so much extra food, but he was suspicious, too. He wanted to believe that it was all for one big Houdini-and-Jackson buffet, but sometimes even dogs know when something seems too good to be true.

I gave him a slice of pizza and pointed toward his couch. "When Hector gets here, he'll probably try to con you out of a seat whining over his broken leg. Don't give an inch."

Chuffing curiously, he trotted over, jumped up, and went to work on his dinner. He'd be surprised when Hector and Meleah, now engaged, showed up along with Abby. Abby he was used to. Add two more people to that, and, well, that was two more people than he'd seen in the house. As I'd thought, things change, and he'd probably adjust faster than I would. But adjust I would. I didn't have much choice after what I'd seen, although half the days I still spent firmly lodged in denial. Blood loss, hallucinations, a statewide secret project to unplug abandoned and dangerous wells—possibly for population control—who knew? But there were the other days, and those days had changed me.

"I was perfectly fine the way I was, right, Hou?" I said aloud. "What's not to love about cynical and sarcastic?"

The dog knew his cue when he heard it and gave a strangled rumble of agreement around his mouthful of cheese. That's when a knock at the door came, and as he had almost two months ago when Hector had shown up on my doorstep, Houdini looked as shocked as if the roof had suddenly fallen in without notice. Once maybe, but twice? Insanity. He'd get used to it, and so would I. Fingers crossed.

I opened the door without bothering to put on my gloves. Hector, Meleah, Abby—they all knew by now why I wasn't a handshaker. They were careful. I didn't have to be on guard with them. But it wasn't Hector, Meleah, or Abby who waited for me.

"Finally," Glory said impatiently. "I am so sick of this thing, you have no idea. I was almost busted by the cops when I tried to sell it. It's a complete leech on my social life. It's nothing but trouble. And now, big brother, it's *your* trouble."

She pushed the blanket-wrapped bundle into my hands so quickly I almost dropped it. As the skin of her hand touched mine, I pulled the warm weight against my chest automatically before I nearly dropped it again.

Since the moment of our childhood separation, Glory had never let me touch her, and she had never touched me. No brother-sister hugs, even when she'd shown up on my doorstep after I'd given up on ever seeing her again. I learned later that she'd checked me out first, to see who I was, if I had enough money to make it worth her while to come calling to take me for everything that wasn't nailed down. I didn't know if she believed that I was psychic or was just Glory being Glory and taking no chances when it came to her uniting with a potential pile of money. With each visit, few that they were, she'd been as careful every time.

Now I knew why.

When her hand touched mine, I saw it.

She saw it, too, in my eyes.

"God, yes, it was me. I wouldn't think you'd need to be psychic to figure *that* out." Her smile was the cruel smile of a five-year-old brat not getting her way. "She wouldn't give me those stupid pink shoes, and I wanted them. They would've looked cute on me." Her red-blond hair was pulled in deceptively cute if Lolita-esque pigtails and she twirled one, as casual as a high school cheerleader. "If she hadn't been so stubborn. Mine, mine, mine—that's all she could say." She gave a shrug delicate and far too pretty to belong to a born monster. "So I took them. Or I tried to. I did get the one, but she fought and screamed, and it just wasn't fun anymore, having a twin. The well was convenient and into the well she had to go." Blue eyes identical to her sister's but as empty as Tess's had been full of every emotion under the sun. "My biggest regret was that I didn't get the other shoe before I pushed her in. But there's always something bright and shiny and new around the corner. You know that, Jackie."

I'd known Glory, the last of my family, was a sociopath the same as Thackery. I'd known she'd done bad things as a teenager, bad things as an adult, and would keep doing them. Bad to worse. But I hadn't thought that at the age of five . . . I'd never thought that a monster was already a monster that young.

"Don't look all grim and holier than thou." She snorted. "You killed Boyd for something he didn't do. Or did you kill him for something he did do? Like stab our bleating sheep of a mother in the throat. She was worthless. I could see how he was tempted. I guess in the end, it's really no one's fault. Can't make an omelet without breaking some eggs, and can't get a pair of pink shoes to save a life."

She was right. I had killed Boyd for something he didn't do . . . and something he did. But my mother wouldn't have attacked him if I hadn't assumed he'd murdered Tess. That one assumption had triggered an avalanche of bloodshed that might not have happened otherwise. Boyd had been an abusive son of a bitch with the potential for murder, but I was the one who'd brought that ugly potential out in the open. Glory had killed Tess—killed our sister—but I'd killed the rest of the family. I had done that. I had brought us all down.

No. *Hell,* no.

I'd read Hector and told him he judged himself too harshly. Was I going to lay a far worse blame on a fourteen-year-old boy? A kid who'd just seen the body of his sister? Boyd had raised a fist to me more than often enough to know what curled in him, dark and gloating, without needing any psychic assistance. He could've taken the knife from my mom. She didn't weigh a third of what he had. Even in her fury, she wasn't a match for him. He didn't have to kill her. And I didn't have to blame myself for shooting him as he tried to do the same to me as he'd done to her.

I didn't have to carry that responsibility at all. Anyone who lived with Boyd, knew Boyd, they would've thought the same. It went wrong and it went bad, but life can. There isn't anything anyone can do to change that. I was right. It was like an avalanche—a horrifying act you couldn't stop or prevent. You could only ride it out and hope to be around when it was done.

Glory . . . that knowledge didn't involve notions of blame or responsibility. Boyd or no Boyd, no one could've guessed or known about Glory. It was nearly impossible to know it now with the confession still hanging before happily curved lips. The last of my family, as dysfunctional as I'd discovered her to be over the years, and now she was gone. Worse, the sister I'd taken care of until she was five, she hadn't existed. That sister had been a lie.

Tess was dead and Glory had never been.

This woman was a stranger and her smile was the smile of a beauty queen as she said, "Have fun with *that.*" With a fingernail painted pearlescent white, she gave a disparaging flick to the blanket. White. The color of purity. Or in some cultures, the color of death. "But don't think it's free, big brother. The only reason I didn't toss it in a Dumpster is knowing what you'd be willing to pay me for it."

It. She only called the bundle it. I suppose that's all she could see.

She named a price and I was certain she'd ask for more in the future, over and over, unless she finally met someone worse than she was. If there was such a thing. It didn't matter. I'd pay the money and I wouldn't miss a penny.

"Call and leave an address. The money will be there in two days. Don't come back here again. Call. If I see your face again, I'll think the river that runs through my front yard is as convenient as any abandoned well." Would I? I didn't know. *Could* I? Yeah, I thought I could. Self-defense I'd done. Defense of the innocent trumped that.

Her smile changed. It was the first uncertain

flicker I'd seen on Glory's face in my life. "Like you have the balls."

"Ask Boyd about that."

A liar at the genetic level, she knew the truth when she heard it. I closed the door in the face of a Reaper walking the earth. Seconds later, I heard a car drive away and felt the shadow of death that had hovered overhead pass away to let the light of a sunset shine through again.

A small gurgle drew my attention to better things.

I looked down at the baby in my arms, sweating lightly over how many times I'd almost dropped it already. Blue eyes, skin the deep golden blush of a ripe peach, and a thick head of curly black hair that was destined to test any brush or comb under the sun. I doubted that Glory had known who the father was, but, like with Hector and Charlie, you get something unique when you mix the best of worlds. Not that Glory was the best of anything, but you couldn't judge a baby by what her mother had done.

I liked babies. Hector would no doubt laugh in disbelief when he heard that, but it was true. People I could often take or leave, but babies, yeah, I liked. They were new, and their feelings all began and ended in wonder. Unless a dirty diaper was involved, but that was easily fixed. I held down a finger to let the small hand wrap around it with a grip of silk. I felt the sheer marvel at everything new and clean in its eyes wash out from it—no, *her*, definitely a girl—as I always did with babies, and then I felt something else. Something so familiar that my chest ached more than it had when I'd been hit with the shotgun blast. My life was changing yet again. It was a phenomenal change and a terrifying one to prove I was up to it.

Second chances come hardly ever. They were miracles in the truest sense of the word. Was I able to handle a miracle?

Have faith, Jackson.

I would. If I couldn't find faith for anything else, I'd find faith for this.

Five years is too short a life, no matter how much that person loved and lived that life to the sky and beyond. You should get a do-over. The rules of childhood games didn't apply to life, but what about after?

Birthday party.

She'd said "birthday party" while pulling Charlie out of thin air: *I'm going to be late for my birthday party.*

"Well,"—I smiled as the grip tightened on my finger—"Happy birthday, Tess.

"Welcome home."

ACKNOWLEDGMENTS

To the incredible woman who birthed me (the world isn't certain she did it any favors, but what does the world know?); Jeff Thurman—my guy in the FBI for the customary weapons, explosives, and general mass-destruction advice; Linda and Richard, whose generosity of spirit knows no bounds; agent Lucienne and editor Adam, without whom this book wouldn't exist; Nini for everything under the sun; Wendy Keebler—copy editor extraordinaire; and, finally, to one of my favorite couples and gurus in all things of geek nature, Michael and Sara.